DANCING FOR JOY

DANCING FOR JOY

James Mitchell

HEADLINE

First published in 1997
by HEADLINE BOOK PUBLISHING

10 9 8 7 6 5 4 3 2 1

British Library Cataloguing in Publication Data

Mitchell, James, 1926-
   Dancing for joy
   1.Upper class - Great Britain - Fiction
   2.Flamenco - Fiction
   3.Love stories
   I.Title
   823.9'14[F]

ISBN 0 7472 1846 3

Typeset by
Letterpart Limited, Reigate, Surrey

Printed and bound in Great Britain by
Mackays of Chatham PLC, Chatham, Kent

HEADLINE BOOK PUBLISHING
A division of Hodder Headline PLC
338 Euston Road
London NW1 3BH

To all my friends in the North

1

Three coffins. Not one; not two. Three. Three funerals too, with three priests *and* a bishop, who somehow contrived to look frivolous in his glittering cope, with a mitre and staff thing – what was it? 'Crosier', that was it. There were three military bands to play the *Marche Fúnèbre* and three sets of buglers to blow the *Last Post*, three sets of mourners too; fluttering black crows, their blackness designed and made in Paris and Savile Row, and all in a cemetery that seemed about the size of the plain of La Mancha. But who was in the coffins? She couldn't ask Mama, because Mama was dead too, and in a coffin of her own, but only one, even if its wood was as smooth as satin, its brass handles gleamed. Mama had been too fond of life to consider the necessity of one coffin, never mind three. At least in her early days. Somebody in the cemetery barked orders and three files of riflemen stepped forward, aimed their weapons at the sky and began to fire in slow, disciplined volleys.

Suddenly Elena said aloud, 'Of course. What a fool I am,' and sat up in bed awake. Each coffin contained one of her husbands. Toby, killed on the hunting field; Charles and Freddy, killed in the war. Too much red wine at dinner the night before; far too much when she considered that she'd eaten on her own. Red wine didn't just make her dream, it made her stupid, too. The odd thing was that the volleys of rifle fire continued; crash after crash: each one louder than the last. She said aloud, 'There's someone at the door, idiot,' rolled from her bed and dragged on a dressing gown, taking care not to look in the dressing-table mirror. She would look terrible and she knew it, and even if it was just the milkman come for his money, he would see how terrible she looked. She opened the door.

It wasn't the milkman. It was a girl – well, young woman – about her own age, but as fair as she was dark. Neatly rather than dashingly dressed, in what she took to be a grey business suit with

1

a blue blouse and a cloche hat with a blue ribbon. Handbag *and* briefcase. Elena eyed her warily. She was in no mood to discuss life insurance or whatever it was the blonde girl had come about.

'Mrs Menendez?' the blonde girl asked, and handed her a business card, and maybe that's what stopped me from crying, Elena thought. I buried Mama just last week, but I'll have to read this card, even so.

'Duckhouse and Allnutt, Solicitors,' she read, and then below; 'Miss Millicent Blenkinsop, representing the above'.

'You *are* Mrs Menendez?' the blonde girl said.

'Lady Mendip,' said Elena, and the blonde girl blinked, and who shall blame her, Elena thought. Anyone looking less like an English aristocrat than me at this precise moment would be hard to imagine.

'This is Flat D?' the blonde girl asked. 'Flat D, 54 Offley Villas?'

'You'd better come in,' said Elena. 'We can't talk about it on the doorstep, whatever it is.' She set her visitor to make tea because the English were hopeless at coffee.

Rent, it seemed. Miss Blenkinsop had come to collect the rent because, as so often in the past, Mama had forgotten to pay it; not because she was hard up – and even if she were she had a rich daughter. Elena washed her face, brushed her hair with the silver brush Mama had cherished so, then began to put on her make-up, and as she did so, she wondered what her three husbands would have made of the Millicent person. Toby would have been appalled, because he had a horror of clever people, and Miss Blenkinsop seemed to be as clever as she was pretty. He would have sent at once for his own lawyer, and refused to say a word till he arrived. Charlie would have invited her to stay for lunch, because Charlie had adored pretty women until the day he died; and Freddy would have telephoned his father at once to ask what he should do, and his father would have said, 'Whatever Elena tells you.'

She chose a dress, white silk with a touch of scarlet, and Freddy's ruby set. She was Lady Mendip after all, and her lord had bought them for her. Then she threaded the last surviving red rose in her hair, and went to pacify the rent collector.

Millicent took one look at her, and blinked again. No question that she looked like a lady now, rather than the shattered apparition who had opened the door, but definitely not an English one. This was a Spanish lady if ever she saw one. She poured tea, and Lady Mendip offered biscuits.

2

'Let's get the money out of the way first,' Lady Mendip said. 'How much did Mama owe you?'

'I have it here,' said Miss Blenkinsop, and produced a bill.

Thirty seven pounds seventeen shillings and sixpence, Elena read. Really, by Mama's standards this was practically cash in advance. She opened her handbag and produced the biggest wad of fivers Millicent had ever seen, and counted off eight of them. Scrupulously Millicent handed over two pound notes and a half crown in return.

'That's better,' Elena said, and then: 'Did no one tell you my mother had died?'

'No,' said Miss Blenkinsop. 'I'm so sorry.'

'It's probably because I don't believe it myself – not all the time. I miss her very much, you see. Too much to face the facts sometimes.'

'What was wrong?' Millicent Blenkinsop asked.

'Spanish flu,' said Lady Mendip. 'It killed so many – and yet she recovered. Or at least we thought she had. Even her doctor. But there were complications. Heart. She died just over a week ago.' Elena swallowed the last of her biscuit and sought in her handbag for cigarettes, offered one to Millicent, then looked at the fair woman and smiled.

When she smiles she looks even prettier and more Spanish, Millicent thought.

'Hardly in deep mourning am I?' she said.

'Your business surely,' said Millicent Blenkinsop.

Again the smile. 'What a nice person you are,' said Lady Mendip, and then: 'Mama made me promise, you see. I look terrible in black. And she loved to show me off, too. She's probably drawing some angel's attention to my rubies this very minute.'

It was funny and witty and almost unbearably sad. Change the subject, Millicent, the fair woman told herself. If you don't you'll soon be crying.

'Are you going to stay on here?' she asked. 'Forgive me. I'm not being nosey. It's just that if you are there'll be legal complications. Transfer of lease. All that.'

'I?' said Lady Mendip. 'Stay here?'

Not that she sounded appalled: simply bewildered. But what on earth's wrong with it? Millicent wondered. Nice part of West 8, handy for Kensington Gardens and the High Street shops, big rooms, elegant furniture. Compared with where she and her

3

mother lived in Pimlico it was a palace. True, the rent was a bit steep, but even so she was a *lady*.

Lady Mendip said, 'Forgive me if I sounded rude. I didn't mean to – you see, I already have a place to live in London. In fact I have three.'

'*Three?*'

'It's just that after Mama died I felt the need to stay here for a little while. To be near her. Just the two of us together. In fact, apart from our priest you are the only person I've seen since the funeral. It was good while it lasted—'

'I'm sorry,' Millicent said again.

'No, no. While it happened naturally, it was good, but to make it last would have been bad, perhaps even sinful. I'm glad you came when you did.' Elena thought for a moment, then said: 'I'll tell you what, why don't you come and see my three houses? They're worth a look if I say it myself. Knightsbridge, Grosvenor Square, Eaton Place. Then we could have lunch.'

'I'd love to,' said Millicent, 'but I doubt if my employers would.'

'You could always telephone this Foulhouse.'

'Duckhouse,' said Millicent. 'Make an excuse you mean?'

'Tell a lie,' said Elena.

Millicent thought for a moment, then said: 'Telling lies shouldn't be a problem. I'm going to be a lawyer after all.' Elena nodded. She really did like this fair, pretty woman. 'But just for the moment I can't think of one that will fit.'

'Tell him about my mother's death,' said Elena. 'Tell him that you found me here and quite ill, and that I must wait for the doctor to give me some pills before we go to the bank, and that you are almost sure the doctor will send me to a nursing home to recuperate, and quite, quite sure that I will pay, because I'm very rich and bank at Coutts.'

'But that's wonderful,' said Millicent, and very likely true, because how many gorgeously dressed young women have their choice of nursing homes in Knightsbridge, Grosvenor Square and Eaton Place?

Elena told her where the telephone was, and went to pack, as Millicent picked up the earpiece and asked for the number. Not Duckhouse, she thought; Allnutt, because though Allnutt was every bit as inquisitive as Duckhouse, he was also a gibbering hypochondriac who found any illness terrifying, and infectious ones the most terrifying of all, and what illness could be more terrifying than the Spanish flu, which had killed even more people than the Great War?

'So I thought it best to go along with the idea,' she heard herself saying. 'She really does seem rich, if her clothes and jewels are anything to go by.'

'Quite,' said Allnutt: 'Quite. But why not a cheque?'

'This is her mother's flat,' said Millicent. 'She doesn't have her cheque book with her.' Really there was nothing to this lying nonsense once you got the hang of it. Then she played her ace. 'Of course, I could always bring her back to the office and we could arrange transport to the nursing home from there.'

'No,' said Allnutt, rather abruptly. 'Take her to the nursing home yourself.' Then, belatedly, he added: 'Shows goodwill, after all.'

Dear Mr Allnutt, Millicent thought. Always so predictable when it came to his own skin. 'If you say so, Mr Allnutt.'

'Oh, I do,' he said.

Elena came in, carrying her suitcase, cloche hat and a velvet coat lined with silk; both made in Paris. She took the telephone, and began to give instructions to someone called Tufnell, then someone called Cook, then hung up the telephone and went to the door of the flat. Millicent carried the suitcase. Coats like Elena's had no business smelling of leather, but Millicent was quite sure that if she had refused to carry the suitcase the other woman would have done it herself: no fuss, no tantrums; simply an acceptance of things as they were. Millicent found that she was beginning to like her very much. They went downstairs to where Elena's car stood waiting and Millicent's last doubts about her wealth and status vanished. It was a Rolls-Royce Silver Ghost, and its chauffeur, Grimshaw, sprang forward to relieve her of the suitcase, leaving her free to climb in and sit on some of the most luxurious upholstery she had ever known. Roses in a little silver vase too, and a lingering memory of Elena's perfume.

As they were going to Knightsbridge, Elena began to think of her first husband, Toby Crick. The Knightsbridge house had been his after all, and very comfortable and pretty it had been, but what a marriage. *What* a marriage. Poor old Toby. A hussar and hopeless in bed. It didn't seem possible but it was true. She'd borne the marks for quite a while: a seventeen-year-old virgin. He'd been a virgin too, rather more than seventeen, but not that much more. He should have gone to Paris or somewhere and had some lessons, but he hadn't. His mother saw to that. And so he'd

5

gone on hurting her, and telling her he was sorry, and how much he loved her. And it was all true: the pain, the sorrow, the love. But it was the pain she remembered, until he'd caught mumps from a schoolboy nephew, and their nights of passion were over. Mumps do that sometimes to an adult male, the doctor had told her. For a while at any rate. Then just to round off a life crammed with incident, poor old Toby had broken his neck on the hunting field. November 1914. She looked out of the window. They had arrived. Elena picked up the speaking tube and told Grimshaw to slow down.

'That's it,' she said to Millicent. 'Number forty-three.'

Forty-three Berwick Street, one of a sumptuous row of terrace houses. Regency, Millicent thought. Probably designed by that chap who did so much work for the Prince Regent – Nash, would it be? – and all of them with their windows cleaned, doors freshly waxed, brasswork glittering: even Number 43, which was so locked, bolted and barred it looked more like a Pentonville for extremely rich criminals than a gentleman's residence.

'I'm so sorry,' Elena said. 'I left Eaton Place in such a hurry I clean forgot to bring the keys. Still it gives you some idea of what it's like.'

'It does indeed,' said Millicent.

'What do you think of it?'

'I think it's wonderful.'

Elena blinked. 'I suppose it is,' she said. The trouble was that Toby hadn't been wonderful at all. Being wonderful had been Charles Lampeter's department. She spoke into the tube once more. 'Grosvenor Square please, Grimshaw,' she said.

More Nash, but on an even grander scale than Berwick Street. Like all the others, Number 17 glittered and gleamed, yet somehow it conveyed affection this time as well as care. She must have really loved the chap who owned this one, Millicent thought, but already Elena had jumped from the car and crossed the pavement. Outside Number 17 was a furniture van, drawn by a team of mules. Nothing else for it, thought Millicent, and jumped out and followed. When she reached her, Elena was obviously furious, which for some reason made her prettier than ever, confronting a tubby and irascible man, who, Millicent was sure, was a soldier in mufti. Around them men in green-baize aprons were carrying furniture from the house to the van.

'If you're poor,' Elena was saying, 'you should beg in the streets. Stealing my property is against the law.'

The tubby man turned scarlet, in a rage so intense that for the moment at least he was speechless.

Millicent looked about her and darted off, and Elena watched her go.

Well, well, she thought. I expected rather more than that, then saw almost at once that she had misjudged her new acquaintance, who returned with a large and reassuring policeman.

The tubby man, still devoid of articulate speech, achieved a kind of turkey gobble instead, and produced from an inside pocket what looked like a scroll which he proceeded to wave at her.

'My God,' said Millicent. 'He's assaulting her,' and ran to Lady Mendip's defence. Even the policeman lengthened his stride – chaps who could turn as red as that were capable of anything – but it wasn't assault. Not yet.

'Will,' the tubby man said at last. 'My cousin's will,' and unfurled it as if he were a herald with the terms of surrender. 'All written down. Signed, sealed and delivered. Isn't that what they say?' he asked the policeman, who was too busy taking out his notebook to answer and thinking: Thank God it's Grosvenor Square. In Lambeth the crowd would be three deep by now.

'Charlie left it all to me. Furniture, house, the lot,' the tubby man said.

The policeman was impressed: 'Name?' he said.

'Pudiphatt,' the tubby man said. 'Sidney Pudiphatt. Major not long ago.' Do no harm to show he wasn't just anybody.

'If you wouldn't mind spelling it, sir,' said the policeman and Pudiphatt did so. He detested spelling out his name, but he had no choice.

The policeman turned to Elena. 'And you madam?'

'Lady Mendip,' said Elena.

Well, if that don't beat cock fighting, Pudiphatt thought. There she stands, claiming what's mine, and all the time she's married again. To a lord, no less.

The policeman turned to Millicent.

'Miss Millicent Blenkinsop,' she said, and then, because it might be useful: 'LL B. I'm a Bachelor of Law, London University.'

'She's my legal adviser,' Elena said, but Pudiphatt scarcely heard her. He was still too busy being furious because Mrs Lampeter – if she *was* Mrs Lampeter – had married into the aristocracy.

7

'Took your time getting here, didn't you, sir?' the policeman said.

'I was in France for three years,' Pudiphatt said. 'Right up to November, 1918. And after that I've been in and out of hospital.'

And we all know why, thought the policeman. Even so, three years. In a way you could say he was lucky, but only in a way.

'I wonder if I might see the will,' said Millicent, and Pudiphatt began to gobble again.

'Sounds reasonable,' said the policeman. 'After all, she is her ladyship's legal adviser.'

Her ladyship, thought Pudiphatt. Crawling already. Reluctantly he handed it over, but Millicent was merciful. She skimmed quickly through it and handed it back.

'Nothing wrong,' she said. 'It's just – did you know Mrs Lampeter had married again?'

'Of course I didn't,' said Pudiphatt. 'I was too damn busy fighting Germans. But what difference does it make?'

Slowly, as if addressing a none-too-bright child, Millicent said, 'Your will is dated 1910 – Lieutenant Lampeter describes himself as a bachelor.'

'Well, so he was,' said Pudiphatt. 'What about it?'

In the same slow, patient voice, Millicent said, 'Your will was revoked. He made another in favour of his wife.' And I hope I'm telling the truth, she thought.

'Ah,' said the policeman, and then, to Elena: 'Where did your husband die, my lady?'

So it's 'my lady' now thought Pudiphatt. Next thing you know he'll be lying in the gutter and begging her to wipe her shoes on him.

'In France,' Elena said.

'I don't wish to pry,' said the policeman, 'but just in case it's asked – what regiment?'

'He was in what he called the Brigade,' Elena said. 'The Coldstream.'

'And where was he killed?'

'The Somme – third day.'

The policeman looked baffled. The Coldstream Guards had been nowhere near the Somme then. They'd had their share, but not the Somme. Not till later.

'He had been – seconded? Is that it?'

The policeman nodded.

'He was a major by then. Acting CO of something called the Tyneside Irish.'

Not a prayer, the policeman thought. Not a bleeding prayer. Even by the Somme's standards the Tyneside Irish had taken a hammering.

'Thank you, my lady,' he said. 'I take that kindly. I really do. I was in the Brigade myself.'

What chance have I got? thought Pudiphatt, and the policeman turned to him once more. Not aloof, not this time. Impatient, and with a hint of menace about him.

'You'd better tell those removal men to put the furniture back where it was. Exactly where it was.'

Pudiphatt nodded to the foreman. It would cost even more money, but he had no choice.

'And while we're at it,' said the policeman, 'how did you get into the house?'

'I had a key,' said Pudiphatt.

The policeman looked at Millicent. 'Is that normal, Miss?'

'Not uncommon,' said Millicent, 'where there's a will involved.'

'All the same,' said the policeman, 'I think we'll give it back to her ladyship. It's her property now, I take it?'

'Yes, indeed,' Millicent said. 'It's all part of the estate. Even a key.'

Pudiphatt wanted to kill her.

'Then you better take charge of it,' said the policeman, 'seeing as you're her ladyship's legal adviser.' He handed it over, then added: 'I'll just take a look round inside. Make sure everything's as it should be. You'll know what to do about the key miss?'

'Oh yes,' said Millicent. 'Thank you, constable. Thank you very much.'

They went inside and Millicent marvelled at the house's glories. Chippendale, Hepplewhite, Sheraton; a painting of a horse by a man called Stubbs, a portrait by Gainsborough, a landscape by a Frenchman called Claude. As they went they replaced the Holland covers, left neatly folded by the men in the green-baize aprons in the places where the furniture had been, and was again. When they had done, Elena motioned Millicent to an uncovered chair, and offered her a cigarette. Millicent took it: she rather felt she'd earned it.

'That business about the key,' Elena said, 'You and that constable sounded rather cryptic. After all, we got it all back.'

Millicent rather liked the sound of that 'we'. All the same she said, 'Not cryptic at all – not to us. We didn't get *the* key back: we got *a* key back.'

'But surely—'

'That Pudiphatt could have had copies made. Probably did.'

'Oh, damn the man,' said Elena, and then: 'You don't happen to know a good locksmith do you?'

'Certainly,' said Millicent. Duckhouse and Allnutt knew a great many locksmiths. Repossessions mostly. 'Shall I call one?' Elena nodded. Chubb, thought Millicent. The place was a treasure house after all. The best was what it needed: even the locks. She made her call, and then once again Elena spoke to Eaton Place, to someone called Walter. He was to come at once to Grosvenor Square and take a taxi.

So, at last Millicent saw 23 Eaton Place, another masterpiece of Georgian brick, but somehow much more elegant than Grosvenor Square's brooding grandeur. Tufnell turned out to be the butler, and Elena told him to bring the champagne.

'Your birthday, Lady Mendip?' Millicent asked.

'No,' Elena said. 'And please call me Elena.'

Quite a concession for one lunch thought Millicent; but all she said was, 'If you'll call me Millicent,' and then the champagne arrived. Delicious, of course, but so strong, and she wasn't used to champagne, and anyway the only hobby Allnutt had was to lecture the Band of Hope on the evils of Demon Drink. Even so, every cautious sip was a delight. And so was the house – or what she had seen of it.

Over lunch Elena began to talk about Freddy, the husband who had owned Eaton Place.

'You'd have loved Freddy,' she said. 'Everybody did.' Not quite as one had loved Charles, but so *nice*.

'And rich, too,' Elena continued, 'which is odd in a way because Freddy's father is still alive. He's the Earl of Chard – but the thing is that Freddy had an uncle – a bachelor uncle – who adored Freddy and left him his little all. Only his little all was rather a lot: this house, the estate in Hampshire. Everything. But he never had time to enjoy it, poor lamb. Killed in France . . .'

She broke off to look suspiciously at her glass. Claret at lunchtime was a good idea, but it exacted its price.

'Even Mama was upset . . . I say even because Mama thought there was only one point in matrimony for young ladies: to make them financially secure . . . Well, I'm that, all right. Mama didn't do too badly as a dancer, but the working life of a dancer isn't all that long, and so she set about marrying me to the nobility and gentry.' She smiled. 'Don't think she made me do what I didn't want to do. I'd have hated being poor. And anyway, I adored Mama.'

Indeed you did, thought Millicent. I can see it in your face every time you speak of her. 'What you say about dancers, I know it's true,' she said. 'My mother used to be one.'

'She *didn't!*' said Elena, but Millicent looked at her watch.

'Oh Lord,' she said. 'Thank you so much for lunch. It was fabulous. But I really must go. I'm hours overdue at the office.'

'No,' said Elena. 'Don't go. Come and work for me instead.'

'Doing what?' For once Millicent sounded wary.

'Being my legal adviser. We could say you were my secretary as well, so that all my friends could say I exploit you. What do you say?'

Millicent hesitated.

'We could give it three months' trial,' Elena said. 'Tenner a week and board.'

It was far more than Duckhouse and Allnutt paid her.

'And after that if we don't get on I'll talk to my own solicitors. They'll find you something.'

I bet they will, thought Millicent. You must be far and away the richest client they've got. All the same, if the first day's anything to go by, this won't just be a job; it'll be an adventure.

Elena rang for Tufnell. 'Tell you what,' she said. 'Let me show you the house, then you can choose which room you want.'

More exquisite grandeur. More Chippendale, Sheraton, Hepplewhite, more mouth-watering silver. Both the rosewood and mahogany had been waxed till they glowed, the silver gleamed. More pictures, too, and a little marble statue that, Millicent learned later, was Greek; second century BC . . . four Canalettos, Millicent noticed, which might have been overdoing it, but not in a house of this size. Two small Turners, and a picture by Titian of a naked lady who was pretty enough, if rather chubby: tubby? Millicent stopped dead in front of the last Canaletto.

'What's wrong?' Elena asked.

'Pudiphatt,' said Millicent. 'He's either an ignoramus or a fool. Probably both.'

'What makes you say so?'

'The pictures in the Grosvenor Square house,' said Millicent. 'He didn't need all those mules and the pantechnicon and men in

11

had to do was let himself in with a key and
...l.'

...said Elena admiringly. 'All the same, I'm glad he's
...e hated to lose any of Charlie's pictures.'

...ondon house the supply of rooms seemed unending, but
...inished at last, and on the way downstairs Elena asked
...licent which room she would like. Millicent suggested a small,
bleak room just below the servants' bedrooms, and Elena was
appalled.

'You can't mean that,' she said. 'No, of course you don't. You're
just being modest, and legal advisers are never that. Come, let me
show you.'

They went down to the second floor, to a room with a southern
exposure, elegant bed, elegant furniture, and a Dutch flower
painting on one wall.

'That's better,' said Elena. 'Now, let me show you your office.'

It was next door. A room rather bigger than Duckhouse's, and
he was senior partner. Bookcases and shelves for her law books,
Turkey carpet, capacious desk, leather chair, more chairs for
visitors, and all polished till they gleamed.

'Freddy's uncle had a friend,' said Elena. 'Cambridge don. He
used to stay here sometimes to work. Now it's yours. What do you
think?' But Millicent was speechless. 'Go and sit behind your
desk,' said Elena. 'Show me how you look.'

Millicent sat, and Elena took one of the visitors' chairs.

'To the manner born,' she said. 'You know it'll be marvellous
having someone here to talk with. It's so boring on one's own.'

A butler, thought Millicent, the footman, Walter, not yet back
from Grosvenor Square, and maybe another on his day off, a
chauffeur, the parlourmaid who had taken Walter's place, cook,
and at least one kitchen maid to help her produce that incredible
lunch, housemaids to make beds and sweep and polish, and she
was lonely. Well, of course she was. A dozen servants at least, but
she couldn't *talk* to them. Millicent lived with her mother and no
servants at all, but they talked all the time . . .

'So you like my house?' said Elena.

'My God, yes.'

'There wasn't anything about it you thought unusual?'

Indeed there had been. Millicent looked at Elena. She was
smiling.

'Did your mother ever practise here?' Millicent asked.

'Never.'

And yet she had a practice studio. A good one, and expensive, but then Elena could afford it, Millicent thought. Gramophone, pianola, a wall that was simply a gigantic mirror, even a barre, bare floorboards and a raised square of hardwood on a miniature stage that was entirely new to her.

'I dance too,' said Elena.

She should have known. Even by the way the dark woman moved, she should have shown. But she'd been much too busy thwarting furniture thieves to give Elena marks out of ten for deportment.

'Mama trained as a classical dancer – not *Swan Lake* or *Les Sylphides* or anything like that. By classical she meant the dances of the old Spanish court – graceful, elegant, quite beautiful, but perhaps just a little demure, though not when Mama did them. Mantilla, a fan and a beautiful smile and you were back in the court of Philip II. Velazquez could have painted her.'

'Her parents must have been proud of her.'

'Not proud, no. Relieved perhaps. You see,' said Elena, 'her dancing had dignity, and a certain – aloofness. A touch-me-not? Isn't that what they say?' Millicent nodded. '*That* they liked very much, and the fact that she was good at it meant that it paid well, too. She and the rest of her troupe travelled all over the place before the war: England, France, Austria, even Imperial Russia, and they were a success wherever they went. Especially in France. And at least from my grandparents' point of view they were a thousand miles from the gypsy dances of Andalucia.

'They adored them,' Elena continued, 'but for my mother to dance them was out of the question.' She smiled then, a smile at once sad and loving. 'And that is why I dance them, because my mother would have liked to dance them too. Flamenco.'

'I'm sorry?' Millicent said.

'It's what we call the gypsy dances. Flamenco. So far as I know I have no gypsy blood, which is considered a serious handicap, but on the other hand the ones who taught me tell me I'm not bad. Not bad at all. Would you like me to show you some?'

'Oh, yes please,' said Millicent.

They went to the studio, where Elena changed her shoes, turned on the pianola, and that was it. She was ready. The pianola crashed out music of a savage power which was like nothing Millicent had ever heard before: 'The Miller's Dance' from *The Three Cornered Hat*, Millicent learned later. Elena responded

13

with a dance that was equally savage, equally powerful, but with its own kind of beauty: wild, demanding, sexually charged. Not a vestige of aloofness there, and yet Millicent could sense beneath it the most demanding of all disciplines, controlling not only Elena's body and feet, but the fingers that snapped, the clapping palms . . . But even that, it seemed, was not the full picture, not quite the real thing. For that she used the gramophone, the most powerful Millicent had ever heard. Guitars; sometimes one, sometimes two, and Elena danced as if the music were a flirtation, even a seduction. To end, Elena charged her shoes yet again, and the guitar became a firework display, climbing, climbing, while on the ground Elena's feet provided the explosion of fire crackers that was like the rattle of rifle fire. Alone or not, Millicent applauded, and Elena curtseyed gracefully, in a way that was entirely Spanish, not English at all.

'*Zapateado*,' she said. 'Shoe dancing. I doubt you'll see anything like it anywhere else in the world. Only in Spain. No. Not even that. Only in Andalucia. You like it, I gather?'

'Oh yes,' said Millicent.

Elena went to a cupboard, took out a towel, and began to dry herself. Young lady or not, she was streaming with sweat, but she still looked pretty. Her dress will need cleaning too, thought Millicent, but what of it? I bet she's got a score of day-dresses at least.

'Do you dance?' Elena asked.

'A little,' said Millicent. 'The basics. Maybe a bit more. But nothing like that.'

Elena nodded at the little hardwood stage. 'Would you like to?'

'Oh yes,' Millicent said again. 'But who would teach me?'

'Well, I would, silly.'

'But I'm supposed to be your legal adviser.'

'We'd find the time,' Elena said. 'It gets a bit boring, dancing alone.'

She went to the cupboard and came up at last with a pair of dancing shoes like her own, elegant leather, with strong, firm heels. 'These should fit you.'

Millicent put them on.

'Come on,' Elena said. 'Let's see if you can do it.'

To the delight of both of them, they found that Millicent could. First the posing of the body in the approved flamenco stance, then the arrogant grace of movement, then the first tentative steps, and as a reward for concentration and hard work, a few more steps to the pianola at the end.

'You did well,' said Elena, but Millicent was looking at the hardwood square.

Elena chuckled. 'No, no,' she said. 'First you crawl, then you walk. But that—' she nodded at the hardwood square, 'that is running in the Olympics . . . I tell you what. Why don't you stay here tonight, have dinner with me? My maid will find you some clothes. It won't be a feast like lunch – not twice in one day – but dancing always makes one hungry. At least it does me.'

That's my lady, Millicent thought. If she likes you, she's happy and she proves it by giving.

'I'd love that,' she said aloud, 'but I ought to let my mother know.'

'Of course,' Elena said. 'Does she have a telephone?'

'Sort of,' said Millicent. It was on the landing outside their flat, and shared with three others, but Elena was far too tactful to demand explanations.

'Use the one in your office,' said Elena, and Millicent got up at once. Never before had she told her mother she was staying with a viscountess.

2

'Are you sure you'll be all right?' Gertie Blenkinsop asked.

'Of course, Mum,' said her daughter. 'She's a lady.'

'Yes, but—' her mother looked at the other doors on the landing. Nobody in sight, but that didn't mean that nobody was listening.

Her daughter visualised her mother, standing by the phone, and realised at once why. Sexually innocent she might be, but she had worked for Duckhouse and Allnutt for almost a year. She knew as much about the theory as any Freudian analyst.

'She isn't one of them, Mum,' she said. 'Honestly.'

Her mother too knew all about Duckhouse and Allnutt. 'You'd know, all right,' she said, 'but then why is she doing all this for you?'

'I helped her handle a tricky situation this morning,' said her daughter, 'but I can't talk about it on the phone.'

'Certainly not,' said Gertie.

'But it isn't just that,' Millicent said. 'We get on together.'

'Still seems funny to me.'

Millicent played her last good card. 'She's mad on dancing,' she said. 'Her mother was a dancer too.'

'I thought you said she was a lady.'

'Well, so are you,' said her daughter.

'Get along with you,' said her mother, but there were no more objections.

In her bedroom Célestine, Elena's maid, had laid out an evening dress of a dark, subtle pink, and a nightdress and negligée of a quite sinful frivolity. Millicent adored all three, then thought about her day as she wallowed in the most luxurious bath she had ever taken. Quite a day. A thief, a constable, a viscountess. (Elena had been right not to press charges. The thief had been family after all.) And dozens of rooms for one person to live in – and that was just London. There was the Hampshire country

17

house as well, with dozens of rooms of its own.

And the dancing. She had adored the dancing from the moment Elena had first begun – and she'd offered to teach her. *And* she was shot of Duckhouse and Allnutt. Far and away the best day of her life since poor Dad had died. She soaped the sponge and stretched out her leg, and just for a second it reminded her that for flamenco, too, there was a price, no matter how young and fit you were.

She dressed and went down to the drawing room, where Elena was drinking champagne. Veuve Clicquot, and what could be more appropriate?

'Help yourself,' she said, and then, as Millicent hesitated: 'One won't hurt you. It's all I usually have.'

'What happens to the rest?' asked Millicent.

'Tufnell drinks it. He's rather fond of champagne.'

Millicent poured out a glassful. At least the rest wouldn't be wasted.

They ate and talked about dancing and went to bed early, which was a relief really. It had been an exhausting day, not least emotionally. Millicent fell asleep almost at once, which was not surprising, she thought next morning. The mattress was the best she had ever lain on. She bathed and dressed in yesterday's suit, made up discreetly, then turned to look at the Dutch flowerpiece on the wall. In no way did that elegant room and her business suit belong together. And yet perhaps they did, she thought. She was a – not a servant exactly – but an employee, and employers did not look like Elena.

Elena was at breakfast: croissants obtained from God knows where, and the most wonderfully aromatic coffee. All the same, Millicent settled for toast and marmalade and tea.

'What shall we do today?' Elena asked.

Really, Millicent thought, I'm more like a companion than a legal adviser. 'I think I should start earning my salary,' she said.

Elena pouted. 'Doing what?'

'First, I think I should tell Duckhouse and Allnutt that they must struggle on without me.'

'Won't that be awkward for you?'

Millicent smiled and shook her head. 'Then, I think I should talk to your solicitors and find out some more about Pudiphatt and Captain Lampeter's will.'

'Yes, of course you must,' said Elena. 'What a fool I am. But surely there'll be time for a dancing lesson?'

'Oh, yes please,' said Millicent.

Phoning Duckhouse and Allnutt was pure delight, as she had known it would be, after a lunch of lobster mayonnaise followed by fresh peaches, with a glass of white burgundy. Of course, she told Duckhouse, told him at once, that she didn't expect any money. Her salary had been fully paid up after all. It wasn't that. It was the fact that she didn't even *try* for any money, and even worse the fact that she wouldn't say where she was going, despite the fact that Duckhouse hinted and hinted, and in the end even asked outright. All she said was: 'I shall miss the old place,' and hung up, and Duckhouse at once sent for Allnutt. Together they spent a frantic and frustrating two hours going through the accounts from the day Miss Millicent Blenkinsop LL B (London) had joined them. Not a ha'penny was missing, which could only mean one of two things: either that Miss Blenkinsop was honest, or that she was far more clever than they were. Duckhouse and Allnutt found it hard to believe that anyone could be that honest, and went through their accounts again.

Millicent persuaded Elena to phone her own solicitors, Messrs Mortimer, Stanhope and Barnes, and was put through to Mr Stanhope at once. Like a bad actress speaking unfamiliar lines, she told him that she had acquired a new personal secretary – not a legal adviser, Millicent insisted; no point in antagonising the whole firm – and that she needed certain information and, of course, she got it. Life was so much easier when one was advising a viscountess, thought Millicent.

Pudiphatt sat brooding in his digs in Earl's Court. About Lady Mendip of course. There could be no doubt that she had cheated him, any more than that the blonde bit with her had – what was the phase? – aided and abetted. All those long words and legal terminology, and that idiot policeman had lapped it up. Well, of course he had. They were both pretty, and one of them at least was rich. What chance had an ex-major living on his pension against that? All the same, that house in Knightsbridge was his, but when he'd gone back for another look later, wary of policemen, the first thing he'd seen was a locksmith changing the locks – after he'd just gone to the expense of having two more copies of the old keys cut. No chance of getting in through the door, and besides, it showed a kind of worldly wisdom unbecoming in young ladies. All the same he had to get possession of his house.

Pudiphatt brooded once more, and then at last it came to him. He poured himself a glass of whisky as a reward for achievement. Information, that was the ticket. In the army the staff could never get enough. Men had died in trench raids just to find out what regiment they were facing after a handover, but once the staff knew, they could plan. And so could he. It would cost money to find out about those two bitches, and he hadn't got all that much, but he had to know. That house was *his*.

Millicent went into the drawing room and said: 'It was just as we thought. You're the sole beneficiary except for a couple of thousand for the oaf, Pudiphatt, and he's already had that.' She advanced into the room a little further to see her mother at ease in a vast armchair covered in silk. Embedded in it, you might say. Not that she was surprised. Her mother would be the last one to pass up the chance to see a dancing viscountess, especially when she had a cast-iron excuse.

'Why, Mum,' she said, 'what brings you here?'

'Brought you some clothes,' said her mum. 'You did say you were staying a while.' The cast-iron excuse.

Gertie looked from her daughter to Lady Mendip, and liked what she saw. Darkly beautiful, determined, but the charm – there was a lot of charm – seemed real enough. Real enough to get three very rich husbands and two more houses just like this. And they all married her, that was the point. During the war all the chaps were getting married, when they weren't away killing Germans. Or being killed. And yet rich as she is, she's fond of our Millie, and it's genuine. No good trying to work out why. Not yet. Early days. All the same, she knew it was true. And it wasn't just because Millie had made herself useful with that daft Pudiphatt. A cheque would have taken care of that.

Elena looked from mother to daughter and could see at once what Millicent would look like in twenty years' time. A little too plump, Mrs Blenkinsop, a little too rounded for current fashion, but she was pretty still, still moved with a dancer's grace.

'So, you don't mind your daughter living with me for a while?' she asked.

'Mind?' said Gertie Blenkinsop. 'Of course not. Beats Pimlico any day.'

'Do you think Dad would have minded?' Millicent asked.

'Not him' said Gertie. 'Not if I didn't.'

'If I may ask,' said Elena, 'what happened to your husband?'

'The North Sea happened,' said Gertie, 'and the North Atlantic. Twice. He was on destroyers. What they call an ERA – Engine Room Artificer. Sort of a petty officer. Blown up three times, and in the middle of winter, and that was once too many, even if you're as tough as my Bert was. Even then it was pneumonia that got him in the end.'

Elena looked at her, and thought at once of her Charlie. 'You must miss him dreadfully,' she said.

'Well, I do,' said Gertie, 'but I try to keep busy.'

The butler came in and brought coffee, and said that cook would like a word. Elena moved with that floating movement that only dancers can achieve, thought Gertie, and not all of them.

'I'll try not to be too long,' she said, and left them.

'So, you're going up in the world,' said Gertie.

'Looks like it.'

'A house in Eaton Place; a viscountess for a mate,' said Gertie. 'You've become one of the nobs, our Millie.'

'A toff anyway,' Millicent said. 'What do you think of her?'

'I like her,' said Gertie. 'I didn't think I would, but I do. Honest as day, that one, but she won't take any nonsense.'

Just like you, Millicent thought. No wonder you like her.

'And from what you tell me, she wasn't always rich like this.' Her hands gestured at the drawing room. 'Not that it shows . . . And so pretty.'

'All of that,' said Millicent. 'And I wish you could see her dance, Mum.'

Elena came in and heard it, and said to Gertie, 'Would you like to?'

'Yes, please. Our Millie told you I used to do a bit in that line. But not like that – musical comedy, that was me. Floradora, The Maid of the Mountains, Chu Chin Chow. Now and again we might do a bit of what our manager said was Spanish. *Fandangos* and that. But I doubt it.' And the Can-Can by private arrangement, she thought, but only if you wanted to. The manager was a very nice man.

'Those days, I was known as Gertie Garnet: stage name. It should have been Dora Diamond. I'd have gone a bit further.' She finished her champagne.

Then Tufnell came in to ask what time lunch would be served, and watched in horror as Gertie went to the cooler and poured herself another glass – and no skimping either.

This time Elena danced in costume: a flounced dress with

21

twiddly bits that would show a bit of leg when she twirled, thought Gertie. White, with scarlet spots the size of saucers, and yet she didn't look vulgar. Maybe she couldn't look vulgar, no matter what she wore or did . . . Elena started the gramophone, and she was off. Like a firework display, thought Gertie. All noise and soaring colour. The last record ended, and Elena looked at Gertie.

'Did you like it?' she asked.

'Loved it,' said Gertie, then, as if by instinct, went to a cupboard and found the towel she knew would be there, and handed it to Elena, who smiled at her.

'You know all about dancers,' she said.

'I should,' said Gertie, and looked at her daughter. 'You're teaching our Millie?' Elena nodded. 'Might I see her too?'

'Mum, I've only had one lesson,' Millicent said.

'I want to see how you look,' said her mother.

She really means to, Elena thought. She really loves her, just as my mother loved me: and so Millicent posed like a gypsy, did a few practice steps, danced to the pianola, and Gertie sighed in relief. She thinks she is going to be good, thought Elena, and so do I, and she invited Gertie to lunch to celebrate.

Lunch was again excellent, and Gertie did it full justice, and thanked her hostess for what had been a memorable morning by any standards.

'Not at all,' said Elena. 'You must come again soon. See what progress Millicent is making.'

Gertie said thank you yet again, but Tufnell eyed her warily.

When Gertie set off for Pimlico at last, Elena and Millicent sat on over their coffee.

'I do like your mother,' Elena said.

'I'm glad.'

'Forgive me,' said Elena, 'but was your father like her?'

'Not a bit,' said Millicent. 'A typical Navy man, my father. Neat, tidy, clever with his hands. A bit strict perhaps, but oh, so generous. His family could have everything he had and I almost did. It was his pension that helped to pay for my studies. They would have paid for my articled clerkship.'

'I'm not sure I quite understand,' said Elena.

'To be a solicitor you have to be an articled clerk,' Millicent explained. 'Work in a solicitor's office; learn the ropes so to speak, then take the qualifying exams. Dad was saving up for that, too – only he died of pneumonia, and most of the pension stopped.'

She smiled. Such a sad smile, thought Elena. 'So, you see, your legal adviser's an impostor.'

'Darling, you could never be that,' said Elena. 'Not even if you practised . . . which reminds me—'

The three months' probation came and went so quickly. Almost from the start Millicent knew she would stay. Never had she had a job that was more congenial, or better paid, and a house that was more like a palace than the flats she'd been used to, but even more than that, she had a friend, because aristocrat or not, million-airess or not, Elena was her friend. She had known it from the moment they had begun their dancing.

The flamenco was going well, too. Elena said so, and Elena wouldn't lie, not about something so dear to her.

'God, it's amazing,' she said one day. 'Not a gypsy, not even a Spaniard, and yet the magic is there.'

Gertie was often there too: sitting in the studio, shouting encouragement, shooing them off to their baths when the practice was over, and off Elena would go, as meekly obedient as Millicent. I know what she's after, her daughter thought. Making herself useful, indispensable even: becoming part of the act: the behind-the-scenes part. And why not? She's awfully good at it.

Barre exercise, for example. My God, how it hurt at first, and how good you felt once you got the hang of it. Even more poise. More grace. No doubt about it, Gertie really had earned her place in the act. Was that what she was after? It would be interesting to find out. In the meantime, Gertie was always there when she was needed – not least because she couldn't bear to be idle – until the moment came when Elena decided that Gertie should be paid for what she did.

At first the older woman was furious, with a dancer's temper and temperament; but Elena continued to look hurt, and the torrent ebbed to a trickle.

'But you're our colleague, our adviser,' she said. 'All advisers are entitled to a fee. They expect it.'

Gertie melted, and worked twice as hard. Worked them twice as hard too, thought Elena, as she cautiously lowered her aching body into a steaming bath.

Inevitably, it was Gertie who first thought of it. It just came to me, she said, one day. The practice had finished: Millicent and Elena, partners now, dancing together: *malagueñas*, *fandangos*, *sevillanas*, and in the middle of it Elena alone, dancing a *zapateado*.

As quickly as Millicent had learned, she was by no means ready for that. Not yet.

'What, Mum?' she asked.

'About your act,' said Gertie. 'It's mostly a double act and that's fine. But double acts means boy and girl stuff, only our Millie should be the boy, because she's a bit taller.'

'But, Mum,' said her daughter, 'when we dance it's only for fun. And exercise of course.'

'Fun!' said her mother witheringly. 'Don't tell me. And if you wanted exercise you could try lifting dumb-bells. You two are good now. You need an audience.'

'You think we're that good?' Elena asked.

'I know it,' Gertie said. 'God knows I've been in the business long enough. You two are ready.'

'But, Mum,' said Millicent again, 'we could hardly go on the music hall.' Even Elena looked shocked.

'I've been thinking about that, too,' said Gertie. 'You can't just go on as you are, hammering hell out of the floorboards.'

'Why can't we?' said Elena.

'Because you're far and away past the exercise stage,' Gertie said. 'What you're doing now – it's art. On the other hand, like our Millie says, you can't go on the music hall, either.'

'So what can we do?' Elena asked.

'That's what I've been thinking about. Charity shows.'

'Ah,' said Elena, but Millicent looked puzzled. 'There are lots of balls and things, especially during the season,' Elena continued. 'Rather grand ones. In a big house or a smart hotel. Entrance by ticket only, and the organisers throw in a dinner and champagne and often a cabaret too, and whatever profit there is goes to a charity: the unemployed, or ex-servicemen, or shoeless children.' She turned to Gertie. 'Is that what you had in mind?'

'That's it,' said Gertie.

'I don't know,' said Millicent.

'What don't you know?' said her mother. 'Don't you want to dance in public? Show the nobs how good you are?'

'I rather think I'd love it,' Millicent said, 'but—' She looked at Elena.

'I rather think I'd love it too,' said Elena, and the two young women smiled at each other, delighted.

'Then that's settled,' said Gertie. However briefly, she was in charge. 'Now about costume. This boy and girl lark. It's always popular. Gets the chaps in the audience all excited – heaven knows why – seeing a girl dressed like a boy dancing with another girl. I mean, look at pantomime. But it does mean they'll put more money in the raffle.'

You've been there already, Elena thought. Done it all. Oh, I do like you.

'Now, about costume. Elena's got the lot, of course she has, but you'll need trousers and a shirt, all that.'

'I'll have some made,' said Elena, and Millicent winced.

'Indeed, you will not,' said Gertie. 'I know a theatrical tailor in the East End who'll do it for a quarter of the price, *and* do a damn good job. Now, let's go back to the studio and check we don't have to alter the choreography a bit if Millie's going to be a chap.'

When Gertie set off back to Pimlico, Elena said, 'I do like your – mum? Isn't that what you call her?'

'That's right.'

'I called mine Mama. In many ways they are so different, but they are alike, too. There is just one thing—' Oh, my God, Millicent thought. What's gone wrong? But it couldn't be that. Elena had just said she liked Mum, and about that of all things she wouldn't lie.

'It's her accent,' said Elena. 'Sometimes it's quite strong – especially when she's excited about something, but it doesn't sound in the least bit Cockney.'

'It isn't,' said Millicent. 'Mum grew up in the North East of England, in a place called Black Sills. The accent there *is* strong, and the dialect. When she's really agitated, even I have to concentrate.'

'You should hear the Spanish the gypsies in Seville speak,' said Elena.

3

That night she dreamed of Toby. She didn't often but at dinner she had drunk rather a lot of claret. (Millicent had drunk very little, but when she'd first come to stay she had drunk none at all.) It was all about adapting, as Millicent's mum said, and maybe that was true of dreaming too. When it came, at last, it was the one she usually had. Honeymoon, then bed as usual, and how nice he had been, even when he hurt her, and there was a paradox for you: but then Toby had been nice, and goodness how Mama had despised him for it. A man's business was to be a *man*, but cavalry officer or not, poor Toby had had no idea how to cope with that kind of manhood.

On the other hand he was rich, and because of all the pain and wriggling and squirming she became rich too, which was why Mama had arranged the marriage, and very right and proper that was.

The funeral had been splendid. The English didn't like that word applied to funerals, but then they'd never seen the Escorial . . . Toby's mother, a widow, had cried throughout. She and her mother had not, and Mrs Crick had detested them for it. Even the magnificence of their mourning clothes was no substitute for tears, it seemed. Not that it mattered.

She had died herself soon afterwards. Heart, poor thing. At least she'd be with her darling Toby, *and* he'd missed the war. Toby would have been hopeless in any war, never mind the unending nightmare that had already begun when he died. Drowsy and half awake, she began to think of Charlie, and the courage he had shown in the trenches. Not that he had told her so: the good ones never told civilians what it was like: least of all their ladies.

'Pretty rotten. Not exactly the Ritz.' That was all you got. A sort of code they had to honour. But after the funeral his brother officers had told her something of what he'd done. There were medals to prove it. And Freddy had been the same. Not like poor dear Toby at all.

Next morning she read in the *Morning Post* that her father-in-law, Lord Chard, and his wife were to give a ball, and wrote to him at once, then went to see Millicent in her office, because the next thing was business after all. She had thought about it long and hard, and had finally decided that it had to be done. She wasn't just Mrs Crick or Mrs Lampeter or Lady Mendip, after all, she was somebody's daughter and she wanted to know whose, now that her mother had gone. He might turn out to be a rascal, of course, but she doubted it. Her mother had been marvellous, but she'd been shrewd, too. If her father had disappeared there had to be a reason, and anyway Millicent would be discreet. She was sure of it. Not only was she her friend, but she had worked for Duckhouse and Allnutt, and from what Millicent had told her, discretion must have been essential to their survival. When she had done, Millicent said, 'Records. There must be records somewhere.'

'Not at my solicitors,' said Elena. 'I asked them.'

'The Knightsbridge house?'

Elena shook her head. 'There's nothing of Mama's there.'

'Your mother's digs?'

Elena thought for a moment: 'It's possible I suppose,' she said at last. 'But Mama didn't like leaving her good stuff in her digs. People might just walk in and help themselves.'

'Grosvenor Square then. Not just the best place for safe-keeping; the only place. Or so you thought. Besides, it might be as well to make sure Pudiphatt hasn't popped in to borrow a set of Chippendale chairs.'

Pudiphatt looked at the mass of paper in front of him. That was what hiring a private detective involved, apparently. Paper. Mostly from Somerset House: copies of birth certificates, death certificates, wills, house deeds, land deeds; a great stack of them, so big he'd had to sober up before he could read them. He could have done most of it himself, he thought, but he still had enough money to get somebody else to do it. Boring work, and if he let somebody else do it that left him free to read *his* books: novels by G.A. Henty and Rider Haggard, poetry by Sir Henry Newbolt, and his favourite, Baden Powell's *Scouting for Boys*. Then there was his whisky, and cheap meals in cheap cafés. God, what a life! But when he'd reclaimed what had been his in the first place, things would all be different . . . The trouble was he knew so little about her. About her dead husbands he knew just about everything, but her – not even a birth certificate. Not even her mother's marriage certificate.

He went once more to look at his house but the locks had all been changed. The new ones were even more formidable than the ones for which he'd held the keys. Best to forget it. All the same, three houses in town and another in Hampshire. It just wasn't bloody fair. He went to the Knightsbridge house then, but they might have known he was coming. It was locked, bolted and barred all over the place. Like a fortress, he thought: like a German pillbox. To get in there he'd need a bloody tank. Better try the other one. True, the Eaton Place house, like this one, had nothing to do with him, not legally, but illegally – that was different. She'd stolen his inheritance after all. Pudiphatt looked around him for a bus stop. A taxi would have been so much easier, but he couldn't afford taxis. He needed the fares for whisky.

They missed Pudiphatt by five minutes, but there was no one to tell them so. The chauffeur opened the door for them and in they went, and everything appeared to be as it should be: neat, tidy, the furniture shrouded in Holland covers. And so much of it.

'It'll take a day at least,' said Millicent. The trouble was, she hadn't got a day. Mum was coming for what she rather grandly called a rehearsal, and Mum was always prompt.

'Oh dear, I'm afraid it will,' said Elena. 'We'll come back soon. I have to know, darling. Honestly I do.'

And so they left, but on the way Elena burrowed under one of the covers and came out with a photograph of a lady in a sumptuous silver frame.

'Your mother?' asked Millicent, and Elena nodded. 'I know it's ridiculous, even impossible,' she said, 'but I couldn't bear it if Pudiphatt got his hands on it, and the frame is silver, after all.'

Pudiphatt had finished his inspection – reconnoitring you might say – when he spotted the Rolls-Royce and bent to tie a shoelace that was already tied. The butler came to the door of the house as the chauffeur opened the car door and saluted. A footman came running to take whatever it was the bitch was carrying. A photograph in a frame, and solid silver by the look of it. More of his money. The frame would pawn for pounds and pounds, but there was nothing doing there. Nothing at all. Eaton Place, too, had more than its share of locks and bolts, and the butler was built like a guardsman, and the other two manservants also had the same dangerous look of ex-soldiers who know how to fight. I would lose, he thought. There isn't a hope; and yet he really would need the money soon.

When they returned there was a message from Lord Chard. He was at his flat in Duke Street, and wanted to talk. Elena went at once to the phone, and Millicent went to her office and the household accounts. Really, to keep Elena and herself alive would have supported a pit village for days.

Elena came to her at last. 'You'll have to change,' she said. 'We're dancing.'

'Lord Chard?'

'He sees nothing wrong in the idea,' said Elena. 'All the same, he wants to see for himself.'

'An audition,' said Millicent. 'Nothing wrong with that. We'll have to do our best.'

They went to change: Elena into one of her beautiful, extrovert dresses: Millicent into a pair of rehearsal trousers and a shirt run up at lightning speed by Mum's tailor, and then Lord Chard arrived. His lordship looked wary. Nothing *infra dig* about Elena dancing in public, he thought; especially with a respectable female with a law degree. All the same, it seemed a bit odd. Yet Elena had been blessed with the kind of realistic common sense that poor old Freddy had never had. Tufnell showed him to the studio door and left him to it. Ah well, he thought. In at the deep end. Mine but to do or die. He knocked and went in. He hadn't had the faintest idea what to expect, but what he got was the sight of two extraordinarily pretty girls facing each other in the classical flamenco pose, absorbing the guitar music from a gramophone that had only just started playing. My God, they're gorgeous he thought, and it was true enough, the dark and the fair who would look lovely wherever they were, but even more so because they were together. The guitar paused, then struck a vivid, angry chord before the guitarist's fingers flew and they were off.

Controlled dementia, Chard thought later, because if the wildness was there, so was the control. This was dancing of a rare quality, and he was their first audience. It finished at last, and Millicent went to the cupboard for towels. He wants more, she thought. It's written all over him – but never give too much at an audition. 'If he wants more let him ask for it,' her mother had said when she told her he was coming, 'and if he doesn't why waste your breath?'

Lord Chard wanted more. 'You were absolutely marvellous,' he was saying.

'Thank you,' said Elena. 'Do excuse us going straight into it like that but we find it's much the best way.'

'Yes, indeed,' said Chard.

'Oh, by the way,' Elena said, 'may I present Miss Millicent Blenkinsop? She's my secretary and legal adviser.'

Lord Chard thought of *his* legal adviser, Mr Sproat, and his secretary, Miss Simkins. Never in a thousand years would either of them look like Millicent Blenkinsop.

'How do you do?' he said.

Millicent dried her hands on the towel. 'How do you do?' she said.

'May I offer you something?' Elena asked. 'Tea? A drink?'

But Lord Chard had promised faithfully to take tea with his wife at the Ritz.

''Fraid not,' he said, 'but when you make your début – it's to be at Hallam Castle. Now mind, I mean that, or I'll never speak to you again.'

'You have our word,' said Elena gravely, and Lord Chard looked at the gramophone, sighed and left them.

'Hallam Castle?' asked Millicent.

'It's his house in Sussex,' said Elena. 'Where they're giving their charity ball. It's one of the events of the season. Oh, Millicent, we've done it.' She flung her arms about her.

'We certainly have,' said Millicent. 'If he'd been an impresario he'd have produced a contract,' and she hugged her friend in return, until Elena broke free.

'I lied to you earlier,' she said.

'Lied?'

'About Mama – and her digs. There's loads of her stuff there – only somehow I couldn't face the idea of going through it. I funked it.'

'I'll be with you,' Millicent said.

'Yes, thank God,' said Elena. 'Otherwise I couldn't do it ever. You're not upset?'

'Of course not,' said Millicent. 'I know how I would have felt if it had been Mum.'

They sat and smoked a rare cigarette before their baths. Cigarettes had to be rare; the dancing saw to that.

Gertie, of course, was delighted to hear about the audition, her one regret that she hadn't been there when it happened. Still, the girls seemed to have handled it well enough between them. All the same, she made them do a bit more when they rehearsed: a fiendishly long time at the barre, and the same flamenco movements over and over until at last they went down to the drawing room for drinks: sherry for Gertie and Elena, white wine and soda for Millicent. Gertie looked at the photograph in the silver frame.

'Is that your mam?' she asked.

'Mam? Oh, Mama,' said Elena. 'Yes.'

'You're the model of her,' Gertie said.

'Then I'm lucky,' said Elena, and Gertie nodded. The photograph said it all. A real bonny'un. 'What name did she use when she danced?' asked Gertie.

'Her own. Margarita Menendez.' It's time to talk, she thought. Millicent is my friend, and so is Gertie – if a favourite aunt can be a friend. It's time they knew more about me.

'My mother wasn't a gypsy,' she said. 'All the best flamenco dancers are, but my mother didn't dance flamenco. Her parents were middle class, her father a not-too-successful lawyer, and they didn't want their daughter to dance at all. It was only because she wanted to do the classic style – the style of the Spanish Court – that they relented. And just as well. Mama turned out to be very, very good and made rather a lot of money.

'The girls were – protected. Dancers had always been fair game, but not it seemed when they came from backgrounds like Mama's. For them a *nudriza* was provided.' Gertie and her daughter looked baffled. 'A *carabina*,' said Elena, and if anything the bafflement intensified. 'A chaperone,' said Elena, and Gertie did her best not to smile. In her dance troupe chaperones had been in very short supply.

Throughout Europe, Spanish music and dancing had become both fashionable and popular, and Mama a rising star. She had been everywhere, in those blissful days before the war: Paris, Vienna, St Petersburg, Rome: but it was in London that she'd met her father. Elena has no idea who he was, thought Gertie, but she was quite sure that he'd married Mama, and that they had been happy. For a while anyway. And why not? Gertie thought. Nobody else would know her mother as she had done. The marriage explained itself, she thought. All those chaperones, but why had the blushing bridegroom been so furtive? A high-up, probably, but who? The Prince of Wales? The Archbishop of Canterbury?

And yet Elena itched to know who her father was. Nothing wrong with that. He was her *father*. And rich too, Gertie thought. A flat in South Kensington couldn't compare with a house in Eaton Place, but it wouldn't be cheap. Millicent had the answer. Once a month, banknotes had been sent to Elena's mother in a plain envelope that paid not only the nursing home, but all the expensive fripperies that rich babies enjoy.

Margarita had given up dancing. She wasn't bored with it exactly, but she preferred the company of Elena, whose existence it would be hard to explain to her fellow dancers. And then her father died, and she took her baby to Malaga, only to find that her mother was dying too. Cholera. A busy time for death considering the year was 1912, thought Gertie. Two years later he'd been working round the clock. Elena and her mother must have escaped the cholera, she thought. A girl's never the same after cholera. She looked at the photograph.

'You know, I've got a feeling I've seen your Mam,' she said. 'We were never on the same bills. Nothing like that. Like I say – Floradora and 'Tell Me Pretty Maiden' and the odd Can-Can if the money was right. That was me. All the same I know I've met her and the reason I'm so sure is that she was every bit as gorgeous as that photograph.' If she remembered she'd have a chat with Millie, but if he'd been a wrong'un she wouldn't say another word. She *liked* Lady Mendip.

It would soon be time to go to Hallam Castle, Elena thought, but first she must do something about her mother's flat: empty it and pay the rent until the end of the month. It proved to be a very difficult thing to do, severing the last link. But how could she not do it? To leave it undone would be morbid indeed. And anyway, she would have Millicent with her, and that would make all the difference.

'So much stuff,' said Millicent, and indeed there was. Above all else, Margarita Menendez had been a hoarder, and being a lady of modest affluence with an eye for the good things in life, what she had hoarded was worth hoarding: theatrical costume, (Elena was delighted because the dresses fitted her), stage make-up, mantillas, dresses, combs. Stage jewellery too, and real jewellery in a locked box for which Elena had the key. (Not that a burglar would have been bothered, Elena thought. He'd simply have walked off with the box.) Other clothes too. Coats, dresses, underwear, stockings, shoes – and a writing desk crammed full of papers, and even more in a secret drawer that Millicent's burglar would have found and opened in minutes. How furious that awful Pudiphatt would have been if he'd known. It was in just such a drawer in just such a writing desk that what Elena had called her 'spare' jewellery had been hidden, and the removal men had been just about to lift it into the van when she appeared with the policeman.

She looked again at the separate piles of clothes: coats, dresses, underwear. Just as well she had brought skips and tea chests, and a lorry to drive them to Eaton Place. Most of the furniture belonged to the landlord, but pieces like the writing desk would go into storage. She wondered what would happen to the clothes . . .

Elena too looked at the neat piles of clothing. Like the charity sale she'd once opened, she thought. It wasn't her mother's life exactly – that had gone, never to return – but rather its setting, its frame. And she didn't need it any more. The days of drinking too much claret and weeping at the sight of Mama's favourite tea gown were over. Better to get rid of them all. She had her dancing now, and her friend who relied on her, just as she relied on Millicent. Carefully they packed the clothes into the skips and containers, and the men with the lorry took them off to Eaton Place. But Millicent hung on to the papers and documents, for a day when Elena would be out, just in case her mum's chap turned out to be awful, and I have to destroy the evidence, she thought. But there was nothing, just bills and papers.

4

The day came at last, and Gertie went with them. How could they dance without their choreographer? asked Elena, but this time, Gertie insisted, she was their dresser. Whatever she was, she too rode in the Rolls-Royce, something she had done far more often than Millie, she thought, especially after Can-Can performances . . .

In the car she chattered incessantly. She had to. Her charges sat tense and silent, Millie rigid, Elena coiled like a spring. Nerves, Gertie thought, and not even first-night nerves. Début nerves as you might say. Ah well, nothing she could do about that. Everybody had to have them once. Like the measles. Not that she was all that worried. Once the music started they'd be fine. She'd bet the rent on it. When they arrived she hurried them into the room set aside for them, then went to bully the band into getting the tempo right. Her charges looked at each other.

'Well,' said Millicent.

'Well, indeed,' said Elena.

'Into the valley of death,' said Millicent, and indeed a lot of the men at the ball had been soldiers, and some of them cavalry at that.

'I sound the most dreadful coward,' said Millicent.

'Not at all,' said Elena. 'Ours but to do or die.'

Millicent brightened at once. 'To blazes with dying,' she said. 'Let's just do.'

The two of them smiled at each other. Triumph or disaster, they would do it together, and in style.

When Gertie came back to them, they were talking about Pudiphatt, and whether it would be a good idea to make an image of him, stick pins in it and say spells. Everything's going to be fine, Gertie thought. She just knew it.

'Time to get changed,' she said, and the two young women removed their dresses. Golly, she's gorgeous Millicent thought,

35

but Mum says I'm a bit of all right too, and nobody would mistake me for a chap, even in shirt and trousers.

Gertie wrapped them in vast bath towels (no one must see the costumes), led them to the improvised stage, and they turned to face each other. Stark black and white with a gleam of scarlet looked at white dotted with huge scarlet spots, improbable earrings, (but just right for the costume) and a carnation threaded into gleaming black hair. Millicent wore a flat-brimmed hat, like a picador's, covering her hair that Mum had plaited into a bullfighter's pigtail. When the time came, she would skim the hat into the wings and the pigtail would whip the air as she danced. All part of the act. Gertie coughed from what wings there were and they took the pose: two dancers frozen in time, like a masterpiece by the early Goya, and slowly, inexorably, the curtains parted and the band began to play. Do or die indeed, thought Millicent; it's too late for anything else, but already the applause had begun, because never before had the audience seen such tempestuous, even angry beauty, as the band's guitarist struck the chord that Gertie had made him practise over and over. The ice that froze the dancers shattered, and they exploded into life: *fandango*, *malagueña*, *sevillana*, and every time more applause as their steps snapped like firecrackers, before Millicent stood back to allow Elena to perform the *zapateado*, the foot-stamping dance that reminded half the men there of machine-gun fire, the dance that Millicent wasn't ready for, not yet. And so she clapped her hands instead, but not like the audience. This was what the gypsies called the *palmas*, that showed that even two palms meeting could be a musical instrument, a kaleidoscope of rhythm and counter rhythm that Elena had taught her, until at last Elena turned to her, arms outstretched, as if she had been away too long from her beloved, and they danced together once more, slowly this time but haughty still, and proud: and so engrossed that they were oblivious to the applause, and the people who made it. There was only each other.

The tempo quickened for the last time, and Millicent took off her hat and flung it into the wings, where Gertie fielded it neatly as the pigtail fell then flew. More applause, but then the tempo slowed and died, and Elena and Millicent turned to face their audience and ceased to be the beings they had created: reverted instead to two very pretty girls who had just performed a work of art as difficult as it was beautiful, and the applause acknowledged it, and one by one the audience rose. As Elena curtseyed and

Millicent bowed, Elena whispered, 'We didn't die, anyway.'

'Into the valley of death and out the other end,' Millicent whispered back. 'It's wonderful.'

Then the curtains closed for the last time and Gertie appeared with two glasses of champagne, and noticed that her daughter drank as Elena did: without thinking, as of right, because they had both offered the best they had, and only the best would do in return. Not that it worried Gertie. There was more than her share still left in the bottle, after she'd mopped the sweat from their faces with hand towels, then wrapped them in those other vast towels like Roman togas and led them to their baths, because young ladies shouldn't even glow, never mind sweat.

'Take your time,' Mum had told them. 'Let the hot water soak it out of you. We don't want you stiff and sore in the morning.'

And take their time they did. Not just hot water, but a huge sponge, and soap and bath salts from Paris. Bliss, thought Millicent.

Out then to dry herself and go into the bedroom reserved for them, where Mum had laid out stockings, underwear, her evening dress. (Elena, it seemed, had taken Mum's advice too. She was still in her bath.) Dry at last, she began to dress. Knickers and brassière first, and golly how marvellous the feel of silk was against her skin. But then it was all marvellous. Stockings next, to be handled gently, cautiously, because they were silk too, and laddered at a glance: but oh the feel of them . . . She looked at the dress: blue with a pattern of white: a gift from Elena. She had loaned her jewellery too: diamond drops for her ears; a diamond and sapphire necklace. What a darling she was.

Then she came in, rosy from the bath, enveloped in her toga towel, and smiled at Millicent, still in her underwear, who thought how lucky some chap would be – and soon by the look of things – for Elena had that air about her that said as plain as speech: I need a nice chap. She shed the towel, patted herself dry, and stretched like a cat, and Millicent stared. It wasn't that she didn't care that she was naked – it probably didn't even occur to her to think about it – but oh, how lovely Elena was. Like that copy of the painting she'd once seen: Giorgione's 'Sleeping Venus'. Elena found her talcum powder, and began to use it. Three chaps, thought Millicent. Three very lucky chaps indeed, except that all three were dead. And me with never a one.

'I think we can say we went down well, Miss Blenkinsop,' said Elena.

'We certainly can, Lady Mendip,' said Millicent.

Elena put out her tongue at her. 'Tomorrow we rest,' she said. 'No rehearsals. Nothing. *Nada*. We gave it our all tonight. We're *entitled* to a rest.' She stretched out her legs and looked at them, as if they were a pair of earrings she was pleased with, thought Millicent. Perhaps even delighted. 'Lord Chard said the Press are here,' she continued.

'What press?' Millicent asked. Not that it bothered her. It was just one more delight.

Elena shrugged, and at once was Spanish: 'Oh – *Tatler*, *Bystander*, magazines from all over. *And* the dailies. *Mail*, *Express*, *Morning Post*, *Mercury*, *Sketch*, all that lot. *The Times*, too, Lord Chard says.'

The Times it seemed was a kind of accolade.

'I hope they won't be too disappointed,' Elena said.

'*Disappointed?*'

Elena said darkly, 'It's my belief they came to see us make a mess of things. A couple of toffs trying to act like Pavlova . . . Only we weren't like that.'

'I should say not,' said Millicent. 'Even Mum says we were at our absolute best.'

Mum, as they both knew to their cost, was their severest critic.

'Well, now we'll have to look our absolute best again,' said Elena. 'They say the camera can't lie, but it knows how to dodge round the truth. Better leave me to do the talking, darling. You just stand there and look scrumptious. It should be pie for you.'

And indeed it was much more Elena's thing than mine, thought Millicent. Elena said so outright – another reason to like her so, and it was true. A widowed viscountess, three times honourably married, dancing like a gypsy in the house of the earl her father-in-law, to raise money for a charity that helped disabled soldiers, and by her side Millicent Blenkinsop, doing her best to look scrumptious, though a course at London University in Law wasn't perhaps the best training for scrumptiousness.

'And what will I be in all this?' she asked.

'My legal adviser, which is what you are,' said Elena. '*And* my dancing partner, because you're that, too. I couldn't cope without you.'

What a darling she is thought Millicent. All the same she felt better when Elena put some clothes on.

Downstairs then to confront the press, who mobbed them at once: flashguns popping, questions showering in a kind of respectful torrent. (Elena's father-in-law was an earl after all, and she a viscountess); but Elena handled it all without any obvious sense of strain: all those weddings, thought Millicent, who then discovered that when she worked as a lawyer she was indeed Millicent Blenkinsop, LL B (Lond), but that when she danced she was Rosario of Elena and Rosario. The press loved that too. They and their readers had a fixed image of what a lady lawyer should look like; horn-rimmed spectacles, hair shingled if not drawn back in a bun, and to discover one who was not only blonde and pretty but danced with a kind of frenzied elegance delighted them.

After that she met the Earl of Chard and his countess, who obviously adored Elena, even if their ways of life were so different. And really, it *was* rather odd. After all, she had been twice a widow before she had even met their son, and yet the fact that they did adore her was obvious. Perhaps it was because while they were together she had made their Freddy happy. Then she watched the countess smile at her daughter-in-law and thought: There's no 'perhaps' about it, and anyway, if Elena liked a man, she would always be a giver.

Francis Boyce was at the ball, Elena noticed. Once Mama had thought he might be Number Four – Mama seemed to think that her daughter could go on marrying into the English nobility and gentry for ever – but for once her daughter had rebelled, telling Mama that a line had to be drawn somewhere, and Francis Boyce was it. Not that he was ghastly: on the contrary. Good looking, clever, unfailingly pleasant, that was Francis. It was just that she didn't like him 'in that way', as the romantic novelists said, and in any case she needed a rest, and when you got down to it she had enough money as it was, without having to worry about how much Francis had. He was in the Stock Exchange, a broker nowadays, so he wouldn't exactly beg for his bread, but even so, the money she had was *hers*, to be spent as *she* liked, though it was nice to do things for Millicent from time to time.

She looked towards him and smiled, and he came to her at once, which was gratifying, even though Millicent was with her, and it was obvious, to her at any rate, that either one of them would do. But Millicent's needs were greater than hers. Millicent needed a nice chap, and above all else, Francis was *nice*, and so she sent them off to dance, and waltzed with the earl instead, because the earl not only waltzed divinely still, he knew exactly how to flirt with a young and pretty woman less than half his age in a way that made them both feel good. At last he asked her if she and her friend intended to continue dancing.

'Would you object?' Elena asked.

'Wouldn't make a ha'porth of difference if I did if your mind's made up, but I don't as it happens.'

'You liked us then?'

'Adored you both,' said the earl. 'I've told you so three times already, but flattery isn't the point. Not this time.'

'Please tell me the point,' she said, and smiled.

'I love it when you smile like that,' said Chard, as a man might say: 'When it comes to champagne, you can't beat Krug,' then continued: 'The point is, I've already had requests for your time and talent. The pair of you.'

'Well, of course the pair of us,' said Elena, and quoted Gertie: 'We're a double act. But what makes you think we'll be wanted?'

'Just you wait till tomorrow's papers appear,' said Chard. 'That alone should do it. And in any case, I'm on the board of other charities too. Not just my poor disabled soldiers. The two of you could help raise the devil of a lot of money. Do a lot of good, too. That is if it isn't too much trouble.'

'Trouble?' said Elena. 'We adore our dancing. Of course we'll do it. And thank you for the offer. It's very flattering.'

'Flattering?' said the earl.

'Not every double act has an earl for a manager,' Elena said, then looked at her friend, supple and easy in Francis Boyce's arms, and happy to be there, and he too was happy because of what he was holding. Love at first sight? She wondered, and indeed he is pleasant and charming, all that, but he wouldn't do for me and just as well. It's far too early for Millicent and me to start quarrelling. Even so, it was time to start thinking about another man. If nothing else, they get to be rather a habit. Lord Chard waltzed beautifully, but he was far too old, besides being married already, and in any case she wasn't at all sure that she wanted to be married again: not yet, anyway. What she wanted was a man.

As she prepared them for bed, Gertie told them she was proud of them, and both young women preened themselves. Receiving praise from Gertie was like extracting gold from a miser . . .

'You went down well with the staff too,' said Gertie.

'They were watching?' Her daughter sounded not so much horrified as bewildered.

40

'Upper servants always see everything,' said Gertie, and this time it was Elena's turn to look startled. 'Now don't start fretting,' said Gertie. 'I'll be here to keep an eye on them so long as I'm wanted.'

'Then you'll be here the devil of a long time,' said Elena.

At that Gertie blushed. A rare event indeed, her daughter thought.

'Thank you, my lady,' Gertie said. Deference too, thought Millicent. Even rarer.

'I hope they fed you properly,' said Elena.

'Same as you,' said Gertie. 'The butler saw to that. Only no Roederer Cristal. We had to make do with Veuve Clicquot.'

'You poor deprived thing,' said Millicent, and Elena chuckled as Gertie tucked them up for the night, and went to find her own room. And very nice too, she thought. Good bed and proper lights, not candles. A proper upper servant's room. All the same she'd better remember to bolt the door. The butler had had that look in his eye. Even so, to have an earl's stately home to stay in – you couldn't top that for class – *and* a Rolls-Royce to take her back to London next day. Something she'd done far more often than Millicent, she thought again, go home in a Rolls-Royce, even if it was in an informal sort of way that she didn't want for Millie. Time to talk to Millie, who was looking even prettier than usual. Could it be that Boyce she'd danced with so much? He'd looked like a nice chap, but all the same there'd be no harm in a chat. Not the birds and the bees – Millie knew all about that in theory – but when you got down to business it wasn't theory you needed, not by a long chalk. Practice, that was the thing you had to have, even if it was painfully acquired. Maybe she'd better ask Elena to have a word, too. She'd know. She must.

Think of tomorrow: think of the nice things: not just the Rolls-Royce but the eggs and bacon cooked by somebody else. And the papers. That the papers would be marvellous she had no doubt at all. And unless she missed her guess there'd be more photographs before long. Gertie got into bed, yawned and stretched. Other things to think about too. Like gossip. All upper servants were good at gossip, and Hallam Castle was no different from anywhere else, except the Castle had an Olympic champion, the housekeeper, that Mrs Tomkins. A lot to think about there, but not yet. Best to talk it over with Millie: after they'd talked about what the birds and bees did to each other: dirty little devils.

Gertie was right about the papers: they were wonderful. Praise lavished from every one. Lord Chard looked up from his devilled bones and *The Times*. 'I hope you're pleased with yourselves,' he said.

'Oh *yes*,' said Elena, and looked at Millicent, smiling.

'Because you should be,' said Lady Chard. She looked at Millicent, who was far too reticent after such a début. 'You don't agree?'

Millicent spread butter and marmalade lavishly on her toast. After bacon too, and eggs, but then dancing always made her ravenous.

'It isn't that, exactly,' she said.

'What then?' The earl this time, but his voice, like his wife's, was kind.

Millicent looked at the great pile of papers, enough for a news-stand, and in every one of them Elena's photograph, and hers, sometimes in costume, sometimes in ball gowns, often both, and all with Elena's interview quoted at length. Elena and Rosario.

'It's just—' she hesitated. 'Suppose we hadn't danced here? Suppose it had been a music hall – even the Alhambra.' The best, Mum had danced there, but Lady Chard looked appalled. Millicent had voiced the unspeakable, even though Lord Chard still smiled. He, too, it would seem knew about the Alhambra.

'Not that we would of course,' said Millicent. 'A viscountess and a legal expert. How could we?' Slowly, imperceptibly almost, Lady Chard began to relax. 'But suppose we'd been a couple of girls who'd decided that they didn't want to work in a factory and took up dancing instead – and made their début last night at the Alhambra? Now, I'm not saying that there wouldn't have been applause – not if they danced like us – curtain calls too – but not like that.' She gestured at the newspapers.

'Clever girl,' said the earl, and Elena too was smiling, but then Elena too was clever. 'But when you think about it, the answer's obvious.'

'Then please share it with us,' said his wife.

'First and most important you're a couple of freaks,' said the earl. 'The most beautiful freaks who ever lived, but still freaks.'

'Because they can dance like that?' his wife asked.

'Because they're a viscountess and a legal expert who can dance like that. Two *ladies* who can dance like that.'

I've just been called a lady, and by an earl, thought Millicent. Mum will be pleased.

'You see the people who came to the ball expected mediocrity at best,' said Chard. 'Something they could be nice about, with the condescension held well in. I'm an earl after all. But you weren't like that. You were brilliant: glittered like diamonds. Which brings us to the snob element. In England there always has to be a snob element. Two ladies doing what you did – and only for their peers. Of course you dazzled them!' He went to the sideboard for kedgeree. 'It's quite simple really.'

Elena went to him and kissed him.

At last they were ready to go: Elena and Millicent side by side, and Gertie facing them in the jump seat. Lady Mendip and her legal adviser, thought Millicent. Two ladies – and she had the word of an earl on it; so sucks boo to Duckhouse and Allnutt. The earl called out that he looked forward to their next appearance, and they waved to him, happy, laughing, and Gertie too was smiling, because she had been part of a triumph. Only the butler looked unhappy, Gertie thought, but that was because he fancied me and I wasn't having any.

5

Pudiphatt wasn't unhappy when he read about them in his newspaper: he was furious. On top of everything else he discovered that, dressed as they were, he desired them, and there was about as much chance of that as there was of his becoming a duke. Now calm down, calm *down*, he told himself. It's only one newspaper after all. Go and check the others. Most likely they won't even mention the bitches. He went to the public library, because he simply didn't have the money to buy great armfuls of newspapers . . . They were in every one, photographs too, and each piece written with a kind of snivelling admiration that made him want to puke. So much for becoming a duke, he thought as he walked across the reading room, then suddenly he stopped dead, and the librarian in charge eyed him warily. There is something about that man, she thought: something I do not like at all, and then to her relief he continued his walk to the exit.

Pudiphatt thought, I'll never be a duke, but I can live like one. Just take back what's mine. Find things out about the pair of them, apply a little pressure – that's all it would take. They were only women after all. They might even be grateful to him for keeping whatever secrets they had, because that there were secrets he had no doubt. The one in the skirt in particular. You couldn't be as rich as she was and not have secrets. He decided to skip lunch and go to his club. Not a very good club: not a very good address either, for a club. Tottenham Court Road. All the same, you did occasionally meet chaps there who knew things.

There was one at the bar that day as it happened. Edwards. Good soldier Edwards, good proper soldier, until 1916 and the Somme, when a lump of German shell had hit him. Took months to heal. After that, after he'd recovered, he'd spent his war in a château at HQ, ADC to some general, which meant hushing up the little French girls his general had developed such a passion for. Pity they were French. All the same, they were foreign and female, just like the aristocrat bitch.

'Afternoon, major,' said Edwards. 'Let me get you a drink.' Very gratifying that "major". He'd had a few already but another wouldn't hurt, even if it was his turn to pay.

'No, no,' said Pudiphatt. 'I'll get these. Scotch?' He told his story about the poor beggars whom he'd lost track of, and who he wanted to mention in his will. And there was a laugh if you like.

'Been to Somerset House have you?' Edwards asked.

'On my way,' said Pudiphatt. He had no idea where Somerset House was, but it would be in the telephone directory.

'They've got all sorts of secrets at Somerset House,' Edwards said. 'All you have to do is ask, and what kind of secret is that?'

Suddenly Pudiphatt was nervous. 'You're not a lawyer, are you?' he asked.

'No, old boy,' Edwards said. 'I'm a reporter on the *Daily Mercury*, with a penchant for being nosy.' He stood up from the bar stool. 'Used to have a penchant for whisky, too. Good thing I stopped. The war's over after all.'

God knows that's true, thought Pudiphatt. And nowadays Edwards was sober. Bit of luck, only one round. He could afford to eat *something*. He went to a pub and ordered a half of bitter and a pie. Both were nasty beyond belief.

Elena had to go for a dress fitting and Millicent and her mother were left together alone. So much to talk about, thought Gertie, but before she could begin her daughter said: 'Elena's just told me I can have any of her mum's dresses I fancy.'

'That's nice,' said Gertie.

'But they're all so old-fashioned,' her daughter said.

'The design is,' said Gertie, 'but not the material. That's beautiful from what you tell me.'

'But so out of date.'

Gertie sighed. Millie might know all about Contract and Real Property, and all those other things that went straight over her mother's head, but when it came to clothes – she sighed again, because it was funny really. She didn't understand clothes, not yet, but she knew exactly how to wear them. Filled out a treat. Like a pint in a pint bottle as you might say.

'We could have them altered,' said Gertie.

'Altered? Do you know somebody who could do that?'

'Mr Bernstein,' said Gertie. Mr Bernstein had made Millie's dancing clothes.

'Do you think he would do it?'

'Let's go and look at them,' her mother said, and they went to the room where they were stored. Silk, satin, chiffon, fine cotton. Mr Bernstein rarely handled material so elegant; so expensive.

'Just give him the chance,' said Gertie. 'Take the lot.'

'Isn't that a bit greedy?'

'They'll only be thrown away otherwise,' Gertie said. 'They're far too what's it for the Salvation Army.'

'Suggestive?'

'I dare say,' said her mother. 'And that reminds me – that housekeeper back at the castle – that Mrs Tomkins – she's a great one for suggestions. She told me that Elena was the dead spit of a lady she'd met when she was in service before the war. Spanish lady.'

'Let's have it,' said her daughter.

Her lawyer's voice, thought Gertie. That meant her Millie was taking it seriously. She concentrated.

It had been a good evening. 'Elena and Rosario', then the dancing, and all the ball gowns to criticise, then supper with the butler and his lordship's valet and Tomkins and her ladyship's maid. Then the two of them slipped away for one more glass of Veuve Clicquot before it was time to put her charges to bed – and if she asks me what I'm doing waiting on my own daughter, I'll clock her one, thought Gertie, but Mrs Tomkins knew it. She didn't.

Instead, she'd begun to talk about when she'd been head parlourmaid in Lord Martin's house in Mount Street, before the war. Nice little house, and Lord Martin no trouble at all. And that was where she'd met the Spanish lady. Not a proper lady, of course. Her being a dancer, how could she be? But ever so nice.

Gertie forced herself to say it. 'His fancy piece?'

'Oh no.' Miss Tomkins sounded shocked. 'I told you. She was *nice*. Just a dinner party. And anyway, Lord Martin was one for the chaps. Especially sailors. Cost him a fortune one way and another. But Lord Martin was one for the arts as well, so he'd invited her. And all the gentlemen guests had treated her like the lady she was. Even if they had eyes in their heads they kept their hands to themselves. Not that it bothered her. Always polite, always smiling, and that was about it. Funny thing, though—'

'Funny?' said Gertie.

'Girl I used to know. Went up in the world, very high up. But never wedlock of course.'

'Of course,' said Gertie.

'In Paris,' said Mrs Tomkins. 'Rue de la Paix would it be?'

It would indeed, thought Gertie, but all she did was shrug.

'She saw this Mrs Menendez, going into a jeweller's shop with a chap a bit older than her but ever so good looking, and well off too. Makes you think, wouldn't you say?'

'It does indeed,' said Gertie, not quite yawning, then swigged down what was left of her champagne. 'Better go and tuck my two ballerinas up,' she said. 'They've had enough excitement for one day.'

Mrs Tomkins looked disappointed. She'd been looking forward to a cosy chat about the ultimate price of a visit to a jeweller's shop in the rue de la Paix. Gertie went over it all again. Rue de la Paix. That was where Mrs Tomkins had seen Elena's mum. In Paris. At the Ritz. With a good looking chap who looked a bit older than her, and well off, too. Proper toff. Better not tell Millie that bit, she thought. Not till it was really necessary. She hadn't yet met Elena's dad, but even so . . . But she told her all the rest.

'Thanks Mum,' said Millicent.

'Any use?' Gertie asked, and her daughter shrugged. Her mother was delighted. Just like me, she thought, and ever so pretty. I wonder if she knows she's doing it?

'Very likely,' her daughter said. 'Another piece in the jigsaw puzzle.'

Gertie went to prepare towels and dancing costumes for the laundry and Millicent went to her office to begin on Margarita's correspondence. She'd been a hoarder all right. There was masses of it. Mercifully most of it was in English, and what wasn't was largely French. She could cope with that. The Spanish stuff was all documents: a passport long expired, death certificates – her parents' – and their wills. It didn't look as if they'd left all that much. At least she had deduced that, but she really must learn Spanish. Slowly, painstakingly, she began to work on the vast litter of paper – a pleasantly familiar task. Pleasant not only because it would be helping Elena – whether she exhibited what she found or suppressed it that was bound to be a pleasure – but because it really was a jigsaw puzzle, and when she put it together, she at least would know the answer to all those questions.

The offers of engagements began to arrive. This charity and that.

Chairwomen of committees, peeresses, even a duchess, wrote to say how grateful they would be if Lady Mendip and Miss Blenkinsop would dance at their charity balls. The trouble was that there were far too many, and Winners and Losers was a hard game to play. All those recommended by Lord Chard, of course (and Elena quite agreed), and the duchess because it never hurt to have a duchess owing you a favour, but after that she had to call in Mum as consultant, Mum whose large, even encyclopaedic knowledge of the nobility and gentry she had at one time found mystifying, but was now endearing.

'No better than she should be.' Wasn't that the phrase? But whatever Mum had been up to, whoever she'd been with, there would have been laughter, and affection and friendship however brief. Of that her daughter was certain. There'd have been comfort too, even luxury, and for that also Millicent was glad. In between the Can-Cans and Floradora her mother had lived well before Dad came along, and why not? They'd both known hardship enough after Dad had died. Not that her Mum and Dad hadn't got on. Mum had adored him till the end . . . She went off to practise. Mum was adamant. The more their fame spread, the better they would have to be. All very gratifying of course, but tiring, too.

A booking in Oxfordshire, and Millicent saw him again. Not at one of the colleges: two ladies dancing unaccompanied by a male, and one of them wearing trousers! That would never do. It was at a small but extremely elegant country house near Blenheim Palace that she saw Francis Boyce again. (At school with the son of the house? she wondered.) Its owner was a retired admiral, which explained why she and Elena were dancing for indigent mariners at a ball organised by his wife. Waited on hand and foot, too, but then they were celebrities now. Below stairs, Gertie also received at least her share of adulation.

They were especially good that evening. Later they discussed it at length and agreed that it was so, but had no idea why. At an elegant manor house in Oxfordshire it was gratifying of *course*, but sometimes it would happen in the practice studio, which was really rather a waste. Even so, Gertie was waiting with hand towels and champagne, and their baths were waiting too. As they dressed Gertie said: 'He's here for more punishment.' Both young women looked bewildered. 'That chap of yours,' said Gertie, taking care to look at neither of them. 'That Francis Boyce.'

'I saw him,' said Millicent.

'Me too,' said Elena. 'When we were taking our curtain calls.'

'This time he's got company,' said Gertie, and left it at that.

Elena was wearing a dress of raging scarlet that only a dark beauty would dare risk, but on her it looked gorgeous, Millicent thought. Yellow-gold hoops in her ears, a necklace and bracelet of the same, and that was it. No jewels at all. Elena herself was the jewel. For Millicent a dress of blue like the sky when dusk first appears, and sapphire ear drops, a sapphire necklace that Elena had lent her. As they entered the ballroom there was a ripple of applause, but they were used to that now, and smiled, and curtseyed slightly, and carried on to where the admiral and his wife were waiting to tell them how marvellous they had been. Very gratifying indeed. As they turned away Francis came towards them, not quite running. He knew from experience how difficult it would be to obtain a dance, but he managed, and went at once to Millicent. Elena smiled. Watching them were two women, one of them like Francis with a bad case of the sulks, and then Elena remembered. Of course! Francis's mama. The other woman was positively scowling. About my age, Elena thought. Brown hair, unremarkable complexion, a dress that was the wrong shade of green – but rather an expensive dress.

'Darling do you mind?' Millicent asked, and Elena winked at her. Why should she mind? For her friend to one-step with Francis would annoy both the sulker and the scowler, she was sure. Besides, there were two men coming towards them: one who looked interesting and the other whom she knew for a fact to be dull beyond belief. He'd been a brother officer of darling Charles.

'Lady Mendip,' he said. 'We met when you were Mrs Lampeter. Do you remember?'

How could I forget? thought Elena. It was hard work just staying awake.

'Of course,' she said.

'May I introduce you to Sir Richard Milburn?' said the dull man, and the interesting man smiled and took her hand as if he'd come to the ball for precisely that.

'I was wondering—' the dull man began, when a woman who looked as if she hunted at least twice a week led him off and steered him into the dance like a hunter approaching a tricky fence.

Again Sir Richard smiled. 'He was hoping to dance with you,' he said.

'Men do sometimes.'

'Well, of course,' Sir Richard said. 'Will I do instead?'

'Let's find out.'

In fact he danced rather well: not showing off, and certainly not pawing, just aware of what he was holding in a polite sort of way, and yet somehow making it clear to her what a pleasure it was.

'Have you known . . . Captain Lushington long?' she asked.

He looked at her unsmiling but was aware of what she had so nearly said, she had no doubt. 'Not long,' he said. 'We ride with the same hunt occasionally.'

That intrigued her. Lushington would certainly hunt, but Sir Richard didn't have the look of a rider to hounds.

Was it his voice, perhaps? Not upper class. No Eton and King's, Winchester and New College, 'privilege my birthright' in that voice. Not lower class either. How could it be? He was Sir Richard after all. And his physique . . . Tall and muscular, certainly, but not with the lean elegance of Lushington, and a scar that ran from his forehead to his neck. Dear God another one, she thought. Chaps who limped, chaps with a sleeve pinned up where once an arm had been, chaps with an eyepatch. The scar was a bad one: fading now, but by no means faded. It would never fade completely, but if it didn't bother Sir Richard – what was his name? Milburn, that was it – why should it bother anyone else? It didn't bother her.

'Were you in the same battalion as Lushington?' she asked.

'Not even the same regiment,' he said. 'Nothing so grand. I was in the army, not the Brigade of Guards.'

'Which regiment?'

It sounded like an interrogation, but it wasn't: simply a request for information, and he accepted it as such.

'The Royal Northumbrians.'

By no means a bad regiment, as line regiments went, but by no means the Coldstream either, as he'd said himself. Not that he gave a damn. By the look of him Sir Richard Milburn wouldn't be all that well known for giving damns.

'Were you a career officer?' she asked him.

'Good Lord, no,' he said. 'I was a sergeant.'

Almost she missed a beat.

'And what do you do now?'

'Undergraduate,' he said. 'Oxford.' He must have been thirty at least. 'I know what you're thinking,' he said. 'And me a grown man. It's just that I like to study.'

The dance ended, and he led her to the buffet and champagne.

Nearby Mrs Boyce was talking to Millicent, or rather haranguing her – being nice would always be difficult for Mrs Boyce – and anyway her eyes remained fixed on Francis and the young woman in green who were enjoying the next dance, or rather the young woman in green was. Francis appeared to be working at it rather, even if he found being nice far more easy than his mother possibly could.

'Poiret,' said Mrs Boyce, 'if I'm not mistaken.'

Well, five out of ten, Millicent thought. For once Poiret too had done a double act – with Mum's friend Mr Bernstein. 'Quite right,' she said.

'It looks delightful,' said Mrs Boyce. 'It really does but – forgive me – don't people find it a little odd for a lawyer to wear a gown made by a couturier so *à la mode* as Poiret?'

'They'd find it even odder if I was a male lawyer,' said Millicent, 'and anyway no one seemed to find it odd when I wore trousers and danced the *malagueña*. In fact they seemed to enjoy it.'

Mrs Boyce blinked. She wasn't used to a counter-attack quite so early in the proceedings. On the other hand there was darling Evadne to think of, and Francis – and herself.

'They look well together, do they not?' she said.

Crude thought Millicent. And leading the witness, too. 'You mean the dancers?' she asked.

'Evadne Petworth and my son,' said Mrs Boyce. Already her voice was beginning to acquire a shrillness that she knew she would regret later, but how could she help it?

Millicent looked at them, apparently for the first time. 'They seem to dance quite nicely,' she said.

'I was not referring simply to the dance,' said Mrs Boyce. 'When I see them like that I feel that they belong together.'

'Really?' said Millicent.

'Yes, really,' said Mrs Boyce, now close to snarling. 'Evadne is charming, and absolutely devoted to Francis. Also, like you, she is very fond of clothes, and being rich she is in a position to afford them.'

'That helps of course,' said Millicent. 'Almost as much as being able to wear them in a manner that does one's designer justice.'

Mrs Boyce discovered that she urgently wanted to scream but, of course, in a ballroom that was unthinkable, even for her.

She had asked him how long he'd been in the army. Three years it seemed: more than sufficient to know what the Western Front was like.

'Was it as bad as they say?' Elena asked.

Like all the best ones he temporised. 'Very likely.'

'Quite ghastly, you mean?'

But he would never tell her the facts, but took refuge instead in simile.

The war – or its after-effects anyway – was like a game of snakes and ladders played in hell. He'd trod on a couple of snakes – his wound stripes – but he'd reached one good ladder too, maybe the best. His father had been a fair to middling accountant, distantly related to a wealthy Northumbrian baronet. The baronet was a bachelor by choice and a baronet by succession. There had been three rather less distant cousins between him and the succession but the war had seen to that, and then it was the baronet's turn, crashing a fighter plane at the age of forty-three because his grandfather had been lord lieutenant of the county. He had opted for bachelorhood, then regretted it. As far as he was concerned accountants had ranked no higher than ratcatchers . . . But then the war had struck, and the accountant's son had rescued a comrade under fire and acquired a Distinguished Conduct Medal, then a Military Medal for doing something damn dangerous in a German trench just before a lump of shell had altered his looks for ever, and it occurred to the baronet that, accountant for a father or not, he had a first-rate second cousin and altered his will accordingly just before he had been killed. Busy time for death, as Richard said, but at least he'd faced death head on. 'Better than riding a hunter,' he'd written in his last letter home.

'And you?' Elena asked. 'What did you do with your life before the war?'

'Just about everything,' said Sir Richard. 'Journalist, sailor, barman, music-hall artist, fairground boxer even – anything except become an accountant.'

Doubtless because he didn't want to be like his father, she thought, even though he'd seemed fond of him, but it was early days to go into that. Instead she asked him if he'd ever been a dancer – he did in fact dance very well – but he'd laughed. He'd sung baritone ballads; patriotic stuff, 'Drake's Drum', 'Glorious Devon'. Not a bad life if you enjoyed singing and travelling.

'Are they what you enjoy most?'

'Not singing,' he said. 'Not since the war. But travelling, yes.

And cricket. And horses. That's why I'm here out of term time. There's a horse I'm after. Bit of a bonus you being here. It's quite obvious you enjoy what you do. You and your friend.'

'You don't think we find it a chore, then?' Elena asked.

'The way you two dance? Of course not. You love it, of course you do. You're brilliant.'

Elena thought that perhaps it was time to take up riding again. Lots of people had told her that she looked good on a horse.

More chaps to dance with: good dancers, bad ones, most indifferent, so that it was a relief to sit out with Lord Chard at last. She looked about her. 'Where's her ladyship?' she asked.

'Card room,' said his lordship. 'Cynthia enjoys a modest flutter now and again. Nothing extravagant. She makes up her mind how much she's prepared to lose, and when that's gone so is she. Not like our friend over there.' He nodded to where Mrs Boyce was deep in conversation with Evadne Petworth; both of them trying to hide the fact that they were watching Millicent and Francis dance.

'No modest flutters for Mrs Boyce,' said his lordship. 'A plunger if ever I saw one.'

'But—' said Elena, and hesitated.

'But what, my dear?'

'If she likes to plunge so, why isn't she in the card room too?' Oh, excuse me—'

'Not at all,' said Chard. 'Cynthia likes a flutter, I like to gossip. No harm in either provided it doesn't go too far . . . The answer to your question is that she's probably broke.'

'*Broke*?'

'For the moment. You'll have observed that Boyce isn't here.'

'Well, yes,' said Elena. There had been no middle-aged men in attendance.

'The reason is that he dislikes gambling, which isn't surprising after the dance she's led him. They've probably had a row.'

'About money?'

'Um,' said his lordship. 'Boyce is well off, extremely so, but he doesn't feel the urge to share the wealth with a Deauville casino or even Ascot bookies come to that.'

'Goodness,' said Elena.

'All very discreet, of course,' said Chard, 'but she knows how to get through it. Hers, not his. She has quite a bit in her own right, and he just lets her get on with it. Not that he could stop her.

Trouble is that until the next lot of dividends comes in, she's broke. Hence, Evadne Petworth.'

'You've lost me,' said Elena.

'Evadne Petworth is scarcely a beauty and she shouldn't wear green,' said his lordship, 'but she does have money. Masses of it.'

'Mrs Boyce is after a loan?' said Elena.

'Mrs Boyce is after a daughter-in-law,' said Chard.

Elena pondered this. 'She wants Francis to marry Evadne Petworth so that she can gamble with her money?'

'A little crude perhaps, but spot on for accuracy.'

'But that's ridiculous.'

'Is it? There was a time when she wanted Francis to marry you for the same reason.'

'And much good it did him.'

'Oh, agreed,' said Chard, 'but then you're as clever as you're beautiful and poor Miss Petworth has neither of these attributes.'

Elena said, 'And Francis isn't exactly *bouleversé*, is he?'

'You'll have observed that Mrs Boyce's personality is forceful, and that her son is, to put it mildly, biddable. How anyone who served with distinction in the late unpleasantness can possibly be biddable is beyond me, but between them he and his mother seem to have achieved that feat.' He laughed. 'Obliged to you for listening,' he said.

'Not at all.'

'It's confidential of course,' said his lordship. 'Not a word to anyone.'

'Of course,' said Elena, and her spirits sunk to her red and gold dancing slippers.

'Except,' said Chard, 'to any close friend to whom you think such information might be useful.' Then without a break: 'Young Milburn seems smitten.' What a darling he was.

'With Miss Petworth, you mean?'

'With you, goose. Mad on hunting.'

'So he tells me,' Elena said.

'Got the worst seat on a horse in the shires, and yet he never comes off. Obstinate, you see. But definitely not biddable.'

A hopeful young man came towards her. She was about to be asked to dance again.

'I did so enjoy our chat,' Elena said.

Next day in the car going home, she and Millicent caught up with their gossip. They had been much too tired the night before. Their dancing had been fine, Elena thought. My friend is really good now. Soon she will be ready for the *zapateado* too, and I shall really have to exert myself, but it was of ballroom dancing and partners that they talked: how handsome he was, and manly, and how the scar made no difference at all – and no more it did, said Gertie. She had seen a few like that after the war, but they had still been men. And then that particular piece of gossip sort of fizzled out. Because we like each other, he and I get on, thought Elena. No conflict, just the acceptance of how pleasant it was to be together: to laugh and talk and dance. Soon they would meet again in London: of course they would. But where was the gossip in that?

Francis was different. Well, of course he was. Much prettier than Richard – not that that mattered. It was just that when he wasn't dancing and laughing with Millicent he had a sort of woebegone look. Plenty of scope for conflict there. Ah well, best get on with it. She told them about Evadne Petworth.

'But that's bizarre,' said Millicent.

'Of course it is,' said Elena, 'but it's happening. Or rather Mrs Boyce is trying to make it happen.'

'I wouldn't give much for her chances,' Millicent said.

Elena looked at her. Something was up. Maybe it was something she didn't want to discuss with her mother – not yet – but something was definitely up.

'From what I hear Mrs Boyce really does have a – what was the word Chard had used? – a forceful personality,' Elena said.

'She may not be the only one,' said Millicent, and Gertie chuckled.

'Good girl,' she said, 'but just make sure he's what you really want before you start any ructions.'

'Yes, of course, mum,' said Millicent, 'but if he is what I really want, I'll have him.'

Elena looked at the intercommunicating window of the Rolls-Royce. It was very firmly shut, and just as well, she thought.

They began to talk about why a particular shade of green could make a particular shade of brunette look like an unlit candle.

6

Pudiphatt began to cultivate Lushington: invited him to his club. He was expensive – champagne his favourite drink – and he was bloody stupid, with the kind of stupidity that wins medals; but he'd been a platoon commander in Lampeter's company. Surely to God he must know *something*. The one good thing was that he was too thick even to realise what he, Pudiphatt, was up to. Against that there was the Pol Roger: he must have forked out for a whole lake full of the stuff.

They had been talking about screen temptresses – Theda Bara high on the list of those Lushington would like to be tempted by – and how they could mess up a chap's life: even a dedicated career soldier's life . . . Take that Spanish female. What a temptress she must have been.

Carefully, patiently, Pudiphatt tried to extract information from whatever Lushington used for a brain . . . Not that the daughter hadn't been a temptress too, Lushington babbled, the one who'd married Lampeter, but her husband seemed worried sick about some family in the North. Noble birth, ancient what's its name. All that.

Lineage, Pudiphatt suggested, and Lushington said very likely.

There had been something about illness, too, but he couldn't remember what; and anyway Lampeter was never one for gossip. All the same it had been on his mind. Pudiphatt left Lushington with the rest of the champagne. Like a very slow gold mine, he thought. You had to work hard to set the wheels turning, but now and again a nugget came to the surface. Debrett, that was the thing. If there wasn't anything in Debrett then that really was the end. On the other hand he had high hopes of Debrett.

Their gentlemen came a-courting, and very correct gentlemen they were, thought Gertie, spying from the hallway. Elena could take care of herself, but Millie had no idea of what was involved,

57

no matter how correct they were. Not like her mother. Better get Elena to have a word soon she thought. If I speak to her straight out she'll start panicking.

It was Francis who called first. Savile Row suit, rose in his lapel and goodness he was pretty, thought Elena. She sat with them primly as a good chaperone should, but he took Millicent to lunch almost at once, and she went to the studio to practise. It was either that or sit and daydream about Richard Milburn, which would have been ridiculous. She had met him only twice after all.

Then she met him again. Savile Row suit, rose in buttonhole, and Millicent's turn to be chaperone before they went off to lunch. Lunch meant that he was serious, she thought, despite the fact that the Savoy Grill had a slightly naughty reputation, but not that naughty. No *cinq à sept*. Not in London. In London naughtiness meant dinner. She wondered if Millicent knew that.

Instead, there was talk, and a ripple of laughter from her sparked by the stories he told, laughter that made her glad she had worn the Vionnet dress of a green not in the least like Miss Petworth's, and the emeralds poor Toby had given her.

The talk was all about Richard, which made him sound like a monster of egotism, but he wasn't. Not at all. His life had been fascinating, and she wanted to *know*. About boxing and singing in a music hall and being a barman and the army, and he talked about them all, except the army.

'Lord Chard says you're mad on hunting,' she said.

He nodded.

'But he also said you had the worst seat in the Shires and yet you hardly ever come off. Mind you, this was between ourselves.'

'Of course,' said Milburn, 'but as for the worst seat – there are some who would say I had the best.'

'Depending on your point of view?'

'Precisely,' said Milburn; 'but a rear-end view of me on a fifteen-hand gelding isn't necessarily seeing me at my best.' She giggled. 'Quite so,' Milburn said, and offered her a cigarette. Just for once she took one, no matter how bad Gertie had said they could be for dancers.

'You see,' said Milburn, 'when my dad inherited the estate we spent more time together than we ever had before. My fault, really. I was always off on my travels. But you can't spend your time pounding some wretch in a fairground booth or throwing him out of a low pub when you're the heir to a baronetcy. So dad and I spent rather a lot of time together.'

'And your mother?' she asked.

'Dead,' said Milburn. 'Spanish flu.'

Oh, my God, she thought. Another one. But he continued as if death, even of someone so close to him, was perfectly natural. And indeed she guessed that he had seen more than his share.

'And it was then I made this startling discovery – startling to me anyway. It wasn't dad I disliked, it was accountancy. There was no need for me to run.'

He smiled then, and she saw how handsome he must have been before the piece of German shell had slashed him, but never pretty. Not like Francis.

'We had an idyllic three months together even if I did do all the talking. But then I always do, don't I?'

But all she did was smile. 'Until it was time to go,' he continued, 'but not because of dad. It was just that sometimes I like to move on. And as I say – dad spotted it, and asked me where I wanted to go, and I said the only place I'd really wanted to go was Australia again, and that was because of some Australian troops I'd met during the war. And so dad sent me there.'

'But why?'

'Dad's whole life was figures. What Hugo – the baronet – couldn't understand was that it was because he was good at them. Tracking down a missing fiver was like Sherlock Holmes finding a murderer. But he enjoyed what I did too. Like going to the pictures, he used to say, and with me as the lead. What he liked best was stories of my time in the tent show.'

'Tent show?'

'Cross between a circus and a fair. Run by a chap called Barton. Took us off to South Africa and Australia. All over the shop. He made a mint – and the rest of us didn't do too badly either. Dad used to look at me as if I was one of H. G. Wells's Martians. You see—'

'Boxing?' asked Elena.

'It's where the money was. Mind you, if it was a big Boer I earned it. If they hadn't been drunk they'd have murdered me. But they always were drunk, thank God, and my God how they hated us – and that made them careless. That helped, too.'

'Hated you?'

'Hated all of us,' said Richard. 'They'd just lost a war against us remember.'

'Oh,' said Elena. 'Of course.' In those days her wars had yet to start. 'And the Australians?'

'Despised us,' said Richard. 'That was foolish too. Never despise your opponent till you know what he can do. The South Africans were mostly miners, I remember. For gold.'

'And the Australians?'

'Stockmen mostly. Boundary riders. Sort of cowboys. They were the ones who taught me to ride. They tried to teach me about cards, too. So did the Boers.'

'They cheated?'

'It was up to them. If they cheated, so did I. When it comes to cheating at cards there's no education like a Tent Show,' said Sir Richard Milburn, Bart.

'But didn't they dislike you?' Elena asked.

'The Boers did. But then the Boers disliked everybody. The Australians and I got on very well after I'd hammered a few.' He saw her look of puzzlement. 'Fought them and beat them.'

'And where did all this happen?' she asked.

'The outback mostly,' he said. 'New South Wales, Queensland. They taught me to ride the wrong way, and I helped them to kill kangaroos.'

She winced. 'Could you bear to do that?'

'No worse than killing Germans,' he said.

'They were the enemy?'

'Of course,' he said. 'The blokes wouldn't do it for fun. None of us would, but these chaps lived on what the cinema calls "ranches".'

'They really were cowboys?'

'They were indeed,' said Richard. 'They called themselves stockmen and the ranch a property – but cowboys is what they are, and the roos eat their grass. Now some of these chaps own thousands of acres – thousands of cattle, too. But once their grass is gone – and roos are very good at eating grass . . .' He shrugged.

'Life was hard?'

'Hard enough,' he said. 'Bewildering too. Like getting into a card game and you don't know the rules.'

Really men were the oddest creatures, she thought. He'd obviously meant it when he said how hard the life had been, and yet he'd enjoyed every minute.

'Let's talk about you,' he said.

'Me?' she said. 'After what you've just told me? Nothing to tell.'

'Nonsense. You can't look as you do and not be fascinating,' he said.

Rushing it a bit, she thought, but he takes his fences flying.

'Mama was Spanish,' she said, 'but surely that's obvious.'

No mention of papa, he noticed, but it was early days . . .

'And she was a dancer. A professional. I told you that.' He nodded. 'When I – became rich – I decided that I would be a dancer too. But not like her. Flamenco.'

'A bit tricky – getting any tuition in London,' he said, and she nodded, approvingly. He really does have brains, she thought. He and Oxford deserve each other.

'I had – have – contacts in the Spanish embassy. They – kept an eye open for me. Isn't that the expression?'

'That's the one,' he said.

'To find me a dancer. Eventually they produced a man called Luis Amaya. He'd come over here to work on some walls and ceilings. Stucco. You know – that very fine plasterwork the Moors used to do. The Alhambra, the Generalife, all that. It's very beautiful – at least I think so – and very difficult.'

'But where would he find Spanish plasterwork here?'

'Surrey,' she said. 'One of Wellington's generals was mad on Spanish architecture: But please do not interrupt.'

He begged pardon.

'Yes, well,' she said, 'but let me finish. Where was I?'

'Surrey,' he said. 'Granada. A craftsman called Amaya.'

She smiled at him. It seemed that he had scored a point. Rather a tricky one. Really we could have been married for years, but that really would be rushing things even more.

'He has a wife called Rosa,' Elena said. 'She is a gypsy and she dances quite well, but she teaches even better, and so—' Her hand made a smooth and elegant gesture that no Englishwoman could ever hope to emulate.

'What happened to them?'

'They went back to Spain,' she said. 'The money in England was fine, but the winter was killing them.' She looked at the ashtray. Somehow it seemed full of cigarette stubs and at once a waiter removed it and supplied a fresh one. And why not? It was too late to practise anyway. One more wouldn't hurt. He lit it for her.

'Like Passchendaele,' she said.

He smiled, but shook his head. 'Out of bounds to ladies,' he said. 'I told you.'

61

I bet I could make you if we went to bed together, she thought, and then: Now, now Elena. Always in a hurry. Headlong that would be.

'You know I was married?' she asked, but of course he did. Freddy's ring was there to see. Perhaps she was punishing him a little, but if so he was ready for her.

'How could you not have been?' he said.

'Three times,' she said, and this time she really did get past his guard.

'I adored Mama till the day she died,' said Elena, 'but she had this *idée fixe* that marriage was the only possible occupation for young ladies – marriage into the nobility – or at least the gentry. And so, somehow or other I met Toby Crick, and somehow or other he proposed. His Mama was not pleased.'

'Why on earth not?'

'She had wanted an English rose. Not a Spanish one. He was in the cavalry.'

Not quite irrelevant, that last sentence. Cavalrymen tended to be the most tremendous swells who married, almost exclusively, the daughters of tremendous swells, to whom money was so plentiful as to be irrelevant.

'Was he killed in France?'

'Melton Mowbray,' she said. 'Or somewhere quite near. November 1914. He was out hunting, poor darling.'

RIP, he thought, but not mourned all that deeply by the sound of things. Not even name, rank and number. Not even what regiment.

'Charlie was killed at the Somme,' said Elena, and Milburn knew at once that Charlie was the ghost he had to lay.

'Infantry?' he asked.

'The Coldstream,' she said, 'but when he – died – he was with the Tyneside Irish. Their CO in fact. Major – acting lieutenant colonel.'

All unknowing, Milburn echoed Millicent's policeman. The Tyneside Irish. Never had a chance, poor bastards.

'And then there was Freddy,' she said.

'Freddy?'

'Viscount Mendip.'

'Another infantryman?'

'Rifle Brigade.'

Not just the top of the milk, he thought. Double cream all three – but it didn't bring them back to life.

'You'd have liked Freddy,' she said. 'Everybody did. He could always make you laugh.' Until he was killed of course. Summer 1918, that had been. She was remembering, he thought. Remembering far too deeply. Freddy and his laughter; Charlie and everything about him. Remembrance that was pain, and useless pain at that, but it was there.

'You poor darling,' he said. 'You didn't have much luck, did you?'

At first that 'darling' had surprised her, then she remembered that he'd been in the theatre, where they all called each other darling. All the same he'd meant it, though she didn't resent the fact . . .

He looked at his watch. It was late; they were the last ones there, their waiter using a napkin to flick the dust from a table already spotless. Milburn paid his bill then escorted Elena back to Eaton Place, where Millicent was entertaining Francis Boyce to tea.

Well, well, well, he thought. Here's a how d'you do, in fact; and what kind of legal secretary did that make her? Not that Elena seemed worried. He accepted a cucumber sandwich and awaited developments. They weren't long in coming. Boyce had to fly, it seemed. A chap from an investment house he simply must see. The chap from the investment house could have waited all week until he and Elena turned up. All the same Milburn left with him to see a man about a horse he simply must see.

Millicent said, 'You don't mind?'

'Mind what?' Elena asked.

'That I gave Francis tea. He sort of just popped in to return a book.'

She nodded to where Arnold Bennett's *Anne of the Five Towns* was prominently displayed.

'Of course I don't mind,' said Elena, took a cigarette from the box on the table and thought of sheep and lambs and then: Head on – it's the only way – like a bull confronting a matador, and anyway she'd promised Gertie. Francis had come to tea. Fine. Nothing wrong with that, but then dinner was mentioned. She'd have to talk to her friend about that, and after Francis had finished saying goodbye she went straight to the point; no hints. Had Millicent fallen in love with Francis? Millicent blushed, and thought perhaps she had.

'Has he ever kissed you?' Elena asked.

'We've only ever met in daylight,' said Millicent, which meant no, it seemed.

'Put his arm around you?'

'Only when we dance,' said Millicent. 'It's very—'

'Very pleasant, having a man's arm around you,' said Elena, then ploughed on grimly. 'He's very nice,' she said.

'Oh, he *is*,' said Millicent.

'But even the nicest ones get urges. The trouble is that sometimes we get them too, and that can lead to complications.'

'Urges?' said Millicent.

'Babies,' said Elena, and Millicent blushed once more.

'I think you'd better see my gynaecologist,' said Elena, not quite irrelevantly.

'His mother wants him to marry Evadne Petworth,' Millicent said. 'She's rich but Francis is poor. And I'm even poorer.'

'He can't be all that poor,' Elena said. 'He's got a house in Hampshire.' She knew this because her mother had told her so, because her mother had wanted her to marry him. Not that she was plain like Evadne.

'It belongs to his father,' said Millicent, 'and his mother gambles quite wildly as you know.'

And indeed she should know. Lord Chard had told her far more about Mrs Boyce than she had told Millicent. All the same she found herself marvelling that anyone who had survived three years of the grimmest war in history should submit to marry money because his mother liked a flutter, but there was no point. It was simply his nature after all.

'Oh dear,' said Millicent. 'I'm in a right old mess, aren't I?'

But there was no point in answering that, either. Even so, Elena was proud of her friend. She hadn't shed a single tear. Rather she had given the impression of one whose birthday would be soon, and who just knew that all her presents would be good ones. And somehow that was worrying too.

Pudiphatt found that he was brooding again, but whose fault was that anyway, except Fate's or God's or whoever it was? And anyway he was drinking too much whisky. Far too much. He poured himself another, and added a little, a very little water. It was those two damn women of course. He hated them both. The dark one, Elena was it? was still firm favourite, but the blonde was coming up fast on the rails; a really promising outsider, except he couldn't stand the sight of either, not even a photograph.

And that was it, he thought. That was bloody it. Their photographs were all he knew. He'd never seen them in costume. In the flesh. *Stay off that word.* All the same that was it. That was bloody it . . . The piece of the dug-out they'd used as a mess, a gramophone that seemed to play nothing but selections from the *Bing Boys*, and *La Vie Parisienne* all over the place. Naked women. Flesh. Usually it didn't bother him, but there had been one – a parody of a Spanish dancer who he'd seen wearing nothing but earrings and castanets, who had struck him as pretty. The thing was he didn't want her to be pretty. He didn't want her in his mind at all. It had taken a week to get rid of her, and now those two had gone and dropped her back in . . . He remembered how Edwards had spotted that he always went back to the Spanish girl. Smart chap, Edwards. Sharp eyes, too. Not that he ever told the others. They were both captains at the time, and Edwards still unmarked, and he, Pudiphatt, had scarcely begun on the whisky. That was 1916, and both of them by then had become impervious to the sound of gunfire: just glad they hadn't been sent to the Somme. Not like poor Charles. 'Still the Señorita?' asked Edwards, but he kept his voice down. Pudiphatt called for whisky.

'At least she's not on the Western Front in a dug-out,' he said.

'She could be in mine any time,' said Edwards. Even the nicest of them, thought Pudiphatt. Even him. Can't get his mind off it. Carnal knowledge would it be? When they charged one of the men with a sex offence? He dropped the magazine on the table.

'Takes your mind off things,' he said.

'With me it's just the opposite,' said Edwards.

Can't they ever think of anything else?

'Big excitement tonight, I hear,' said Edwards. 'Trench raid.'

Pudiphatt was silent.

'I hear you volunteered,' said Trenlow.

'You heard correctly.'

Edwards shook his head in bewilderment. 'Why the rush?' he said at last.

'It's what we're here for.'

'Yes, but—' Edwards was still bewildered. 'Why volunteer?'

'Why not?' said Pudiphatt. 'Wouldn't you?'

'I've learned to wait till I'm asked,' said Edwards, and called for two more drinks.

Pudiphatt was far and away the strangest man in the battalion, he thought, yet maybe he's right to volunteer for death after all.

As he says, it's what we're here for. German high explosives can kill you just as surely as a German bayonet. He raised his glass. 'Good luck,' he said.

Pudiphatt went to his bunk, if you could call it that. More like a bed of pain . . . The problem was what to read. He pulled out the ammunition box that contained his books. No need to worry about hiding them. Some of the chaps had books that made *La Vie Parisienne* read like tracts. They left each others' books alone.

His books were his treasures, he thought, acquired, sometimes painfully, over the years: treasure hoarded as a miser hoards gold: A.E.W. Mason, Stanley Weyman, Henty and Kipling, although Kipling could be a bit difficult sometimes. *Treasure Island*, and that Italian-sounding chap who wrote rather well about pirates, although he would keep dragging women into it. Trust an eye-tie . . . Rider Haggard was safer. True, there was *She* to be considered, but she was a goddess and goddesses didn't count, surely? Then there was the poetry. Mostly Sir Henry Newbolt, but my God he could write the stuff. 'The Gatling's jammed and the colonel's dead.' And then 'The voice of a schoolboy rallied the ranks, Play up and play the game.'

A boy had saved them. Probably a prefect two terms ago he thought, as he so often did. Out there on the foothills of the Himalayas. Probably got his colours for cricket long before the rest of the team, and now he was out there, ready to face the Pathans or whoever they were: bronzed, golden haired and young. My God so young . . . The Pathans tortured their prisoners. *Stay off that*. This was a clean war with clean wounds and a clean death. Immaculate. The nearest woman a hundred miles away. Not like the Western Front at all.

Baden Powell. He was the chap. *Scouting for Boys*. He could teach them all they needed to know about sex. Give it a miss. And yet he'd heard things about BP. Chaps talking about him, sniggering. It was just rumours of course and he tried not to listen, but all the same . . . Discipline a bit strict for the younger ones, they said, and anyway why wasn't he in France instead of teaching the older ones how to defend railway bridges the Germans would never attack anyway? And all that DYB DOB business . . . Still, bringing in the *Jungle Books* was nice. Bageera, Baloo, all that. DYB, DYB, DYB meant the Wolf Cubs. Wide-eyed and angelic no doubt while they learned about Shere Khan and Mougli and the Banda log, but far too young for the North-West Frontier. He'd been a Wolf Cub himself, and all he ever dreamed about was roly poly pudding and the school being struck by lightning and going home for the hols. Home was rotten too, but not quite so bad as school. School was awful. Dark green paint, and footer even when there was snow on the ground, and lavatories that were like the cubicles of a brothel that must have been designed in hell. He knew all about that. He'd inspected one just before a court martial. And always, wherever you went, even the library, even the lavatories for God's sake, the smell of the kind of gravy that made him feel sick. And Whacker Phizakerly. The headmaster. Whacker for two reasons, so the older chaps said. First and obviously because he knew how to whack: tell you to take your trousers down as soon as look at you. And secondly (though you had to whisper this), because he came from Liverpool. Not only that but he'd been to university there. Not Oxford; not Cambridge. *Liverpool*. It pleased him sometimes: a very little. He'd played for his House once, but he was a left-hander, and the way the Whacker saw it, being left-handed was the Eighth Deadly Sin, so that was that, except he'd been beaten for it . . . Home was just a bit better. His mother was a permanent invalid and he the only nurse, and his father could talk of nothing but school bills, but he wasn't nearly so good at walloping as the Whacker. And there were the books. Hidden of course. His parents would have confiscated them at the drop of a hat, or sent them off to China to teach the slant-eyed orphans to read, but by then he'd become good at hiding things . . .

Did nothing good ever happen to me? he wondered. Even his regiment was awful, and the sixth battalion at that . . .

But of course something good had happened, he thought. Charles had happened: Charles who really had been bronzed and fit and young. Always just back from somewhere: Kashmir (wild duck), Bengal (tigers), and wild boar just about everywhere. Pig sticking and tent pegging, polo and gymkhanas. A life of bliss compared with his, but he'd never grudged it. Cousin Charles (once removed in fact, but no need to go into all that) had been kind, thoughtful, considerate, and above all he was a gentleman. He'd seen quite a lot of gentlemen just recently, he thought. Peers' sons, some of them. Ten thousand a year men. Chaps with names every bit as weird as Phizakerly. Foljambe, Marchbanks, Folliott, Cholmondeley. But nobody laughed at them. They were toffs, as the men said, and rich toffs at that. All the same, Charles could lose most of them: at least as much as money, and an ancestry as long as theirs. The Lampeters had been squires on the Welsh borders for six hundred years, Pudiphatt knew. He'd looked it up in Debrett, because however loosely, he belonged in it too. In the old days he'd have been squire to Charlie's Knight: jousts; crusades: taking their archers to France to slaughter the French at Agincourt. It was all in Henty.

7

Every time he had leave Charles would turn up at that little
garrison town in the Midlands, and even before the war the place
was awful. Even so, Charles always came, and when the Guard
turned out they crashed to the kind of attention that, he,
Pudiphatt, never got. Not that he grudged it . . . And always, or
so his memory seemed to recall it, Charles would take him out to
dinner, and always to a new restaurant. Charles could find a
restaurant as a spaniel could pick up a pheasant.

'And how are you these days?' he would ask, and Pudiphatt
would tell him, happily smiling. All lies of course. Impossible to
tell Charles what his life was really like: his school (Charles had
been to Eton), or his regiment (Charles was in the Coldstream).
Better, far better, to smile and tell lies. But Charles would talk too,
about India mostly, and Egypt. Not much to shoot in Egypt, but
there was racing and occasional game. For real game you had to
go to South Africa: lion, leopard, buffalo – and deer. About a
thousand varieties of deer, or so it seemed. Made him sound like
a mass murderer, Pudiphatt thought, but he wasn't. Not really.
Most of what he shot was trophies. When he'd got one he moved
on. Massacres weren't his line at all. Once Charles had asked him
what he, Pudiphatt, shot.

'Game birds,' he'd said. 'Out on the moors.' He'd be lucky to be
invited out twice in a season, and yet he was a damn good shot.
Everybody said so.

'What guns do you use?' Charles had asked.

'Churchills.'

'Nice guns,' Charles had said. Whatever he could borrow would
be nearer the truth, so long as they suited a left-hander. Then
they'd ordered: eaten well: drunk even better – claret called
Château d'Estournel perhaps. And all the time they'd talk; about
the next war mostly. Would there be one? Charles was utterly
certain that there would be. The only question was what kind.

He'd been surprised that there would be a choice, but Charles was adamant that there was. Open-order movement on the one hand, the way we'd fought since Wellington's time. Or it might be under cover, because the Germans were experts with machine-guns.

Pudiphatt hoped it would be open order, and so did Charles, but in the end they'd had both. Charles knew his drill and a fat lot of good it had done him. Haig, he thought, who'd had nothing to do with it. Not his fault. He wasn't a coward. It was just that Haig had been so far away, like a star, he thought, and not the nearest one at that. He'd seen him now and then, riding with his staff on the kind of horse that would cost him a year's pay at least. No sign of lances . . . sabres although the rumour was that he still hankered after them. No sign that he knew a damn thing about trenches, nor about warfare either. (At the Somme the men had carried full packs as well as rifle, bayonet and ammunition, through mud that was more liquid than solid.) But then Haig didn't much care for the war they were actually fighting; the one the Germans insisted on. He much preferred the one in his imagination – bugles, horses and all. If it weren't for them Charles might be still alive: so sod them.

They'd gone to France on the same day, and Charles had bought one last lunch, and a claret called Château Gruaud Larose that Charles said sang on the palate like a choir of angels, and he wasn't far off at that, Pudiphatt thought.

Over lunch Charles said, 'I'm leaving you rather a lot of money.'

'You don't have to,' Pudiphatt said.

'One of the reasons why I'm doing it.' He ate a little more salmon. 'Be honest. It will cheer you up.'

'No end,' said Pudiphatt.

'There are you are then.' They found a taxi, and took their kit, and porters came running. (Porters always came running when Charles appeared.) His kit he kept with him, but his boat sailed two hours later. Near the buffet a Salvation Army band had appeared, all polished boots and gleaming brass. The very band in fact that Haig would have chosen to go with the lances and sabres – except that there were women as well, and Haig would never have allowed women in his cavalry. They were singing 'Rock of Ages', and some of the singers were his own men, passing the time while they waited for the buffet to open. They stared rather when they saw him and Charles together, but then people often did. It never bothered him. He was proud of Charles.

Then a guard shouted, a whistle shrilled, and Charles turned to him: offered his hand. 'Looks like it's *au revoir* old chap,' he said, clapped him on the shoulder and walked past the barrier.

Pudiphatt watched him go, bronzed and golden-haired and young, he thought. My God, so young, then promptly wished he hadn't and said the Lord's Prayer because the spirits might be evil. He and Charles never saw each other again, but then the war was like that. You got used to such things: you had to. Except that he never really got used to missing Charles.

There in the dug-out he remembered others he had liked and who were dead. He'd even watched some of them die, but in the end he'd forgotten them. But not Charles. Never Charles. In his mind he began to remember his battles: Mons, Loos, Amiens. Steady under fire, his colonel had called him, and it was gratifying at that: gratifying too, because Charles had got it right. It had been open order to start with. Only one thing wrong with that. They were marching the wrong way. They weren't on their way to Berlin: it was Paris. If the war really was going to be over by Christmas, it would be because we lost he thought. He checked the men's health obsessively – Nanny Pudiphatt they called him – but they were the only regulars his battalion had, and even they were beginning to wilt, hard as they were. Feet that didn't want to walk any more, exhausted bodies that *couldn't* walk: even a couple of doses of clap. How on earth had they managed that in the middle of a route march? And then the Germans decided it was time they sent for the machine-guns like a pianist who feels that he has practised enough, and was ready for the concert, and it was then that the digging began. Nobody dug the way they did. Dig like badgers and live like rats. No better than school in fact, except there was no Phizakerley. (Phizakerley when last heard of had been organising comforts for the troops and there would be no prizes for guessing who got the best ones). Well, that just about took care of everything, he thought. Just time to say the Lord's Prayer (to his bewilderment he found that he was losing his faith, but even so, why leave anything to chance?) His eyes closed, and he relaxed at once. When Edwards looked in on him twenty minutes later, Pudiphatt was already asleep, his breathing as gentle and silent as a baby's. Once again Edwards found himself shaking his head in bewilderment. One so often did when contemplating Pudiphatt . . .

Pudiphatt awoke next day and found himself famous. No other way to put it, Edwards thought. Their raid had begun at 0130,

71

exactly as planned, and Pudiphatt had led back the survivors, plus a handful of prisoners, at 0251. Debriefing them with the colonel, the adjutant, and a chap from the staff, then Pudiphatt went off to his dug-out and slept exactly as he had before. When he woke up his mess was *en fête*: carefully hoarded champers, whisky, even cognac . . . Pudiphatt, it would seem, was a hero. This man from the staff said so, the adjutant said so, even the colonel said so. The magic letters MC glittered in the air. The first Military cross since 1916, when Barlow had won one, but now Barlow was dead: killed at Ypres while the Virgin in the cathedral looked down. Edwards thought: Really, I must stop all this pathos or whatever it is. This is a *war* for God's sake, not one of Pudiphatt's novels. He took a glass of champagne and went to where Pudiphatt was drinking Scotch: one in his hand and two to go, the two donors talking to each other as if Pudiphatt was on his own rather than at a party in his honour, and yet . . .

'Enjoying yourself?' Edwards asked.

Pudiphatt smiled. 'Top hole,' he said.

Alone or in a group he was happy, it would seem, but wasn't there a bit of condescension, and why not? After all he'd shown the others how to play to win.

Keep it light, thought Edwards. 'Rough, was it?' he asked.

'Just a bit,' said Pudiphatt, 'and yet I'll tell you something—' and then was silent, but he spoke at last. 'The men I chose,' he said, 'mostly miners. Tough. Almost out of control most of the time, which is why I got so much out of them.'

No fool, Pudiphatt, thought Edwards, but then why should he be just because he reads Henty and Henry Newbolt?

'Chaps who got drunk every Saturday night and hammered the daylights out of each other. They didn't care.'

'Care?'

'Who got hurt. Who lived and who died, for that matter. Just went straight in. God, they were nasty.'

'Better not let the colonel hear you say that.'

'Of course not.' Pudiphatt picked up the next whisky, but his voice was low pitched, even so. 'I was nasty too – but it got us what he wanted.' He began to brood again and Edwards thought, I wonder what he's thinking of now? But he couldn't possibly know.

Pudiphatt was wondering how he could let Phizakerley know, and Charles.

One more dance recital she thought, and then time for a rest. Once she thought that she would never tire of dancing, but that was just the point. She wasn't tired of dancing: just tired. Millicent's mother, Gertie, would never tire of striving for perfection, being bossy, but then being bossy didn't weary the boss. Time for a rest at last. Belgrave Square this time, a damn great barracks, but at least the ballroom was adequate for their audience: the improvised stage even more so. Nothing wrong there. And Millicent had tried out *zapateado* for the first time. Nothing wrong there, either. Quite the opposite. If Millicent continued to improve like that she, Elena, would have to try even harder, and oh, my poor legs, thought Elena. All very gratifying in fact, and yet there was something up. Like summer lightning that flickers then disappears, and all seems well – until it comes back.

Millicent was dancing with Francis while she sat out with Richard, and that should have been all right too, except that Mrs Boyce and Evadne Petworth were sitting out too, like vultures waiting for a corpse – but that really wasn't quite fair. At least Evadne wasn't wearing her green. This time it was a pretty strident shade of blue, which suited her better: well, a little better anyway. But the thing was that they both looked happy while Millicent and Francis danced together, and *they* didn't look happy at all.

'Intrigued by the delectable Miss Petworth?' asked Richard.

'Is that how you would describe her?'

'Of course not,' said Richard, 'but a lot of chaps here would.'

'What sort of chaps?' It seemed incredible.

'Hard-up chaps. She's just been left another sackful of the stuff. I read it in *The Times*. Want to dance?'

All very well for you, she thought. The only exercise you've taken was to go riding with me. A black gelding he'd called Noche he said, in honour of her, and a bad tempered so-and-so if ever she saw one: and Richard with that impossible seat. Saddle too big and stirrups too long; and yet Noche knew past doubting who was boss. It had been a good ride, not least because every one stared so, waiting for Richard to be thrown. He disappointed them every time. Somehow she got to her feet without visible signs of pain. He deserved his waltz a) because she was so fond of him; b) because he waltzed jolly well.

Francis waltzed well, too, but not that night. That night he did everything but waltz well, and serve him jolly well right too,

Millicent thought, after the things he'd said. The idea! At least he'd made all the right noises about the *zapateado*, but even so— He still couldn't grasp the fact that it was exhausting as well as difficult, and even when he came near he just wondered why she didn't give it up. He'd said so: actually said so. His mother had been even worse, but then she'd expected that.

Why doesn't she just charge admission? his mother had asked, and when Francis said they did, but the money went to orphans, shoeless children, wounded ex-soldiers, all Mrs Boyce said was that it sounded most unladylike. Not what dear Evadne would dream of doing. Millicent knew it for a fact because she'd made him tell her. She was getting good at making him tell things. His mother was like a tank, she thought, and all poor Francis had to fire back was a bow and arrow at best. Even so . . .

'You don't seem very happy tonight,' said Francis.

'Of course I'm not.'

'It's my mother isn't it?' he said. 'It's always my mother.'

Then get another one. She danced in silence. He couldn't bear that when they quarrelled.

'It doesn't have to be like this,' he said, but still she didn't speak.

'What I mean is – it's all because I have to be nice to Evadne – isn't it?'

'Have to?'

'I've explained that,' Francis said.

'Then explain it again.'

'But it's so simple.'

'Then allow for my stupidity. Explain it again.'

She was telling him that she was at least as clever as he was, and far cleverer than Evadne Petworth.

'Just for the moment as I say, Mummy thinks I should be – nice to Evadne—'

'And you think so too?'

Never argue with a lawyer, he thought. They know all the right questions.

'Not think, exactly. No. It's just – well, she is my mother, after all.'

'And why does your – mummy think you should be nice to Evadne?'

Like being on a rack, he thought. At Vimy Ridge I was mentioned in dispatches, and now mere women are tearing me apart.

'Of course, if you don't want to tell me—'

That card took the trick. Not to tell her would mean that mummy had won.

'Not must be nice,' he said. 'Have to be nice.'

Better, she thought. Not much, but a little.

'Evadne's always been rich,' he said, 'and since last week she's even richer.'

'Am I to wish you joy?'

'No!'

He didn't shout, but for a ballroom his voice was loud indeed.

'The thing is – this is all rather squalid—'

'Money usually is,' said Millicent.

'Mummy's – a bit short just at the moment; and she's got the idea – please believe me. It wasn't mine. I swear it.'

'What idea?'

'If Evadne thought that I might be fond of her, mummy might be able to borrow some cash.'

'While there you stand,' said Millicent, 'up on the auction block, and only a fig leaf to cover your shame.'

'Millicent *please*,' he said. 'It wouldn't be that bad.'

'Wouldn't it?'

'We could still meet. We'll have to be discreet, that's all.'

'On the sly, you mean?'

'No, I don't mean on the sly. We love each other – or at least you said we did.'

Then the music stopped and she left him, because if she spoke the entire ballroom *would* have heard.

It was their habit to discuss the evening in the car on the way home: women's dresses, the clumsiness or otherwise of the males, the band's inadequacies: but that night they couldn't. There were far more important things to discuss than people and bands, and Gertie was there, sharp and caring. Gertie who had already begun to suspect that something was wrong, but in the end even Gertie had to go back to Pimlico, and they went into the house.

Millicent had wondered if Elena would mind if she went to her room to see her, but being Elena it hadn't worked like that. Almost before she had finished undressing, Elena tapped at the door and wandered in, like a dog not quite sure of its welcome. A quite adorable dog.

'I hope you don't mind,' she said, 'but you looked as if you might want to talk.'

'I must talk,' said Millicent.

Elena produced cigarettes. 'School's out,' she said. 'Jolly hols.

Let's enjoy life.' Then she looked at Millicent. 'No,' she said. 'You're never going to enjoy life again, are you?'

But already Millicent was dragging down the smoke. 'Oh, I know it's going to sound melodramatic and all that,' she said at last.

'Let's see,' said Elena, and out it all came: Evadne, Mrs Boyce, Francis. The whole sorry mess.

'Not melodramatic at all,' said Elena at last.

'If only he hadn't said those stupid things, stupid things about our flat,' said Millicent. 'You know we had one?'

'I guessed,' said Elena.

'In Hammersmith,' said Millicent. 'Snug and sweet. Amorous of course, of course, but friendly too. He made it sound like a love-nest for a kept woman. Bloody fool.'

A good sign that last bit, thought Elena. In such cases strong language was always a good sign.

'My dear,' she said, 'hasn't it occurred to you that men are capable of all sorts of stupidity?'

'Well, yes,' said Millicent. 'But that—'

'A bit much, I agree,' said Elena, 'but he was under a lot of pressure after all.' She hesitated, then: 'You're saying that if he were stronger you wouldn't be nearly so fond of him . . .'

Millicent took her time to think about that. It was one of the reasons she was such a good lawyer. She took her time.

'In logic you're right, of course. But this isn't logic. It's me.'

Suddenly, without warning, she burst into tears, and Elena scooped her up and held her like a child, until at last the tears became a kind of shuddering, and even the shuddering eased, when Elena left her briefly to fetch a glass of brandy.

'I hate that stuff,' said Millicent.

'So I should hope,' Elena said. 'And anyway, you're supposed to hate it. It's medicine,' and tucked her up in bed as Millicent sipped. There was a good chance that she would sleep, she thought: emotions like that were always exhausting. I mean, look at Toby.

Millicent lay on her bed and looked at the Dutch flower painting, and for some reason felt better . . .

Elena lunched with Richard, in no doubt that she could trust Richard: the only man she had trusted in that way since Charles. When she had done she said, 'It's a mess, isn't it?'

'Weird,' he said, and thought about it. Thought about it

seriously, darling man. 'Sad and yet farcical too,' he said at last.

'*Farcical*?'

'Well, there's no doubt Francis insulted Millicent quite dreadfully and reduced himself to despair while doing it.' He sipped his wine.

'Interesting, that. It's usually the woman's rôle!'

'That isn't very nice,' Elena said.

'None of it's nice. Deceiving one woman you'll be engaged to while another one continues to be your mistress. That isn't nice at all; which is why the farce is so useful.'

'*What farce*?' She was beginning to lose her temper.

'Why, Mrs Boyce. The Demon Queen in the pantomime and Mr Boyce, who contrives never to be there whether he's wanted or not, or even Francis, scuttling from one English rose to another like a lover in a low comedy who's about to reveal his all. Of course there's farce. And a good thing too.'

'At least Millicent isn't in it,' said Elena.

'More like Nemesis, our Millie,' said Richard, and Elena concentrated. She would have to look up Nemesis in the dictionary.

'But her mother is. Blissfully unaware, the rest of them think. But she isn't. Not Gertie. Let one of them put the wrong foot forward and she'll blow up like gelignite.'

He looked at her face, that showed nothing but sadness. Gone too far this time, matey, he thought – but she had asked, and she was one of the few who expected answers.

'Finish it,' she said.

So she knows there's more. As clever as she's beautiful. 'At our own place. By ourselves,' he said, and when they got there: 'Evadne what's it,' he said.

'*Evadne*?'

'Well, of course Evadne,' said Richard. 'Where does that leave her?'

'Oh,' said Millicent.

'Oh is right,' said Richard. 'A girl who wears the wrong sort of dresses, and even in the right ones she'd fail. A plain, rich girl hankering after a poor, handsome man. Which is she – farcical or sad? *What* is she, come to that? Witty, clever, artistic, stupid? We don't know, do we? All we do know is that she's in full cry after Francis, who doesn't even see her except as a lump of money his mother wants.'

'Oh, dear God,' said Elena, and looked sadder than ever.

Very gently Richard said, 'You did ask.'

'Yes, I did,' she said, 'and I invited your opinion. What will happen to her?'

'I doubt if it will be that bad,' said Richard. 'She really is extremely rich. Even if Francis gets away, there are lots more pretty young men. Some of them quite well connected. She'll simply buy one of them.'

'Buy,' Elena said. 'Like a new frock; new hat. You don't mince your words. And don't tell me that I did ask. I know I did.'

'We're a blunt lot we Northerners,' he said. 'Is that what you're saying?'

'I'm saying I want you to finish about Evadne.'

'It may not be that bad,' he said. 'Not if she wants power, because that's really what one kind of love is. Power. Domination of one half by the other. And we're not back in the nineteenth century. Nowadays a woman's money's her own.'

He looked at her face. The worried look again.

'And don't start fretting about some pretty fellow waiting in the wings for Francis to make his final bow,' Richard said. 'None of it's happened yet.'

Quick as a lizard she put her tongue out at him. It's going to be all right, she thought.

'Men do that,' she said. 'I know. It's quite often on the agenda when I go to see Stanhope and so on.' Stanhope and so on he took to be her lawyers. 'What shall we do now?' she asked.

There could be no doubt that she loved the place. Chelsea, but not exactly the naughty part, and a flat that was mostly a vast bedroom, a bathroom built for two, and a fridge. He had wanted to tell her why he hadn't hurried: how much better it was to court her, but in love at least she was more percipient than he and kissed him until at last he embraced her, began to remove her clothes, and marvelled at the gift she gave him so freely: the most elegantly beautiful body he had ever seen.

He was every bit as delightful as Charles had been, she thought. Not better, not worse. Just strong and tender and inventive, and only in that was he like Charles. My sergeant and my major . . . While they rested she said, 'You're not going to nag me any more?'

'Nag you?'

'About my sad farce.'

'That's their problem,' he said. 'They'll either solve it or they won't, but either way if they want help we'll give it – but only if they ask.'

'Millicent's bound to ask,' said Elena.

'Then we'll help her.'

'Is she so pretty?'

'I've no idea,' said Richard, 'but she's the best friend you've got. Of course I'll help her.'

He began to touch her in the places where she specially liked to be touched, till even Millicent was forgotten. Altogether a most satisfactory afternoon, she thought, when at last she went to the bathroom, then called him to her so that they might bathe together.

She would, if he asked her nicely, share Francis's bed, she had told Elena, but for how long she was by no means sure. Some instinct had told her he'd be good at it, and she was right. Just the one for a virgin. Gentle and loving and persuasive. Strong too, when she was ready for his strength. Elena listened gravely, and asked if her friend had remembered to do what the gynaecologist had told her. Hardly Hearts and Flowers thought Millicent, but practical. She set great store by practicality and said she had. Elena embraced her.

'You know,' Millicent said, 'it's really rather pleasant once you get the hang of it.'

Elena looked startled. 'You've settled for Francis then?' she asked.

Millicent looked startled in her turn. 'Of course not,' she said, 'but he has his uses.'

Elena blinked.

Even so he obviously did have his uses until some time before Mrs Barber-Binns' party. There could be no doubts about it, Elena thought. Sunny smiles and sweetness and light to the point where Elena simply knew it couldn't last, nor did it. Smiles where there had been tears . . .

Richard was right about Gertie, but then he was quite often right about things, she thought. She'd just have to get used to it. Gertie called on her one morning when Millicent was with Stanhope and so on to discuss her articles. But then Stanhope and so on had somehow got the idea that Elena was paying, and wanted all her money that they could get, in a genteel sort of way. Not in the least like Duckhouse and Allnutt. Even so, Millicent was determined that Stanhope and so on would get as little as possible: hence the long meetings, and the lunches for which Stanhope and so on always paid.

Gertie said, 'I'm worried about her.' Elena waited. 'I know you told me what Millie and that Boyce is up to, and I'm grateful, but then it's only natural. It isn't that.'

'What then?'

'She isn't happy any more, and when she came to work for you I'd never seen her so happy. Not since her dad died. Then misery, like you wouldn't believe, and now it's smiles again. What's up, my lady – or can't you tell me?'

My lady. That meant it really was important – to Gertie at least.

'Of course I can tell you,' said Elena, and did so. Gertie heard her out in silence, then exploded.

'So what you're saying is that he's playing fast and loose with our Millie, and courting this Evadne at the same time.' She brooded for a moment, then: 'The bastard,' she said.

'He's just pretending with Miss Petworth,' said Elena.

'That's as maybe,' said Gertie. 'Pretending won't last long, you'll see. He's a bastard all right.'

Oh dear, Elena thought. Suppose she's right. She might well be, and wished that she could phone Richard. The trouble was that Richard was at Oxford, schooling his new horse, and staying at Christ Church, where phone calls from females didn't exactly make them delirious.

'What are we going to do?' Gertie asked, and then: 'No, that's nonsense. It's hardly your fault, after all.'

'Well, of course it is,' said Elena. 'We're in this together, like everything else. It's how we handle it, that's all.'

'Thank you, my lady,' said Gertie.

'Though from what she told me, Millicent's solved the problem by herself.'

'How?' asked Gertie, intrigued.

Millicent's mother had an expression that Elena was rather fond of. Now if ever seemed the time to use it.

'She told Francis to push off.'

At once, Gertie seemed to swell with pride. Her own daughter had known precisely what to say, and without any help from her mum what's more. 'By, that's wonderful,' she said, and then: 'Sorry about the language. Again. It just sort of slipped out.'

'Don't give it another thought,' said Elena. 'I used far worse in Spanish when I first heard.'

There were articles to be discussed, and a trip to Spain, but after 'Push off' Gertie seemed to find them trivial indeed. For the time being at any rate.

8

Pudiphatt thought: Something's up. He had taken to doing what he called a recce outside each of the three houses in turn, and there could be no doubt that storm clouds were gathering. First the old bitch, the young bitch's mother, though it had to be said she left Eaton Place far more cheerful than when she arrived. Still, she'd been miserable for a while, and that was something. The young bitch went about with a face like thunder, which was gratifying indeed, while her ladyship, the thieving tart who had robbed him of his inheritance – it was difficult to say. Half the time she looked well enough, but the other half she looked as if she wouldn't be happy till she'd kicked a large number of dogs.

He hadn't seen either of their chaps, either. Not that that amounted to anything, not with three ex-soldiers waiting on her hand and foot, and in the kitchen a fourth, with muscles like a wrestler and the nastiest looking chef's knife he'd ever seen. All the same, something was up, and that could only be good news for Sidney Pudiphatt. He settled down to wait for the young bitch, and she didn't keep him long. Been out for lunch, he thought, which is more than he had. All the same it didn't make him angry for once, not when something was up and soon afterwards it turned out to be worth the visit, not that he could see how to use it to his advantage; not yet, but all the same it was something to chew on. Instead of lunch he thought.

Millicent was saying, 'Why are lawyers all so greedy?'

'You'll be one yourself soon,' said Elena, 'then you'll be greedy too.' She offered cigarettes: 'Your mama came to see me.' Best to get that out of the way. One should never have secrets unless it's absolutely necessary, *her* mama had said, and she was right. All the same, was papa a necessary secret?

'Was it awful?' Millicent asked.

81

'Your mama's never awful,' Elena said. 'I just told her every-thing, and she thoroughly approved. She even called Francis a bastard.' Millicent looked horrified, and Elena hurried on: 'But then he *is* a bastard.' She remember another of Richard's words: 'In the colloquial sense, that is.' At once Millicent looked relieved.

'What else did you do?' she asked. 'Dance practice?'

'Far too tired,' said Elena. 'I read these.' She held up a bundle of letters. 'From Charlie. At the Somme. Trouble is he doesn't tell me much, and I'd dearly love to know what happened there.'

Millicent said: 'Darling, do you really want to know? It was all pretty ghastly there.'

'I have to know,' said Elena. 'I loved him rather a lot.'

No arguing with that. Elena was sweet and thoughtful and kind, but she was also the boss.

'I'll look in at Foyle's and see what books they've got,' said Millicent, and wondered: Why now? Major Lampeter had been dead for years. Can it be because of Richard? Does she love him rather a lot too? Not in any morbid way, not Elena. She wasn't a ghoul. It was just that there were so many men in her life and she wanted to know all about them. It was only natural after all. Then Francis arrived. One of life's little worries? she wondered, though for the life of her she didn't know whether she wanted to see him or not.

'You'll have to see him,' said Elena. 'Otherwise he'll haunt the place.'

'He may do that anyway,' Millicent said. 'Not that I'll encour-age him.'

In that case he hasn't a prayer, thought Elena. 'Do you want me to stay?'

'Perhaps just to start with,' said Millicent, and Elena settled herself. Like a seat at a matinée, she thought. All that was needed was the box of chocs . . .

Grey suit, rose in his buttonhole, regimental tie, like always. Only the worried look was wrong. No. Not worried. Terrified. Like a rabbit confronting the most beautiful ferret in the world. At last he became aware that Elena was there too.

'Oh,' he said.

Elena was not used to young men saying 'Oh' because she was in the room, and resolved to stay for a while, even if it was Millicent's turn. Her friend spoke with the voice of one who has been pestered almost beyond endurance.

'What is it this time, Francis?' she said, and then to Elena, 'He phones, you know. I've asked him not to, but he will do it. Some of us have to work, I tell him, but he doesn't seem to hear. Perhaps he isn't all that bright.'

She spoke as if Francis were in his father's house in Hampshire, and some would call it bad tactics but not me. Millicent needed to know precisely how sorry Francis was. Very sorry indeed by the look of him: a little grovelling would do no harm. Besides, this is punishment too, Elena thought. It hurts.

Born idiot, Millicent thought. Such stupidity could only be hereditary. But useful. Like that time when I made use of him: that first time. All right and proper of course. Lunch, despite Elena's theories, then talk of a matinée, but the matinée was at his flat, and only two performers and no audience except each other.

Later she was to realise how marvellous he had been: gentle, caring, doing his best to keep the pain to a minimum, and though there was pain, gracious what pleasure followed. Francis knew what he was doing, but now wasn't the time to think about that. Of course, being Francis he had begged her not to tell anyone – 'Our secret,' he called it – but all she had done was to say 'Francis', in a reproachful sort of way, and tell Elena at the first opportunity. After all, she hadn't *promised*. Elena had sent her at once to her gynaecologist, and that made two for a start.

Later too she wondered what would happen if she was pregnant. She had no doubt that she could make him marry her. If his mother could dominate him then so could she. But it wasn't that. All that writhing and squirming were all very well, but she'd sooner be a solicitor, even before the storm clouds gathered, worthy and aimless yet furious, like demented sheep . . .

Back to the chit-chat, Millicent thought, and waited. She didn't have to wait long.

'You know I'm sorry,' he said. 'I've told you and told you. Only you never seem to listen.'

Millicent looked at Elena. Always the same, the look said. Sorry, sorry, sorry. *What* a waste of time.

'All right, Francis,' she said at last. 'You're sorry. May I get back to work now please?'

'I want to talk,' said Francis. 'Please let us talk.'

That's for me, Elena thought, and looked at Millicent, who nodded almost imperceptibly, and rose to her feet.

'I have things to do anyway,' she said, 'but please make it quick. Millicent really does have lots of things to do. She isn't here to gossip with idle young men.'

That hurt: she was sure of it. Francis bitterly resented the implication that his adored Millicent had to work for a living, and he himself wasn't really idle. He went to the Stock Exchange quite often. She risked a look at Millicent, who was obviously delighted with what she'd said. She went back to her reading. Charlie had written an awful lot of letters before it happened. Almost all of them were about love, which was delightful, though it told her nothing about the Somme.

'The bitch,' said Francis, and for once he had surprised her. Astounded her even.

'*Elena*?' she said.

'Well, of course Elena. Talking of you as if you were a servant.'

'Well, so I am a servant,' Millicent said. 'Or at any rate she pays me. She is also my best friend, and I'd like to think I'm hers.'

So, of course, Francis had to start apologising all over again, until at last she interrupted him.

'It amounts to this,' she said, in her best University Debating Society voice. 'You're sorry. You've poured out more words than the Oxford Dictionary, but in effect that's all you've said. You're sorry. Just two words. Three if you're being formal. Very well. I take note of your words. Will you please go now?'

He sat, appalled. He hadn't finished: scarcely begun.

'Very well,' said Millicent, 'let me help you, though God knows why I should.'

'Let me just tell you,' he began. 'It's important. My whole life—'

But not mine, she thought, and said aloud, 'Do try to be quiet, Francis. It isn't all that difficult, once you've had some practice.'

He squirmed in his chair. If he was silent how could he explain? But one word from him he was sure and she would ring for Tufnell.

'At Sunday School they taught us a lot about being sorry. Taking another child's sweets, coveting her dolly, putting a drawing-pin on teacher's chair: these were *sins*, and for sins one says sorry to the child or to the teacher, and to God. But being sorry isn't the end of it. By no means. If you're sorry, really sorry, you have to be repentant too: say extra prayers: do extra homework, particularly in a subject you don't like. And even that isn't the end. Last, but not least, comes the restitution.'

'Restitution?' said Francis, but it was just one word and she ignored it.

'Paying back. Paying for the toy you broke: the book you borrowed and forgot to return. Now it's up to you.

'You're sorry. God knows you've said so often enough. But what about penitence? Restitution?' She was waiting, and her very silence demanded an answer.

'But how can I make restitution for what I did?'

'Think about it,' Millicent said. 'God isn't that cruel. He always knows a way for you to find.'

But Francis knew already. There was a way, but it was a very high price indeed.

'I'll think about it,' he said, and Millicent rang for Tufnell.

After a discreet interval, Elena came back in. 'How was it?' she asked.

'I think we're making progress,' Millicent said. She looked hard all through. 'The trouble is he's so *nice*,' she continued. 'I had to force myself, rather. It's that bloody mother of his. I'm worried she may have broken him completely, and if she has I shan't be able to put him together again.'

Like Humpty Dumpty thought Elena, but really, Millicent was in the most frightful rage: her bosom heaving far too much for mid-afternoon. I simply must take her to that corsetière in New Bond Street, she thought. In Spain she wouldn't last five minutes. But all she said was, 'Darling do you think you could bear to go to Foyle's?'

Millicent looked at her. Her friend had been crying. 'Of course,' she said. 'A good brisk walk is just what I need to work off Mrs Boyce.'

Pudiphatt watched her go from the shelter of a doorway, striding out like a Goth marching on Rome. There had to be something in it. Had to. All those comings and goings, including the boyfriend, the pretty one, who had arrived looking dejected, and left looking appalled. The trouble was, he couldn't work out what was in it for him, no matter how sure he might be that it was there. And then he had a piece of luck. He was close, he knew he was, and even if he couldn't afford round-the-clock surveillance, he could at least watch from time to time. He'd even bought a bicycle – a jolting bone-shaker from a second-hand shop – to make it easier. Good disguise, too. If a policeman came he could always pretend to be blowing up a tyre. Only it wasn't a policeman; it was the other boyfriend. Neat day clothes and a bruiser's face. Pudiphatt, an expert in such matters, had known at once that he would be dangerous: coldly, methodically dangerous. The taxi horn hooted, and she appeared at once, the thief who took his property, then the taxi started its journey and Pudiphatt followed. The traffic was so bad that Pudiphatt had no difficulty in keeping up, even on the rusting wreck which was the only transport he owned. It should be a Rolls-Royce Silver Ghost, he thought, and maybe quite soon it will be.

'I'm sorry I interrupted your holiday,' she said. So serious.

'I don't think Noche is,' said Richard.

'You worked him hard?'

'No more than he needed.'

Small talk, and seated decorously apart. The inside of a taxi was not their arena.

'The thing was that I needed you,' said Elena.

'And so you sent for me. Sensible girl.'

The taxi arrived and he paid it off while Pudiphatt made a note of its number and the address of the Chelsea house. No need to do more, he thought. He knew very well what they were there for. Disgusting. Yet with those two it might be beautiful, too. He started on the long ride back to Eaton Place. Might as well check on what the other bitch was up to . . .

She lay on her bed, naked, because he liked her to be naked: elegant, shapely, luscious as a plum. Such breasts, such hips, and no bulging dancer's calves, despite Gertie's urgings to practise. What he couldn't understand was why she should like to look at him too. His body was all right, toughened by the boxing ring and the outback, but his face looked as if he had lost an argument with a butcher's cleaver, and yet she loved to touch it. Ah well, it was a gift. Never question a gift. He embraced her instead, and his hands cupped her breasts, watching as they firmed, the nipples hardened.

'All over,' she said. 'Like last time. Please.'

But why thank him for doing what he so longed to do? She responded at once: moist and eager, yielding, and their love began before she had even touched him. But there was no need to touch. This was her hour and they both knew it. It took so long, he thought, because he willed himself to prolong it almost past endurance, until at last she writhed once more, once more cried out, as together passion left them, and only love was left.

Elena went to the bathroom, and when she came back he had opened champagne from the fridge.

'Loosening my tongue?' she asked.

'Do I need to?'

She shook her head, the seriousness gone. She was smiling.

'Come here please, darling,' she said, and he went to her, and she stroked his scarred face.

'You don't mind?' she asked yet again.

'Not if you don't.' Together they sipped their wine.

'It's difficult,' she said.

'Then tell it if you want to,' said Richard. 'I'll listen. But only if you want to.'

'Charlie,' she said

'What about him?'

'The only other man I ever met who was even remotely like you.'

I knew it from the start, he thought. My only rival. And even though he'd dead he still has power.

'Born November, 1885. KIA July, 1916. Isn't that what you say?"

'It's what the Australians say,' he said. 'Killed In Action.'

'They sent me a telegram,' said Elena. 'Hundreds of women must have received telegrams then. Thousands.'

'The Somme,' said Richard.

'Like a mincing machine,' said Elena. 'Thousands of British men just funnelled in. And the French at Verdun.'

'Germans too.'

'Oh,' said Elena. It was obvious that she'd never thought of that before. But she went on, unheeding. 'And Charlie just one more piece of meat . . . He wrote me letters. Dozens of them, but he never mentioned the Somme.'

'I told you we didn't,' said Richard, and she nodded gravely, like a child about to join the grown-ups.

'Only I want to know,' said Elena. 'Oh, I know it was years ago and I never bothered before, but I want to know. *I have to know.* Millicent says—'

'What does Millicent say?' Richard's voice was gentle, loving.

'She thinks it's because of you.'

Even from beyond the grave, Richard thought. What a man he must have been.

'Not that I'm comparing you,' she said. 'That's impossible. Like comparing a mountain with the sea.'

'What then?' His voice was still gently loving.

'I lost one of you,' she said. 'I couldn't bear to lose the other.'

He put his arms around her. 'You won't,' he said. 'Not unless Noche's too crafty for me, and he won't be. Not after what you've just said.'

'But that isn't all,' she said. 'You were in it, too . . .' He waited. 'You could have died. Charlie did. The two best men I—' her voice faded, then resumed. 'I want to know why men do this to each other. How . . .'

You want the secret of the universe, thought Richard.

'Millicent bought some books for me and I'm trying. I really am. But so far it doesn't make any sense.'

If it did it would be Charlie holding you, not me, he thought and then: Delayed reaction. She must have mourned him, she loved him so, but some of it had gone down deep, too deep, until I came along and dragged it up to the daylight.

'You don't mind me telling you all this?' she asked.

Of course I mind, he thought, but it's impossible to say so.

'He must have been a remarkable man to inspire such love,' he said.

Her arms embraced him.

'Well, so he was,' said Elena, 'and I'm a very lucky girl.'

'Lucky? His voice was wary.

'In love,' she said. 'Once I had Charlie. Now I've got you.'

But I'm not like that, he thought. It's all very well for Charlie the paladin, his armour ever shining bright: but I'm still alive: still vulnerable. Even so, now was not the time to tell her.

'There must be someone I can ask,' she said. 'Someone who knows.' She was fretting again.

'Tufnell,' he said.

'Tufnell?'

'He was in the Coldstream,' said Richard. 'He went with – your Charlie, to the Somme.'

'But how do you know this?' she asked.

'He told me.'

'You always tell each other,' she said: but never the woman.

Still she continued to hold him: her hands explored. First the scar, then down and down.

Catharsis, he thought. Pity and fear. Her very own brand. Pity for the dead: fear that others had been so close. Then his body stirred and he thought: stop thinking like a scholar. You're supposed to be a lover, too.

Love her. It was a beautifully easy thing to do.

As they bathed, she said, 'Would you like a photograph?'

He was bewildered. She liked it when he was bewildered; he who was so clever.

'Of what?' he asked.

'Of me, silly—'

'Well, of course,' he said.

'Only there's a catch. Millicent will be in it, too. We'll be wearing our costumes. Elena and Rosario.'

'All right,' he said. 'Only I want a separate one as well. Just you.'

She smiled then. It was like the act of love.

'What about Francis?' he asked.

'What about him?'

'How many copies will he get?'

'If Francis were a mouse at a banquet for a hundred people, he wouldn't even get a crumb of mousetrap cheese.'

'That bad?' said Richard, and of course she told him. If she didn't how could he advise her?

'Poor Francis,' she said. 'Poor, stupid Francis.' She waited, but this time it seemed that he had nothing to say.

'There must be something he can do,' Elena said at last.

'Does she want him to?'

And there's the hell of it, Elena thought. I simply don't know. But then his brow wrinkled, which did extraordinary things to his scar, then cleared. It was a gesture that she was already beginning to know.

'Restitution,' he said at last.

'What about it?'

'Isn't that one of the words she used to him?'

'There were three,' she said. 'First being sorry, then repentance, and then restitution last of all, but how he could possibly make restitution for what he had done?'

'All the same, I think he knows,' said Richard. 'He isn't always a fool, you know. Just lazy.'

One of the problems about loving Richard, she thought, was that she had to think sometimes. But it was worth it.

'No more than I'm a fool,' she said.

'Nor are you lazy,' said Richard. 'You just proved it.'

Her body, her whole being, took on the luscious look that she had reserved only for him.

'She wants him to surrender,' said Elena. 'Go to her: bid money goodbye.'

'Good girl,' said Richard, and almost Elena blushed. After all they had just done together . . .

9

There was to be one more party. Pretty little Mrs Barber-Binns had written to Elena to say how flat the season was – hence the party – and though she quite realised that darling Elena and Rosario were unable to dance, she still dared to hope that the two most gifted dancers of her acquaintance would be available for next year's season.

Elena wore a gown by Lanvin, Millicent one by Chanel and Bernstein – but not Francis's jewels. To wear them would be a sign of surrender, and Elena had agreed at once, and so she wore sapphires that had belonged to Elena's mama, rather fine ones: because they were the only kind Elena's mother had liked.

On the way, Elena told her about Tufnell.

'But why him?' Millicent asked.

'Because he was there. With Charlie.'

'Really with him? Quite close?'

A sergeant in the same battalion, it seemed, who had gone with him to the Tyneside Irish, and of course she was sure because Richard had found out and made Tufnell tell.

'Made him?' said Millicent.

'Yes, indeed,' said Elena, because although Tufnell wasn't a gentleman he was a thoroughly decent man. Elena had chosen an afternoon when Gertie had had a headache and left rather a lot of champagne so that at least Tufnell's tongue was loosened. But even so he'd hated it because Richard was persuasive and he had liked Charles enormously.

'Like hell,' said Elena. 'A hell that Dante hadn't thought of, but like it even so.'

It was the mud that made it like that, of course. First of July and the rain unrelenting in a long, wet summer that lasted till November, but even on that first day it made life hell.

Some of the Tyneside Irish literally drowned in the stuff, and the last sounds they heard were the rattle of German machine-guns, the crunch of German high explosive. And all the time they carried something called a full-pack, which General Haig thought they would need when they breached the German lines, let in the cavalry, and advanced on Alsace-Lorraine. In fact, all the packs did was drag them down even faster. A lot of the men, the brighter ones, got rid of their packs quite early, and many of the rest soon followed. Charles acted as if he'd never even seen it. He'd come to command men, not mud larks.

They died, of course. Some of them drawn up by companies, some in scattered groups: but the German guns were greedy, and took whatever they could find. Sixty per cent, eighty per cent, once even a hundred per cent – but that was later . . .

'But how could they go on?' Elena had asked. 'They must have known what was waiting.'

'The ones who could still see did,' said Tufnell, 'and the rest could hear. We could all walk or crawl. It was pride drove them, miss, pride because they were men, and a few like your husband to lead them. More like angels with flaming swords than men. So long as they were there, we followed.'

'And then?'

'Your husband stopped one, my lady. Well, it stood to reason he would – he was taking even more risks than the rest of us.'

'Go on,' Elena said.

'When he fell, we just stopped. No surrender. None of that. We were there and we stayed there. But it was like our legs had gone – wouldn't move. We just lay where we were, except a few of us crawled forward to the major and made sure the mud didn't swallow him too.'

'You were one of them?' Elena said.

'Yes, my lady,' said Tufnell. 'I had great respect for the major.'

'Thank you,' Elena said. 'You told me the truth and I'm grateful. It must have been ghastly for you – reliving it like that.'

'You're welcome, my lady,' said Tufnell.

'Just one thing,' said Elena. 'That hundred per cent casualties. Surely that's not possible?'

'It was at the Somme, my lady. Anything was possible there,' Tufnell said. "B" company drove in the farthest – into the German lines, and the platoon that was leading – the Germans opened up on them with their artillery. There was nothing left, my lady. You'd have been pushed to find a button.'

'But my husband,' said Elena. 'He didn't command "B" company.'

'He commanded us all, my lady,' said Tufnell. 'Good fighters, those Geordies, but the major made them more than that. They were men to be proud of.'

'But they were wiped out.'

'That was the staff, miss, all the way up to General Haig. No better than murderers. But us and the major – it was terrible, my lady, but we didn't run.'

'Thank you, Tufnell,' said Elena. 'That really is all.'

'You're welcome, my lady.'

In his voice was triumph: in hers despair.

What Charlie had done was magnificent, of course. Not just the killing of Germans but being there, being what he was. And his men had admired him for it, even loved him, and yet it could be argued that he had squandered his men's lives, like chips on a roulette wheel: when an even greater man, St Francis, say, would have fought no more. But her man had been great enough. Tufnell had even made her proud of him. It wasn't Tufnell's fault that he had horrified her, too. And Richard had been like that. She was sure of it. Richard had been in places called Vimy Ridge and Passchendaele, that hadn't been all that much better than the Somme. The only difference was he'd survived them both . . . Tufnell had been proud to have been at the Somme: she was sure of it. He'd been in the army for two more years, seen much more action, acquired another wound stripe: but all the rest of it had been a very nasty job, and nothing more. But in the Somme he took pride: one of Major Lampeter's boys, he called himself. It said it all.

'It must have been ghastly,' said Millicent. 'How could men do such things to each other?'

'We'd have to turn into men to find out,' said Elena, and willed herself back to the present, which was Cadogan Square and a party with music and pretty little Mrs Barber-Binns being flatteringly attentive. Richard was already there, and Francis. Richard looked happy; Francis did not. Even so, Richard took one look at her and took her to the buffet, and champagne.

'You talked to Tufnell,' he said.

'How did you know?'

'It's in your face. That isn't a face that belongs at a party.' Somehow she achieved a smile.

'Better,' he said. 'But not much.'

I'm trying she thought, but please don't be hard on me. You've seen it.

'It isn't easy,' she said.

'Then we won't talk about it.' Darling Richard.

She looked at the merry throng. Well, at least they *seemed* merry. They couldn't feel worse than she did. Francis, mother ignored, Miss Petworth ignored, was talking anxiously to Millicent, who appeared bored, so that Francis looked even less merry than she felt, and for such a trivial reason. All he had to do was say a sentence. The thought was pleasing, and she smiled once more.

'Much better,' said Richard, and then: 'There's a chap over there who would rather like a word with you and Millicent.' He nodded to where a ruddy faced man was talking to Mr Barber-Binns, their host.

'Any particular reason?'

'I'd like it to come as a surprise.'

'A pleasant one?'

'Very possibly,' said Richard. Elena went to collect her friend, who, it seemed, had just lobbed another grenade.

'Spain?' Francis said. He sounded horrified.

'Elena loves it.'

'And will you love it?'

'If I don't go, how can I find out?' said Millicent.

'You'll be away for weeks,' Francis said.

'Absolutely ages,' Millicent agreed.

'But you know how much I—'

'I,' said Millicent. 'Personal pronoun. First person singular. All egotists love it, but with you it's becoming an addiction.' She turned to Elena. 'Do you need something, darling?'

'I don't *think* so,' said Elena. 'It's just that Richard wants us to meet someone.'

'I'll come at once.' Millicent contrived to imply that whoever the newcomer was, at least he wouldn't be Francis.

'May we talk later?' said Francis.

'At least you asked,' said Millicent. 'A few minutes if I'm not too busy.' She followed Elena to the ruddy faced man.

'What a pleasure it is to meet you both,' the ruddy faced man was saying.

'Too kind,' said Elena. They hadn't met, but he reminded her of someone quite different from himself.

Millicent knew precisely who he was, thought Elena, which is why she looks so wary.

'I'm David Boyce,' he said.

Of course, thought Elena. Not nearly so pretty as his son, but with a lot more steel, and by no means at home at a party. He should be on his broad acres in Hampshire, Elena thought, having a pop at something or other with a twelve bore; considering the possibility of trout, or even a salmon.

'Just think,' Boyce was saying: 'Elena and Rosario. My lucky night.'

Not lucky at all, thought Elena. You knew we'd be here, or why bother coming? A bit hard on Millicent though.

'Shall we sit?' she asked.

To find seats they must walk by Francis, whose reactions might be worth seeing. In fact they were those of a man who had been cuffed, rather playfully, by a world heavyweight boxing champion.

'Perhaps I'd better leave you to it,' said Richard.

'No – please,' said Boyce. 'It's a party, after all.' Then he walked past his son as if he were invisible. Boyce turned to the two pretty women and nodded to Richard. 'He's got a horse called Noche,' he said. 'Marvellous brute.' He turned to Richard. 'You're the only man I know who can ride him. But you manage.'

'He can be difficult sometimes,' Richard said.

'A lot of creatures can,' said Boyce, not quite looking at his son, 'but one has to get on with it, if one wants to keep the creature cooperative.'

The band began to play 'Always' . . .

> 'When the things you planned,
> 'Need a helping hand,
> 'I will understand . . .'

'It applies even when the creature is human,' said Boyce.

'If you please, I would like to dance,' said Elena, and Boyce let her and Richard go. Millicent was his target, after all.

'What a tartar,' said Elena, and then, 'Oh, my God.' Mrs Boyce and Darling Evadne had just joined Francis, but beyond staring at them long and hard, as if he were counting them, his father showed no reaction.

To Millicent he was saying, 'My son is such a creature. I assume you knew I meant my son?'

'Of course,' Millicent said.

'Of course. You're by no means a fool . . . He always means well, and quite often he does well. Mentioned in dispatches. All that.'

'So I hear.'

'May one ask how?'

'Elena told me. Her second husband – Charlie Lampeter – was in the Coldstream too.'

'And was killed,' Millicent nodded. 'Francis was wounded. Twice. He did well then.'

'No doubt,' said Millicent.

'You are thinking of the present – not all those years ago?'

The woman beside him waited. From the corner of her eye she could see that Francis was wriggling between Mrs Boyce and Evadne like a newly landed fish.

'He went to that first ball to see you and Lady Mendip dance. Of course he did,' said Boyce. 'But he also wanted to see how the money was raised. He does a bit in that line himself you see. Does well.'

Still she made no answer.

'You're not helping me,' Boyce said.

'Perhaps I don't wish to.'

'Give me five more minutes and we'll find out.'

'Very well,' Millicent said.

'He can be bullied,' said Boyce. 'His mother can do it. I can do it – though I don't. Not often – and I dare say you could do it too.'

I was right, thought Millicent. He really is very bright.

'But he loves us, don't you see? All three. He knows perfectly well that his mother needs – or wants – money, and she needs him to get it. She weeps, and makes scenes and he capitulates – at least he always did in the past. Then you came along, and he fell in love. He was always a lady's man – but with you he fell in love. You see why, of course.'

'He really is very pretty,' Millicent said, and Boyce winced.

'Not that pretty,' he said. 'That's between the two of you after all. What I'm saying is, he admires you: your strength, your ability, your determination.'

'You seem to know an awful lot about us.'

'He told me,' said Boyce. 'I may have sounded hard on him earlier, but I love my son, and now and again we can talk. This business with his mother. This time he'll resist it. I know he will.'

'And come to me instead?'

'Of course,' said Boyce. 'He can't serve you both after all.' She waited. 'What I mean is, Francis *knows* he must choose, and I'm certain I'm right. Now that being so, surely you can find it in your heart—'

'You said he means well,' Millicent said.

'So he does,' said Boyce.

'It could be his epitaph,' said Millicent. ' "He Meant Well".'

Boyce seemed to swell with rage. 'What the devil do you mean?' he asked.

'He wants us both,' said Millicent. 'He just told me. Twenty minutes ago.'

A lot to think about, snuggling there among the pillows. Really masses to think about. Richard first, Elena decided, because it was always Richard first. 'This Spanish business,' he called it. Why on earth did she bother? And considering their times together in Chelsea it was a more than valid question. But there were reasons, even so: because she hadn't seen Andalusia for so long: because she'd promised Millicent: because she wanted to go. And the last, far and away the most important. Richard must learn that though she was his lover, she was by no means his property. And indeed he had begun to learn it already, but then Richard didn't have a mother whose idea of heaven was to be seated at a roulette wheel that invariably returned the numbers she backed. Not that he would have taken a ha'porth of notice if he had.

Tufnell now: she had thought there might be trouble there (and of her own making, which was bad). But Tufnell had forgiven her, partly because she was young and pretty, and even more because she'd been Charlie's choice. He had even managed to overlook the fact that Gertie drank the champagne he'd regarded as his own. And last of course was Millicent. Top of the bill. The others seemed to regard her as a sad figure: Francis's father, even his mother and Evadne, to whom she represented a dark force of destruction. Even Richard felt pity for her, but then perhaps she desired pity. She had gone up to her bed dry eyed, but even so . . . The whole business *was* comedy: perhaps even farce. All this fuss because a middle-aged woman wanted to go to Deauville Casino and chuck her money away. What was it but a cause for laughter? Darling Evadne, too. (The wrong shade of yellow this time. On her it resembled nothing so much as an Ugly Sister attending the wrong ball.) But what about the widows and orphans, the shoeless children, the wounded ex-servicemen they had danced for? There was the cause for tears. Which reminded her that Tufnell had said something very interesting. Richard was always making a fuss about what a nondescript regiment he had belonged to – 'like the rude mechanicals with rifles'. But in fact, the Royal Northumbrians was an old and honourable body of men, and really quite smart, though not of course to be compared with the Coldstream. She would tease him about that: maybe even coax him into telling her why he told such whoppers. Very ordinary, he'd called them, as if he'd ever belong to *anything* very ordinary. She yawned, then her eyelids fluttered, her eyes closed at last . . .

Pudiphatt thought he'd best bide his time. Not something that infantry officers were all that used to – usually life alternated between almost total inertia and frantic activity – but it had to be done. The trouble was that the Chelsea flat wasn't enough. Endless scope for moral disapproval, all that, but nothing criminal: nothing serious enough to get her dispossessed from his house in Grosvenor Square. Definitely more info needed, but his usual sources had dried up. Lushington too stupid, Edwards far and away too smart. He'd have to find another one, but where? In the meantime, he wrote down what he'd got, in the form of a letter. After all, he could always post it if nothing better offered, and ruin her day, if not her week.

'I know all about your goings on at 81 Rosewood Mansions, Chelsea, and the fact that you call yourself Smythe; still, better than Smith, I suppose. Just. But not the sort of thing one would expect from Charlie's widow. *Kindly get out of my house.* S. Pudiphatt, Major (Ret.).'

He addressed an envelope and stuck a stamp on it, but he neither sealed nor posted it. More info definitely needed, and stamps did cost money. He went to the library and Debrett and the Army List instead. There had to be *something*.

Richard was the one chosen to look after the houses: Knightsbridge, Grosvenor Square, Eaton Place. A bit much, he grumbled. He only wanted to mount guard when his princess was in residence. All the same he agreed. His princess was worried, and he couldn't have that. And Elena really was worried. Before this nonsense all she'd done was leave Tufnell in charge and go off when she wanted, for as long as she wanted . . .

Damn Pudiphatt anyway, she thought, but there was no doubt

that he had power to hurt; if not to break and enter. Not that she'd regarded the three houses as shrines to three demi-gods, but they'd been warm places, secure places, where she was happy and safe with her man of the moment. Even Toby had given her happiness, once he'd contracted mumps. The thought of her houses being desecrated was appalling, and so she took the problem to Richard. More and more she found it easiest to take her problems to Richard, who listened to her and was serious. If Richard listened at all, he listened seriously.

'You want me to arrange things so that he won't get in?' he asked at last.

'Will that be easy?'

'Damn difficult,' he said at last, 'but I'll have a pop at it. One thing – there are plenty of able-bodied men about the place.'

Tufnell, she thought, and the footmen Walter and the new one Frederick, Grimes the chauffeur, and Nicolas, her chef, a cube-shaped French Basque of uncertain temper and an impressive collection of kitchen knives.

'And you?' she asked.

'If it makes you any happier,' he said. 'The three best hotels in London. But if I did, there'd be talk. Masses of it.'

'I thought of that,' she said. 'Best if you just organised it.'

'Very well,' Richard said.

'Because there already is talk,' said Elena. 'Not to the point. How could it be? Sort of shapeless.'

'Inchoate,' said Richard.

'No doubt. But it's there.'

'Millicent?'

Elena nodded. 'She and David Boyce did talk rather intensely at the Barber-Binns' party.'

'And we did leave them to it rather obviously.'

'There's more,' Elena said. 'After we left, Mr and Mrs Boyce had the most colossal row – not raving and screaming – just hissing whispers and filthy looks.'

'And all the worse for that,' said Richard.

'Evadne thought so. She burst into tears.'

'Oh, dear God,' Richard said.

'And after that, the rumours started. Some of them are quite weird.'

'Tell me the weirdest.'

'Probably the one where Mr Boyce has fallen madly in love with Millicent, and vice versa I may say, and Boyce senior is about to leave his wife and set up house with Millicent somewhere abroad.'

'At least it's inventive.'

'The sort of thing you watch at the cinema,' said Elena. 'Have you any?'

They were in bed together in Chelsea, and he began to stroke her in the way she specially liked. Soon it would be time to forget about Millicent and the Boyces.

'There's the one where the older Boyce has lost all his money, and he's going to leave Mrs Boyce and Francis and let them get on with it – and live off Evadne instead.'

'Mrs Boyce never seems part of the happy ending,' said Elena.

'Does it bother you?'

'Not at all,' she said. 'It's Millicent I worry about.'

'Has she heard any of this nonsense?'

'Almost all of it,' said Elena.

'But how could she?' Richard asked.

'I told her,' said Elena, and Richard looked at his lady, awe-struck. Here was plain speaking indeed. 'Far better she should know,' Elena said. 'She agrees with me about that. Just wishes it had never happened, that's all.'

'We all agree on that,' said Richard, but then Elena did something so delicious that the world and its problems ceased to exist.

Pudiphatt tinkered with his bicycle and watched the Chelsea flat. Curtain windows drawn like always. They certainly got their money's worth out of the place, but even so – Smythe indeed. And she had once been married to a Lampeter. She would pay for that. She would pay for everything.

Gertie came to call, a little tearful because they were off to Spain and she wasn't. She'd always been one for a trip abroad. Elena did her best to be soothing. Next time, she said. But that wasn't all. All this rubbish about her Millie. At least, it was all rubbish what she heard . . . Elena rang for champagne and Tufnell brought it at once. He could see that Gertie was upset.

'No backbone,' said Gertie. 'Bloody spineless.' And then, 'Beg pardon my lady.'

'Yes, well. It's true enough I suppose,' Elena said, 'but try not to say it when there are other people present.'

All very well for you, thought Gertie – but look what you drew out of the bran tub – Sir Richard Milburn no less – and look what my poor Millie got.

'Mr Boyce isn't exactly a coward, you know,' said Elena. 'He did very well in the War.'

Because he bloody had to, thought Gertie, and then: Come on, old girl. Other people had said so. What's the matter with you? At odds with everybody, *and* thinking nasty about my lady that's been so good to you. *And* luckier . . . That was the point. It was her Millie who was getting the short straw every time.

'How will it all end, my lady?' she asked, and Elena shrugged.

Beautiful, thought Gertie. Really beautiful. The whole body one long continuous flow.

'That's rather up to young Mr Boyce,' she said.

Spineless wonder, thought Gertie, but Millie was a beauty too. Round and fragrant as a peach. She'd seen her. If anybody could put some guts into him it would be Millie. All the same: 'It makes him look so stupid,' she said.

'He loves his mother,' Elena said.

'Just like I loved mine and you loved yours. But that isn't the way to show it.' She got to her feet. 'Ah well. Best get back to Pimlico. Unless you—' Her eyes looked up to the ceiling: to where the studio and the barre were waiting.

'We're resting for now,' said Elena. 'Let's leave it till we get back from Spain. We may have learned some new tricks by then.'

And won't Sir Richard be pleased, thought the older woman, and then, for shame Gertie Blenkinsop.

He was in the public library going through the Army List when it hit him. He didn't get many of those lightning flashes these days, but when he did they were still damned accurate . . . The point was this. He shouldn't be trying to ferret out facts about the Coldstream of a decade ago. The Rifle Brigade. That's where he should be. Freddy what's it. Lord Mendip. Well, of course he should. Stands to reason. She didn't talk much about dear Charlie, but she must have mentioned him to her viscount from time to time. And there was another thing, he thought. Not just a house in Eaton Place, but a manor in Hampshire, too. Stick to the point, Sidney old chap, he admonished himself. Your turn will come. But please, God, make it soon.

The list gave him the number of Mendip's battalion, and the adjutant of the moment, and Pudiphatt wrote off at once while he was still sober. After that he could do nothing but wait. Officers, NCO's, Other Ranks. They were all there. But not how well they'd know Mendip: served, obeyed him, gone on leave with him. Not even whether they were alive or dead. All he could do was wait.

Richard's days seemed unending, he thought. Together he and Tufnell went over the house and ordered replacements where they were needed: locks, bolts, bars, grilles. He had been worried about Tufnell at first, conscious that he, Richard, might appear much too obsessed with the house's safety, but Tufnell had taken it without a blink. There had been an outbreak of cat-burglars that year: good ones too. One of her ladyship's acquaintances had lost five thousand pounds in jewellery alone. Much better to fit new locks. Cheaper too.

And then more drills. Where to assemble if any alarm sounded, or unexpected parcels arrived, and how to dispose of the post. Small things, fiddly things, but how much better he felt after they had all been done, except that there were still Knightsbridge and Grosvenor Square to be seen to. Elena was right. Pudiphatt *was* a damn nuisance. Still, the labourer was worthy of his hire, especially when the hirer was Elena. A bit too frequently some would say, but then soon he wouldn't be seeing her for weeks and weeks. Try that for mortifying the flesh. That afternoon she told him about Gertie's visit.

'So she thinks it's ridiculous too?' he asked, when she at last had mercy on him.

'Painful too,' said Elena. 'Millicent's her daughter after all.'

'It's all Boyce's fault?' Richard suggested.

'And his mother's,' said Elena.

'A bit hard wouldn't you say?' said Richard. 'One might as well blame the tide for going out.'

'Not if you're Millicent's mother.' Richard nodded. Point taken.

'How are the fortifications?'

'One down. Two to go.'

'You do think it's necessary?'

'The devil of it is we don't know,' said Richard. 'Pudiphatt's as erratic as a grouse in flight. Better safe . . .'

She nodded. It was a boring job and he worked hard at it, even if she did do her best to repay him.

'Which reminds me, I ought to go up to Northumberland. Take a look at the place.'

'You think Tufnell can cope?'

'An ex-sergeant in the Coldstream? Of course he can cope.'

'Let's see if you can too,' she said, and he embraced her in the way she adored: the strength so obviously there, but never the threat of pain.

When they had done she said, 'Tufnell.'

'What about him?'

If I sound impatient who could wonder, he thought. What she was doing so deftly should have left no time for butlers.

'Sergeant in the Coldstream. And you a sergeant in the Royal Northumbrians.'

So that was what she was after, he thought. All those teasing hints of the last few days, and off to Spain so very soon, and frantic to know before she left.

'Charlie was in the Coldstream too,' she said.

Major Lampeter. A God, an Olympian to those of us below. Yet even so he was dead.

'You're not ashamed, are you?' she asked.

'Of what?' His bewilderment, she was sure, was genuine.

'Your regiment.'

'Of course I'm not ashamed. They were a fine bunch of lads.'

'Not that,' she said. 'The fact that they weren't the Guards. Is that why you – play them down?'

And yet she fought fair, he thought. She always fights fair. The delicate caress continued. Even so, it's a bit much. First a butler, now a whole bloody regiment.

'Disparage them you mean? I thought I'd stopped that. I'm trying to – I was trying to get away from it, you see. The War. That meant my company, my battalion, the regiment. An old one. Raised in the seventeenth century. Fought in Canada and India. With Wellington in Spain – and Waterloo. A proud lot. Even arrogant sometimes. And I was proud to be there with them.'

'Then when it was over I missed them. The living – what was left of us – and the dead. And to say I missed the dead was like saying I missed the war. And so I – disparaged them as I say. Ran away. Even as far as Australia. But it couldn't be done. They came with me. Then one night in The Outback I saw sense. How could I disparage men I admired so much? So I tried to stop – and mostly I succeeded and I'm proud of them instead. Not out loud of course – they'd hate that even more than I would – but in my heart and in my head, I'm proud.'

She twisted among the sheets to look at him; to absorb what he had told her.

'At last,' she said. 'Have you told this to anyone else?'

103

'Of course not.'
Another silence then: 'I love you so much,' she said.

Millicent thought: Two more days, and not a word. I've lost him.
His mother was too strong. And then the letter came, addressed
to Miss Millicent Blenkinsop, LL B. About as decorous as you
could get, except that the envelope was attached to a bouquet that
wouldn't have disgraced the Prince of Wales's wedding, if he ever
got around to it, and buried deep in the roses a little square
parcel; a most interesting parcel . . . She took the lot to her office
and rang the bell, and a parlourmaid appeared almost at once
with a vase. There were never any secrets in a house of that size.

'They're lovely miss,' said the parlourmaid, and didn't even wait
to find out who they were from. The answer must be written all
over them, thought Millicent.

And indeed, they were lovely, but the letter surpassed them.
Francis, *of course*, and the letter written so cleverly, but then
Francis had the brains to use, once he stopped listening to his
mother being stupid in other words.

Darling Millicent (he wrote), *This is probably the most difficult letter I shall ever send you, because you're right. Of course
you are. I am much too fond of the first person singular,
especially after I've talked with mother. But how to avoid it?
Can love find a way even in this?*

Oh, the cunning darling, she thought as she read, because love
had found a way.

Every 'I' in the letter had been crossed out, and the word 'one'
put in its place: *'One shall always love you.'* One *is* much too fond
of the first person singular: on and on in page after page. Clever,
clever Francis. And sometimes it was funny: *one loved you from
the moment one first saw you,* and sometimes it was sad, then
happy, as when he referred to his mother – *But what was one to do,
given one's nature? Turn to you, of course, because beneath all the
silliness, the disgraceful (and foolish) suggestion that one might
have you both, there was something else: the implication that you
alone could help. And of course you did. Oh, how nasty the medicine
was, but it cured one in a way that nothing else could, and one
thanks you for it, most profusely.*

And so on and so on. And sometimes she wanted to laugh, and
sometimes she wanted to cry – or even both together – but always

she knew that he was struggling to tell her the truth, that he loved her and wanted her, and it had nothing to do with his mother. So far as his mother was concerned, O-U-T spells out, as they used to say in the Infants' School. At least for now.

But he finished at last. *'Well, that's it,'* he wrote: *Another lesson you taught one. Say what you have to say, mean it, and be quiet. Listen instead. One loves you to the depths of one's being, you see, and silence isn't easy, but it's essential sometimes. One knows that now. God bless you, my darling. Even if one never saw you again one will go on loving you: even though one longs so desperately to see you. One loves you. Oh, my God, how one loves you.*
    Francis.

There was a PS. Somehow she had known there would be. Francis had only just begun to learn how to guard his tongue: being Francis he never would quite, but it was worth reading.

The little box is another proof of it; he wrote. *One's love. The love that fills one's whole being. In law it may not be admissible, (it would take you to put one right on that) but in love it is stronger than steel. Believe that.* Please. *You see Evadne has discovered Billy Cathcart (Eton and the 11th Hussars), and poor Billy has a country house, a hunting lodge and his mess bills to support. Not to mention the kind of race horses that mean well, but what's the use of that when others win all the time? The question is valid, frighteningly so. One used to be that way one's self you see. Evadne's defection means that mummy has only one's self to turn to for money. One's little all. Only she can't get at it – not unless she burgles Asprey's. Again, one's love. 'F'.*

Millicent opened the parcel. Inside was a little box, and inside the box a diamond necklace that was not only proof that he had disobeyed his mother, but a stupefying, even heart-rending gift. She looked at her watch: the working day was over, and she picked up the telephone and dialled Francis's number. First a telephonist, then a secretary, then Francis.

'Hello,' he said, but his voice was wary.

'One would like to see you,' Millicent said.

'But you're sure it's all right?' said Elena.

'Quite sure,' said Millicent, and Elena looked at her because to be quite sure meant that there was no going back.

'But why aren't you out with him?' asked Elena.

'He says he should have a chat with his mother.'

'And will he?' Millicent nodded. 'Dear God!' said Elena. Quite sure wasn't in it. And yet she knew that it was true only for the moment. It was most unwise to assume that nothing would change. It was true, for the present, and that would have to do.

'*We'll* celebrate then. Just the two of us,' she said at last.

'I really ought to finish my packing,' said Millicent.

'Célèstine is doing it now,' said Elena, and it was Millicent's turn to be awestruck. Somebody else to do the packing, even for one's friends. Yet another proof of how rich Elena was . . .

'So you've made it up,' said Richard. They were having drinks at the Savoy – the Grill. Soon it would be supper.

'Didn't I tell you?' said Francis.

'Impossible to say,' Richard said. 'You were rather incoherent at the time.'

'And who shall blame me?' said Francis. 'I'd just left my mother after what she calls "one of our little chats" – or used to call.'

'You've escaped then?'

'She may not think so, but I know so.'

Happy, thought Richard. Euphoric even. Just the man to help keep an eye on houses in Knightsbridge and Grosvenor Square and Eaton Place.

'If you'll excuse me,' said Francis. 'I think I should give Millicent a call.'

'Of course,' said Richard. 'Off you toddle.'

And off Francis toddled, bliss and achievement in every toddling step, and why not? thought Richard. He's earned his happiness. Mounting guard on West End houses would keep.

10

It was of course every bit as good as she'd expected it to be, thought Millicent, from the Pullman to Southampton to the suite on the ship: 'The Empress of the Orient', but that was true. The Empress often did venture as far as India, or Hong Kong, or the Dutch East Indies, but for them at any rate the voyage ended at Malaga. Calm seas, luxury all about them, stewards whose one *raison d'être* seemed to be to cater for their every whim. Bliss. No personal maid to do the unpacking, but that was taken care of too. A stewardess did it instead. Millicent decided that she must do something really nice for Elena, which seemed impossible, though perhaps it wasn't. Not completely. She must work at it. In the meantime there were lunches, dinners, parties, and oh, how grateful she was to Francis for the diamonds; to Elena whose mother's dresses continued to look like Hartnell, Vionnet, Chanel, thanks to Mr Bernstein. Greedy bitch, she thought, but how could she be anything else on a P and O cruise? The gracious and beautiful Lady Mendip, returning on a visit to her ancestral home and artistic inspiration, and her friend and partner, the beautiful Miss Blenkinsop, 'our modern Portia?' That was from the gossip column in one of the dailies, and really, if I read much more of this tripe I'll start to believe it, she thought. Not that it wasn't true of Elena. She *was* beautiful, and they were going to mug up for what you might call the Advanced Flamenco Course after all. Even so, Elena seemed so happy, which was odd when you considered that Richard was already hundreds of miles away. She mentioned it one night when they changed for dinner. 'Caviar,' said Elena. 'Foie gras. And all those eligible young men who aren't a patch on Richard.'

She looked at all the invitations on display and the flowers, quite a lot of which were her friend's.

'But if they're not a patch—' Millicent began.

'That's just it,' said Elena. 'Comparison. They're all hopeless, poor darlings, but even so, one has to dance.' Carefully, sparingly she applied more lipstick. No Elena and Rosario. Not that night. Millicent didn't see it like that. She knew how delightful Francis was, and it didn't take the short-comings of others to prove it. She looked at her friend: cream and scarlet silk, and rubies: huge drop earrings and necklace, and a tortoiseshell comb in her hair, set with what looked like diamonds because they were diamonds. Elena looked in her dressing-table mirror.

'Do you think I ought to change?' she asked anxiously.

'Of course not,' said Millicent. 'You look gorgeous.'

'I look Spanish,' said Elena, and Millicent looked at the mirror in her turn.

Blue and creamy white cut on the cross, like Vionnet, (*clever* Mr Bernstein), and Francis's bounty. 'I don't,' she said.

'English rose, that's you,' said Elena. 'Blue for your eyes and cream for your complexion.' She looked at the peaches that went so often with cream, but they were neatly tucked away inside the New Bond Street bra.

'Darling what's wrong?' said Millicent.

'Nothing's *wrong* exactly,' said Elena, 'but someone might ask us to dance, and for the first time in my life I don't want to.'

So she does miss him, thought Millicent. As an exercise in logic it was contorted at best, but Millicent knew she was right. Nowadays, Elena danced only for Sir Richard Milburn, no matter who else was there. She persevered. 'I'm hardly dressed for it,' she said.

'They could ask for a solo – even ask you to change. Stop at nothing some of them.' But this was nonsense, and she knew it was and smiled.

'Which reminds me,' said Millicent. 'Why did you let Célèstine pack our costumes if dancing is out?'

'There's a man I heard of in Seville,' said Elena. 'Best portrait photographer there is, I'm told. Off to Paris any minute. They say that theatre photographs are his best thing and I thought we might find out. Something for our chaps.'

'Marvellous idea,' said Millicent, and rose to her feet with that flowing elegance that her mother and generations of Spanish gypsies had taught her.

'Will you excuse me darling?' she said. 'I forgot I wanted a word with the purser.' It was his party that night, and Elena looked at her, the dark eyes lustrous, beautiful, but for that moment shrewd, too. 'Bless you darling,' she said.

You never had to draw pictures for Elena.

The letter came: a splendid letter. He might have written it himself. From the Rifle Brigade adjutant, Captain Henshaw. First a compliment about his MC, then a reference to Lord Mendip. A tremendous loss to the regiment. Good to know that his friend would be writing a little memoir about him. For private circulation, the adjutant trusted. Couldn't be more private, thought Pudiphatt. Even so, I'll write and tell him so. Seems a decent young chap. Thoroughly decent. Best keep him sweet, he might need him again – especially as he'd told him about Rifleman Stobbs, one Mendip's batman. He found some writing paper that wasn't too awful, and began the letter at once. When it was done he made a copy for what he'd labelled the Lampeter file and read it through. Coming along nicely, he thought, but best to post off the adjutant's letter at once, before he forgot. He put the file together again, then found his hat and stick. Time for a spot of exercise. At least he wouldn't have to ride that damn bike.

He was tired when he got back (could the pillar box really be so far?) but a couple of whiskies soon put that right. There was cheese in the dish – the good stuff – and butter, and bread too, still fresh enough to toast. No need to go to some rotten pub. He'd get enough of that once he managed to track down ex-Rifleman Stobbs . . . Carefully, methodically, he took one more look at the file then put it all back together. Made him feel good, that file. Justice was about to be done at last, and he poured another whisky because he deserved it. Then suddenly he froze. Something was wrong, perhaps badly wrong, like counting his men in after a raid and finding that one was missing.

And, of course, what was wrong was obvious. The letter to the Rifle Brigade adjutant. He held it in his hand, and yet he'd posted it. He was sure he had. His memory wasn't that bad. Not yet. Better check. Go through the file again. He'd been to the pillar box: he would swear to it, and of course he had. He'd posted the letter about the love nest.

Well, that was what letters were for: posting. Only with this one the timing was wrong. First he should have talked with Stobbs. Pudiphatt tried to remember whether he'd signed it or not, but of course he had. He enjoyed writing S. Pudiphatt, Major, (Retired) at the end. Vanity. Such a vulgar sin. What to do about it, that was the thing, but the answer was obvious. He could hardly go and ask for the damn thing back. Next morning, when he was sober, he cycled over to Eaton Place, and had a tiny piece of luck. The postman was there and liked a chat, it seemed.

'Nice morning,' he said, and Pudiphatt nodded. The postman had Other Rank written all over him.

'Could do with a break though,' said the postman.

'Holiday?' Pudiphatt asked.

'Fat chance,' said the postman. 'Not like some.'

He looked towards the door with its glowing knocker that the housemaid was polishing yet again. Not just a postman but a Red, thought Pudiphatt, and what's worse he thinks I'm one too. All the same, he had to listen. It was his duty to listen.

'Gone abroad,' said the postman. 'Leastways that's what *she* tells me.' He nodded at the housemaid.

'Somewhere nice?' Pudiphatt asked. It was killing him.

'Cruise,' the postman said. 'End up in Spain. All right for some. Still – they're a couple of good lookers.'

As a piece of logic it was ridiculous, but it was useful.

Later she was to discover that their cruise was like every other, even in a P and O suite: a kaleidoscope of visits to ruins, temples, mosques, all beautiful, but seen at breakneck speed, and in between, long periods of a quite delicious idleness. Like the war, she thought, the way one of Elena's books had described it: waiting, fearing, anticipating, and then the bombardment, except that they were bombarded with beauty, or at any rate spectacle: in Monte Carlo, Nice, Cannes and then, at last, Malaga, the first taste of the real thing, said Elena: an hors-d'oeuvre of what was to come. And indeed a lot of it *was* beautiful: the cathedral, the lighthouse, the Gibralfaro, the Moorish castle: but she hadn't come there for lighthouses. A little place quite near the docks – but not too near: too near the docks was social suicide . . . The house where Elena's grandparents had lived and died.

'But *why*?' Elena asked.

'There may be papers there,' said Millicent.

'But that's *working*.'

She makes it sound like cheating at cards, Millicent thought, but all the same she had her way: went to the little house, while all around her Malaga glittered and crashed, heat like a blow, and a noise like a boiler factory: tramcars, carts, lorries, and people screaming at each other as if each sentence were the prelude to a fight, and yet they seemed friendly enough.

The house at last, cool and dim after the street. Fringes and velvet-covered furniture, all of which needed dusting, and photographs of Elena and her mother. Pictures too, most of which were rather ghastly, but one that wasn't ghastly at all. It wasn't even on a wall, but inside a locked drawer. Just as well Elena had given her the keys, even if Duckhouse and Allnutt had taught her rather a lot about locked drawers. It would never do to burgle Elena's grandparents' house. She looked at the picture: she knew something about pictures: art appreciation, her only other interest when she read law.

Pencil sketch. Seventeenth century, would it be? And done by a master – but not Velazquez. It was too self-consciously charming for that. Murillo, possibly. But whoever it was, first rate – and valuable, she thought, the last vestiges of Duckhouse and Allnutt prodding, nudging.

From her handbag she took a nail file, scissors, a fruit knife: the only burglars' tools a P and O suite could provide, and looked once more at the picture, a boy reading a book to a laughing blind man, then turned it over. Somebody else had been there too, and long after Murillo. Taking the back off wasn't nearly as tricky as she'd feared – and there it was. Another pencil sketch of another laughing man. Not in Murillo's class, but the man looked nice, even so. No name, no signature, but it was a start. She reassembled the sketch and Duckhouse and Allnutt prodded and nudged again.

Don't leave it here, they said. It's messy. Perhaps even evidence. Millicent wrapped it in a cloth, found an old shopping bag and put it in that. I wouldn't have left it here anyway, she told Duckhouse and Allnutt. It belongs to Elena. Time to go . . .

My life is never easy, straightforward, Pudiphatt thought. No easy tube ride in an off-peak hour: more like a bloody switchback. And then: Those last few days must have hurt. I rarely use words like that – not even inside my own head.

Out of habit he had cycled to Eaton Place to watch the changing of the Guard routine, and he the most unlikely Christopher Robin, but this time only the pretty, elegant one came out, and looked around him for a taxi. Had he, too, read the letter to the titled bitch, he wondered? Well, of course he had. Another bloody switch back . . . then a policeman appeared, and Pudiphatt went through the motions of pumping up a tyre. Stobbs had disappeared. It sounded melodramatic, but he *had*.

The Rifle Brigade's adjutant had sent him his last address, but he wasn't at his lodgings, or any of what the *Police Gazette* used to call his 'known haunts'. Not that learning even about Stobbs' absence had been easy. His acquaintances had been taciturn to a man, even furtive. Prison, he thought, the damn fool's in prison, and I'm about to be the confidant of a criminal – if I'm lucky. *Lucky*! He'd gone through the local papers for months back, but there'd been no mention of a Stobbs, which argued that the offence had been minor, and soon he would catch up with him, but even so – he'd have to be nice to him, which was awful . . .

Elena stirred in her easy chair. Soon be time to change. As always when she was troubled she'd been thinking of Freddy; even dreaming of him when at last she dozed, because Freddy had always been so soothing: like a warm bath just right for tempera-ture. She'd remembered the one time that he had come to *her* for comfort. They'd been chatting over a drink before dinner, about a couple of chaps he'd known at school. He often did talk about chaps he'd known at school, but it didn't bother her. Even that could be entertaining. But not that time. One chap had been in the Navy and his ship had sunk and he was dead.

'Brian,' he said. 'That was his name. His chum was called Ian. We used to make jokes about them – and sailors.' Elena waited. 'They were – They—'

'Were what?' she asked him.

'Homosexuals.'

'Well, of course they were,' said Elena. 'Sailors indeed. But you were only joking after all. You weren't to know. And anyway, a damn sight more men are heterosexuals—'

'Even so – one can't help thinking.'

'That it's your fault? You weren't in command of the 'U' boat or whatever it is. Don't be silly, Freddy. You're not silly. So don't start now.'

'You don't mind queers, then?'

'Well, of course not,' she said. 'My mother was a dancer.'

'I know that,' said Freddy, 'but what's that got to do with queers?'

She looked at him sharply, but no: he means it, she thought. He really means it. Gently she explained the facts of life to him as they applied to dancers.

'Oh, good,' he said, when she had done. 'Not for poor old Brian, of course, but it means I can tell you about Uncle Freddy.'

'He was one?' Elena asked.

'Yes, he was,' said Freddy. He sounded angry, almost defiant. Not like Freddy at all. 'But how the devil did you know?'

'He was at our wedding,' Elena said. 'And anyway, I just knew. Mama did too.'

'You mean you told her?'

Still angry, she thought, but this was obviously a big thing in his life. Be gentle: be patient.

'I told you she was a dancer.'

'Yes, you did,' said Freddy. 'Sorry.'

Three more days before he goes back to the trenches, and yet he can be so contrite. So sweet.

'He left me all this,' Freddy said. They were in the Hampshire house, and his gesture took in the drawing room, the gardens, the trout stream beyond. 'He loved me, you see. I don't mean—'

'Of course you don't mean,' said Elena. 'He was your uncle. Your father's brother.'

'He was rather more than that,' said Freddy.

'You mean you loved him too.'

'Yes, I did,' said Freddy, but this time there was no defiance: simply the acceptance of a fact kept hidden far too long, but now out in the open. 'After Cambridge he gave it up,' he said.

'Eton and King's?' Elena asked.

'Well, of course,' said Freddy, but he was smiling as he said it. 'He'd just got back from a shooting trip – Kenya. We dined together.'

Elena waited. Uncle Freddy hadn't looked like a man who enjoyed slaughter.

'It wasn't really shooting,' Freddy said. 'More an excuse for wandering about. Africa and India mostly. He covered a lot of ground: saw a lot of people. Photographs, masses of them. He took his guns because he didn't want to look conspicuous.' Almost Elena giggled. Carrying his rifles as a kind of anonymity – but she stopped herself in time. Half the young men in Europe were doing it that very minute.

'For the pot, yes,' said Freddy 'and if there was a rogue loose he'd kill that too. The locals used to beg him to do it.'

'Rogue?'

'Predator. Big cats, mostly. Leopard, tiger, lion. A few live on past their natural span, but they get too old to hunt deer, and so they vary their diet, so to speak.'

'And they eat what?'

113

'Man,' said Freddy. 'Woman, too. And children.'

'Dear God,' said Elena.

'They were hungry,' Freddy said simply. To him it was a part of the natural order. Not a subject for debate. No point.

'Uncle Freddy was good at Shikar – hunting,' said Freddy. 'Good at tracking, good at keeping out of the way of a charging leopard, and a damn good shot.' He smiled, remembering. 'Anyway we drank rather a lot of port – the Cockburn's '93, I remember – I finished the last of it this leave – and he told me why he hunted and travelled so much.'

'And why did he?'

'He enjoyed it, as I say, but he said it took his mind off things too.'

'What things?'

'His salad days,' said Freddy.

'When he was green in judgement?'

'Exactly,' Freddy said. 'Never at Eton. Those little boys were no temptation. His target was tigers, not rabbits. But in the hols, and then at Cambridge. Sailors too, for all I know. "I was a right little whore," he told me. "Quantity not quality. That's what I was after." Then when he went down – he took a first by the way. My father couldn't believe it – he came to London and just kept on going, so to speak. Until he woke up one morning with someone quite nasty, even by his standards, looked at himself in the mirror, then threw out the nasty, had a bath, and took the next train to Cambridge.'

'Why Cambridge?'

'He didn't know,' Freddy said. 'Never could tell me. All he knew was he had to go, so he went. Straight to King's.'

'His old college?'

'Yes,' Freddy said, 'but it wasn't that. Well, not precisely. At first he wandered round and looked at everything. The Backs and the river, the library, the hall. But that was just putting it off,' he said.

'But why should it?'

'Because it was about to change his life and it terrified him. All the same, he went to the chapel, but again that wasn't why: not precisely. He looked at it, he said, looked and looked as if it was for the first time. As if it was the only thing he'd ever seen. And then he went inside. The choir was just finishing a rehearsal: Bach. Strong and beautiful, he said, and then silence. Silence even more profound than the music – and then suddenly, he knew.'

He paused to look at her, but she said, 'Please go on, Freddy.'

'No more sex, not much drinking and a lot of hard work. He was going to be a parson. Not that it wouldn't have its compensations. He'd be "High", he said – dragging up in a cope, music – perhaps Thomas Tallis when the bishop couldn't hear, incense, even a Mother's Union banner. Still the camp talk, but he smiled as he said it. For him the old way of life was dead. The new one was a resurrection, you see. And he did become a priest.'

'Of course he did,' said Elena. 'He married us.'

'I'm the only one he ever told,' Freddy said.

'And now you've told me.'

'Well, of course,' Freddy said. 'It was us together. He married us as you say.'

Darling Freddy you'd never talked like that before, she thought. Or since. But then it wasn't you talking. It was your uncle.

'I hope I didn't – bore you?' he said.

'Of course not. It was wonderful.'

'And then he died,' Freddy said. 'A sniper got him. Neuve Chapel, wasn't it? But before he died he'd bewildered the whole battalion.'

'Bewildered?'

'What was a toff of a parson doing in trench mud? And such a parson. Well, he showed them what. He was very popular after that, until—'

'He was happy,' said Elena.

'As a sandboy,' Freddy said. 'Whatever that is.'

Then he began to talk about the jolly times they'd have when 'it' was over. To Freddy the war was always 'it'. He was killed at Vimy Ridge six weeks later, and the widow's times weren't all that jolly, until she met Richard. She yawned and wriggled and stretched and Millicent came in. Missing him, thought Millicent. She always does the Salome stuff when she's missing him.

'Did you have a lovely time, darling?' Elena asked.

'Two – maybe three,' said Millicent.

Hopeful suitors, Elena thought. They always kept count of the suitors, and two maybe three wasn't bad for a sun deck. But that wasn't the point.

'You really saw nothing?' she said.

'Not a thing,' Millicent said, 'and I truly did look everywhere.'

It hurt her, it really did, when she lied, but first she had to be sure.

'I found something though.' She opened her bag and the drawing wrapped in a cloth.

'At my grandmother's house?'

Millicent nodded. 'You'd never seen it before?' she asked.

'Never. It's valuable, isn't it?'

'If it's what I think it is.'

'It never belonged to my grandparents.'

'You seem so sure,' said Millicent.

'Valuable,' said Elena. 'Elegant, too. Beautiful.'

'If it had been in that house, Mama would have seen it. She was elegant and beautiful too.'

Not for a court of law, thought Millicent, but it will do for me.

'It must have been his,' said Elena. 'My father's. He must have given it to her.' She seemed utterly sure.

'I think so too,' said Millicent, and all the evidence was there. Not just the artist, but the setting: a patio and a Moorish garden, and a guitar lying at the blind man's feet.

'Let me hold it,' said Elena, and Millicent gave it to her, and Elena stared at it as if it just might, by some miracle, reveal her father. Tears welled in her eyes, but she brushed them away almost angrily, as if they had no business there.

'It isn't much,' she said, 'but it's a start.'

'We're getting there,' said Millicent.

'You really mean that?'

'I really do.'

11

Getting there. Not all that easy, thought Milburn. Not with Elena. She would make up her own mind. No good trying to break her to bridle either. Elena was one who'd have to be persuaded. He stirred in the saddle and his mount, a big and active grey mare called Misty, stamped impatiently. Standing about was not what she was for.

'Just give me a minute,' said Milburn. After all, Noche would have been even more impatient, if anything . . . He looked about him. Broad acres, though perhaps not as broad as Elena's, and certainly not as fertile. But there was the coal. Coal almost limitless. Black gold – but Elena's was the real stuff: in Coutts and Company's vaults. And the house. But Elena already had four. At least no-one can say I married her for her money, he thought. If she ever does marry me. At the moment she'd sooner dance.

Not that she didn't like him. Without liking at least there would be no Chelsea flat. It was just that she had to dance, had to, and everything else must wait its turn. But he was used to waiting. The war had taught him that at least. He turned the grey, clapped heels to her and cantered home. A light lunch, and another attack on Euripides. Soon he'd be going back to Oxford. Better not go unprepared.

The switchback was going up for a change, he thought, and not before bloody time. Then – No. Don't be rude about it. Never be rude to Fate: and it was going up after all. Another letter from the Rifles' adjutant. Nice man. Pudiphatt hoped he had fair hair . . . To begin with Stobbs hadn't been in Pentonville or Wormwood Scrubs or wherever they put them. He'd been in hospital: military hospital. As a matter of fact he'd been in one himself – officers only, of course – but for him it had been nightmares, fantasies, the things inside your head that made you scream. For Stobbs it had been shrapnel that had to be removed from his chest or else he would die – but not, please God, before Pudiphatt had settled the matter of that aristocratic bitch. The next step was to find him, but the adjutant had helped him there, too. Lodging in the Clapham area, he said. Shouldn't be too difficult; an ex-Serviceman, just out of hospital, living on his own. He was definitely getting there . . .

Culture, thought Millicent. Everywhere you turned. Culture and more culture. Elena simply went when she felt like it, but Millicent found she had to go. Was it being a Protestant, or was it because God alone knew when she'd get another chance? Whatever it was she went: camera, Baedeker guide and all. Even sensible shoes. Far too hot for Andalucia: but easy to walk in, and such a comfort when one took them off. She slogged on because it was her duty, she thought. 'Stern daughter of the Voice of God?' but it was far too hot for Wordsworth, too.

At least those Moors had understood about the heat: the Alcázar in Seville, the Alhambra and the Generalife in Granada – those heavenly gardens too – the Great Mosque in Cordoba. Elena had told her the proverb: He who has not seen Seville has not seen a marvel . . . That's as maybe, thought Millicent, her mother's daughter. They certainly hadn't been cool. But the culture – altogether too much of it. No doubt back in London she would look at her photographs, read her guide book, but here it was like a diet of cream cakes, breakfast, lunch, tea and dinner.

Then, at last, there was respite, even a treat. Elena ventured out into the heat finally, and they went to see her photographer: but first she looked at her friend's face, slowly, carefully.

Oh, my God, thought Millicent. Have I caught the plague or something?'

'Darling,' Elena said, 'on the way we must buy you a bigger hat. If we're not careful, you will be sunburnt.'

To be sunburnt, it seemed, was far worse than the plague.

Enrique Oliverès was delightful. Not all photographers were, according to Elena: some were bullies, but Oliverès relied on charm. Queer, of course, but then he was in what Millicent's mama called the business, and pretty (it was part of the charm), and he loved the costumes. Even the pansies, thought Millicent. Two pretty girls dressed like Goya's models, and one of them about as feminine as a girl can be, the other dressed like a man and yet obviously, ineradicably, a girl, and they went down like ninepins. Every tune. And thank God for that, thought Millicent.

Oliverès took picture after picture. But at last even he had had enough, and produced cakes and wine instead. Millicent avoided the cakes – they were stuffed with cream – but drank the wine.

'So you like it?' Elena asked. Millicent did, it seemed.

'Varga Siciliana, and an old one too. The best Spain can offer.'

'It's expensive?' Millicent asked.

'Vastly,' said Elena. 'Cost more than his bill probably, and that won't be exactly centimos.'

'Golly.'

'But it isn't just that. It's rare. The vineyard is minute, you see. He must like us.'

You know he does, thought Millicent, and he worked jolly hard. But when it came to delivering the pictures, my God, they were slow – like Duckhouse and Allnutt with a rich client ... Until one day Elena came out of her bath stark naked, and said, 'I've decided.'

I do wish she wouldn't do that, Millicent thought. Their hotel was stuffed with servants and a lot of them were male: page boys, waiters. I mean, she's as gorgeous as ever, but a little rich for a waiter's blood. She handed her friend a bath towel.

'Decided what, darling?'

'Today is the day I lose my temper. But first we'll prepare for it.'

They were speaking Spanish, because Millicent needed the practice and it all sounded deliciously menacing, even if the preparations meant a specially good lunch and rather a lot of wine. Then they took a carriage to Oliverès's studio, and Oliverès, wise in the ways of dancers, was nowhere to be found. Not that Elena cared. They had his chief assistant, who would do just as well, if not better. What happened next reminded Millicent of nothing so much as her father's description of an oil tanker hit by a torpedo: first the impact, then the explosion, then the flames and fragments soaring like a firework display. The assistant, who was almost as pretty as his master, then ruined his make-up by bursting into tears.

'*Mañana*,' he sobbed. '*Mañana*,' and Elena had mercy at last. One passing reference to what would happen if it wasn't *mañana*, and she left him to his tears. He had lots of work to do.

Outside the studio Millicent looked at her friend, awestruck. Elena was smiling.

'I really enjoyed that,' she said, 'but now we must go and rest. We have lots to see tonight.'

119

We have lots to see every night, thought Millicent, and it's marvellous.

For once it was cool, and they both had fans if the heat came back, if only on a visit, but more importantly, there were the gypsies: in cafés, in patios, even on the streets. They didn't care where: a few pesetas and they would dance. They danced like the artists they were, thought Millicent: the women like queens, the men kings waiting for a distant throne, the guitarists virtuosi to a man, and the singers all with that wailing cry, part triumph, part lament. And all of it superb: polished, practised, and gleaming like fine gold. Incredible. Even the hand clapping. There was nobody in London who could clap hands as they could. I'm probably the best, she thought, and even I plod like a tortoise in a race for gazelles. And yet it was bliss, even if she knew the gazelles would always win. She looked at Elena, who obviously thought so too. Not to be them, of course not, she had four houses and a fortune, but just to know it was there: to be able at least to try.

She smiled at Millicent. 'You're not discouraged?'

'No point,' said Millicent. 'I enjoy it. It exists,' and again Elena smiled. Now part of her will be forever Spanish, she thought; now that she's seen it, in Seville, Granada, Cordoba; it will always be there.

They went to the bullfight too. Elena had worried about the bullfight: so many English people went, then hated it. Mostly English naval officers, she remembered. La Linea, just across the border from Gibraltar, or in Ronda, up in the mountains. They hated it, especially when the horses were ripped and torn: the bulls – on a good day – killed with elegance and grace. How awful to kill an animal for pleasure, they said, although most of them hunted foxes . . . She had shrugged, she remembered, and Mama had laughed, and somehow, sheepishly, they had smiled, but then as Gertie said, sailors would accept almost anything from a pretty woman . . .

Millicent wasn't like that. She enjoyed the bulls: not as entertainment; a corrida wasn't entertainment, and Millicent had known at once that it was not. It was the dancing rhythm of it, the smooth movement of the matador's body that she enjoyed. Another way to dance: the most terrifying way . . . And that to Elena was it. Dancing with a bull whose name was Death, and yet dancing with grace. And sometimes dying, and that was the point. By watching the matadors one learned: about Freddy and Charles and perhaps about Richard too, for that he had been close to death she had no doubt. There had been altogether too much dying. After the corrida in Seville – the grandest of all – she said to Millicent: 'Darling would you mind if we went home soon?'

'Not at all,' said Millicent.

'You're sure?'

'It was a holiday,' said Millicent. 'All holidays end sometime and anyway, you've already given me three good reasons for going back.'

'Three?'

'Stanhope, Mortimer and Barnes,' said Millicent, and Elena giggled.

'That doesn't mean you'll have to stop dancing, even if there are three of them.'

'Of course not,' said Millicent. 'I shall feel a little shy, that's all.'

'Why feel shy?'

'After what we've seen here,' Millicent said.

Tattered finery, glass instead of jewels, and yet they walked like queens. And with reason. A waiter brought them coffee, and she relaxed. At least her friend had her clothes on.

'The ones we dance for won't see us like that,' said Elena.

'Why won't they?'

'They've never been to Spain,' said Elena, and yawned and wriggled.

Missing Richard again, thought Millicent, and why not? I'm missing Francis. Time to go back.

Another P and O boat, more parties, more suitors to collect. But not in competition; not like deck tennis. With the suitors they hunted as a pair, because it worked even better: like a couple of elegant staghounds scenting a herd of rather clumsy deer. Because one of us is dark and the other fair? Millicent wondered. But who cared why? It was fun – even if it wasn't precisely why Dad had sent her to the University. But she doubted whether it would have bothered him. After all he'd been a sailor.

Her mother loved it. Of course she did. She'd been a notable staghound in her day . . . Rather a choppy voyage back, and the thought of mum one of the things that sustained her, that and Francis, but they had neither of them been sick; not like some of the sailors at the corrida . . . But it hadn't been too bad. The Customs Officer had seen their pictures in a magazine and let them through at once, and Grimshaw and a porter were waiting.

The drive from Southampton was lengthy, but they were in a

Rolls after all: there was comfort, and then Eaton Square, and Tufnell so pleased to see them: Francis and Richard too; and absolutely no sign of burglars, said Francis. No cut purses, no footpads, no scurvy knaves. Jokes, thought Elena. From Francis. Gracious he must be happy, and of course he was. They all were. And the next day their bodies would be excited too. She looked at Millicent.

'Darling, you're crying,' she said.

'Just happiness,' said Millicent.

'That's all right then.'

'And all because of you.'

'I thought perhaps Francis might have something to do with it.'

'If it hadn't been for you I'd never have met Francis,' said Millicent.

'But I overslept at my mother's house and you did.'

Though whether that's good luck or not, thought Elena, and then: No, not tonight. My friend has saved her tears. And she's strong enough to cope even with happiness. Spain had proved that.

'He loved his photograph,' she said.

'They both did.'

Soon, she told herself. Honestly God. Soon. On my solemn word. Just let me speak to mum first.

Next day Mrs Blenkinsop arrived in state: silk dress, what she called her Floradora hat – she was much too old for a cloche, she said – and a taxi all the way from Pimlico; money no object. And at the end of it all, the photograph. Millicent had been out early that morning to have it framed. Solid silver Gertie noticed, but it was the picture she loved.

'Richard wants us to sit for a painting, too,' her daughter said.

'And will I get one?'

'Of course,' said Millicent.

'What a good daughter I have,' said Gertie, 'but something's bothering you. Let's have it.'

'Not bothering me exactly,' said her daughter, but then Tufnell came in with champagne. Gertie, to his relief, drank sherry that her daughter had brought from Spain. It was true that she drank champagne herself, but Miss Blenkinsop never drank much . . .

When he'd gone, Gertie asked, 'Is it about Elena?'

It was true that Elena was out with Richard, but it never pays to shout, Gertie thought. Not when it comes to *l'amour*.

'She and Sir Richard haven't quarrelled?'

'Oh no,' said Millicent. Even the idea seemed to horrify her.

Not like you and Francis, thought Gertie. Always a barney with you two. But then you enjoy it, don't you? But that's because you win.. 'What then?' she asked.

Millicent showed her the Murillo sketch.

'Lovely,' said Gertie, 'but it's her property after all. Nowt to worry about.'

All the same it was getting to her, thought Millicent. The lapse into the Geordie accent showed that.

'I found this behind the frame,' she said, and handed over the sketch of the other laughing man.

Gertie looked long and hard. 'And who's he when he's at home?' she asked.

'I rather think it's Elena's father,' said Millicent. 'And so does Elena.'

Right little Sherlock Holmes, thought Gertie. All the same she's got brains. Just like her dad.

'Ring any bells?' Millicent asked.

'Have a heart,' said her mother. 'One sketch – and not even a good one. All the same, there's a look of somebody. Maybe after I've had a think . . .'

'How about this one?'

Millicent passed her a photograph. A man and a woman together, drinking coffee outside a café – pricey one. The woman was Elena's mother. Outside the rue de la Paix. Dancers in Paris never strayed far from the rue de la Paix if they could help it.

'Great God Almighty,' said Gertie. She knew it was blasphemous, but then she'd had a bit of a shock. 'Where did you get it?'

'Behind another picture frame. The one with Elena's mum.' She smiled. 'They seemed to use them instead of safes. Know him?'

'I should think I do,' said Gertie. 'Well, not to say know him. We met at parties a few times. He was nice.'

His name, mum, *please*, thought Millicent. It was a scream, but only inside her head. When mum set off down Memory Lane she couldn't be rushed.

'Name of Channing,' her mother said at last. 'Adam Channing. No. Aylmer, Lord Aylmer Channing as a matter of fact, on account of his father was a duke. Duke of Bellingham, up our way, only you wouldn't think so, not if you knew his house, and then mine. Still, like I say, a nice man . . . where were they?'

'In France,' said Millicent. 'Almost thirty years ago. Still, it's all perfectly legal.'

123

'You'd know all right,' said Gertie, 'but how do you know?'

'That was in the safe too,' said Millicent. 'The photo frame – beside the picture.'

'Sounds like love all right,' said Gertie. 'But why didn't she tell her daughter?'

'She died very quickly,' Elena said.

'No doubt she did,' said her mother. 'That flu. They were dropping like flies, excuse me for saying it, but what I meant was – why make it a secret? They were married after all.'

'Maybe he was ashamed of her,' said Millicent.

'Then he wouldn't have married her.'

My mother may not be strong on logic, but when it comes to common sense she's unbeatable, her daughter thought.

'You wouldn't happen to know if he's still alive?' Millicent asked.

'Of course he's alive,' said her mother. 'All the Channings live to be eighty at least. Or do you mean the war?' Millicent nodded. 'He was a soldier right enough. Grenadiers. Only he missed a lot of the big one. He'd been off to fight the Boers, and when he came back he was raving.'

'Mad?'

'As a hatter. Living his life out in Bellingham Castle. Never leaves it now, poor feller . . . He went back for the big one, then he went funny again. You've said nothing to Elena?'

'Not a word.'

'But it's her *dad*,' said Gertie.

'I had to talk to you first.'

Gertie nodded. 'No harm in being sure when you can.' She looked again at the sketch, and then the photograph. 'You'll have to tell her soon.'

'Today,' said Millicent, and her mother nodded again then was silent, both women staring into the future as if it were an abyss.

When all was said and done, this was a big thing. The biggest. Not like borrowing a lipstick or a dollop of perfume from someone else's dressing table. This was Elena's *dad* and Millicent had known about it for days: suspected it for weeks. Yet how could she stay silent? The secret was out now and it would stay out. Somehow, somewhere, somebody would find it.

Millicent thought, she's my friend, the one who brought me here, set me free from Duckhouse and Allnutt, took me on a cruise, paid for my articles. And how did I repay her? Lies and concealment and treating her like a child who couldn't be trusted.

124

She's the best friend I ever had, and not just because she's rich. She'll be furious, she thought, and Elena knew all about fury. She'd seen her in action in Seville . . . Once she told Millicent that of all the sins, betrayal was the worst. Well, she'd betrayed her all right. Her best and only friend.

Her mother said, 'Would you like me to stay here for when you tell her?'

Somehow, Millicent managed a smile. What a mother. All the same: 'No mum,' she said. 'This is one I have to tackle myself.' Her mother left her chair and kissed her.

And still the switchback climbed. He'd rung the military hospital records and they'd heard him out at once. Crisp voice, authoritative manner – and two whiskies and no more till he'd heard what they had to say, which was so good that he'd bought another bottle. He'd been seconded from the West Kents he said, to bring the records of the Rifle Brigade's wounded up to date, and they'd mislaid one – Rifleman Stobbs. A long pause while somebody looked through files and produced a Corporal Lipton as a conjuror might produce a rabbit. Brief thanks – the West Kents might respect the Rifle Brigade but they wouldn't grovel – and then Lipton. The important thing was that Lipton had a permanent address – a downstairs flat in Stepney, and that meant he could be talked to: soon. A God awful place that part of Stepney, but he hadn't come as a health visitor after all. A tuppenny notebook from Woolworth's, a fountain pen and he was in disguise. Pudiphatt knocked on the door of 83 Lord Roberts Street, and it was opened at once but not all the way: by a man.

'Who goes there?' said a voice from inside.

'Friend,' said Pudiphatt, because what else was there to say?

Slowly, warily, the door opened, and Pudiphatt found himself looking at ex-Corporal Lipton. Mad as a hatter, thought Pudiphatt. Still, it takes one to know one, and he'd done at least his share in that department.

'Advance friend and be recognised,' said Lipton in a voice that alternated between a rumble and a squeak, and the man himself once big and powerful, but now the very medals he wore on his coat, shiny beyond belief, seemed to drag him down.

'Major Pudiphatt, West Kents,' said Pudiphatt. 'Liaising with the Rifle Brigade.' Stupid to give his own name, he thought, but perhaps even more stupid not to.

'That's as maybe,' said Lipton. 'I had a mate fell for that one at

Loos. A month ago would it be? Six weeks? . . . I could take you straight to his grave.'

The Battle of Loos had been ten years ago, thought Pudiphatt. Before even my time. No wonder Lipton was crazy.

'About your case,' he said, and produced his notebook.

'Case?' said Lipton. 'Full pack's what we had,' and then, 'Oh, case . . . Let's see some identification, major.'

Even what was left of Lipton looked powerful, formidable. Pudiphatt went through his pockets and produced a card with his name on it, and a letter from the War Office marked OHMS. Lipton took them from him and read them, his lips moving as he read.

'This doesn't say nothing about the Rifle Brigade,' he said.

'Well, it wouldn't,' said Pudiphatt. 'I told you. I was in the West Kents.'

'Oh, ah,' said Lipton, and handed back Pudiphatt's papers. As he did so a car backfired in the next street, and Lipton jumped about a foot, then: 'That sentry's nervous,' he said.

Pudiphatt forced himself to say something.

Anything.

'New battalion,' he said at last. 'They haven't been out long.'

'Ten minutes is enough for me,' said Lipton, and then, 'You'd better come in.'

It seems I've passed the test, whatever it is, thought Pudiphatt. 'Thanks.' He said.

'Oh, ah,' said Lipton and led the way inside.

The place was glittering clean, he noticed. Canvas on the floor gleaming, carpet swept. Lipton? He wondered. He still had the strength for it. Then they went into what was obviously the 'best' room: chairs and sofa covered in horse hair, and on the mantelpiece a photograph of Lipton with the rank of Rifleman, but with all the glory of pre-war dress uniform. On one wall a Union Jack was pinned, on another the poster of Kitchener pointing his finger and saying: 'Your Country needs you.' Well, it certainly got poor Lipton, Pudiphatt thought, and me too for a while, and maybe a second time if I don't watch it.

'Passchendaele was a bastard,' said Lipton. 'All that mud. Were you there?'

Oh, God, thought Pudiphatt, but before he could lie Lipton continued. He wasn't there for a chat, he was there to remember.

'I got stuck in it,' he said. 'Little Jackie Collins nearly drowned. Took three of us to drag him out. And then a sniper got him.

Waste of time.' On and on it went: Passchendaele, Cambrai, the Hindenburg Line. All over the place: not just in space but in time, too. Loos, the Marne, First Ypres. No wonder the man was demented. But the remorseless flow was dammed at last. A door slammed, there were footsteps in the passage, then a woman came in, angry yet defensive. Lipton's mother? Pudiphatt wondered. Maybe it was his wife. Years and years of Lipton would age any woman. Gently, he told his lies again, and the woman relaxed. Disconcertingly, in the middle of it all, Lipton fell asleep – but then any old soldier would get some kip when he could.

'So you've come to get him more money?' the woman asked.

'I've come to try anyway.'

'It's what they all say.' The woman's voice held no hope at all.

'I mean really try,' said Pudiphatt. 'He's the most deserving case I've ever seen, Mrs—'

'Lipton,' she said. 'I'm his wife.' She looked at her sleeping husband. 'He's a good man really. Never ever lays a finger on me. Not even when he's—'

'When he's what, Mrs Lipton?'

'Like he is.'

'Only I'll need an independent witness. Corroboration. From somebody that really knows him.'

'They're mostly dead,' said his wife. 'Let's ask him.' Her hand reached out, but he was awake before she touched him.

'This gentleman has to ask a few questions,' his wife said.

'Oh, ah,' said Lipton.

'About who your pals are.'

'Dick Rogers,' said Lipton at once.

'Killed at Cambrai.'

'Billy Jackson.'

'Missing presumed killed. Wipers would it be?'

'Wipers it was,' said Lipton, but the list went on.

'Mrs Lipton seemed to know it as well as he did, but then she'd heard it often enough.

'What about that man you was in hospital with – before they moved you?'

'Charlie Stobbs?' said Lipton. 'Rotten soldier. Bone idle he was – even on parade.'

Cautiously, Pudiphatt said, 'But he finished up as Lord Mendip's batman. He must have been a smart one.'

'Not smart,' said Lipton. To be smart was praiseworthy – 'Crafty.'

Casually Mrs Lipton asked: 'Where's his home, Bert?'

'Doubt if he's got one,' Lipton said, 'except the Black Horse in Wellington Street.'

Slower, but still climbing, thought Pudiphatt, and promised himself that when he got home he really would write to the War Office, even if he hadn't been in the West Kents. Lipton had given more than enough for his country. It was time he got something back, and he, Pudiphatt, would say so. And *then* the fresh bottle of whisky.

12

She told her at once: there was no other way. Let it wait and when the time came she'd be tongue-tied. The trouble was Elena looked so *happy*. Well, of course she does. Millicent thought. She's spent nearly all day with her chap.

'There's something we have to talk about,' she said.

'Is there darling?'

No shrugs, no squirming, but her mind and even more, her body, were on a bed in Chelsea.

''Fraid so.'

Her friend sounded so *serious*. Elena dragged her mind back to Eaton Place, took out cigarettes, and offered one to Millicent, who took it. It must be serious.

'Let's have it then,' she said, and out it all came. The Murillo sketch, the picture frame and marriage lines.

'You have them here?' Elena asked.

'Of course.'

'Let me see them, please.' No sign of what she was thinking. None at all—

For a long long time she held them and stared at them: especially the picture of her mother and father, then the marriage lines last of all, but she read them and re-read them as if committing them to memory.

'This is, what do you call it – valid?' she asked, her voice still expressionless.

'Perfect,' said Millicent.

Then Elena proceeded to amaze her friend and perhaps even herself by bursting into tears. And that was altogether too much. Rage or not, Millicent went to her friend and embraced her.

'Darling – what's wrong?' she asked.

'You did all this yourself?'

Indeed I did, thought Millicent. Solo. Unaided. But all she did was nod. That would never do. 'I promise you I meant it—; she

129

began, but Elena motioned her to silence, the sobs became hiccups, then ceased.

'How can I ever thank you?' she asked.

'Thank me?' But Elena motioned her to silence again. She wanted to talk, not listen.

'It was all like some ghastly treasure hunt,' she said. 'Oh, I knew the treasure would be wonderful if I found it – but suppose I failed? I honestly don't think I could have borne it. So I kept putting it off instead. The pieces were there. I knew that too. I just couldn't bring myself to fit them together.

'And all the time you were working at it too, quietly, not a word so as not to upset me, not to raise false hopes, and it was only when you held all the pieces that you – that you – oh God bless you, darling,' and she reached out for Millicent and hugged her and hugged her, and Millicent returned the embrace.

Say nothing, she told herself. It isn't cowardice. Your friend is happy. Happy all over. Let her stay that way.

At last, Elena said, 'Do we know who he is? This Aylmer Channing?' Millicent told her. 'And still not a word,' Elena smiled. 'No Spaniard could do that. Not even a half-Spaniard. Is he well, my father?'

Gently, Millicent explained what had happened to him, and Elena heard her out in silence, then sighed.

'At least he's alive,' she said. 'But how do you know all this?'

'My mother met him, years ago,' said Millicent; she found it was somehow impossible to keep silent. 'They weren't – lovers or anything: just met at parties. And she and her old cronies still meet now and then, and gossip.'

'Do you know how I could reach him?'

'Best to ask Lord Chard.'

'Of course,' said Elena. 'I can't think, you see. Not just at the moment. Just as well I have you to do it for me.'

At last I'm beginning to understand the meaning of the word hypocrite, but I'll make it up to you darling. I swear I will.

'Seeing Francis tonight?' Elena asked, and Millicent nodded. But it won't be like you and Richard, she thought. No relaxing bliss, no long-lost fathers. Only a mother all too readily available. She wished that Mrs Boyce would leave the country. Timbuktu, she'd heard, was delightful at this time of year.

'Always a pleasure to feed you,' said Lord Chard. He was doing so in the House of Lords, where Elena was wearing a dress of what he could only think of as twilight blue – the only blue that became her, and pearls, and looked as edible as the food in front of them. By God, she's happy, his lordship thought. What's up?

'You don't mind the chaps staring at you?' he asked.

'Is that what they're doing?'

'They worship you you see,' said Chard. 'From afar. A lot of them have looked at dancers in their time, but never worshipped them. Not like you and that partner of yours. They worship her too.'

'We're not goddesses,' said Elena.

'You're ladies,' said the earl. 'Ladies who can dance like no lady I ever saw before. Now, tell me what I can do for you.' Elena told him. 'Poor chap,' said Chard. 'He was one of the most promising soldiers I ever met. Would have been a general when the next one came along.' Though he did act on the staff, Chard thought. 'Only just not crazy and a staff officer. Your best bet's Bellingham,' he continued.

'The duke?' said Elena. 'He's in London?'

'Of course he is,' said Chard. 'The House is sitting. Very keen, Bellingham. Especially coal mines and things.'

Elena decided to let that one wait until she saw the duke, or talked to Millicent.

'He'll ask for a quid pro quo though,' Chard said. 'Bound to.'

'What quid pro quo?'

'He's giving a ball,' said Chard. 'One of the tribe's just got engaged.'

'Tribe?'

'Female Bellingham. There must be dozens.' He astonished them both by quoting Shakespeare. ' "Not single spies but in battalions." '

'Why not?' said Elena. 'We're dancers.'

'Thought you said you wanted to rest for a while.'

'That was before we went to Spain,' Elena said. 'We saw marvellous things there. We'd rather like to try some. Besides—' Chard waited. 'I rather think the music will be better . . .'

She discussed it with Millicent.

'Better?' asked her friend, intrigued.

'I went to the Spanish embassy before lunch. Please don't be angry with me for not telling.'

Coals of fire, thought Millicent.

'There's a man there who was a friend of mama's. They've found a guitar player, he says.'

131

'Who has?'

'The embassy. He's from Cadíz. Wants to go to Mexico – only someone stole nearly all his money in France. His name is Pedrillito.'

'Little Peter.'

'Very little Peter – except when he plays.'

'He must be good.'

'Darling,' said Elena, 'if there's a gypsy heaven that's the kind of music they'll play there.'

Millicent was working and Elena and Gertie were sitting gossiping before the fire in the little sitting room, which was early Victorian and relaxing, a cosy, elegant room.

Tufnell had poured champagne for Gertie and sulked just a little as he did so, but not too much. Gertie always left him a glassful . . .

'All different them days,' Gertie was saying. 'I'm glad our Millie missed it.'

'Where was this?' Elena asked, although she knew pretty well. Gertie did so enjoy remembering. 'Black Sills Colliery,' said Gertie. 'Up North. Terrible place that was. Mind you I didn't think so at the time – not knowing any better. And Black Sills could have been worse after all.'

'How worse?'

'We had the Channings,' said Gertie. 'The Duke of Bellingham's lot. They owned it. Owned half the county come to that. That's what saved us.'

'But how could it?' Elena asked.

'Good works,' said Gertie. 'They had it like it was a disease. Incurable, thank God . . . Not that we needed it. Not for years. Me da was always fit and well but – for them that wasn't, the Channings was always there. Two of them anyway. Lord Arthur and Lady Mary. Not like their neighbour – Sir Harry Webb. He owned pits, too. All the toffs did up there. But with him – get sick and you were out. That's what workhouses are for, he'd say.'

'Good God,' said Elena.

'I mind once – remember I should say – when I was a bairn out playing and Webb came by on his horse just as Lord Arthur came by on his, and Webb tossed me a shilling when Lord Arthur could see. If I'd had the money I would have had it framed. A rare item, a shilling from Sir Harry. Very rare.'

'Morning, Channing, he says, and Lord Arthur rode on as if he'd never ever seen him, and I got away quick before he could take his shilling back.'

'What happened to him?' Elena asked.

'He died,' said Gertie. 'But not in the workhouse.'

'And who—'

'All in good time,' said Gertie. 'There's a lot went on in Black Sills.' Elena begged pardon. 'Like me da,' continued Gertie. 'Papa you would say. Big chap for a pitman – what you'd call a miner. Earned good money down by. Underground that is. And he did earn it. Very near six foot, me da, and the seam – the coal face – four foot six at best.'

'But how on earth did he manage?'

'He stooped,' said Gertie. 'Like all the rest. But him being tall made it harder.' She sipped her champagne. 'When I was little he used to take his bath in front of the fire, and I saw his back many's the time. Like he'd been flogged. And not all that long ago either. But that isn't how he made his real money . . .'

'How did he do that?' Elena asked, and thought, I'm like a KC leading a witness.

'Whippets,' said Gertie. 'Little titchy greyhounds that go after hares. Miners is daft on them. Them and racing pigeons. Fighting cocks too, but Lord Arthur put a stop to that.'

'Your father bred whippets?'

'The best,' said Gertie. 'Chaps used to come from miles around. The whippets weren't cheap, but they were winners. Daft on them. One set of chaps out Ashington way, they even formed a what have you.'

'A syndicate?'

'That's the one,' said Gertie. 'Mind you, they reckoned the dog was worth it. Won three races on the trot.' She settled back in her chair. 'So there we were, happy as pigs in muck because we knew no better and anyway there was roast beef on the table every Sunday and all the beer me da could shift – though he was never a drinker like some. There was school, too.'

'In the village?'

'That's right. Mind you, I liked school – within reason. Learned me twelve times and joined-up writing. Read *Uncle Tom's Cabin*.' She smiled. 'A bit like Black Sills, we thought. All the men, they were black, too . . . I did all right at school. Not like our Millie. She was outstanding – one of these days I'll tell you about her – if you want to hear.'

133

'Of course I do,' said Elena. 'She's my partner, but go on about Black Sills for now.'

'Funny place,' Gertie said. 'Anywhere else we'd have been slaves, but for Black Sills we were middle class. Till da fell ill.'

'An accident?'

Gertie shook her head. 'Pneumoconiosis.'

'I'm sorry?'

'Pitmen's disease,' said Gertie. 'On account of what they breathe down by. It isn't just air, you see. There's stone dust and coal dust as well. Well, da survived for nigh on thirty years – he'd been down the pits since he was twelve – but it got him in the end. Gasping for breath, coughing black muck. Oh, I'm sorry.'

'Why should you be?' said Elena. 'It's what happened. Please go on.'

'Mam sent for the doctor. Dad told her not to – pitmen has a horror of doctors – but she did anyway. First time she'd ever disobeyed him. Anyway he comes to the cottage on his bicycle and goes over da as if he was a lump of meat, and when he'd done he looks at mam and says, 'He's got pneumoconiosis,' and then because we're only ignorant pit-folk he gives us a translation, us that had seen it all our lives. 'Dust disease,' he said. 'Breathing. Bad cough. I'll write you our a prescription for some cough syrup.' There wasn't a cough syrup in the world could save da, and the doctor knew it, and so did me mam – and anyway cough syrup was a tanner a bottle – sixpence – and from then on we'd have to start counting the pennies, never mind the sixpences. "We'll see," said Mam, and the doctor knew when he was beat and got back on his bike. It was only then when the door was shut that Mam started to cry . . .

'Somehow, the day got over and we seemed to take turns in crying, but Da had to be fed. Broth it was usually, on account of he couldn't swallow much else except maybe a custard for afters and tea – and then there came a knock at the door and I went to answer. Nobody was afraid to open the door in them days, and anyway – what did we have worth stealing? So I opened the door and there was this chap.'

'Another doctor?'

'About a million times better than a doctor,' said Gertie. 'It was Lord Arthur Channing.

'Big feller, Lord Arthur,' said Gertie. 'The Channings was all big. But nice with it. "Can I come in?" he says. My mother was standing behind me. "Yes, please come in, sir," she says and in he came.

134

' "I'm sorry to hear about your troubles," he says, and me mam just looked at him. Not upset or anything. Just like mam believed it.

' "Thanks," says mam.

' "The thing is, we may be able to do something about it," and I thought, got a miracle up your sleeve have you? But Mam looked as if he might at that.

' "We sir?" she says.

' "Me and my brother," said Lord Arthur. "The duke. I've just talked to him on the phone from the colliery office."

' "Yes sir?"

' "We've heard your husband's good with dogs."

' "Whippets," said Mam – meaning not your sort of dog at all.

' "A dog's a dog," Lord Arthur says. "Now the thing is this. I take it your husband wouldn't want to go back to the pit even if he could?"

' "He would not," said Mam, in the tone of voice you shouldn't use to a lord, but Lord Arthur didn't even blink.

' "Quite right too," he said. "So we thought maybe he'd like to come and help us with the dogs instead."

' "What dogs?" said me mam. It sounded champion, but she liked things above board, me mam.

' "The ones at Bellingham Castle," said Lord Arthur. "We've got two kinds – indoors and outdoors. The indoor ones is mostly little 'uns – pugs, Pomeranians, Pekinese, poodles: all the p's in fact. We wouldn't want to bother him with them – but the outside dogs are just what he'll need I'd say. They're of two kinds too: the ones that hunt – only we call them hounds – and the ones we take shooting. Spaniels mostly: the big ones. Clumbers. And Labradors. They need work of course, a lot of work – mostly walking. We've got other chaps for that. Your husband would do the other things: the tricky things. Grooming, obedience, walking to heel. What would he say to that do you think?"

'My mother was looking at him as if he was an angel with a sack of gold. "Best ask him yourself, sir," she said at last, "if you wouldn't mind." Then she took him to their bedroom. When she came back she said, "Pray Gertie. Just pray." And I prayed. Lord Arthur was back in no time. Dad had been asleep, but he woke up sharp enough when Lord Arthur said his piece.

' "And what did he say?" Mam asked him.

' "He said, 'When do I start?" ' Lord Arthur, and he and Mam smiled at each other like conspirators.

' "There be a chap along tomorrow to arrange the details," said Lord Arthur. "Our agent. But if you need any money to tide you over—"

' "No, thank you, sir," said Mam. "We'll manage."

'Always one for paying her own way, me mam. And she could. But Lord Arthur just smiled, because what he was thinking was "whippets", only he was far too good-mannered to say so. Then he changed the subject. "There's someone outside wants a word," he said. "My sister, Lady Mary. I'll send her in shall I?"

'But Mam went to the door herself, and I went with her to gaze at a lady in a riding habit, with a groom to take care of her horse and Lord Arthur's. Not to mention his own. It was beyond belief. A fine lady sitting on a bench outside a miner's cottage, waiting for her brother to finish and it was her turn.

' "I'll leave you to it then," Lord Arthur says.

'What Lady Mary had come about was school. Well, it had to be. All the estate children went to it, and very nice too. Miles better than the one in Black Sills. Even curtains on the windows: ones we made ourselves. There was reading, writing and arithmetic – well, of course there was. By the time they'd done with me I could tackle long division and copper plate writing as good as the boys. At reading they were doing *Treasure Island* and I fell in love with Jim Hawkins – even if he was a bit thick. There was other things too, like housekeeping and bathing a baby and cookery, and the teachers that nice – unless you were cheeky, then they gave you what for and why not? You'd asked for it . . . The school even had a posh name – The Lady Mary Channing School at Bellingham Castle. There were girls got good jobs just because they'd been there, and it sounded nice. And so it was. There was even some stuff called eurhythmics. Sort of dancing that was, invented by a Froggy called Dalcroze, and I loved it. I would have done it till I dropped. They very near had to take a whip to me to get me back to long division. I loved that school, and I worshipped Lady Mary.'

'She was the only one?' Elena asked.

'Lord Arthur kept an eye on the boys, but it was mostly her. The other Channings were easy going, kind even, like I said, but all they really cared about was field sports and running the country – and the girls getting engaged.'

'Didn't Lady Mary—'

Gertie shook her head: 'She didn't want a nursery – she wanted a schoolful. Lord Arthur the same. And yet they were neither of them queer. None of that. It was just as if God had put them into this world to look after the likes of us, so they did it.'

'They never married?'

'Not them,' said Gertie. 'I don't suppose the idea ever entered their heads. And even if it did – good works was better. Lady Mary even looked after me mam.'

'Just like Lord Arthur took care of your husband,' said Elena.

'Exactly,' said Gertie, 'and one day after we were settled she sends for Mam and says, "I hear you were a country girl before you married."

' "Yes, my lady," says Mam. "I worked on a farm out Alnwick way."

'Don't ask me how she heard. Lady Mary heard everything – eventually – only you never took offence.

' "And what did you like best?" she asked. "The dairy?"

' "Sewing," says Mam. "Rydale Moor Farm was a big place. Gentleman's residence. Sewing room. All that."

' "We'll try you out," says Lady Mary.

' "You think I'll be up to it, my lady?"

' "I've seen your daughter at school," Lady Mary says. "Always neat. Sometimes a bit more than that. Let's try and see what happens."

'Now, what Lady Mary was offering wasn't just money. Far from it. If you worked at the Castle – superior servant Mam would be – then she'd be looked after till the day she died, no matter what happened to Da, and I reckon both women knew it, but all Mam said was, "Thank you my lady," and all Lady Mary did was wave her hand in a way that meant "You're welcome I'm sure." '

'And did your mother get the job?'

'Yes,' said Gertie, 'she did. A dab hand with a needle, me mam. And Lady Mary knew it. This wasn't charity. It was money paid for work done. Mam was in her element.'

'She sounds rather wonderful, your Lady Mary,' said Elena.

'All of that,' said Gertie, 'but then so was me mam.'

There was a tap at the door, a no-nonsense tap that said I know you're sitting there all warm and cosy, but some of us have work to do, decisions to make, and Millicent came in. One look at her daughter's face and Gertie knew it was time to be off. The rest would have to keep.

'Sorry to interrupt,' said Millicent, 'but I've been having a word with your lawyers. Their Mr Barnes.'

Dimly Elena remembered that Barnes was the one who looked after the will, as Gertie got to her feet.

'Time I was shaping,' she said, and Millicent knew Mam had been at the memories again. Her Geordie accent was always broad after she'd remembered Black Sills.

'Bye, bye, Mum,' she said and smiled, but Gertie left them even so, and Elena braced herself for the dry-as-dust executors and codicils and goodbye whippets and good works and sewing rooms.

'Nothing serious I hope,' she said.

'Well, yes,' said Millicent. 'But not worrying, I promise you.' Elena waited.

'It's Pudiphatt,' said Millicent.

'It always is these days,' said Elena. 'What's he done now?'

'That drawing,' said her friend. 'The Murillo.'

'It belonged to my father,' said Elena. 'I know it did.'

'So do I,' said Millicent, 'but supposing Pudiphatt found out about it? I'm not saying it's probable, or even likely, but it seemed a possibility. The man was a born snooper after all. A remote chance but – it was there. Not that Charles owned it – just that it had once been in the Grosvenor Square house. Think of the fuss he'd make. The sort of publicity.'

'Not like the dancing,' said Elena.

'Not in the least.'

'So what's Barnes going to do about it?'

'Barnes?' Millicent sounded horrified.

'But—'

'Barnes is useless,' said Millicent. 'All he can think about is his house in Richmond and his golf club and getting his son into Oundle. Being respectable.'

Impossible to imitate the venom she put into that last word.

'Then who—' said Elena, and then: 'You?'

'Well, of course, me,' said her friend.

'I won't have you taking risks,' said Elena.

She really means it, thought Millicent, and loved her the more.

'No risks,' she said. 'Let me tell you why. First I had Barnes go through the inventory of pictures. There was no Murillo drawing.'

'You didn't tell him why?'

'Of course not. I said it was just an idea you'd got into your head. Barnes loves it when women get ideas into their heads. It means there's no room left for business – and, anyway, it's your money. So he humoured you via me and went off to the golf club.'

'And what will you do?' Elena asked warily.

'Use a private detective.'

'*What*?' To Elena, private detectives were little better than professional co-respondents.

'We need to know more about Pudiphatt,' said Millicent. 'Like the five thousand your husband left him.'

'Charles would know what he was doing.' For once Elena sounded defensive.

'Certainly,' said Millicent, meaning it. 'But why five thou? It's an odd sum when you think of it. Either too much or too little.'

Elena considered this. 'I'm beginning to see what you mean,' she said. 'At least I think I can.'

'What we need is more facts about Pudiphatt,' said Millicent. 'His relationship with your husband, why he was left money in the first place. All that. And we need a detective to find out.'

'But where would you get one?' Elena began, and then, 'Oh! Foulhouse and Thingummy.'

'Duckhouse and Allnutt,' said Millicent. 'Exactly. Not that I need bother with them. I'll do it on my own.'

'It *is* risky,' said Elena.

'It's what I want to do,' said her friend and thought: I owe you far more than that.

'You do it then,' said Elena. 'Will it take long?'

'The report should be waiting for us when we get back from the North.'

'If we go,' said Elena. 'The duke hasn't asked us yet.'

'He will,' said Millicent. 'I mean, just look at you.' Love and dancing she thought. An unbeatable combination.

'Let's talk about your mother,' Elena said.

'What about her?'

'Is she happy in Pimlico?'

'Where she lives now she is,' said Millicent. 'Nice little house, and all her old cronies nearby. *And* there's a telephone. Besides, there's the tram for the cemetery and shops quite near.'

'*Cemetery*?'

'It's where Dad is,' said Millicent. 'She likes to go there for a chat with him sometimes. She always says it's because he can't answer back now – but there's far more to it than that.'

'May I ask what?' Elena asked.

'Of course,' Millicent said. 'You can ask me anything. You know that . . . They loved each other – not just the way people say they do. They really meant it. Love that was passionate of course, but – I can't think how else to put it. Profound as well. To the depths of their beings.' She shuddered then. 'Love isn't just Hollywood, you know. Real-life chorus girls can get it too. And even sailors.'

'But can she manage?' Elena asked. 'I worry about her, you know.'

'Between us she can,' said Millicent. 'Thanks to you. Between us she manages.'

'You help her?'

'Well, of course,' said Millicent. 'We look after our own. Always have.'

Like your mother and grandmother before you, Elena thought. Your mother told me so herself.

'And anyway,' said Millicent, 'if I had to I could always pawn the odd bit of jewellery.' What an extraordinary ménage it is, thought Elena. Millicent and Francis. And yet it seems to work. Millicent clearly enjoys it . . .

What to wear was a problem, even if she had wardrobes full of dresses to choose from, for this was tea at the Ritz after all, *and* with a duke. In the end she settled for a masterpiece by Erté (she knew it was a masterpiece: the great man had told her so himself), in a strong yet subtle shade of pink. Just the thing to show off the ruby bracelet and earrings Freddy had given her, but not the necklace: not even for the Ritz and a duke: it was tea after all, and so she chose a ruby brooch instead: rather a nice one that Charles had given her. When she had dressed and made-up she went down to Millicent's room. No harm in a second opinion, and Millicent's reaction was all one could wish.

'Good enough for a duke?' Elena asked.

'Good enough for an emperor,' said Millicent.

And yet the duke was – wary. Still young – forty perhaps – really quite handsome, and the most eligible bachelor in the kingdom, and she in all her finery, and yet he was wary, and getting more so as the tea progressed, until she understood why. It was when dukes were *away* from their castles that they were under siege. Inside they felt protected and secure, but when they ventured out people wanted them to give them things: especially pretty girls. An engagement ring was the ideal, but even gifts bestowed on less formal occasions were acceptable, provided they cost enough, and His Grace's wealth was enormous . . . The problem would be to persuade him that she had no wish to be a duchess: that the role of viscountess was more than adequate. He wouldn't believe it, which made him sound pompous, but it wasn't that. Not vain glory. Wariness still. After all, she was a *very* pretty girl that afternoon, and so she should have been. It had taken absolute hours – and it hadn't worked. Time for attack. She took the French marriage certificate and her parents' photograph from her handbag, and handed them to him. Even the way he took them was wary, until he looked and read.

'Good Lord,' said his Grace, and then, 'How well they look together,' and she began to like him. 'Chard tells me your name is Elena,' he said, and offered his hand. 'I'm Oswin. Excuse the informality, but we are sort of cousins.' She took it.

'A pleasure to meet you Oswin,' she said, and he blinked, knowing he still had more to do.

'And such a charming and talented cousin,' he said. 'Famous too. But you've no wish to talk about that.'

'I want to talk about my father.'

'Of course,' said the duke. 'You want to see him, in fact.' She nodded.

'Not up to me,' said His Grace. 'If it were, you'd be on the next train for Newcastle – but I'll tell you what. I'll phone his doctor and let you know tonight, though I can't foresee any objections. You'll be just the tonic he needs. What any man needs, come to that.'

Wariness paid for.

'So we're going North,' said Millicent, and Elena nodded. 'Are you nervous?'

'Terrified,' said Elena, 'but I've got to go.'

'*Terrified?*'

'Suppose it doesn't work?' said Elena. 'It seems it's possible. My poor father still locked away from reality inside a room he hardly ever leaves.'

'At least he won't be worse,' said Millicent. 'And you'll have tried.'

I don't want to try, thought Elena. I want to succeed. I don't care what he was like before – but he must have been nice. Mama had loved him.

'The duke wants a favour in return,' she said.

'Mum says dukes always do,' said Millicent. 'It's to stop other people asking for favours all the time.'

'He wants us to dance. One of his sisters is getting engaged so there's a ball, and we'll be the cabaret.'

'Hardly a favour,' said Millicent, 'unless you don't want to?'

'Of course I want to.' Even if my father gets no better, she thought. At least I'll be dancing for him.

'Who are you taking?'

'Your mama, and Pedrillito,' said Elena. 'All we need, really. They're the best.'

'Not Richard?'

'He came off Noche yesterday. Put his knee out. Now he's scouring the country looking for some bone-setter or other. He should have stuck to his Ancient Greeks.'

But she smiles as she says it, thought Millicent. No fits of the vapours, and definitely no malice.

'Francis will want to come too,' she said.

'Well, of course,' said Elena. 'But it's Invitation Only.'

'It's never stopped him in the past,' said Millicent, 'but I don't want people to get the idea that we're engaged.'

13

Gertie enjoyed the train journey: first-class Pullman, and no
shortage of champagne, and Elena to talk to while Millicent
worked at papers. Difficult-looking papers, tied with pink ribbon,
and she reads them as easily as if they were a novel by Elinor
Glyn. She sighed. Best leave it. Some mysteries were better left
unsolved. She turned back to Elena instead.

'Where was I?' she asked.

'The rich Channings,' said Elena.

'Well, so they are rich,' Gertie said. 'You'll know what that's
like, being rich yourself.' And then: 'Beg pardon, my lady. It's the
champagne talking.'

'Oh, get on with it,' said Elena, and Gertie got on with it.

'Not just the land,' she said, 'though it seemed like half the
county. There was the railway as well, to take the coal to the ships
– the port.'

'To Black Sills, in fact,' said Elena.

'Well, once upon a time,' said Gertie, 'but it was awkward. It
would be. As well as being nasty.'

'Awkward?'

'Not enough draught for the colliers. The ships that took the
coal to London. And the rocks. That's the sills, it seems. Great
layers of rock and coal that could rip up a collier like opening a
tin. After the second one this duke's grandfather came over and
decided it just wouldn't do.'

'He went elsewhere?'

'Elsewhere meant paying, and he wasn't having that. He built
his own instead.'

'A whole port?'

'A whole port. Docks and berths and staithes, and the houses
for the folk that worked them. Very nice houses too, they tell me.
All very modern. Folks queued up to work there. Port Bellingham.'

'But it must have cost a fortune.'

'He had a fortune.'

'And lost it?'

'Channings don't lose fortunes. They make them. Think about it. First off he saved all the port fees he'd have to pay, then chaps like Webb wanted to use it – and they had to pay too. And not just colliers. Tramp ships, general cargo, they all came to Port Bellingham because it was cheap – and His Grace made money. *And* the children. And not just the good works. Eton and Harrow and Oxford and Cambridge, and the cavalry and the Guards. Foxhounds and hunters, and dresses from Paris for the girls. Jewellery too. Money by the ship load, and it all came from under the ground, then it was in the bank. I'm not sure he didn't own the bank as well.'

I'm rich, thought Elena, but I'm not that rich. I doubt if anybody is except maybe the king.

'And that's the Channings,' said Gertie. 'The whole story.'

Well, maybe not quite, that she thought. I danced the can can at a party one of them gave, and went to Paris with another. But not like your mam, me lady. Best was my chap, and we both knew it.

'Did you ever see Black Sills again?' Elena asked.

'Just the once,' Gertie. 'It was a good place to leave. Nothing good ever came out of it.'

Without looking up from her papers, Millicent said, 'Dad did.'

'And that'll do from you, my lady,' Gertie said. 'This is my tale and I'll do the telling. So just you get on with your homework. Your da's for later.'

Unseen by her mother, Millicent put out her tongue, and Elena had to struggle hard not to giggle. Gertie coughed.

'About the Webbs,' she said. 'They were none of them like Sir Richard.'

'And what's he like?' asked Elena, intrigued.

You know all about him, Gertie thought. Far more than I'll ever know. You just want – what's the word? – reassurance, that's it.

'Big and easy going and good looking, and far more likely to laugh than threaten. Not that I'd want to threaten him, the size he is. But he's not like the Webbs at all. Most of them were right—'

It was her daughter's turn to clear her throat.

'Right so and so's,' said Gertie. 'Great ones for the local girls. What they called the talent.'

'Tell us about Sir Harry's brother and you,' said Millicent, her eyes still on her papers.

'Took a fancy to me,' said Gertie. 'And me not even fourteen. Used to follow me everywhere until—'

'Lord Arthur intervened?'

'He would have done,' said Gertie, 'if he'd known. But he didn't. It was Da.'

'Your father?' Elena sounded incredulous.

'Not up to it, you mean? But like I keep saying, the Castle wasn't Black Sills. Fresh air, good food, exercise – aye even that. Da was back on his feet – even walking the dogs. He had a couple of them out when he found us. Prince and Pirate. Both friends of mine. We got on fine. I used to walk them, too. Prince was a gent if ever there was one. But not Pirate. He would have torn Frank Webb's throat out, and even Prince would have bitten him. Only he didn't have to. Da told them to sit, and they sat, for all the world like spectators at a boxing match, and Da fetched Frank Webb a clout you could have heard in West Hartlepool.

'Young Webb lay down for a bit getting his strength back, then he somehow got to his feet.

' "You insolent swine," he said, "I'll have you up for assault."

' "And I'll have you up," says Da.

' "*Me*? What am I supposed to have done?"

' "Attempted rape," says Da. "Look fine in the *Bellingham Echo* would that."

' "Your word against mine," young Webb said. "Who'd believe you?"

' "I've no idea," says Da. "I'll have to ask Lord Arthur while our Gertie asks Lady Mary."

'And that hurt too, being bested by a common pitman, and him three years at Cambridge.

' "I'll forget it this time," he says to Da, "but don't do it again."

' "And the same to you," says Da.

'Next thing I know me and Mam was up in front of Lady Mary in her sitting room. How she'd got to hear about it I don't know, but like I told you, Lady Mary always got to hear everything, and she came straight out with it because that was the only way she knew.

'At last she said, "So what it amounts to is Gertie's at risk."

' "He won't try it again my lady," says Mam.

' "No, not him," says my lady. "But there'll be others. After all, she's a very pretty girl."

'That made me blush, because nobody had ever said that about me before.

' "And it's almost time for her to leave school. We'll have to find her something."

'Dairy? I wondered. Sewing room? I prayed it wouldn't be the dairy.

' "She's quick," Lady Mary said, "but she'd never make a teacher. Dancing – that's what she's good at."

' "So she is," said Mam, and Lady Mary looked at her. Two hounds that had found the scent and were going straight for it.

' "You've got an idea?" she asked.

' "I was looking through her school reports last night," says Mam. "And every time it was 'Eurythmics Outstanding'. Now, from what she tells me it isn't easy."

' "Monsieur Dalcroze didn't believe in making things easy," Lady Mary said. "What he believed in was elegance, beauty, grace." And I started to blush again.

' "Just so, my lady," said Mam. "Now I've heard there's a school in Newcastle that teaches dancing. Not just Eurythmics. Everything."

' "So there is," said Lady Mary. "Madame Louise's School of Dance. It's rather a good one."

' "I want to send her there," says Mam.

' "It isn't cheap," Lady Mary said, and I could see what she was after. Free schooling was one thing, but dancing classes, clothes, shoes – that was a bit more than free school.

' "We'll manage," says Mam. "Just loan us the money and we'll pay you back – I swear it."

' "You know how much it is?" Lady Mary said. Mam nodded. "And you'll take on that debt all by yourself?"

' "There'll be me man as well, and our Gertie once she starts earning."

'Lady Mary turned to me. "What a lucky girl you are," she said, "to have parents who love you."

' "Yes, my lady," I said. It was all that I could manage, but it seemed to be enough for Lady Mary. She smiled at me.

' "You'd better go," she said. "Leave your mother and me to take care of the details." Details! By the time she'd finished she'd paid out more than I'd ever dreamed of – and all because my mother loved me. If it wasn't for her I'd never even have got started. Her and that smack on the jaw Da gave Frank Webb.'

Her daughter looked out of the carriage window, then began to shuffle her papers together.

'Soon be in Newcastle,' she said. 'Better get ourselves ready.'

Trust our Millicent, Gertie thought. Just when we were getting to one of the good bits. All the same, she too was a very pretty girl.

His Grace was there to meet her himself, which meant that he took her seriously. Meant that he thought it important, too. There was even a kind of entourage: the doctor, and papa's personal footman, and a butler who was more like an archbishop.

Oswin said, 'I think we'd better go to him at once,' and turned to the doctor. 'Don't you?'

'Lord Aylmer's been thoroughly prepared, your Grace.'

What with that and the butler who looked like an archbishop, Elena thought of Confirmation classes. Anything rather than the ordeal to come, but that would never do. She owed Mama at least one ordeal.

Papa was in a room in the East Wing, and he should have been cold except for the rug on his knees and the fire roaring. (Coal would never be a problem to this family.) Now that's enough, she told herself. Get on with it. But it was her papa who spoke.

'Why Margarita,' he said. 'How young you look.' His voice was a deep baritone, and he spoke in Spanish. He must have learned it for Mama's sake.

'I'm her daughter, sir,' she said. 'Elena.'

'It's been so long you see,' her father said. But he didn't tell her why, not then, but said, 'You don't mind us speaking Spanish?'

'I love it, sir.'

'Old family custom – or it will be. Besides, it prevents the busybodies from eavesdropping. I don't talk much, but when I do he writes it all down.' He looked at the doctor, then away.

'But why should he?'

'I rather think he's writing a book. *Melancholia and the English Nobility* or some such thing.'

'How dare he?'

She turned on the doctor and her father said hastily, 'No need to get excited. Before you came back I scarcely uttered, which meant he has nothing to write about. But you – you're like your mama you see. Temper and all. She died, didn't she?'

'Complications after the flu sir,' said Elena.

'She was rather good at complications,' said her father. 'But usually they were nice ones. I mean, you were a complication, and look at you.'

'Sir?'

'So pretty, so elegant, so quick. Just like your mama. Do you like me enough to give me a kiss on so short an acquaintance?'

'Of course, sir,' said Elena and kissed him.

'So fragrant too,' he said, and then, 'Do you know why I live like this?'

'No, sir.'

'A Boer decided that I'd lived too long, and shot me. Only he made rather a botch of it. Got my head all right – God knows it was big enough in those days – but the wrong part, if you follow me. When I came out of hospital I felt odd. Distinctly odd. And I went on feeling odd for ages and ages, so I came back here. Elephants' Graveyard.' He paused for a moment. 'Whatever that means. I was happier here,' he said, 'and Oswin didn't mind. Only after Mary and Arthur died I had no one to talk to. And so I didn't. Not for days, sometimes. Until the Germans started another war to take my mind off things . . .'

The doctor cleared his throat. A warning. Like those boats on the lake that Millicent had told her about. 'Come in Number Five, your time is up.' Well, not yet it isn't, thought Elena. Not for Papa. I'll see to that.

They went out, doctor, duke and daughter, and the doctor seemed inclined to linger rather – all that Spanish – so that the duke got rid of him and led her to what once had been Lady Mary's sitting room.

'Your friend's there,' he said, 'and your – trainer would it be?'

'*Régisseuse*,' said Elena. 'She's also my friend's mother.'

'Looks as if she knows her stuff,' said the duke. Make of that what you will, Elena thought. Gertie was saddened by the news of Lady Mary's death, and her brother's. There had been so many deaths, but Lady Mary had been special . . .'

'So he was all right?' Millicent said at last.

'Used up a month's supply of words while I was there,' the duke said.

Goodness, how happy my friend looks, thought Millicent. Best ask her now.

'No headaches?' she asked. 'No sign of his sickness?'

'None,' Elena said.

'Elephant's Graveyard?' said Gertie, and then her hand went to her mouth. 'Oh, I'm sorry. I didn't mean—'

'He was talking about the worst time,' said Elena, 'when he'd had no one. And like the elephants he went back to his own place to die.'

And yet he'd had Mama, she thought, and me too by then . . . But she must wait. She who found waiting so difficult. But one day he would tell her – in his own time. She knew it.

'Only he didn't,' said Millicent. 'He's well and talking to you. It's marvellous.'

Gertie opened her mouth, took one look at her daughter, and shut it again, then they gossiped about the show they would give, until it was time to visit more sick. Richard and his dislocated kneecap. No fear of the elephant's graveyard for a dislocated kneecap.

They went in the duke's Rolls-Royce, she and her friend. This one's bigger than mine, she thought, but then there are so many Channings. She began to think of her papa. If only he would tell her just one thing, she thought – but he'd kept his secret for twenty years. He needs *time*.

'How wild the countryside is here,' said Millicent. Prim and correct she sat beside Elena. The window that separated them from the chauffeur wide open, so what could she talk about except the weather or the view?

'And yet—' said Elena.

'Yes, darling?'

Darling, thought the chauffeur. To a viscountess. That made her a lady too. Something to let fall in a casual way over supper in the servants' hall. The butler, Henshaw, and the rest would have to listen to him for a change.

'It has its own grandeur,' said Elena. They drove through moorland so sparse that even the sheep who grazed it had to forage like invading troops: not like Bellingham's lush pasture at all. They passed the ruins of a peel tower – a fortified farmhouse – and behind it in the distance the giant outline of a pit shaft.

'It has its own irony too,' said Millicent, then they crested a hill and Milburn Hall lay waiting just below them. Not quite so grim as the peel tower or even the pit, thought Millicent. Somebody had done their best with what the eighteenth century called 'improvements', and the formal gardens around it looked well tended, but nothing like her gardens in Hampshire. How could they be?

Richard was waiting for them, even if he did limp a little, and conveyed rather more than a hint of embrocation, and Elena smiled, though not entirely with malice.

'I know,' said Richard, 'but we all come off occasionally if the horse is any good.'

He shook hands in a formal way because his own butler was watching, but this one was more like a sergeant major than an archbishop.

'Drinks in the drawing room, Moscrop,' said Richard.

'Sir!' said the butler, and did everything but snap to attention.

A dark room, oak panelled, the furniture covered in hide that even papa's elephants might have approved: no pictures, only prints; and flowers displayed as if for a bereavement, and yet . . . Moscrop produced dry martinis cheerfully enough, and not the public penance Archbishop Henshaw would have made of them.

'Was he in your regiment?' Millicent asked.

Richard grinned. 'Fourth battalion,' he said. 'I was a sergeant, and he was my Regimental Sergeant Major in those days. All a bit different now, no doubt, but it doesn't bother him, and it certainly doesn't bother me.'

'Why should it?' said Millicent, and opened her briefcase, took out yet more papers.

'I keep meaning to do something about this room,' Richard said, 'but it's not something I'm awfully good at – interior design.'

He looked hopefully at Elena, but all she did was smile, as Millicent took her papers to a table big enough to hold them.

'How is he?' Richard asked, and she smiled again, and oh, so happily, he thought. Good sign. The best.

'Tell me about yourself first,' she said.

'As I say, I came off,' said Richard.

'Noche restless?'

'Full of frisk,' said Richard.

'All the same, somebody seems to have put you together again.'

'Rather faster than Humpty Dumpty,' said Richard. 'It was Eckie as a matter of fact.'

'Eckie?'

'Used to bill himself as El Equilibrio,' said Richard. 'In the days when he was a tight-rope walker. We met at the tent show. Not in the colonies. Vale of Evesham. Number One tour as you might say. He was pretty good – only one night he put his shoulder out and decided to give it up.'

'Lost his taste for it?' Elena was doing her best to be tactful.

'He put his shoulder back himself. Nothing to it, he said. So he read a couple of books and started practising on the others. Acrobats, trapeze, artists, tumblers. They're always having trouble with their joints. Even the contortionists.'

Elena tried and failed to think what a contortionist could do to his body that would need the services of a bone-setter.

'How interesting,' she said.

'Of course his fame soon spread as they say. Word of mouth I believe they call it. He gets calls from all over England. Decent of him to come to Oxford at such short notice.'

'Wasn't it?' said Elena.

'And not so much of your polished irony,' said Richard. 'At least he put you together again. Too bad you'll miss the ball.'

'Better than all the King's Horses and all the King's Men,' said Richard. 'And who says I'll miss the ball? I promised Francis I'd go with him. Moral support.'

'How on earth did he wangle an invitation?'

'One of the duke's aunts by marriage is his godmother.'

'So long as you leave off the embrocation,' said Elena.

He smiled, then was serious. 'Your father,' he said.

She told him everything, and he listened as intently as if it were the final briefing before his platoon went over the top . . . 'And that's it,' she said at last.

'It seems it amounts to this,' said Richard. 'He was glad to see you. Overjoyed, in fact.' He lowered his voice to a whisper. 'Believe me, I know how he feels.' And then, more loudly, 'And at the end of it all he looked much better, because of you. Talked for more than anyone could remember. Because of you. So we know for a fact you're good for him.'

'There's one topic he never mentioned,' said Elena. Millicent was there, but what did that matter? She had no secrets from Millicent. Nor it seemed did Richard.

'Let's look at that,' he said. 'First we know it wasn't snobbery.'

'We're totally sure?'

'Totally,' Richard said. 'You've carried that load for long enough. It's time to put it down.'

'But who told you?' Elena asked.

'Nobody. For those of us who love you it's just obvious, that's all.' He looked at Millicent, her documents forgotten. Silently she nodded her agreement.

'But how can you *know*?'

'No man who despised his wife, wished he had never married her, would talk about her as he did.'

'But he didn't—'

'He talked about you,' said Richard, 'but it was all Margarita really.'

Suddenly she knew it was true, and the load she had carried fell at last.

'Then why his silence?' she asked, even so. 'For years and years.'

'For much of it he seems to have been locked in even more silence,' said Richard, 'as if his whole past life was a prison, and there was no escape. And then gradually he began to see that there was a choice. He spoke just a little, and his mind was clear, even if the habit of silence was still strong. *His mind was clear.* He was past the stage of madness, dementia, catatonic withdrawal – whatever the psychiatrists might call it. He'd regained the ability to choose – to talk or not to as he placed.'

'But so often he chose silence,' said Elena.

'Of course. All his loved ones were dead. Perhaps even in the war we fought together. There was no one left to tell how it feels to be shot by a Boer farmer who isn't quite up to it.'

'There was me,' said Elena.

'And you were happy,' said Richard. 'From what you tell me I bet he read every word the papers had to say. He knew that you were happy and so he was too.'

'And proud, too, the way she tells it,' said Millicent. 'And so he should be. His daughter's brilliant.'

Now I call that handsome. I really do, Milburn thought. You're half of the act, after all – and never a word about yourself.

'But he didn't say it,' Elena said.

'Because you're all tied up with your mum,' said Richard. 'A bit cryptic, I agree – but just think. Two beautiful women, both dancers, and both with the need to love him. It would be a tricky one for an expert, never mind the prisoner who's just been released after all those years. But he'll solve it.'

'I pray to God he does,' said Elena. 'But what makes you so sure?'

'Because he must,' said Richard. 'Once that's done there's no more prison door. There isn't even a prison.'

Elena turned to her friend. 'I know it's changing the subject, but this may be important.' Millicent waited. 'Do you mind Francis being here?'

'Of course not,' said Millicent. 'He's my chap. It's just that he's rather low on my list of priorities at the moment.'

'His mother and father are off to Deauville,' said Richard. 'He told me.'

Elena went to him. 'Richard my dear,' she said, 'this is going to sound like the most confounded cheek after all the things you've done for me. Ordering a man out of his own drawing room. But I need to cry you see, and Millicent's the only one who can help me.'

'Of course,' said Richard. 'I need to put on more embrocation anyway.'

She smiled then and he left them, and as the doors closed the weeping began.

14

The Black Lion in Wellington Street was by no means his idea of what a pub should be: no champagne, no roast beef sandwiches, no oak panels and sporting prints. Beer and grime, that was the Black Lion. All the same he found Stobbs there at the second time of asking. Of course, he only pretended to know nothing about the mysterious major, Pudiphatt was sure. Lipton would have seen to that, or more likely his wife. This was Stobbs's game after all. He would have to play it according to Stobbs's rules.

The first it seemed was alcohol, in what Pudiphatt feared might be an unremitting stream. A small man, thin to the point of emaciation, and the face of a fox who had fled every hound in the pack, and yet he was on his third rum and peppermint while his host began on his second whisky. Where on earth does he put it? Pudiphatt wondered, and told yet again the tale of Lord Mendip and the memoir to be printed oh so privately, while Stobbs nodded in sympathy and didn't believe a word of it, thought Pudiphatt.

Even so, he had to give some excuse. He couldn't just walk up, state his demands and ask how much. Life was never that easy. Still, it started well enough. Mendip a fine officer and Stobbs proud to be his batman, good lady devastated. All that. Hazy memories of Lady M's ma having some connection up North, but what that was appeared hard to recall, after so many years. Pudiphatt pressed, but Stobbs grew coy. Long time ago. Lord M. had been talking to one of his brother officers. Stobbs remembered that . . . but which one? There's been so many, said Stobbs, suddenly tearful, and most of them gone so quickly. Lord M. had managed nearly two years. Why was that? Pudiphatt asked, over and over, but all Stobbs could manage was, 'Years ago . . . So many years,' like a needle stuck in a gramophone record. His only other words were, 'None of us is perfect,' and at that Major Pud-whatnot went real doolalley, but that was all he got. Stobbs was far less drunk than he seemed.

Let's wait for the return match, he thought, in no doubt that there'd be one. This Pud geezer was avid. All the same, better to let him wait, grow even hungrier.

Belatedly he remembered his promise to visit his aged mother, even though Pudiphatt knew as well as he did that Stobbs had no next of kin. None at all. As he finished his whisky he thought how much he detested the smell of rum and peppermint . . .

She was so desperate to finish the story of her life, but now was not the time and she knew it, what with Elena seeing her dad for the first time she could remember, and even if he'd looked well, he couldn't be that well. Better to wait, thought Gertie, and concentrate on the arrangements for the night's show. Elena had told her it was a sort of gift to her father – though she'd never tell her audience. All the same it had to be as near perfect as Gertie could make it, which meant that she would apply the spit and polish, and that meant a bad time for the indoor servants: fur flying all over the place. But the little stage glowed like jewellery; that was the point: even the brass supports for the curtains gleamed, and the hardwood floor had been waxed and polished to a sheen that satisfied even Gertie. Time for just one more rehearsal, but first she inspected the place for eavesdroppers and spies, and only then did she allow Pedrillito in.

Pedrillito was their dark horse, so to speak: what gave the act its really authentic touch – a genuine gypsy Spanish guitarist. True the little man was moody and untidy and took baths only under threat, but that made him even more a gypsy. Just look at him now, Gertie thought: in need of a shave, reeking of cheap cologne, clothes that fitted him well enough, but far too old, and that made him more like a gypsy too. He looked about him; for Elena or Millie, Gertie thought: the only ones who spoke Spanish, but they weren't there, and so he smiled at her instead and lit a cigarette. He had a really beautiful smile, which was why Gertie allowed it: that and the fact that he'd remembered to bring an ashtray. The first time he hadn't and Gertie's yells could have been heard in the deer park. Black tobacco, black as a kitchen hob and an acrid smell like no other. It smelled like Spain, Elena had told her, that and the cheap cologne. Add a dash of garlic, and you were back in Seville. He lit the cigarette and smiled at her again, and for the hundredth time Gertie forgave him. He looked so – what was the word Millie had used? – vulnerable, that was it. Not that he was. Tough as fighting bull meat little Pedro, but oh, that smile.

He picked up his guitar, and became at once a different being: a man in love, and the guitar his lady, then very softly he began to play. Only the staff could hear him at this time of day, and they should be hard at it in the ballroom. Once and only once she'd been asked if Pedrillito was the one who played the guitar, and she'd said no at once. The guitar music was a record used for rehearsals, and Pedrillito was the man they'd brought to wind up the gramophone. It was Spanish, she explained. It needed a Spanish expert to control it. And the bloody fools had believed it. The guitar sighed like a woman who'd been treated just right. Now, now Gertie, she told herself, you're nearly old enough to be his mother. All the same, he had a lovely touch. Gramophones indeed.

Then the two of them came in, dressed for rehearsal. Her girls. In her mind she always thought of them as that: the ones she'd threatened, yelled at and occasionally coaxed, even petted when they'd been specially good, but that didn't happen often. Petting was rationed. Too much petting and maybe they wouldn't try as hard. As it was they tried like whippets overhauling a hare. Millie adjusted her hat and Elena spoke to Pedrillito as his fingers disentangled the melody of the *Sevillana* he was playing, and he smiled at her, then her daughter, and then herself once more. No fool, little Pedro, she thought. He knows fine well who'll have to fight with cook for his supper. Then Millie leaped on to the little stage (sometimes trousers could be so useful), and helped up Elena, wary of the flounces on her skirts. The *Sevillana* whispered once more and died, then Pedrillito struck the *razgueardo*, the sweep across the open strings, as Millie and Elena faced each other, their gaze intense and yet proud, too. Noble. Because this was Spain, thought Gertie. They're back in Spain. Northumberland might never have existed. Then the guitar tempo quickened, its sound grew louder, and the two girls danced.

Pedrillito puffed on his cigarette as he played. They didn't mind if he smoked at rehearsal, and just as well. But not during performances, though they didn't bother if he drank red wine from a *pórron*. More authentic, they called it. And tobacco negro wasn't? But they weren't bad dancers. They had started too late, and they weren't Spanish gypsies, but they weren't bad even so. And they loved it just as he did. The fair girl, most irresistible of

157

caballeros, stepped back, hands clapping, and the guitar, a man now, strong, elegant, brave, began to flirt with the dark one. Easy stuff, Pedrillito thought, but satisfying. The dark one looked well at least.

More duets, then the fair one on her own, and then the two of them just once more, before they finished at last and he lit another cigarette.

'Very nice girls,' said Gertie, and he smiled at her as if he understood, then his fingers touched the strings again, he played once more that first, lovesick tune.

'You mean it?' said Elena.

'Of course I mean it,' said Gertie. 'Dancing's not something I tell lies about.' Her voice grew softer. 'Your father should be proud,' she said. 'What you're giving him – money couldn't buy it.' And that's enough petting.

'Time for your baths, the pair of you,' she said. 'Then I'll give you a rub. We can't have you catching pneumonia. You've got a show to do.'

'Yes, but no embrocation,' Elena said.

After the rub she felt marvellous. Like boxers must feel she thought, when they've been trained to a hair and know that that night they'll win; then she wrapped her bath towel around her and went into the dressing room she shared with Millicent.

'Oh, dear God, thought Millicent, not in the nude again, as the towel began to slip. Not that it bothers me. Not any more. I must be getting used to it.

Then the towel fell away, and Millicent thought, she's gorgeous, as she so often did, but this time Elena was specially gorgeous, her whole body ablaze with life, as if nothing was impossible, as if one step would take her to the moon. My God, Richard's lucky she thought, but then Francis doesn't do too badly in that line either – provided he's a good boy and does as he's told. She turned to Elena.

'Ready?' she asked.

'Can't wait,' Elena said.

As Gertie smuggled them on to the stage the music of the foxtrot finished, chairs scraped as expensively covered bottoms seated themselves, the curtain slowly rose to the loudest applause yet. But then this was Spain. The magic carpet had done its stuff. Pedrillito took a gulp of red wine, struck a chord, and there was even more applause. Albeniz, de Falla, the music said, and because Spain was sight as well as sound, Goya – perhaps even

Murillo – and all done by music, and two young and supple bodies.

They had never known such a night. It seemed as if they couldn't go wrong, but then they didn't go wrong, not once, not that night, and as the last applause thundered, the last bows were taken, and Millicent whispered, still smiling, 'Happy, your lady-ship?'

'Ecstatic,' Elena said. 'I hope you are too.'

Millicent quoted her father. 'Not arf,' she said.

They went to bathe and change, and then to the ballroom and even more applause. The duke came up to greet them; gabbling, almost incoherent with delight and pride, for not only had he provided the best show in the castle's history, it featured a member of his family. And never a hint of vulgarity, profession-alism.

He achieved articulate speech at last. 'Superb, Elena. Superb.'

'Thank you, Oswin,' said Elena.

'But it's true,' said the duke. 'It's true. I mean, I'd heard the usual chatter, read the illustrated papers – but the reality.' He threw up his hands, became once more a very tongue-tied peer.

'And that partner of yours, Miss Blenkinsop,' said the duke. 'You can't really tell me she's a lawyer?'

'Indeed I can,' said Elena. 'And a good one. You thought she was a good dancer, too?'

'I thought she was superb.'

Could it be that her ducal relative was smitten as well as tongue-tied?

'And her mother was involved in it too, you tell me?'

'Ballet mistress. *Régisseuse*. Indeed she was in it.'

'She used to live here, you know. She and her parents worked for us. They were very good people. We were lucky to get them.'

Once again she was being reminded what a jolly nice lot the Channings were. Well, I'd better take care to be jolly nice as well, she thought. After all, I'm a Channing.

'I wonder,' said the duke, 'if I may suggest a little light supper for a few of us after the others have gone? Sort of a dormy feast, so to speak.'

'Jolly good idea,' said Elena, and wondered who the others would be as the duke nodded to Henshaw. The butler bowed in return. So it's all a put-up job, she thought. If we'd flopped I'd be eating the same canapés as the others. Not that they'd be that bad . . .

'I wonder if Miss Blenkinsop would like to come,' said the duke.

'Ask her yourself,' said Elena, and nodded to where Millicent talked with Francis, who seemed tense, but then talk of Deauville always upset him.

'I hardly like to intrude,' the duke said, and Elena beckoned to her friend, who came over to them at once. Such a dear girl, Elena, thought the duke, but unfortunately she was a relative and it wasn't the same somehow. Then Elena introduced them. The duke was far too cunning to talk at once of dormy feasts, if that was what he'd intended. It was music he spoke of and how well she and Elena had danced. Francis was on his own and that would never do. Elena walked over to him with that graceful ease her mother had first taught her.

'Francis, my dear,' she said, 'how splendid of you to come all this way.'

'Three hundred miles just for one ball,' Francis said.

He spoke of it as if it were a five-mile point, and at the end of it the fox had escaped.

'I hope you thought the ball was worth it?'

Love made Francis Byronic, as well she knew, but there were limits. Francis did his best to pull himself together.

'Oh yes,' he said. 'Wonderful. It's just that my private life has been rather a mess lately, but that's no reason to take it out on anybody else.' He glanced to where Millicent chattered and smiled. And now on top of everything else I've got a duke to cope with, the glance said. But in fact he didn't. When at last he was introduced to Bellingham he attempted to explain away his moodiness as the onset of a headache, and the duke pounced. Had just the thing for a headache. Never failed. Powder. Mix it with water, then a large Scotch and he'd sleep before he'd finished tying his pyjamas. Only thing was – take it at once. Longer you waiter, the longer it took to work. Stood to reason.

Feeling bewildered, Francis climbed into Richard's motor car to be driven to his house. Even more bewildered, he realised that Richard would not be coming with him. Richard could see no reason why he should forego a jolly good supper for a headache, real or imaginary. He danced with Elena instead.

'Was he in a foul temper?' she asked. 'He was frantic to be, only he couldn't. He'd brought it on himself after all.'

Elena pondered the fact that even if dukes could no longer have lesser mortals hanged, they could still get away with highway robbery. Headache powders indeed! And yet she'd be willing to bet that he had some, and that they'd do what he said. This was a duke with all his buttons on.

'Who's coming to this debauch?' she asked.

'The dormy feast?' She nodded. 'You, Millicent, the duke and me,' said Richard.

'It's a debauch,' she said.

'*Un parti carré* at least,' he conceded. 'And I agree. If that isn't a debauch, it's close. Do you mind?'

'Should be fun,' she said.

'Does Millicent think so?'

'When it comes to sex, I never know what Millicent thinks,' said Elena. 'That's because I never ask. But I do know she's in the mood for a party.' And that's another thing, she thought. 'You were wonderful' were the first words the duke had spoken, and Francis hadn't said a word. Not to her, anyway. The duke was well ahead on points. Then the duke's guests left, and she went with Richard to a breakfast parlour and the dormy feast was waiting. And such a feast. Caviare, foie gras, lobster, smoked salmon, cold chicken, salad, and bread from the castle's own ovens, peaches, nectarines and grapes from its conservatory. Champagne that had to be Krug, and a red wine that made Richard gasp aloud. Burgundy, it seemed, and such a Burgundy. Domaine de la Romanée Conti, and fifteen years old. Everything perfect in fact, except that Henshaw sulked rather because he was missing a supper for the upper servants, and God alone knew how much they'd leave him. The duke sent him away almost at once.

'Serve ourselves,' he said. 'No harm in roughing it for once,' and Henshaw left then, sulking once more because he wasn't wanted.

'Moody chap,' said the duke. 'They can ruin a good party, the moody ones.'

This was so breathtakingly frank that Elena almost gasped aloud, but all Millicent did was smile.

There could be no denying that it was fun. Richard told suitably edited stories about tent shows in the colonies, and the duke managed to make even estate management like an episode in a French farce, and the two friends listened, ate, drank and were happy, not least because two eligible young men were working hard to make them so. Vaguely, at the back of her mind, Millicent wondered for whom the foie gras had been meant originally, but it didn't worry her. She was the one who was eating it . . . But at last they could eat no more, not even foie gras, not even caviare, even

161

though they were the first she had ever tasted – on dry land anyway – and she longed to be hungry again so that she could start again. Go easy on the Krug she told herself, even though that too was a first. Vintage . . . Poor old Francis.

The men refused port but finished the Burgundy, and the duke listened for once about the rigours of life at London University, with only Art Appreciation to relieve them.

'This place is stuffed with art,' he said. 'Got a Holbein tucked away somewhere. Care to see it?'

'Oh, yes please,' said Millicent, and rose at once, and the duke followed, leaving Richard to his Burgundy, Elena to her champagne.

'Got a Titian, too,' said the duke. 'We might take a look later, if you're not too exhausted.' The door closed behind them.

'Well,' said Elena, but all Richard did was smile.

'I'm jolly grateful to him,' he said. 'I've got you to myself.'

'Yes, of course,' said Elena, 'but it was the way he did it. In Spain—'

'We're not in Spain,' said Richard. 'We're in an enchanted castle in Northumberland – where he owns everything in sight.'

'Enchanted?'

'If that's the way they act then it's enchanted. And anyway—'

'Yes, darling?'

Richard smiled once more. It was his night, too, he thought. When he'd said he'd got her to himself she'd said, 'Yes, of course,' as if it were the only way to be. And now 'darling'. All the same—

'I'll have to go soon,' he said.

'But why?'

'Francis.'

Elena grimaced, yet still looked beautiful. 'He does have the knack of getting in the way,' she said.

'Not of the duke.'

The grimace became a giggle, then, 'All the same,' she said, 'what am I supposed to do about them?' She nodded towards the door.

'Why nothing,' said Richard. 'What can you do? She's a big girl now.'

Indeed she is, thought Elena, and even if she started late she's making up for lost time. All the same, I love her dearly, and I won't have her hurt. Perhaps it was love that made Richard so perceptive.

162

'She'll be all right,' he said. 'His Grace won't handle her the way he did Francis.'

'But what will happen?'

'Up to her,' said Richard. 'But she'll be the one who makes the pace. He won't force her.'

'You know all about it, don't you?'

'A little.'

Tent shows have a lot to answer for, she thought, but then so do the nobility and gentry.

'You're wrong about one thing,' she said.

'Only one?'

She put out her tongue at him. 'When you said the duke owns everything in sight, he doesn't own Millicent. Nobody does.'

'You're right,' he said. 'It's like holding four aces when the best the others can do is a full house. Let's talk about us.'

They found her evening cloak, and went outside where he embraced her, and they wished they were in the Chelsea flat.

'Even so,' he said at last, 'I have to go.'

'Oh, sod Francis,' said Elena, and Richard blinked.

'Who taught you to say that?' he asked

'You did,' said Elena.

'I must have been tight.'

'Just a bit.'

'I love you so much,' he said. 'It makes me nervous, you see.'

And just as well, she thought. From time to time I'll need four aces too. Then she kissed him – the best one of the night – but even so he had to leave her.

She went to her room. Well, where else? she thought. Playing hide and seek with a Holbein was a game for two, or had they reached the Titian stage by now? The trouble was, she knew she wouldn't sleep if she went to bed. Three in the morning and her mind was racing: supper, dukes, tent shows, castles – and Richard. Darling Richard. And her father. First him, then Richard. But no Millicent. Things were complicated enough without the next instalment of Millicent's Life and Times . . . Perhaps she would be able to persuade the doctor to let them dance for her father. He had adored to see Mama dance, and after that supper they really would need the exercise. She yawned and wished that she had brought Célèstine with her. Perhaps she would be able to sleep after all . . .

There was a tap at the door and she called come in. Pedrillito, clean, neat by his standards, not even smoking. He began to speak as he came into the room, and by the time he had finished

Elena wondered if she would ever sleep again. But why me? She wondered, and why at three in the morning? But the answer to that was obvious. It was the only chance Pedrillito had. When he had finished all she could do was sit, dazed, and realise how Richard must have felt when a hefty farm labourer had managed to land a good one for a change.

'I surprised you,' Pedrillito said.

'Well, yes,' said Elena, and thanked God that the poor man spoke only Spanish. Even if there *were* eavesdroppers, they wouldn't understand a word.

'I surprised myself,' said Pedrillito, 'but when such things happen it is best to say so at once.'

Best for whom? Elena thought bitterly, but that was unfair. She'd felt the same when it happened to her.

'But you'll speak for me?' Pedrillito asked.

'Not tonight,' Elena said firmly. 'It's far too late. Better tomorrow. I'll see what I can do.'

He bowed, graceful as a *hidalgo*. 'You are very kind,' he said.

Be that as it may, she thought, I'm a woman in a hell of a fix. She felt even more like poor Richard when – what was it he called it – the haymaker had landed for once, and he hadn't yet managed to counterpunch. Then the door opened and Gertie came in. Now's not the time she thought, but Gertie had brought coffee and at that moment she would have accepted coffee from the devil himself.

'Bless you darling,' she said, and Gertie pounced. 'Wasn't that the little guitar player I saw?' she asked. 'Bit late for a recital.'

'First chance he had,' said Elena. You know what today's been like,' and Gertie nodded. Fraught wasn't the word.

'He's worried about his guitar,' said Elena, lying frantically. 'It may need a new bridge. They're made in Spain. He doesn't think he'll get one in England.'

'Soho,' said Gertie. 'They've got everything foreign there. I'll take him myself once we get back to town,' then changed the subject. 'Good supper was it?'

'The best.'

'It would be. We had a good one too. The butler and the valet and the housekeeper and me. Mrs Hoskins – the housekeeper – she could remember my mam and dad and me when I was little. I hear Millie clicked with the duke.'

Oh, my God, thought Elena, another one. But Gertie too was merciful.

'But that'll keep till tomorrow,' Gertie said. 'Would you like to know some more about when I was a dancer?'

A bedtime story, thought Elena. Just what I need. 'Once upon a time . . .'

'Yes, please,' she said, and Gertie poured more coffee.

'Let's see,' said Gertie. 'Last time we talked I was at dancing school. Did well, too. I loved it there. Maybe that was why I was popular, too. Not the pet of the place – nothing like that – but the other girls liked me. We got on. And then one day – I was just turned sixteen I remember – Madame Louise sent for me and I wondered what I was supposed to have done. Those days she was mostly records and accounts. It was Reg who ran the school.'

'Reg?'

'*Régisseur, Maître de ballet,*' said Gertie. 'Pansy of course, but nice with it. Not bitchy like some. He used to be a dancer, but he wasn't all that good. Natural born teacher, that was Reg. He had a friend in London who really could dance. Freddy. But we'll get to him later. Where was I?'

'Madame Louise.'

'She sent for me and I couldn't think why. I was a good little girl in them days. Only it wasn't that.'

'What then?'

'Big show at the Variety Theatre. Cast of hundreds. Well, twenty anyway. Only one of them had had a fall. Pulled a tendon. They needed a replacement quick.'

'You?'

'I was petrified,' said Gertie. 'I mean, apart from a couple of weeks in the chorus – another poor girl pulled a tendon – I'd never even faced a proper audience, and here I was playing second lead. I mean, I know Reg was there every night to coach me – chaperon me too. Their star comic was as randy as a stoat – it was still a what-d'you-call-it.'

'An ordeal,' said Elena.

'That's the one. Only the funny thing was I was all right as soon as I faced that audience. Enjoyed it even. It was like I was coming home. Well, you know the feeling.'

And indeed I do, thought Elena.

'I went down well. No question . . . Even when I sang. I've got no voice at all, but Madame and Reg taught me how to cheat. I did all right.'

'Six weeks' regular wages. On the nail every week. Money to pay back Lady Mary. Then the show moved on. Number One

Tour they were. Never less than a month in one place. They wanted to take me with them, but Reg said no, and quite right too.'

'Why was that?' Elena asked.

'Well, for a start, the other girl's tendon got better and she wanted her job back – and where would that leave me? – not to mention she was queen of the comedian's harem. Not for me. And anyway, Reg reckoned I was ready for London.

'Sounds daft, I know, and me just out of school – but the Newcastle papers had given me good notices, and the word was out by then, and anyway, Reg's friend Freddy knew all about me.'

'Freddy the dancer?'

'Had been,' said Gertie, 'but not when I met him. He was doing the same as Reg.'

'But if he was so good—'

'Had an argument with a hansom cab and lost,' said Gertie. 'It healed all right, but a dancer's got to be perfect. Once one of the bits is broken and stuck together, we're never the same. Anyway, me and Freddy got on, just like me and Reg. Proper big sister. Even got me a start in the show he was doing in that place by the Haymarket. It's gone dark now.'

'Gone dark?' said Elena.

'Closed,' said Gertie. 'It was bright enough when I was there . . . Anyway, Freddy got me a start. Not second lead, nothing like that – but a foot in the door, as Freddy said. Solo spot in the second half and my name in the programme.'

'How marvellous,' said Elena.

'Well, it was,' said Gertie. 'Mind you, he had to throw a tantrum to get it.' Her face softened as she remembered. 'He could throw you a lovely tantrum. Prompt books flying, make-up tubes coming at you like bullets. He'd even lie down and scream. Afterwards he used to say it was because he was a fairy, but it wasn't. Not really.'

'What was it then?'

'He enjoyed it,' Gertie said. 'Anyway, it got me the job. Management decided it was cheaper to pay me than have Freddy throwing things and screaming he couldn't cope – and maybe meaning it. Mind you I turned out to be worth it in the end.'

'Then what happened?' said Elena, and her eyelids drooped a little.

'I fell in love,' said Gertie. 'Let's get you out of that dress and your nightie on,' and Elena submitted. She was weary at last –

and no wonder, she thought, and now silk next to her skin, linen sheets that smelled of lavender. Bliss.

'Your first time?' she asked.

'There has to be one,' said Gertie. 'You know that.'

And indeed she did. 'Nice?' she asked.

'Lovely,' said Gertie. 'Freddy saw to that.'

'*Freddy?*'

'My big sister,' said Gertie. 'I told you. Put poor old Rupert through it as if he was asking for my hand in marriage.'

' "He'll do," he said. "Loving. Thoughtful. Nice boy." They were all boys to him.'

'Who were?' said Elena, more sleepy still.

'My chaps,' said Gertie. 'I was always one for the chaps after that.'

Like mother, like daughter? Elena wondered, and then, quoting Gertie, Look who's talking.

'I lost it in a little hotel out Henley way,' Gertie said.

'Lost what?'

'You know fine well,' said Gertie. 'But it was worth it. And not just on account of Rupert being so nice. There were the presents too, and suppers at Romano's, the Trocadero, the Café Royal. To a girl like me it was—'

'Like fairyland?'

'I nearly said that to Freddy once,' said Gertie, 'only I stopped myself just in time.' They both giggled.

'Then my mother wrote to me,' said Gertie. 'Never much of a hand at writing, but she made herself do it.'

'Must have been important,' said Elena, not quite yawning.

'My uncle Joe had died,' Gertie said. 'Her brother.'

'Miner?'

'Only one that wasn't,' said Gertie. 'A sailor. Mind you he sailed in colliers. Them little boats that carry coal. It was what killed him.'

'Overwork?'

'They could all have died of that,' Gertie said. 'It was a storm at sea that did for him. Off Black Sills. It would be. Mind you, that was how I met my Bert.'

'I don't think I—' Elena began. Sleep was closer than ever.

'Mam asked me to go to the funeral,' Gertie said, 'and I went. Freddy fixed that. "Does you credit," he said. He even fixed my blacks.'

'Blacks?'

'Mourning,' said Gertie. 'Found some in costume that fitted, so all I missed was a few days' wages – but Rupert made up for that – or was it Harry by then? Anyway, up to Black Sills I went – last time I ever saw the place. And just as well after the Trocadero – talk about contrast.

'They'd arranged a concert,' she continued. 'No disrespect. Nothing like that. The dead had all been buried at sea – but most of them left wives and bairns – and the ones that were hurt too. They all needed money. So Mam had a word with Uncle Joe's pastor – strict Primitives Uncle Joe and his wife – and he said he could see nothing wrong with it.'

Elena learned later that Primitives were a breakaway sect of Methodism with an unrelenting awareness of sin. To win their pastor over must have been a victory indeed.

'Wrong with what?' she asked.

'Me singing and dancing at the concert – though nothing vulgar. Anyway, that was where I first saw Bert. He was engine room artificer on the 'Speedwell' – the destroyer that rescued Uncle Joe's collier, and damn near foundered themselves doing it.'

15

Time to end it, Stobbs thought. Rum and pep was all very well, but soon the tap would run dry. He could read the signs. There'd have to be a – what did the French call it? – a *pourboire*, that was it. With a *pourboire* he could go to the Ring of Bells. Two pretty barmaids at the Ring of Bells and one of them could be obliging after hours . . . Not that he hadn't earned it. All them truths and half-truths and lies. Ah well. To work, to work.

'Funny thing about his lordship,' he said. 'What you might call interesting.'

Major what's-his-name was on to it at once.

'Interesting? How – interesting?'

'I'll have to think,' said Stobbs. 'Trouble is, I owe this geezer a fiver, and he likes to be paid, and I'm a bit short at the moment. I mean, what you want is all here—' he tapped his forehead '—but it's a bit of a jumble. This geezer who wants his fiver back could jumble anything.'

Pudiphatt sighed, and took a fiver from his wallet. He was quite sure that Stobbs was lying, but for once Stobbs told the truth. Horses were hell, and unpaid bookies even worse. The fiver might have looked lonely inside the major's wallet, but his need for it was even greater.

'Thank you, sir,' he said, and waited till Major Thingamy bought him another. Enjoy it, he thought. There won't be any more where that came from.

Pudiphatt sipped, 'Get on with it, man,' and Rifleman Stobbs got on with it. This loony had been a good officer once.

'Of course it's rumours,' said Stobbs, and Pudiphatt nodded. Without rumours the army couldn't function.

'But there's rumours and rumours,' said Stobbs. 'And this lot sounded right, if you follow me?'

'Get *on*,' said Pudiphatt again.

'Drink,' said Stobbs. 'Of course, all the officers did – just like

169

me – but then Captain Mendip really started hitting it. Sudden like.'

In his mind he thought, Sorry captain. You were a real nice bloke and it's all lies anyway – or most of it. But oh, my Gawd I need five quid.

'Couldn't handle it,' said Stobbs. 'Not even in the trenches. And anyway he didn't even try . . . And then it was girls.'

'*Girls*?' Major What-Not hadn't minded drink, but the girls horrified him.

'Off he'd go behind the lines, every chance he got.'

'You're sure?'

'I used to take care of his kit, sir, what with being his batman. Scent. His uniform used to reek of it.'

Major Who's-is looked appalled.

'And then—'

Stobbs hesitated: what he had to say had truth in it.

'Get on man. I shan't tell you again,' said the major.

And just where do you think you are? Stobbs wondered. Beaumont Hamel? Wipers? Certainly not the Black Lion in 1924.

'It was about his wife, sir. More her mum, really. All mixed up with some posh family in the North. That's all I got, but they say it bothered him no end.'

'Why he started drinking you mean?'

'Could be,' said Stobbs. 'By then he was a mess, sir. Drunk half the day and all night. And then he—'

'He what?'

'He started dodging the column, sir. Shirking.'

All lies of course, but five pounds was five pounds.

'Good God,' said the major.

'Saw it myself, sir, being his batman . . . And that's all sir. Sorry.'

'It's enough. Cut along,' said Major What's-it. Already he was plotting and planning, but there were two things he had to *know*. One was if the Rifle Brigade had been in the places Stobbs said they were – after six years memory grew hazy – and hence, if Mendip had had the opportunity for drunkenness, lechery and cowardice, Stobbs had sworn that he had shown. The other was this well-born Northern family Mendip had grown so interested in – well, one of them anyway. A pub was not the place to consider such problems. Home and his own armchair, his own Scotch. At leas the could be quiet there. But what choice did he have?

He fell asleep at his own fireside – quite often did these days as a matter of fact – but when he woke up – three in the morning and the start of a headache – he had the answer, or at least the means of solving the problem. Daisy Pemberton. Not the ideal solution – not even a nice one, but she would know. Had to. She had been cousin Charles's – *chère amie*, bit of fluff, bird in the hand, so to speak, until he met the foreign bitch. She would know. Bound to. But he'd have to do it right. Cautiously, he made his way, first to aspirins then bed. For this he'd have to look the part. British officer in mufti, clean and spruce and neat. The same story, he thought, only with Charles instead of Mendip. It had worked well enough with Stobbs after all. With a woman there would be no trouble. Not that Daisy Pemberton was without surprises. To begin with there was her address. Ex-chorus girls with a fondness for the chaps didn't usually live in St John's Wood. Hackney and the kind of pubs there, the ones that sold cheap gin, were far more likely. But it was St John's Wood. A nuisance really. One didn't arrive at that kind of address by bicycle. A bus, and then a walk. They were the only way, even if more and more he was finding walking difficult, even detestable. He who had once actually looked forward to a route march. Not any more.

The house, and it was a house, if a small one, had been polished till it glowed. No suggestion of a flat for Daisy. Mahogany door waxed that day, brass door knob that could have been gold, and a neat and elegant housemaid who bade him wait in the hall while she enquired, but his luck was in, it seemed. Miss Pemberton would see him.

She was even more neatly elegant than her maid, even more golden than her door knob – but then her gold really was gold. Rather too much of it for mid-afternoon, thought Pudiphatt, but he was a petitioner after all. He smiled.

'Major Pudiphatt,' she said, and turned his visiting card over in her hands. With that gone he had three left. She looked at the one she held.

'A friend of Charles you say.'

'Relative too, actually,' said Pudiphatt. 'Second cousin.'

She looked at him more closely then, awarding marks for what he wore, he thought. Apparently he'd done well, but even so . . .

'And living in West Kensington,' she said. 'Rather a long way from Grosvenor Square.'

Now this was rude. Damn rude in fact, but she was a pretty

171

woman, if mature, and well used to getting away with far more rudeness than that.

'We weren't the rich branch of the family,' Pudiphatt said, and she nodded, point taken.

'And you've come to talk about Charles,' she said. Again the private memoir was produced for inspection, and she didn't believe a word of it.

'And you intend to publish this?' she asked.

Pudiphatt changed the story at once. He couldn't have said why. Impulse. But now and again impulses worked. Follow it, he thought.

'Oh no, no,' he said. 'Typed, but that's all.'

'So much trouble for a few pieces of typescript,' said Miss Pemberton. 'No one will see it, after all.'

'I'll see it,' said Pudiphatt. 'Write it too. My memorial to Charles. And when I do, other may see it. Read about the man they knew.'

And to himself he thought, I'll do it. As soon as I live in Grosvenor Square . . .

'He was a real man all right,' said Miss Pemberton.

'Indeed he was,' said Pudiphatt, his voice easy, relaxed. Big and tall, blue eyed and fair. He knew very well what she was hinting at: that he was queer and Charles the unrequited love of his life. Sexual love. Well, he could handle that, because it wasn't true. He waited, and his silence impressed Daisy Pemberton more than a torrent of words.

'He was my friend too,' she said, 'and what you say is true. But how can I help you?'

Pudiphatt put Charles back in his box of daydreams and returned to his real world, the grubby world of half-truths and deceptions.

Carefully he said, 'The way you remember him. The things you know about him that will show what a splendid person he was. All that. I want you to tell me.'

'There are some things I couldn't possibly tell you,' said Miss Pemberton.

'Well, of course,' said Pudiphatt, easy still, though the thought of Charles and that gold-beaded strumpet revolted him.

'Time together,' he said. 'Time in London parks and gardens. And restaurants: he loved them too. And laughter.'

She looked at him, questioning.

'Where Charles was there was always laughter.' Her eyes were

172

on his, but she was thinking back, and remembering at last.

'Yes, there was,' she said. 'I can even remember how he laughed, and I'd love to help you, honestly. But how can I, in my position?' She didn't even say what her position was, but they both knew.

'Just your initials,' he said. 'A made-up name if you want. The name doesn't matter, so long as you're there.'

'You'd let me see it when it's finished? Perhaps even alter it?' She was hooked. He had her by God.

'Word of a gentleman,' he said.

'That'll do me,' said Miss Pemberton. 'Ask your questions.'

Out it all came. At first she'd seemed reluctant, even coy, but soon it was more like a tap turned on full. How they'd met – after a first-night party at Daly's. The show had flopped, but she hadn't: not with him. And Paris and Deauville at weekends – though he wouldn't let her gamble, and just as well. Skindle's on Sundays in summer, and a wonderful week in Nice when he had leave and she was between shows.

'And always just the two of you?' Pudiphatt asked.

'Oh no,' said Miss Pemberton. 'There were parties all over the place. Not that Charlie ever looked at another girl. Not till his darling Elena appeared. He looked at her hard enough.' She sighed. 'But that was all right – or it should have been. I had this rule: once they're engaged it's over. It seemed Charlie had the same rule.'

'Why did you say it should have been all right?'

'Charlie was a hard one to kiss goodbye,' said Miss Pemberton. 'The hardest of them all.' She rang for tea. Earl Grey. Very nice. And ginger biscuits, just right. This one had learned about behaviour.

'His darling Elena married again,' he said.

'Indeed she did,' said Miss Pemberton. 'Habit she had – getting married. This one was a viscount. Mendip—'

Again Pudiphatt responded to an impulse. 'Nice chap, so they say.'

'Who told you?' But Miss Pemberton cared little for viscounts. 'A bit too fond of whisky, maybe.'

'Most of us were,' Pudiphatt said.

'How long were you in France?' she asked him.

'Three years.'

'Good God!' said Miss Pemberton. 'Why aren't you dead? Even so, it's time you stopped. Or you will be.' She sipped her Earl

Grey. 'She had another chap, too. Or so they say. One of the Channings. Or her mother had.'

Again Pudiphatt was silent: again she approved.

'One of the Duke of Bellingham's lot – they're all rolling in it.' She paused. It was her turn for silence.

'Mendip must have been rolling in it too,' said Pudiphatt, and she nodded, pleased.

'You're wondering if this is all – relevant? Is that the word?'

'Well, yes,' said Pudiphatt. He'd hoped for more about the Channings, but he'd had all he would get. The rest he'd have to dig for on his own, or the silly cow would start to get suspicious.

'Because it does dishonour Charles's memory,' said Miss Pemberton, and he forgave her at once. 'She's a dancer too, and so's that partner of hers. Good ones so the papers say. Both their mothers were dancers. Very refined, her ladyship's mother, or so they tell me. Not like the other one. Gertie Garnet. What a name.' She snorted. 'All the same—' Pudiphatt waited, and again she was pleased. He was the best listener she'd met in years. That might be useful.

'She was a stunner,' said Miss Pemberton,' and stunners are the ones who get the chaps. Not that she got Charles, but I had to watch him like a hawk. How did you find me?'

Change of subject, he thought. Quick change. Like an interrogation.

'Entertainments Directory,' said Pudiphatt, and she nodded, not displeased.

'I like to keep in touch,' she said. 'Mind you, I'm in a different business now.'

'You don't dance any more?'

'Not even for fun,' said Miss Pemberton. 'Last time I even tried I was terrible. Diabolic. These days I'm an investigator. Private. Know what that is?'

'Sounds like a detective,' said Pudiphatt.

'It *is* a detective. Only I specialise. Discretion Guaranteed. That's my motto.'

'Sounds interesting.'

'And so it is,' Miss Pemberton said. 'It's the way I get to hear about dukes and viscounts.'

'I see,' said Pudiphatt.

'Of course you do,' said Miss Pemberton. 'You're not a fool. Chaps. That's what I specialise in. And dear little rosebuds like me and Gertie that couldn't wait to be roses. Hanky panky,

174

naughtiness, divorce. That's what I specialise in. Pays better than the chorus, believe me.'

'I can see it does,' said Pudiphatt.

'Maybe you could specialise, too,' Miss Pemberton said.

'*Me*?' More amazement than outrage, Miss Pemberton thought. All right there.

'Certainly you,' she said. 'Born nosy, good listener, do your research before you start. You were born to be an investigator. What's your first name?'

'Sidney,' he said.

'Sidney Pudiphatt.' She said it as if the two names belonged together and so they did. He hated both. 'Tell you what,' she said. 'You go and write your memoir and let me see it. Oh, don't worry. I know you'll do it: the affection's there all right, but there's nosiness too. Isn't there Sidney? Anyway, you go and write it and lay off the Scotch for a bit and I might have something for you. Something rather good.'

On the bus going home he thought about it long and hard. She'd meant it all right. Work he could do, liked doing come to that, and at the end of the day a neat little house like hers. A nice offer. Very nice indeed. How was she to know a house in Grosvenor Square was waiting for him? Bit of luck her being in the line she was: quite a lot of juice in Daisy Pemberton, and she'd even squeezed it herself. The fact that Mendip drank, for instance. She confirmed that. True, they all drank, but even so . . . Then the Channing connection. Stobbs had known about it, too, but Miss Pemberton had been far more precise. True it meant dreary hunts in libraries and record offices – that and bothering the Rifle Brigade adjutant again – but it was the only road that led to Grosvenor Square.

The private detective had been no threat; the five thousand no more than conscience money because Charles had pitied Pudiphatt to the point where even pity was insulting.

And as for Pudiphatt himself – more than half-crazy after three years in France, and with a drink problem that imperilled his reason. Private clinics, once upon a time, but now there was no money for private clinics or very little else. A danger to all and sundry, the mad major. She passed it all on to Harry Edwards. No dramas there. It was what Elena told her about Pedrillito that incensed her.

'He wants what?' she yelled.

It was true that her friend was on full volume, but she had something to yell about. All the same, I'm starting a headache, thought Elena.

'I told you,' she said to Millicent. 'He wants to marry your mother, and yelling won't help. Honestly it won't.'

Millicent looked at her, then put her hand to Elena's forehead.

'You've started the curse, haven't you?' she said.

Elena nodded.

'I'll get the aspirin,' said Millicent and did so. 'It was such a shock, you see,' she said. 'I mean, he doesn't even speak English. I take it he was serious.'

'Absolutely,' said Elena.

'Oh, sod it,' Millicent said, and then, 'How did he think he'd support mum?'

'By playing his guitar.'

'In London?'

Easy, thought Elena. It isn't his fault. It isn't anybody's fault.

'There's a part of France near Spain,' she said. 'Around Bayonne. They're mad about Spanish things there. The bulls even. Pedrillito reckons he could do well there, and when he'd made enough money they'd go to Mexico. Gypsy music's all the rage there.'

'Mexico? Mum doesn't speak a word of Spanish. Not a word—'

'He reckons he'd teach her. Then later on—' She hesitated, but Millicent said. 'Finish it please.'

'They'd come back to Bayonne. Start a dancing school. He thinks you'd help them,' said Elena.

'But why on earth should I?'

'You're her daughter.'

Millicent gasped as if her friend had hit her. 'He's a clever one,' she said at last.

'He's a man in love,' Elena said, and then, 'You'll have to tell your mother.'

'You'll be with me?'

'If you want me to be.'

'Oh yes,' said Millicent, and shook her head like a boxer who's been punished too much. 'I can't even make up my mind whether this is tragedy or farce.'

Bit of both Elena thought, but didn't say so. 'Let's tell her now,' she said.

'You feel up to it?'

'Best to get it over with,' said Elena, and sent for Gertie, plied her with sherry, and told her everything. Millicent had asked her to speak, not only because her Spanish wasn't up to it, but because it was Elena he had told. And anyway, she couldn't trust herself to do the talking . . .

When Elena had done, Gertie said, 'But that's marvellous.'

'*Marvellous*?' Millicent sounded appalled, but Elena wasn't. Gertie had a right to feel marvellous. She was loved after all, by a man much younger than herself, a man of great talent. Of course it was marvellous.

'Mind you, I knew something was up,' said Gertie.

'But how could you?' said her daughter. 'He doesn't speak a word of English.'

'He's got eyes,' said Gertie. 'He can look. Those eyes told me things. Quite a bit in fact. And anyway, he used to play a little tune while the two of you were talking. That tune was for me.'

Oh, it was, it was, Elena thought. But how to say so without upsetting her friend?

'He loves me all right,' said Gertie.

'And you?' Millicent's heart was in her mouth when she asked.

'He's a very nice boy,' said Gertie, and Millicent sighed her relief. 'Nice' was exactly the word she needed. 'There was a time . . . But not now.'

'Why not now?' Elena asked.

'Too old,' Gertie. 'Six months of rapture, and then he'll move on. He may not mean to, but he will. Believe me, I've seen it.'

'Yes,' her daughter said. 'I daresay you have.' But her voice was loving.

'Not me, mind you,' said Gertie, 'but I've seen it all the same. Mexico? Not a hope. Not that I'm all that keen to go there.' She turned to Elena. 'Tell him no, please,' she said. 'Only let him down lightly. He really is a nice boy.'

'I'll do the best I can,' Elena said. 'I can't say more.'

For a moment Gertie became formal. 'Thank you, my lady,' she said. Then the parlourmaid came in. Miss Blenkinsop, it seemed, was wanted on the telephone. A Mr Barnes.

Millicent got to her feet, and for a moment Gertie thought her daughter might use what she called language.

'One of your solicitors,' she said to Elena. 'Probably lost half a crown and wants us to find it before he goes to the golf course.' Then the maid shut the door and she added, 'Bloody fool.'

All the same, Elena thought. It was her mother's life we were talking about. Supposing it had been your mother's? But she knew that was impossible.

'Ready for bed again?' Gertie asked.

'Yes, but not to sleep,' said Elena. 'I want you to finish the story about you and Bert first.'

Gertie, who had been brooding on what might have been, cheered up at once.

'You really want to hear it?' she asked.

'It's not just a good story, it's true,' said Elena. 'Of course I want to hear it.'

'True every word,' said Gertie. 'If Bert had come across him, that little Pedro wouldn't have lasted five minutes.'

And make what you can out of that, thought Elena.

'Of course, we went our own ways,' said Gertie. 'Nothing else for it – what with him putting into Cape Town or Fremantle or Aden, and me in Monte Carlo or Nice on somebody's yacht. 'But whenever he was in England – like Devonport or Portsmouth – he'd be straight round to see me. Top priority he said I was. And so was he. We could have gone on like that for years.'

'But you didn't?'

'The war came,' said Gertie. 'When it started we said it wouldn't make any difference – but it did. Mind you, he was lucky at first. Two solid years of U-boats and what Jerry called armed raiders, and my Bert without as much as a scratch. He was a Chief Engine Room Artificer by then. And then he got one. 1917, that would be, and what a scratch that was. Single-ship duel, he called it. His cruiser against a German. Bert's ship sank the other one, but they took a mauling first. Bert nearly lost a leg, only they patched him up somewhere or other. Halifax Nova Scotia would it be? They did a marvellous job, he said, but all the same he limped till he died . . .

'Back to Blighty then. Sick leave. Lovely. What I mean is, he wasn't all that sick. He couldn't have been. We got married. Mind you, Millie was getting on a bit, but it wasn't that.'

'What was it?' Elena asked.

'Being together. Sounds daft I know – him hundreds of miles away half the time. But it wasn't. We were together all right, daft or not.'

Elena thought of her father in South Africa: her mother in London. 'Not daft at all,' she said.

'When he went back they put him on convoys. A destroyer – the *Daffodil*. Sister ship to the *Speedwell*, the one he'd been on when I first met him – only she went down in 1915.' She brooded for a moment.

'Anyway he was happy enough on the *Daffodil*,' said Gertie.

'But how could he be?' said Elena. 'He'd been wounded. Badly wounded.'

'This was 1917,' said Gertie, 'and he could still walk. By 1917 they used to say if you can walk you're in. Anyway down in the engine room he was the boss. He liked being the boss,' she smiled, remembering. 'But I liked being the boss, too. Even if I was worrying myself sick . . .'

'Anyway he limped on, as you might say. Till February 1918, and then a U-boat got them. *Daffodil* went down in minutes, only Bert had a lifebelt on and a wounded sailor in his arms, and where either had come from he had no idea. All he could remember was the cold. Bitter, he said it was. Then a ship's boat reached him and they sailed on to New York, and the MO told him another hour in the water and he'd have died.

' "Only I didn't stay another hour," he said. "I was warm and snug." Her eyes half closed. She was quoting from a letter, and close to tears.

' "All I needed was you," he said, "but then you're what I always need. What a lucky chap I am." I reckon what he meant was I was always there when needed. Wouldn't you say?'

'Well, of course,' said Elena, 'because you always were.'

'More sick leave,' said Gertie. 'Theatres and watching other people for a change, nice restaurants and bars, and all snug and warm, too, because one sniff of the cold and his teeth used to chatter like those castanets of yours. All the same, we were happy – until the next medical. In the May, that was. Fit, they said. Fit! The tulips were out and he still wore two of everything, but he had to go. He even reckoned it was right. Chaps like me were in short supply, he said. Short supply! He was one in a million.'

This time the tears really did flow.

'Come here,' said Elena, and Gertie went. 'I want to give you a hug.'

Her body still shapely beneath the underwear, Elena thought, but it was all for her Bert. Pedrillito didn't come into it at all . . .

Gertie went back to her chair. 'He felt better when the summer came,' she said, 'and anyway, we knew the war was going to end. All the same he was still passed fit. Chaps like him were scarcer than ever. Another country. Norway this time. Pit props. They sailed in the September. Had to make a detour – the place was alive with U-Boats – so they went North into the Atlantic, almost as far as the Arctic Ocean, to a place called Kristansund, where the merchantmen could pick up their cargo. Only poor Bert never got there.

'Trouble is, it was cold, even in September. Bitter. Worse than the last time. Five hundred miles from port Bert reckoned they were when Jerry got him. This time he was in a light cruiser – *HMS Invictus*. Daft name for a warship. It means 'invincible, unconquered', only it wasn't. Went down as easy as *Daffodil*.

'Regular repeat performance, Bert reckoned. Over the side, then the lifebelt, then the wounded sailor to hold on to, only this time he could remember where they came from. Not that it mattered. All he could think about was the sailor, and how cold he was. The trouble was he was in the sea even longer. The Atlantic's a big place to find two men, and one of them wounded. Even then it was Jerry who found them first.

'The first Bert knew was the conning-tower coming up, and men firing at them with a machine-gun. Daft, Bert reckoned. All that trouble for just two men. But then the Germans were daft from time to time, he said. After all those years of war they were just like the rest of us. They were still good shots though. Bullets slapping into the sea all round them, except for one that hit his shoulder. And there was nothing he could do. You can't dodge bullets, and you can't swim away either. Not with a wounded sailor in tow. All he could do was swear a lot, and I bet he did a thorough job, being Bert. But the Germans had been barmy, that was the point, and a destroyer heard them and came charging over, firing everything they'd got. Bert said they were more danger than the Jerry machine-gun. But in the end, Bert reckoned there was a good chance they'd sunk the U-Boat, and turned their attention to their own side. And just as well, Bert reckoned. On the way down, the U-Boat had sprung an oil leak, and he and his mate were getting more than their share. But they were taken aboard to the sick bay. Waste of time with the sailor – two bullets from the U-Boat on top of everything else – but they patched Bert up and piled all their spare blankets on him, and brought him back to Blighty. To me.

'They put him in the naval hospital for a while, then gave him a medical board, but it was useless. Even the admiralty couldn't find a use for him then, the state he was in. So it was back to the old routine, so to speak. Him in front of a roaring fire, with a rug round his knees, till he started to get his strength back. Then he did the housework when I landed a job.'

'*He* did?' said Elena.

'Sailors is marvellous at housework. I reckon it's because of their being so handy, and knowing how to polish. Then he got well enough to take a little walk, then one day some woman gave him a white feather.'

'Why on earth did she do that?' Elena asked.

'It was nearly always a woman,' Gertie said. 'If they saw a youngish feller in civvies in London, instead of a uniform at the Front or the High Seas. Telling him he was a coward, you see, but Bert just laughed and tucked it into his lapel. Me, I could have scratched her eyes out, and our Millie would have done even worse.'

'How was she in all this?'

'Being illegitimate you mean?'

Elena shrugged. For a long time she'd thought that she too was illegitimate.

'How did she cope?' Elena asked.

'So long as Bert was there she was happy,' said Gertie, 'and even when he wasn't, he used to write her the most marvellous letters. And the presents from abroad! She must have had the best collection of dolls in national costume for miles. Of course, we told her how things were first chance we got. She was bridesmaid at our wedding, though mind you, it was miles away from where we lived – but she looked lovely.

'And then as she grew up Bert helped her with her homework – especially the maths. He was good at maths. All sailors are. Bit of French, too. I reckon that went back to his bachelor days, before him and me were serious. She used to wear his medals too, on Armistice Day, on her Girl Guide uniform. She was that proud of him.'

'You didn't say he had medals,' said Elena.

'For gallantry and service, the citations said. Our Millie had more medals than anybody else in her class. Then one day—' she hesitated.

Please, go on – if you can,' said Elena.

'He'd been talking about a place called Brisbane in Australia,' said Gertie. 'How it was always warm there and we'd get ourselves jobs and be happy.'

'And Millicent?'

'Didn't give a damn so long as she went too . . . Then suddenly he began to talk as if we were already in Australia, and I knew straight off. Went to a phone box and talked with the naval hospital. They sent a doctor at once. By car. They were very proud of Bert. Nothing was too good for him. Only—'

'Please, go on,' Elena said again.

'Only nothing was any good,' said Gertie. 'Pneumonia. That was what he had.'

'We can take him into hospital,' says the doctor. 'Only I think he'd rather stay here.'

' "To die?" I said. That might have sounded like a cheek, but the doctor didn't think so.

' "Yes, Mrs Blenkinsop," he said. "I'm afraid I do."

'And so Bert died in our bed, and Millie and I made what she called an interesting discovery.

'Bert died for his country – of course he did – but more than anything else, we were his country. His wife and daughter. And after he'd gone it wasn't just his heart that stopped. It was the money as well.'

'In a way you could say it was our own fault. We'd never learned how to save money, just how to spend it. Not just on ourselves. There was coaching and extra tuition for Millie too. Cost a mint. Not that it was grudged. It got her into university.

'Thank God he lived to see that, and her graduation. Cap and gown. All that. Miss Millicent Blenkinsop LL B (Hons.) And first-class honours at that. Proud as peacocks, the pair of us. But it all cost money. And then we were alone, and there wasn't any.

'It was our Millie who sorted it out – or tried to. All I could do was cry. She cried too, but she worked out how we were going to live, too. It wouldn't be easy. Nearly all my prezzies – jewellery I mean – was gone – and on top of that there was only my pension as a war widow, and a fiver we'd found in Bert's wallet, and Millie said, "It isn't enough. Nothing like."

' "To pay for your articles you mean?" I said, and she nodded. "But it's what you've worked so hard for."

' "It's what I can't have," said Millie. "Look, Mum, we'll have just about enough to pay the rent and rates. We'll eat regular – regularly is what she said – but there won't be any restaurants. No theatres either. Saturday matinée at the pictures, that's us. And even for that I'll have to get a job."

' "What job?"

' "Shorthand typist," Millie said.

'It was Bert who made her do it, and it fair bothered me at the time. Even more extra money. But it came to me the moment she said it. It was our lifeline.

'Not that I liked the idea. Our Millie, a shorthand typist. She should have been *a solicitor*. And then you came along and she will be.' But the tears hovered once more.

'What's wrong with that?' Elena asked.

'All that money,' Gertie said.

'It was a present,' said Elena. 'And even if you don't see it like that you can always pay me back a bit at a time. After all, you paid Lady Mary back. It seems as if the Blenkinsops always pay their debt to the aristocracy.'

It was a struggle, but at last Gertie smiled. 'Thank you, my lady,' she said, and then: 'So that's the end of my story. End of my life, really. But it couldn't be. I sharp saw that. Not while I had our Millie it couldn't. I love her as much as I loved Bert – and that's what saved me.'

'And her, too, I've no doubt,' said Elena. 'What gorgeous women you are, the pair of you.'

16

Next day was the day of the telegram. Elena took it from Tufnell. She was sitting with Gertie in the day room while Millicent in her office fed bits of Barnes into a mincing machine, and Gertie took one look at the buff-coloured envelope and said, 'Oh God.' Like everybody else with a close acquaintance of the war she had learned to dread telegrams, and yet Elena opened this one unperturbed.

It was a beautiful telegram. 'Northumberland is still magnificent,' she read, 'but I could do with a change of company. Please may I stay with you for a while? Papa.'

Only one answer, of course, but first she had to know if it was possible, and telephoned the duke.

'My God, yes,' said Oswin. He sounded like a man mopping his forehead.

'He's better?'

'*Better*?' said Oswin. 'He's just off on a five-mile walk. That doctor of his – I'm worried sick about him.'

'But why?'

'He has to go with Aylmer and he hates walking. Especially five miles a day across the fells carrying a game bag. You see, Aylmer always take a shotgun, and the doctor hates guns too.'

'Will he let papa come to me?' asked Elena.

'He'd stoke the engine of the train if he had to.'

'And he can talk?'

'I should just about think he can,' said Oswin.

'Then why send a telegram? Why not phone?'

'He says he likes to look at people when they're talking.'

'It isn't such a bad idea at that,' said Elena. 'Especially if it's papa and me.'

When she hung up at last, Gertie had gone. Elena's father was the uncle of a duke after all. Better have a sort through her clothes just in case. Elena sent word that she would see her housekeeper and butler in ten minutes at most. It was her father's first visit after all, and the house had to be perfect. As she waited and planned, Millicent came in. Elena recognised at once the look on her face, and now was not the time. On the other hand, she'd handled the news of her father's reappearance in the world brilliantly, and her first week at Elena's lawyers she had made it plain to the golf-mad Mr Barnes that retrieving seventy-three pounds six shillings and five pence was far more important than four ball, and quite right too. But that wasn't the real reason for her visit.

'Francis?' asked Elena, and of course it was Francis. He was being difficult it seemed. Again.

'The duke?' Elena asked.

'Who else? Though why he should be jealous of a duke in Northumberland when he was no more than a mile away I fail to understand.'

'Because he's rich,' said Elena, 'with a house in London, and my father's nephew. He'll be here soon.'

Millicent thought. A bit jumbled but, 'Your father? You mean he's coming to town?'

'In a few days' from now. So's the duke. He wants to take us dancing, if we can find the time.'

'Us?' Millicent asked, and none too gently either. Try to be more specific: that was the message.

'You, me, Richard,' said Elena. 'Only I may not be able to go because papa's coming to stay.'

'Your father,' her friend said. 'Oh, darling, how marvellous.'

And there you had her, the other Millicent, thought Elena: the one who had handled the press release about papa and herself as if his absence had been no more than a rather lengthy recuperation from a wound acquired in the service of his country. The fact that the recuperation had lasted for years had been ignored as irrelevant. Loving daughter and heroic father reunited. That was the theme; helped no doubt by the duke's ownership of twenty per cent of a popular daily, the *Messenger*, and the Herculean efforts of an up-and-coming young journalist, Harry Edwards. But the planning and execution had all been Millicent's. One could endure quite a lot of Francis and his difficulties for that.

'—and the phone calls,' Millicent was saying. 'You wouldn't believe the phone calls. And you know how expensive they are.'

'From abroad?' Elena asked.

'Deauville.'

Oh dear, thought Elena. 'She's still there then?'

'His mother? She's there all right. Probably won to start with. She quite often does. But when she starts to lose she hasn't the sense to leave.'

'Is that what he phones about?'

'Oswin,' said Millicent. 'That's what he phones about.'

'But I thought he'd given up all that possessive business.'

'He seems to have forgotten. And when I reminded him about Evadne Thingummy and me, he said that was different.'

'Maybe it is,' said Elena.

Her friend looked at her squarely and honestly. 'Elena, listen to me,' she said. 'I'm the daughter of a sailor and a dancer – and now a duke's being nice to me. Can you imagine how that feels? I don't know whether I want to take it further, not yet, but he's a duke and he's nice. Foie gras and caviare and champagne for *me*. And if he gives it because of the way I look – I don't care.'

'How like your mother you are,' said Elena.

'I could do worse,' said Millicent, 'but I bet she never had a Francis round her neck like a millstone.'

'You want to finish with him?'

'I don't *think* so,' said Millicent, 'but I just don't know. Oh, Elena, what the hell am I going to do?'

'Give it time,' said Elena. 'Don't rush it – enjoy it. And if Francis keeps going on about it, give that time too.' She thought of a saying of Richard's. 'He may have wounds, but they're self-inflicted after all.'

Millicent kissed her. 'Thanks darling,' she said, and then the housekeeper and butler appeared.

Her father was due at Eaton Place at seven, and before that she and Millicent and her mother met for cocktails in the drawing room.

'May I ask a question?' Gertie asked. For once she looked shy.

'Well, of course,' said Elena.

'Do you want me here when your father comes? If I'll be in the way, please say so.'

'How could you be in the way?' said Elena. 'You're our *maîtresse de ballet*.'

'Thank you,' said Gertie, but there was no 'My lady'. This was colleague talking to colleague. 'In that case,' she continued, 'what about little Pedro?'

Elena gasped, her hand went to her mouth. 'Oh, my dear,' she

said. 'I'm so sorry. I quite forgot to tell you. I settled him after
lunch.'

'You did?' Millicent was impressed. 'What did you say?'

'Naturally, I told him how fond of him your mother was, but
she couldn't marry anybody – not even a man she was fond of.'

'But why not?' Gertie asked.

'Because part of the reason for getting married is to have
children, and you couldn't. Not any more.'

'But why not?' Gertie asked, but her daughter had already
worked out the answer to that one.

'Too old,' she said.

'Indeed I'm not,' said Gertie, indignant.

Her daughter embraced her. 'He's out of the way,' she said. 'Be
happy.' And then to Elena, 'Do go on, darling.'

'I wish you could have seen his face,' said Elena. 'He was doing
sums. I could almost hear him counting. I'm twenty-seven, he was
thinking, and she could be fifteen years older. Maybe more.'

'How *dare* he,' said Gertie.

'Yes, but he agreed,' said Elena. 'Gypsies marry to have babies
too.'

'No irregular attachments?' Millicent asked.

'Well, of course,' said Elena. 'They're not just gypsies. A lot of
them are artists too. But the babies come first. And then he asked
me to tell you how much he still loved you, but from a distance.'

'Worshipped from afar in fact,' said Millicent.

'Now that's enough, our Millie,' her mother said, then to Elena:
'Please go on.'

'How you'd been an inspiration to him,' Elena said.

'That little tune he played?'

'That's the one. He has plans for that little tune. "One day it
will be big. My best," he said. "No matter what else happens in
my life." And then he gave notice.'

'*Gave notice*?' Millicent was appalled.

'That's what it amounted to. Because of your mama, you see.
She may be unattainable, but she'd be so close.' Gertie's sigh was
ecstatic. 'So he wants to go to Bayonne.'

'But how will we manage?' Millicent asked.

'He has a cousin in Granada. Antonio. "Almost as good as
me," he said. I liked the "almost" – and asked me to write to him,
and I did. Pedrillito will stay till he comes.'

'Oh, the poor, sweet lamb,' said Gertie, and wiped her eyes.
Millicent looked at her carefully, but her mother wept as she did

at the cinema sometimes, for an orphan in a storm . . .

Papa looked at the women in front of him. 'My lucky day,' he said, and indeed they were a sight worth seeing: one older woman, still elegant, still pretty, and two younger ones at the height of their beauty. He raised his glass.

'To the three Graces,' he said, then peered more closely at the mature beauty flanked by youth.

'Good Lord,' he said. 'It's Gertie Bewick.'

'That takes me back a bit,' said Gertie.

'You used to live on the estate,' said Lord Aylmer. 'Your father was the best dog trainer we ever had.' He continued remembering and never once was the word 'servant' used. No wonder the Channings were held in such affection.

'But why this Garnet business?' her father asked.

'My stage name,' said Gertie. 'I know it sounds a bit funny, but it's meant to be. I used to be the soubrette you see – dance for 'em, sing for 'em, and make them chuckle too. But I always looked pretty.'

'I bet you did. You've looked pretty since the day I first saw you.' Gertie looked delighted. Two in one day – and both of them distinguished in their way. At her age.

'But Blenkinsop,' said Lord Aylmer. 'That wasn't a stage name, surely?'

'Married name,' said Gertie. 'Millie's dad.' And then, before Lord Aylmer could ask: 'In the Navy. Died of wounds. Leastways, that's what I call it. On the certificate it says pneumonia – but it was hours and hours in the freezing cold – that's what killed him. Big an enemy as the U-Boats, the cold.'

'Quite right,' Lord Aylmer said.

Gertie finished her drink. That night Elena and her father were dining tête-à-tête, while she and her daughter dined in her daughter's room, served by a footman – another marvel in her life, which, quite recently, had been crammed full of marvels. She left them to it.

'And that's about it, really,' said Elena's father. 'There's not a lot to tell. Not much worth the telling when all you do is sit and think.'

'My father will take his port here,' said Elena. 'I'll stay with him.'

'Good idea,' said Lord Aylmer, and Tufnell bowed, fetched the decanter and left them to it.

'You did rather more than just sit and think,' said Elena.

'Being on the staff you mean?' Elena nodded. 'Who told you?'

'Oswin,' said Elena. 'He's very proud of you.'

'God knows why,' said her father. 'He was a fighting soldier for more than two years. The thing is—' He poured more port then lounged back in his chair. He isn't tired of talking yet, thought Elena. Maybe he never will be again.

'—Oswin's father was killed. The eighth duke. Lovely chap – even if he was my brother. Do anything for anybody. Even help us to get rid of our ghastly mediaeval names. Only he couldn't, apparently.' He sighed. 'Where was I?'

'Your brother the duke.'

'We were close,' said her father. 'Loved each other in fact. Nothing wrong with that.'

'Of course not,' Elena said, and her father looked at her, then was satisfied.

'Then he was killed. Shell splinters, but a flame thrower was involved too.

'I'd been going through a period of remission. Acting sanely. Even sensibly compared with some poor chaps. So I came up to London and saw a chum at the War Office.'

'It was that easy?' Elena asked.

'It should have been damn difficult, but I had some useful strings to pull. My nephew the duke, all that, and in the end my chum said, "Not the trenches, but there's a vacancy on the staff in old Richardson's division." We'd both been at school with Tim Richardson. Not a bad sort of feller, but no brains at all. He needed a good staff. Even me.'

If you could walk you were in. Just as Gertie had said.

'What my old chum meant was the staff would keep me out of harm's way. Just the place for a loony with a duke for a nephew. But it didn't work out like that.'

'It couldn't,' Elena said. 'Not with you.'

Her father smiled his thanks. 'I was good at staff work, if I says it as shouldn't,' he said. 'Earned my fodder, so to speak. Got a citation. Then the war ended and so did my remission. The trappists mustered, and I rejoined.'

'Did my mother know about this?' Elena asked.

'She knew everything,' said her father, 'but not tonight my dear. I've had enough for one night.'

'Of course,' said Elena and thought, his beloved brother butchered like that. But he'd had his revenge. That's another thing about us Channings. We may believe in forgiveness, but we believe in vengeance too.

'From what I hear, you were rather busy as well,' her father said.

'All that matrimony you mean? That was mama's idea. She thought I was the sort of girl who needed looking after.'

'But I looked after you,' said her papa. 'You know I did. And it was a pleasure as well as a duty.'

'Well, of course,' Elena said, 'only mama somehow got the idea I should be looked after in the arms of a gent. The lawfully wedded arms, that is to say.'

'Your mama did get ideas,' said her father. 'Forgive me if I say they weren't always good ideas,'

'This one was,' said Elena. 'I married Major Lampeter.'

'Was he killed?' papa asked.

'They all were,' said his daughter, 'all three,' and Lord Aylmer blinked. Three seemed to be overdoing it rather.

'Though I doubt whether Toby Crick is in Valhalla with the other two. He was killed on the hunting field.'

Papa's lips twitched. This Crick hadn't been even second favourite.

'Mind you, there were compensations,' said Elena, then hesitated.

'Oh, get on with it,' said her father, and Elena was delighted. It was exactly what a father would say.

'Booty,' she said. 'Loot.'

'Now, that will do,' said her father. 'You're not a pirate, any more than I am.'

'Maybe not a pirate,' Elena said, 'but I'm disgracefully rich. Do you know I own a manor in Hampshire and three houses in London?' And one of them coveted by a maniac, she thought. There was a pause, companionable at first, but it lengthened into a silence that was menacing.

'There's something we have to settle,' her father said, 'and until we do we can never again be as we were five minutes ago.'

She was frightened, terrified. Supposing it was something really dreadful? All the same, it had to be settled, whatever it was. She folded her hands and waited.

'Yes, papa,' she said.

Richard said, 'You told him I was coming to discuss a ride in the Row,' and Elena nodded. 'What did he say?'

'How kind,' said Elena. 'I doubt if he even heard me. Then he said, "I'm tired. I don't want to talk any more," and went off to bed.'

'Let me see if I've got it right,' Richard said. 'The obstacle to their marriage was that she was a Catholic, and he wasn't, and he wouldn't turn.'

'Indeed he wouldn't,' said Elena. 'He's a very devout Anglican. He could see no reason why he should become an unreliable Catholic. His words, not mine. But to mama it meant she was damned.'

'So neither of them would budge, but they managed to make a life together – of sorts. Except that she wouldn't acknowledge him.'

'Too ashamed,' said Elena.

'Dear God what a mess,' said Richard. 'And then you came along. His best chance to try for a solution, only he went off to the wars instead.'

'And mama was ill. Nerves the doctors called it, but it was all in her mind. She believed papa would burn.'

'*Burn?*'

But it was his brother who had burned.

'Eternally,' said Elena. 'She couldn't stand it. She loved him so much, you see. When I was old enough we used to pray together. The same prayer over and over. Holy Margaret – her patron Saint – intercede for us. Please God don't let papa go to hell for ever.'

Richard looked at her. Night after night as a tiny child, reciting all this, and yet she was so sane.

'Because one of us had done it already. Married a foreigner, a Protestant. My great-aunt Pilar. And the Protestant – he was a German – deserted her, and took all her money. And then she grew ill – cancer – and died of it. Agony, mama said. But to her, Aunt Pilar's pain was only the beginning.

'Good God,' said Richard once more, and then: 'Post-natal depression – you must have heard of it. It affects some women once a child is born. My guess is that for a while your mama was as sick as your father.'

'You seem to know a lot about it,' she said.

'I once knew someone who had it rather badly,' he said.

Someone he loved, Elena thought, but now was not the time. Instead she said, 'It might explain the money too.'

'Go on,' said Richard.

'Aunt Pilar lost all hers, so she made me marry mine. But not

192

with a German. The money it seemed was not so important.'

'You've told it all now?' he said, and she nodded.

'Want me to tell you the most important bit?'

'Please.'

'I don't want to talk any more.'

Elena gasped. The implications of those words were appalling.

'But *he* must. You must make him. Now,' said Richard.

'But how can I?'

'He's your father and you love him, and he loves you. And God knows he needs you.' He took her hands and kissed her, very gently. 'It's your only chance, my love.'

17

He was in his bed, but he lay awake. Wide awake.

'I told you I didn't want to talk any more,' he said.

She went to him and kissed his cheek. 'I've been thinking of you and mama,' she said. 'Such nonsense.'

He shot up as if she'd jabbed a needle into him. '*Nonsense?*'

'Oh, not between you and mama. I was thinking of me. I do you know, sometimes.'

Papa lay back on the bed. 'I'm sorry, child,' he said. 'Was I being selfish?'

'I don't *think* so,' said Elena. 'But never mind if you were. The point is this. I may look like mama, but I'm not Margarita, I'm me. Elena. And I don't believe in a word you've told me, except the bit about the goodness of God. And there wasn't much of that, was there? Only pain and suffering for ever. Well, that's not the way I see it. God is love, the priests say, and I believe them in *that* at least. And his blessed Mother – she's love too. Or don't you believe that, papa?'

'Well, of course,' her father said. 'It's just—'

For once she interrupted him. 'God's either love or He's a red-hot coal,' she said. 'I can't believe He's both. Notice what I said. *I* can't. Me, me, me. Now, if you can, I can't help you. If you suffer in silence because mama believed it, I still can't help you. Because I'm not Margarita. I'm me. Me. Me. And she had her beliefs and I have mine, and they coincided very rarely.' She was terrified of what she must say next, but it had to be said. 'It's up to you. Nobody else on God's earth can say it for you.'

He was silent for so long that she thought he'd reverted to the catatonic trance his doctor had talked of at such length, but he spoke at last.

'I loved her,' he said. 'I shall always love her. But she was human, fallible, she could make mistakes. She made one about you. And so did I, God forgive me.'

195

'But you couldn't help it,' said Elena. 'Neither of you could.'

'You mean she was mad too? But hers was at least the madness of faith. *Torquemada*, the hermits in the desert – even Saint Joan perhaps. But mine was just – I'd had enough. I couldn't go back to face Saint Joan. Maybe I should be grateful to that Boer farmer.'

'Papa!' said Elena.

'I said "maybe",' her father said. 'It wasn't just your mother. When the bullet hit me the entire world became too much.' Elena waited. 'I just couldn't cope with it. Not even the tiniest bit. And so I legged it: ran away and dug a hole and never even thought of coming out – until you came along and dragged me out.' But he was smiling as he said it. 'You may have cause to regret it,' he said. 'I can be a very boring conversationalist, if my memory serves me correctly.'

'I'll risk that,' said Elena.

'Good girl,' her father said, and yawned. 'Don't worry, I haven't rejoined the Trappists,' he said again. 'Just sleepy.'

Elena tucked him up, and went to the door.

'I say,' said her father, and Elena turned. 'Do you and your young man always have such profound conversations when you arrange a ride in the Row for elderly persons?'

Elena stared. A joke from papa at such a time. A victory in fact, and no small one either.

'I thank you,' Lord Aylmer said. 'Deeply. Profoundly. With my whole being in fact. I shall pray for you as soon as I wake – God likes one's prayers to make sense. God bless you, daughter.'

'And you, father.'

Lord Aylmer eased himself under the blankets. 'She'll understand,' he said. 'I know she will. I shall pray for her as well.'

'Me too, papa,' said Elena.

He knew all about it. It was in all the gossip columns after all. That young feller Edwards had been particularly busy. His stuff was signed, too. He must be getting on in the world. Soon to be a sub-editor. Wasn't that what he'd said? All the same it seemed a pity that he should join the others in such a chorus of lies. For that they were lies he had no doubt. It stood to reason.

To begin with, there was the suggestion that the Spanish bitch's parents were married. In France of all places. Well, everybody knew what 'married in France' meant. His brother officers had told him often enough. A hotel bedroom in Montparnasse, that's

what married in France meant. Besides, both Stobbs and the
Pemberton bitch had said so. Well, maybe it wasn't what they'd
said, precisely, but it was what they meant, and newspapers were
never fussy about what lies they told, and anyway the Channing
family owned a goodish chunk of the *Daily Mercury*, so it had
done what it was told and the rest had followed like sheep.

Even so, what about Mendip and his drinking and dodging the
column? Not a word. Typical, thought Pudiphatt. Typical. The
thing was he hadn't heard from the Rifles' new adjutant yet. The
old one would have written like a shot, and that was typical, too.
Nothing for it but to hang on. Ah well, he'd done enough of that
in his time. The trouble was that soon he'd have to take the
Pemberton bitch's advice: not because he wanted a little house in
St John's Wood – his address was Grosvenor Square, his house
vast, but because he was almost broke. Barely enough to keep him
in whisky, and soon not enough even for that – and then what? In
his mind he screamed at the Rifles' new adjutant: come on. Come
on.

What he needed was a treat. A treat would cheer him up no
end. The trouble was that treats cost money. But not that much.
Not this time. A very large Scotch from a bottle he'd already paid
for, and a phone call. Only tuppence, a phone call, and it would
be tuppence well spent. First he went over in his mind what he
would say, the facts and then the lies. There had to be lies, but
soon there would be treats. He was sure of it. He picked up the
phone and asked for the number.

A man's voice and then a pause, and then another man's voice,
another pause. All designed to put him off, he thought. Well, it
wasn't going to work, not this time. This time it was a *treat*. Then
a woman's voice. At last. 'Lady Mendip's house,' it said.

Well, of course it is, he thought. Silly cow. You own it and you
may think you own one in Grosvenor Square, but you're wrong,
believe me. W-R-O-N-G.

'Now, look here,' he began, and she interrupted him then and
there. Typical woman.

'This is Lady Mendip's legal adviser, Miss Blenkinsop.'

As if I cared, he thought. I wouldn't care if she emptied the
Spanish bitch's bath water . . .

'You'll do,' he said. 'I detest you too.'

Millicent looked at the telephone earpiece, but she'd heard
right, she knew she had.

'Then please be quick,' she said. 'I have several urgent calls to make. Some of them are important.' Pudiphatt blinked. Answering back had not been in his script.

'Tell her bloody ladyship,' he said at last, 'that I want her out of Grosvenor Square and the deeds made over to me by next week.'

'Don't be absurd,' the legal woman said.

'It isn't absurd at all,' said Pudiphatt. 'If she doesn't move out, I'll tell the lot. Now don't forget: better if you write it down. Out next week and the deeds made over to me. And no lawyers.' He paused to let *that* sink in.

'That's it,' he said at last.

'Or else you tell all?'

'Exactly,' said Pudiphatt.

'And just what is all?'

'Her mother's cavortings with the Channing feller. Every detail.'

'Oh, that,' said Millicent and hung up.

She hung up, thought Pudiphatt. On me. And I hadn't even started on that feller Mendip. Not that it mattered all that much. He could discharge that barrel some other time. But to hang up on me. Damn it, he thought. I was a major.

Millicent reached for her notebook. It was all nonsense, she thought. Maybe even the beginning of lunacy. All the same, better to have it on paper. And anyway he'd suggested it himself. Yet another thing to worry Elena with . . . At least she'd said nothing about the letter he'd written. Strictly speaking she should have done, but it was altogether too nasty. She'd burned it instead – and no harm done in all probability. After all, he'd said nothing about it when he phoned. Probably forgotten it. He was very near the edge and perhaps the more dangerous because of it. All the same, she'd have to tell Elena about the phone call, or would she? Elena was so happy.

'What a handsome father I've got,' said Elena, and indeed he still looked good in riding kit. 'Elderly indeed.'

'I felt elderly enough after our little chat last night.' He yawned and stretched. Tired but happy, his daughter thought. 'Tricky one, but now it's over I never felt better,' said her father. 'All the same I'll never ride like this feller.' He nodded to Richard.

'Most people don't want to,' Richard said.

'Most extraordinary sight I ever saw,' said Lord Aylmer. 'That big black brute of his tried to throw him – there in the Row.'

Elena looked at Richard, alarmed.

'No, no,' said her father. 'I did say tried. I doubt if it lasted two minutes.'

'But why bring Noche?' Elena asked. 'There are plenty of good hacks for hire.' As she spoke, Millicent joined them, and they could hear the sound of a guitar being tuned.

'Showing off,' said Richard. 'Serves me right.'

The guitar began to play, with a kind of bewildered beauty: Why did you refuse me? It said, and Gertie rose and left them, muttering about costumes, but already tears were welling. Elena turned to her father.

'It's Pedrillito's tune for Gertie,' she said. 'He loves her, but he thinks it best to go.' Her father nodded, gravely.

'You don't find it funny?' Millicent asked.

'Of course not,' said Lord Aylmer, and sat back, brooding.

I know quite a bit about love, he thought. It sent the two of us mad: gave Margarita her very own preview of hell, and locked me in my cell like an anchorite. Dangerous stuff if you're unlucky. If you're lucky – he looked at his daughter and Richard – it's Château Margaux . . .

Better tell her, thought Millicent. If Lord Aylmer ever hears – she went to Elena.

Elena said, 'Francis again?' but Millicent shook her head.

'Pudiphatt,' said Millicent. 'If I could just have a word—'

'Here,' said Elena. 'Richard knows all about it – and papa should . . . What now? The Grosvenor Square house again?'

Papa should know. So much for tact. 'He wants to move in next week. Otherwise he'll expose you and your father.'

'Dear God!' said Lord Aylmer.

'How did he sound?' Elena asked.

'Crazy,' said Millicent, 'but quite determined.' She looked at Lord Aylmer, who seemed well enough, and Millicent was glad. Apart from anything else, he hadn't laughed at mum's romance.

'You want me to go there?' Richard asked.

'No rush,' said Millicent. 'He specifically said next week.' She glanced at her notes. 'Twice.'

Richard topped up Lord Aylmer's sherry glass, and began to explain about Pudiphatt as Elena went to her friend.

'But Francis did phone you, didn't he?' she said.

'Oh, my God, he never stops,' said her friend.

'Deauville?'

'Still there,' said Millicent. 'Some rigmarole about fog in the Channel. It might well be true, but the point is he should have been back here before the fog fell.'

'But he did write that marvellous letter.'

Millicent looked at her friend. Such a darling, but far and away too soft hearted.

'Last month,' she said, 'and nothing else since except bed. And even then half the time his mind was on other things – mostly his mother.' She smiled. 'Ah well – plenty more fish in the sea.'

'And some of them rather grand ones,' said Elena.

'The duke? He wants to take me to Paris.'

'Did he say why?'

'Yes, he did. Because that's where Cartier's is.'

'Golly,' said Elena. 'You do live.'

'That's not all,' said Millicent.

'It isn't?'

'Harry Edwards. He's a journalist.'

'Of course he is. I remember. He wrote those pieces about papa and me. They were good.'

'I'm glad you think so,' said Millicent. 'You're dining with him tomorrow night.'

'I am?'

'First reserve,' said her friend. 'Since Francis is still in his fog—' she shrugged, and Elena wondered if Mr Edwards was first reserve for other things besides dinner parties.

'You'll like him,' said Millicent. 'He's rather sweet,' *Rather more than dinner parties*.

'He's already given me a prezzie,' Millicent said.

'Cartier? From a journalist?'

'No, no. He's got me elected to a club in Fleet Street. Very exclusive. Only lawyers and journalists need apply. I didn't think he'd get me past the committee, not having qualified yet. But he did. I'm down on their books as a managing clerk.'

'Did the committee see you personally?'

'Oh yes,' said Millicent. 'It's a sort of viva. As tough as taking a degree. A lot more fun though.'

'Which dress did you wear?'

'The cream and pink.'

'No wonder they let you in,' said Elena, and for the first time in ages Millicent smiled. 'Did you tell Francis?' Millicent nodded. 'And did he approve?'

'He did not,' said Millicent. 'Mr Fogbound thinks it's all terribly unladylike, and from what I gather his mother thinks so too.'

Richard and Lord Aylmer came over to join them, and there was no more to be said.

'Sad in a way, very sad,' said Lord Aylmer, 'but it's a damn nuisance as well.' He turned to Millicent. 'You did well that first time – finding a policeman. And every other time too, I gather. Even so, he's got to be stopped before the press get hold of it.'

'The press have got hold of it,' said Millicent.

'That chap Edwards?' said Lord Aylmer.

'But how did you know?'

'He seems to be specialising in us Channings just for the moment,' said Lord Aylmer. 'But he won't use it. He works for the *Daily Mercury* after all. Even the duke wouldn't wear that one, easy going as he is.'

Elena looked at her friend. How tangled her love life was becoming. Her father turned to Richard.

'You seem quite sure he's mad,' he said.

'After three and a half years of Beaumont Hamel and Vimy Ridge and third Ypres he couldn't be anything else,' Richard said.

'But my daughter tells me you did three years yourself, and you're not mad,' said his lordship.

'You'd better talk that over with Noche,' said Richard, and the others smiled, but not his lordship.

'What my quack used to call therapy,' he said. 'It's possible . . . Is he violent?'

'Not any more,' said Richard, 'but he was once. Brave, too. He got an MC for it.'

'Chap to watch,' said his lordship, and smiled. 'Tell you what. I'll do the watching and you do the restraining. Watching's a staff job.'

Pudiphatt wasn't in the least violent over lunch: short in the temper, disconnected in conversation, and for some reason behind it all, embarrassed. They were in a restaurant in the West End – a ferociously expensive one by Pudiphatt's standards, and the major wasn't wearing the gold cuff links with the regimental crest he'd worn last time. The price of the lunch?

The cause for embarrassment too, if Edwards had but known it. They were a gift, like so much else, from Charles, and now he was going to use the pawnshop's money to tell lies to a nice enough young man. Hence the embarrassment. But it was essential too: hence the lunch.

The trouble is he really believes he's making sense, thought

Harry Edwards, whereas in fact rage was making him incoherent: rage and the dawning suspicion that he might lose his fight. Impossible of course, his whole being seemed to say, and yet, and yet . . .

Edwards let him ramble on while he devoured terrine, tournedos and a really first rate St Estephe. No sense in wasting good food and drink.

'Got a story for you,' the major began, spooning up soup.

Once upon a time, thought Harry Edwards, and so it proved.

'In the first place, the newspapers were liars.'

Nothing wrong with that, thought Edwards. It's how we sell them after all. But which newspapers? What news? Though the answer was inevitable.

'That business about Cousin Charles and the house in Grosvenor Square, for instance, and Lord Mendip,' said Pudiphatt. 'Only rumours they said. Even you said it – no offence, dear boy.'

'None taken,' said Edwards. 'But surely it's true? They are only rumours after all.'

The Rifles' new adjutant had said it, too, despite what Stobbs had told him – *and* the Pemberton bitch, which rather went to show that the new adjutant had seen no active service. Didn't even know that rumour was far and away the best source of information the army had.

'But that's just the point,' said Pudiphatt, and went on to deliver a lecture about how vital rumour was.

'But surely—' Edwards began, but Pudiphatt ploughed on, unstoppable. Like a tank.

'A very grave injustice had been done as the newspapers well know, and yet the newspapers say nothing. The dead dishonoured, the living vilified, and yet the newspapers say nothing.'

He's off again, Edwards thought. A high price to pay, even for steak like that. Nice phrase though, about the living and the dead. And the poor chap obviously needed a spell in one of these rest homes he went to. He did his best to listen, but found he couldn't because it didn't make sense. And then suddenly it did, and horrendous sense it was.

'The only way,' Pudiphatt was saying. 'Go right to the top.'

'The Channings?' How could anyone in their right minds confront the Channings about the *Daily Mercury*? – but then Pudiphatt wasn't in his right mind.

'No, no,' Pudiphatt said, 'that's staff work. Behind-the-lines stuff. The battalion commander, that's the ticket.' The poor boy still looked bewildered. 'Your editor,' he said.

Oh, God, not Sexton, thought Edwards. He'll be worse than the Channings and a damn sight ruder.

'So the situation is this,' Pudiphatt was saying. 'You will go to your editor and explain things, and I—'

'Go to the editor?' How to explain to this sad, mad person that it would be like a bog Irish priest strolling in for a word with the Pope. Yet if Pudiphatt went on like that he'd have to.

'He has an office surely?' said Pudiphatt. 'See him there.'

'But—' Edwards began.

'Now, that's an order,' said Pudiphatt. 'I'm your company commander after all.'

'But I can't,' said Edwards, and at once Pudiphatt's cheeks grew mottled, his eyes glittered with fury. 'You refuse to obey an order from your superior officer?' he roared.

Very loud, thought Edwards. Already people were staring, and God alone could say what mischief he'd be up to if I let him roam loose outside.

'No, no, sir,' he said, his voice conciliatory, 'of course not. It's just that it may take a little time. He's the CO after all.'

'It has to be today,' said Pudiphatt, but he didn't say why; not then, not ever. Knowing what his fate would be, perhaps. Not wanting to. Having to.

'Mad you say?' said Sexton.

'Not raving. Not yet anyway.'

'All in good time, eh?' said Sexton. 'But we can't use it as well you know, even if he thinks he's a teapot. I'm surprised at you, Edwards. The Channings are involved.' Sounds like he isn't the only looney. Soon he'll turn mottled too, Edwards thought, and scurried into speech.

'Not the story, no,' Edwards said.

'None of the other papers would touch it either.'

'Of course not, sir. The thing is – he talks very wildly, but even so – the British Broadcasting Company—'

Sexton sat unmoved. 'Foreign newspapers,' said Edwards.

'*What?*' At the mention of newspapers Sexton was very moved indeed.

'*The New York Times, Le Figaro, Die Welt*,' said Edwards.

'He can get to them?'

'He's connected to the Lampeter family,' said Edwards. 'They have newspaper contacts – rather a lot – and after all a duke is involved. An English duke at that. *Le Figaro* would have a field day. So would the others.'

All true, he thought, and all irrelevant. The Lampeters would run a mile if they so much as saw Pudiphatt coming.

'Your point being?' said Sexton.

'Libel,' said Edwards. 'Suing.'

Sexton said something uncouth, then: 'You think the Channings would sue?'

'No,' said Edwards. 'They'd make us do that. And maybe Lady Mendip too, *and* Miss Blenkinsop.'

'Who the hell is—'

'Lady Mendip's legal adviser, sir.'

'Legal?' Edwards nodded. 'God what a mess.' He looked at Edwards. Bright lad. Frantic to get on. In ten years' time he'd be editor. Not that I'm worried, he thought. I'll be retired by then. 'Think you can clean it up?' he asked. 'The mess I mean.'

'Yes, sir.'

Sexton liked that. No coyness, no waiting to be coaxed. Just a straight affirmative. And if he couldn't he'd have said that too.

'I'll let you get on with it then,' he said, and then, 'Lady Mendip's giving one of her dancing do's tonight. Want to go?'

I'm already going, thought Edwards. My favourite lady's dancing too. All the same, no need to share all my secrets.

'Could be useful,' he said. 'Contacts and so on. But please don't ask me to review the dancing.'

Sexton smiled. 'Of course not. We've got a couple of fairies to do that.' Anybody's for a kiss and a cuddle, he thought. Sixpence each. Five for two bob. Not like you, young man. At least I hope not.

'I'll be off then,' said Edwards. 'White tie, is it?' He knew very well it was.

'Mind you look smart,' said Sexton. 'Give my regards to Lord Aylmer, and not a word about the foreign press.'

We'll see about that, thought Edwards.

Only eight for dinner – Lady Mendip, Millicent, her mother, and a distant connection of the Channings – Zoe Barton. Her father owned a biggish estate in Bucks. Was there anybody who owned more than five thousand acres who wasn't related to the Channings? The late Lord Mendip certainly had been, and Lampeter too, no doubt. The men were Lord Aylmer, the duke himself, Richard Milburn, and me, Harry Edwards, trying to look as if I belonged, but what I'm here for is to snoop. No Francis

Boyce. The duke would be pleased about that, and I'm not exactly in despair. All the same two dogs and only one bone, and the other dog with a pedigree longer than a supreme champion's at Crufts. Still, if you never ask—

Dinner was excellent. Well, of course it was. Elena's chef had seen to that – but even so Elena and Millicent ate very little, to Lord Aylmer's surprise. But that was because they were about to dance, Gertie explained. They'd make up for it at supper.

Elena and Lord Aylmer went to the ballroom to greet the early guests, and Edwards waited until it was possible to invite the surviving Channing to stroll on the terrace. Pudiphatt, he explained, and the duke sighed. Millicent was dancing with a chap he'd never liked, but the dance was almost ended. All the same he went with Uncle Aylmer to be told about Pudiphatt, damn the man.

Mad – well, of course he was. Known fact. All the same, Edwards was doing something about it. He'd discovered that it was possible to have the mad major put away for a bit. One of those military hospitals that specialised in – well – loonies. Not only that, but Edwards had persuaded him that very afternoon to an indefinite stay. A week to put his affairs in order, then off he'd toddle. The ideal solution. Vaguely the duke wondered if Edwards had ever been to Staff College. Uncle Aylmer certainly had, and approved without a doubt. So did he, come to that. Not that he'd ever been to Staff College. Cavalry had been his choice, and none of your Blues and Royals either. A yeomanry regiment, and a good choice it had been. Palestine and General Allenby, and a cavalry charge, a whole division of them. Australians mostly, and by God could they ride. Best day out he'd ever had. Even a day with the Beaufort was nothing to it . . . He called himself to order. He was letting his mind wander, and knew all too well why. All the same the chap had brains.

'Plus a small pension,' Edwards was saying.

'Found among Major Lampeter's papers. No doubt he was taking care of it for him.'

And we all know who found it, thought the duke. Millicent bless her. As clever as she's beautiful.

'Will it be enough?' he asked. 'I don't mind contributing.'

'More than adequate,' said Edwards. 'He assured me himself.'

How to tell a duke that what Pudiphatt had really said was that he wouldn't take anyone's damn charity?

'So it amounts to this,' he said. 'The major's withdrawn from circulation at least long enough for the duke's business manager to do something about *Le Figaro* and the rest.'

'Well done, old chap,' said Lord Aylmer.

'Yes, indeed,' said the duke, hoping he sounded sincere.

18

Time for the dance recital. A lot of people had paid a lot of money to see them, but it was Elena's father they danced for, and the charity he had chosen as beneficiaries – shell-shocked officers and men. A little extra for Pudiphatt, thought Millicent, as she took the Goya pose with Elena, now so familiar to London Society. Even so, the applause roared out, then Pedrillito struck the opening chords on his guitar and the dancing began.

Gertie, watching from the wings, thought: They've never danced better. But then she loves her father, and why not? He's a lovely man. And far more style than – she interrupted herself. Later, she thought. Save that for later. See what the night brings. Just look at your girls. And indeed they were worth looking at: a performance quite flawless, so that when they finished at last, the applause was deafening as the audience begged and pleaded for more, but they had no more to give. One more bow, one more elegant curtsey, and they were gone to the wings where Gertie waited with towels and champagne, before transforming them from Elena and Rosario to Lady Mendip and Miss Blenkinsop, LL B.

'Wonderful,' said Gertie, 'wonderful,' and Elena went to her bath in a daze of happiness because her father had applauded more loudly than anybody else, and talked excitedly to the people on either side of him as he did so. 'My daughter,' he'd be saying. 'My daughter.' And then, rather belatedly 'and her friend Miss Blenkinsop'. Darling papa. Miss Blenkinsop danced almost exclusively with Harry Edwards and Oswin. No Foggy Francis to worry about, thank God, and it wasn't every day that a duke fetched her toast and caviare and smoked salmon. No Krug, but Harry assured her that the Roederer Cristal reserved by Tufnell for the chosen few was as good, and indeed it was. Dancing really did give one an appetite, she thought, and not just for food and drink. She smiled at her attendant lords, and Zoe Barton wondered what they saw in her, but the answer was obvious. She wasn't just beautiful, she was a star.

Sitting out with Lord Aylmer, Gertie watched, and saw at once what her daughter was up to. It was as good as a play. No – not a play, like the pictures: all sight and no sound. There was even music: the band provided that, and she could understand every move. I should know, she thought. I've done a bit in that line myself. All the same, two really good looking chaps, and one of them a duke. Eeny, meeny, miny—

'Penny for them,' Lord Aylmer said.

Her eyes still on her daughter, Gertie said, 'Just thinking what a good night it's been.' Millie smiled at that Mr Edwards. Never a truer word, she thought.

'Best night I've had in years,' Lord Aylmer said. 'Did me proud all three. All four, I should say.'

'Four?'

'Elena, your daughter, the little guitarist, and you.'

'But I did nothing.'

'You did the devil of a lot,' Lord Aylmer said. 'Trained them, drilled them or whatever you call it, even got them started. I'm more grateful than I can say.'

'What will you do tomorrow night?' Gertie asked. Millie dancing with the duke this time, and that Mr Edwards far from happy.

'The four of them are off to the Savoy to dance,' Lord Aylmer said. 'They invited me, too. Nice of them, but—' he shrugged. 'It's me for the Guards' Club,' he said.

Doesn't sound exactly bliss, thought Gertie. Millie was chatting with both her chaps, while she drank champagne and ate lobster salad. And no wonder, she thought. Dancing can make you ravenous, the way you burn off the energy . . . Now she was smiling at both of them, giving each one just as much as the other. Like kids sharing sweets. And then the laughter . . . Got it off to a 'T', she thought. Just like me before I met Bert. And why not? That Francis will never make a Bert. Not in a thousand years. Nor would Lord Aylmer, but even so . . .

'There's a sort of club I know,' she said. 'Soho. Mews off Compton Street – but all very respectable. Caters for our generation, and very nice too. Even the music. All that. Good food. Good wine.'

'Sounds delightful,' Lord Aylmer said.

'All of that.' She looked straight ahead. 'We could go there, if you don't fancy the Guards' Club.'

'A bit short notice surely.'

'I'm known there,' said Gertie, and Lord Aylmer tensed. 'What I mean is the ones that own it are chums – old pro's like me.'

Lord Aylmer relaxed. 'I'd love to take you there, and not so much of the "old". But I thought little Pepe sulked if you went out without him.'

'So he does,' said Gertie, 'and I don't want to hurt him. Especially just now. But—'

'But what?'

'Elena said you'd been on – the Staff, did she call it?'

'So I was, not being fit for anything else.'

'That meant bossing whole armies about, according to Elena.'

'A division anyway.'

'A heck of a lot of fellers, whatever you call it.'

'Oh thousands,' Lord Aylmer said.

'There you are then,' Gertie, who had had rather a lot of Roederer Cristal, lapsed into silence as if her point were made.

'Gertie,' Lord Aylmer said. 'My dear.'

My dear, Gertie thought. We're coming along nicely.

'I don't think you'd quite finished,' Lord Aylmer said.

'Good lord, you're right,' said Gertie. 'What I meant to say was a chap who could go bossing a whole division should be able to see off one little Spaniard.'

'I'll have to think,' said Lord Aylmer.

'So long as you do it before tomorrow night,' said Gertie.

In the end she decided on Harry Edwards. He'd been working jolly hard and deserved a treat. Besides, she and the duke would be off to Paris soon – Cartier's and all that – and as Elena said, she needed a holiday, *and* she'd leave enough work for young Mr Barnes to keep him away from the golf club. So Harry Edwards it would be.

Rather too much like her for comfort, but a nice man all the same. She lured Elena to their dressing room to tell her she'd be spending the night in Hammersmith, and all Elena did was grin. What an employer. What a friend, she thought, because all she said was 'Don't you ever get tired?' and then, 'Have you told Gertie?'

'Later,' said Millicent. 'Too late tonight. Not that it'll bother her. If she doesn't know already.'

'But how could she?' Elena asked.

'There isn't much mum doesn't know about girls and chaps together,' said Millicent.

Gertie did already know, but she'd gone off to bed early. Too much champagne, and in any case tomorrow night would be even better than tonight, if her luck was in . . .

Best to take her by surprise and go round at once, he thought. True, Elena was giving a ball, but the packet had made good time, and just as well after all those delays, and for a ball it wasn't all *that* late. She'd still be there; Millicent never left a ball till the end.

The butler – Tufnell wasn't it? – blinked when he saw his lounge suit, but was otherwise impassive and said he'd see: even let him in as far as the hall, where he could watch the dancers. It would be all right, he thought, and there'd be so much to tell. Mummy absolutely stony broke after a bad run at chemmy, but he, Francis, as steadfast as one of the burghers of Calais. Not a penny would he advance, well, not until he'd spoken to Millicent, and even then, hers would be the decision. He waited and listened to the music. 'I Want To Be Happy'. And so do I, he thought, and I will, too. Then Elena came to him in a ball dress of green that seemed to have been designed specially to enhance the glory of her emeralds. Perhaps it had been. Not far off Lord Aylmer stood hovering but Elena would need no protection from him.

'Francis what a surprise,' said Elena.

Francis murmured about calm seas and a fog that had lifted at last.

'But why call at this hour?' Elena asked.

'Well, to be frank,' said Francis, 'Millicent and I had a bit of a tiff before I set off for Deauville – and I thought it might be a good idea to set matters right.'

'But so late,' said Elena, 'and at a ball, too.'

'Not late for a ball surely?' said Francis. 'And I really would like to settle matters.'

His voice had risen slightly, and Lord Aylmer strode over to them.

'Something wrong?' he asked, and looked at Francis, his eyes all too aware of a chap who tries to enter a ballroom in a lounge suit. A chap moreover who hadn't been invited.

Oh God, Francis thought. I'm muffing it.

'Mr Boyce rather wanted a word with Millicent,' said Elena. 'I haven't had time to explain that she'd gone to bed early. Headache,' she explained.

From where he stood, Lord Aylmer could see his nephew dancing, not altogether blissfully, with Zoe Barton. Of Millicent there was no sign, so it might well be true, except that that smart young feller from the *Daily Mercury* was nowhere to be seen either.

'Ah,' said Lord Aylmer, and Elena looked at him warily. Already she knew enough about her father to realise that not only did he know what was going on: he was enjoying it. She hurried into speech.

'I honestly think it would be better if you came back tomorrow,' she said.

'But not in the evening,' said her father, in that same ready-to-be-amused voice. 'I understand she has an engagement tomorrow evening – if she's well enough that is.'

'Millicent's headaches never last long,' said Elena. 'Come to tea.'

He wanted to argue. His business with Millicent was vital, even urgent, but Lord Aylmer had rung for Tufnell, who besides being a very large butler had served as a Guardsman.

'I'll call you a taxi, sir,' he said, in a voice there was no denying.

Harry Edwards had been appalled when she told him he must leave: gratifyingly so in fact, but he was a clever young man who used his brains, thought Millicent, and dressed almost as quickly as she did herself. She'd make it up to him, she thought. She owed him that much at least, and besides, they were scarcely halfway through what had promised to be a quite delicious encounter. Definitely she would make it up to him . . .

Edwards made his way towards his own flat in South Kensington. Lust, affection, and a duke in the background took rather a lot of assimilating. Vaguely he wondered what his chances of a taxi would be. Not good, he thought. Not at that hour of the night, but even as he thought it one rattled to a halt and Francis Boyce got out, not happy at all. Edwards flagged it down as Boyce banged on the knocker like a timpanist practising fortissimi. One rival making use of another one's transport. Symbolism there, thought Edwards, with irony, but just at the moment he was much too tired to consider what it might mean . . .

The door opened at once, which surprised him. After Eaton Place and all that nonsense about headaches he had known at once where Millicent would be and he'd been right. But not about what she wore: a tailor-made coat and skirt. By no means the negligée of his imaginings.

'Oh, it's you,' she said. 'You'd better come in, I suppose.'

Hardly, Darling I've missed you so, but he followed her inside, into the living room. She'd made coffee for herself he noticed, but there was none for him.

'Now look here,' he said, 'I've travelled God knows how many miles to see you and—'

She interrupted him ruthlessly.

'Can it be,' she said, 'can it really be, that you've tracked me down at this time of night just to make a speech crammed full of the first person singular?'

But he was in too deep for apologies. 'Yes it can,' he said. 'In the first place I thought you'd be at Elena's ball, not in our flat.'

Our flat was a good'un she thought. He always fights harder after a spell with Mummy.

'And who told you I'd be here?' she asked.

'Nobody,' said Francis. 'I worked it out.'

'And did you work out why I'm here?'

'Perhaps,' he said, 'but I'm hoping I'm wrong.'

Another good punch, she thought. Mummy *has* trained him well. And now *you're* going to hurt him, Millie Blenkinsop, because there's no other way.

'While you were being fogbound in France,' she said, 'Pudiphatt popped out of the woodwork.'

'I don't understand,' Francis said.

'Of course not,' said Millicent. 'I hadn't finished. He tried to speak to Elena but he got me instead. He sounded madder than ever, and so I had a word with the bobby on the beat over here. Though how he got my address—' Something I should have done ages ago, she thought. I'm having far too good a time, but that's no excuse. 'The policeman called him a prowler, but he sounded like Pudiphatt. Tonight he thought he'd got him, and the station phoned to ask us to send someone round. At the height of a ball? The night of our dance recital in Lord Aylmer's honour? There was nothing else for it. I came here myself.'

'You should have sent for me as soon as it started,' Francis said.

'Chance would have been a fine thing,' said Millicent.

No need to go on about plucky little women. He could work that out for himself. And even if it wasn't true, it sounded right.

'You'd have come marching through the snow and ice with a banner labelled Excelsior, no doubt.'

'Damn it I didn't know,' he said. 'How could I?'

'You preferred your mother's company to mine,' she said, and sighed: one of her patient, long-suffering ones. 'Very well. Since you're here, let's get on with it.'

'Now isn't the time,' he said.

'But you've just come God knows how many miles to tell me about it,' she said. 'How can it not be the time?'

It took him forever, but he got it out at last.

'You here, in our flat,' he began, but she wouldn't let him try that one a second time.

'What's the matter with here?' she began and then, after a pause: 'Oh, *I see*. You thought I'd brought another chap here.'

'I didn't say—' he began.

'But you thought,' said Millicent. 'Who was it, Francis? The Duke of Bellingham? Lord Aylmer? Though, mind you, Lord Aylmer must have been something special in his day.'

Francis scowled. My goodness, he was possessive. Even conjecture could do it.

'Of course not,' he said.

'Or His Grace?'

'He's a duke,' said Francis. 'He wouldn't.'

'He's a man,' said Millicent, but Francis merely shrugged. Dukes, it seemed were immune.

'Who then,' she asked. 'There must be someone to explain all this fuss.'

'I told you,' said Francis. 'Now isn't the time.'

She ignored him, pretending to think hard. At last she said, 'Could it be, could it possibly be that you're jealous of Harry Edwards?'

'You were seeing a lot of him while I was in Deauville,' he said.

'I was seeing a lot of His Grace, too, and for the same reason. Trying to avoid a scandal, as you well know. After all, the Channings are Elena's family too, it seems. I worked at it flat out, and so did Mr Edwards. And I must say he knows what he's doing – and it wasn't making love to me.'

Very pleasant lust, she thought, but not love. Once more she pretended to think. 'And anyway, since you live in Deauville, how did you know I was seeing Edwards? Who told you? Your mother? Hearing from some crony writing from London?'

'Damn it, she thought we were engaged,' said Francis. 'So did I for that matter. Are we?'

'You tell me,' said Millicent. 'You in Deauville with Mummy, and me in London working my socks off. You tell me, Francis dear.'

'You keep dragging Mummy into it.'

213

'Nobody drags your mummy,' Millicent said. 'She pushes hard and the rest of us make room.'

'You're not wearing my ring,' he said.

'So we *are* engaged?' He made no answer. 'You don't mean to say she's found you another one?' said Millicent.

'She's found a girl she thinks I might be happy with,' said Francis.

'Which means Mummy will be happy with her too,' said Millicent. 'But will you be happy with her?'

'I don't know,' he said. His voice was a wail.

'And am I to be told who she is?'

Daisy Hudspeth. Father in trade, and well on his way to his first million. Trust Mummy. But in the meantime she wanted Francis's diamonds back. Not a hope.

'Well, are we or aren't we?' she asked. No answer. 'What I mean is, am I to stay in this pre-marital limbo indefinitely? Not engaged and not not engaged? Put the poor maiden out of her misery. Well, perhaps not maiden precisely—'

'I suppose that's my fault too,' he said, and that annoyed her. It really did.

'Well, at least half of it was,' she said. 'I was there at the time – or had you forgotten?'

He flushed at that: a dark, unpleasing red. 'I'm sorry,' he said. 'I didn't mean—'

'You never mean,' said Millicent. 'Shut up and listen.'

He sat up then, ramrod straight, as if he were up back at school and in front of his housemaster, accused of smoking cigarettes, charge not yet proven.

'The last time we played this little scene – no wonder it goes so well by the way. So many performances – I warned you. Do it again and I'll leave you. Do you remember that?'

He flushed at that. He's afraid I'll tell him to leave, she thought.

'I meant it then. You'd hurt me very badly' – he had too – 'but on second thoughts maybe that was moving too quickly. I'll give you a little while to tell me if it's yes or no. Three or four days. That should be enough . . . Well?'

'And if it's yes, will you have me back?'

Suddenly she was yelling. 'I don't bloody know,' she said, 'but at least I won't have you thrown out on your ear, which is what I want to do now. Take me home.'

'I beg your pardon?' said Francis.

This time her long suffering sigh wasn't acting.

'Take me to Eaton Place,' she said. 'I call it home because I live there. Go and find a cab, preferably with a wheel at each corner, and *take me home.*'

Gertie set her stitches neatly and precisely, the way Lady Mary had taught her all those years ago. A present for Elena, a handkerchief, and it had to be just right. It would be for her birthday, after all. Soon be our Millie's, she thought, but it wouldn't be a handkerchief she wanted. Asprey's at least, but preferably Cartier. And she'd get there. You had to hand it to Millie. Like a juggler. Three chaps in the air at the same time. A coronet, a notebook and pen, and a – what would Francis be? A money bag? But would it be full enough? Not that it mattered. At the end of the day she'd get what she wanted. Just like me, she thought, and if at the end of the day a couple of chaps' feelings were hurt, well that was a risk chaps had to take when they played with the big girls.

Lord Aylmer came up and joined her. Not much chance of his feelings being hurt, she thought, but then she didn't want to hurt them.

'Any luck?' she asked.

'Quite a lot,' said Lord Aylmer. 'Any chance of a cup of tea?' She rang for Tufnell.

Lord Aylmer settled in his chair. 'Spanish gypsies can be tricky, according to my daughter. But then I remembered that English gypsies knew a thing or two as well. Travellers' Green . . . Do you remember?'

'They used to camp there, according to my dad,' said Gertie. 'Always poaching,' he said.

'Those lurchers were even better poachers than their owners,' said Lord Aylmer. 'Rabbits and hares mostly, but they weren't above the odd partridge. You could warn them till you were black in the face. The game still went.

'Most of them were Catholics, but they feared neither God nor Devil. The only thing that bothered them was priests. Couldn't stand a priest. For some reason priests frightened the life out of them.'

A parlourmaid arrived, and Gertie poured tea, made sure the cucumber sandwiches were within easy reach. He's enjoying this, Gertie thought, and why not? So far it's all true.

'So we sent for Mr Perkins – you remember him?'

'The chaplain,' said Gertie.

'Quite right,' said Lord Aylmer. 'He was High.'

'High?' said Gertie.

'High Church. Went over to Rome eventually, but the point is he had all the regalia. Robes and things. So we coaxed him into wearing them then walking past the camp – and that's all it took. By next morning they were gone.'

'I see,' said Gertie.

'I bet you do,' said Lord Aylmer. 'You're as clever as you're pretty.'

'Oh, get on with it,' said Gertie, by no means displeased.

'So I thought – if it works for English gypsies, why not Spanish? And I went to the studio where he was practising. Just as well I speak a little Spanish. Anyway, I just happened to mention we had a priest looking in tonight and he nearly dropped his guitar.'

'Didn't he ask why?'

'He did. No fool, little Pepe. I said this was the day we hold a service to commemorate the dead.'

'Is it?' Gertie asked.

'No idea,' said Lord Aylmer, 'but it shook him. Shook him badly . . . Then I told him that after a glass of sherry we'd be going to the church, and invited him along. There'd be a lot more priests there, and afterwards they'd be coming back here for a light supper. I suggested he look in and play the guitar for them. Unique opportunity, I said.'

'And what did he say?'

'That he rather thought he'd made arrangements to go to the cinema.'

'Clever you,' said Gertie. 'Never mind the staff. You'd have finished up with the general's job.'

'Useful things cinemas,' said Lord Aylmer. 'What I mean is the words don't matter. The story's in the pictures.' He finished the sandwiches and selected an éclair.

'All the same he's rather sad,' said Gertie.

'That may well be,' said Lord Aylmer. 'But I'm not. Not if you'll let me take you to this club of yours . . .'

'He's so wet,' said Millicent. 'Absolutely soggy.'

All the same, what her friend had done was disgraceful, Elena thought, and Millicent was hazily aware of it too. But only hazily. Millicent would never just stand there looking pathetic. She'd go on the attack at once. Indeed, had already done so.

'All the same—' said Elena.

'Oh, I know,' said Millicent. 'All those threats and lies. But I can't help fighting any more than Francis can help looking pathetic.' Suddenly her look softened: became worried even. 'You're not too angry are you?'

But what she meant was, Oh, my God, I don't want to lose your friendship. I couldn't bear it. And especially not for a weed like Francis.

Elena shrugged. 'As you say, it's the way you are,' she said, 'and heaven knows, I've been glad of it sometimes. But—'

Yet again Millicent sighed, but not as she'd sighed for Francis. 'Yes, darling?'

'Couldn't you let him down more lightly – just once?'

'Honestly, I try,' said Millicent. 'I try every time. It's just that when he gets to a certain point I let fly. Not that I'm proud of myself. In a weird sort of way he *makes* me do it.'

'What about Harry Edwards? Or the duke for that matter?'

'The duke would just walk away. Peace and quiet are what he likes – and oddly enough he gets them. Even from me.'

'And Harry Edwards?'

'He'd hit me back – literally or metaphorically,' Millicent said and added, relishing the thought: 'He'd be good at it too. He's just been on the phone to me as a matter of fact.' She smiled at the look on Elena's face. 'No, no. Not ardour, just business. It seems the mad major's committed himself to that mental home in Berkshire. Quite likes it apparently—'

'Oh good,' said Elena.

'Yes, isn't it? Let's talk about what we're going to wear tonight.'

In the end she settled for a blue that was as aggressively beautiful as herself: the colour of peacocks, and a design by Mr Bernstein that echoed Erté, but not enough to sue, and her – or Francis's – diamonds. Elena wore yellow of a pale softness: the only yellow that was kind to her dark skin, designed by Marthe Caillot as yet another setting for her emeralds. She looked first at her friend, then herself in the mirror.

'We'll do,' she said, to Millicent's relief. Next to her mother, Elena was the most ruthless critic she knew.

The Rolls-Royce was waiting to take them to the Savoy, and a look on their lovers' faces showed how much they agreed with Elena: dinner at once, and champagne, and dancing between courses; one steps and foxtrots and the Black Bottom, and always the Charleston, because, thought Millicent, at the end of the day there was no other dance quite like it.

All that and people staring, because they were really rather famous and could dance like Spanish gypsies as well as English roses. It was all most satisfactory thought Millicent, and Harry could dance quite well, and Richard could dance brilliantly, when he put his mind to it. He didn't always.

Harry, she thought, I owe a debt to Harry. He'd been awfully sweet about it, which was pleasing, and yet frantic with frustration which was even more pleasing. Definitely she owed Harry a debt, which she determined to repay as soon as possible: perhaps even that night.

Richard said, 'Your father certainly knows how to ride.'

'He said the same about you,' said Elena.

'Yes, but – he wants to ride Noche,' said Richard. She had been relaxed in his arms, a foxtrot for a change, and perfect for relaxing, but now she stiffened.

'And will you let him?' she asked.

'My best girl's father?' he said. 'Not if I can help it. Trouble is' – he thought of Gertie and how close they'd become so quickly – 'your father seems rather good at getting what he wants. I'd better sell him.'

'Sell Noche,' said Elena, 'but you can't.' It would be, she knew, a tremendous sacrifice.

'He is rather a one man horse,' said Richard. Just as I'm rather a one man woman Elena thought, but kept it to herself. No sense in rushing things.

'We can't have him killing a perfect stranger,' said Richard. 'Tell you what. I'll send him back to Oxford tomorrow – soon be the hunting season after all – and give him croup or the staggers or something, and by the time he's recovered your father may have thought of something else.'

Some*body* else, thought Elena. But all the same, what a darling he was.

Altogether a delightful evening, Millicent thought. Soothing, relaxing, utterly devoid of excitement for a change. And then it happened. It was Richard who saw it first, but then sergeants saw most things first, which was why they were sergeants: but Millicent was on to it almost as quickly, and at once her jaw sagged, her eyes stared astounded, so that for once that elegant, imperturbable young lady looked neither elegant nor imperturbable. And no wonder. On the other side of the room two people were being ushered to a table. A young woman unknown to her and Francis Boyce.

'Good God,' said Richard, and he and Harry Edwards stared, awestruck by Francis's rash courage.

'I'd never have believed it,' Richard said.

'From what you've told me, neither would I,' said Harry Edwards.

Elena waited in silence. It was definitely her friend's move. She would follow her lead of course, but this time it was her friend who must give it. Usually it happened at once: Millicent silently competent, ready to strike, eager even. But not this time. First she reassembled her beauty as a mechanic might repair a car, so that her jaw was back in place, her eyes no longer popped, but were part of the cool composure that contributed so much to her beauty.

'Well, well, well,' she said, and accepted a cigarette from Edwards' case. She needs it, thought Elena, and so do I, come to that, and took one, allowing Richard to light it.

'The Savoy of all places,' said Millicent. 'I've never been insulted at the Savoy before.'

'First time for everything,' said Richard, and she glowered enough to imperil that cool and competent beauty.

'And who's the lady?' said Millicent. 'Miss Daisy Hudspeth do you suppose?'

'Well, of course,' said Elena, who knew all about Miss Hudspeth, and Harry Edwards and Richard, who knew just enough, nodded in agreement.

'Quite pretty,' Millicent said. 'Just like him.' She turned on Richard. 'And what did you mean, first time for everything?'

'He means that you're adorable in the Savoy too,' said Edwards.

Oh, I do like him, Elena thought.

'So. It's fifteen all,' said Millicent, 'and Francis to serve. But you and I can give him a game. Can't we, darling?'

'Damn right we can,' said her Harry, and Millicent smiled at him. She had no doubt that Francis would be watching.

Richard looked again at Francis and said, 'Good God!' because as soon as Francis realised he'd caught their eye he raised his champagne glass in a toast.

'How to destroy him,' Millicent mused. 'Saint Sebastian shot full of arrows or Saint Lawrence on his grid iron? Decisions. Decisions.'

It's gone very deep thought Elena, and I'm not surprised, but she did ask for it . . .

They danced once more then Elena suddenly sensed someone was watching them. Millicent sensed it too and looked towards her as Miss Hudspeth signalled.

'Will you—?' the look asked.

'Might as well,' Millicent signalled in return. 'If you never ask you never learn,' and excused herself to the men, who stood up dutifully, then looked at each other, bewildered, though to the women it had been as plain as a page of typescript. Millicent went towards the 'Ladies' and within seconds Miss Hudspeth followed.

At least it's empty, thought Millicent, and touched up her lips as Miss Hudspeth came in.

'This is most kind of you,' she said. Millicent said nothing, just waited.

Always wait before you speak. That had been one of Duckhouse's, and jolly useful it had been, even if Duckhouse was an old bastard.

'I wanted a word about Francis,' said Miss Hudspeth, 'obviously,' and Millicent nodded because what else could it be?

'I rather gathered – forgive me – that you and he were considered a pair.'

'No apologies necessary,' Millicent said. 'We were. But quite briefly.'

Just long enough for him to take my virtue, she thought, though I did aid and abet rather.

'Then you're no longer—?'

'I told him that was rather up to him. Yesterday. On his return from Deauville. I take it he's made his choice. The queen is dead, long live the queen. Is that it? But just a teeny bit hasty, wouldn't you say?'

'You mean you didn't know about me?'

'Not the foggiest,' said Millicent.

'Good God,' said Miss Hudspeth. It was at that point that Millicent began to believe her. 'But I've been seeing him for weeks.'

'No doubt he thought it more tactful not to tell me.'

'It was because of his mother you see,' and Millicent nodded. Most things about him were because of his mother, but even so she waited once more.

'I think it's to do with the fact that I'm rich,' said Miss Hudspeth.

Of course it was, Evadne what's-it was rich, too. Probably others as well, though Darling Francis seems a dab hand at keeping them hidden. Aloud she said, 'I'm not.'

'Then why—' Miss Hudspeth blushed a not unpleasing pink. 'I'm sorry,' she said.

'Don't be,' said Millicent. 'I think probably because we fell in love without his mother's knowledge. At least, I thought we did. Love's young dream. All that.'

'Love?' said Miss Hudspeth.

'Well, I thought so at the time,' said Millicent, and again she shrugged.

'If I may ask—' Miss Hudspeth said.

'We'll see.'

'What was it that made you like him so?'

'He was so sweet,' said Millicent, 'and malleable. Like clay under one's hand. I felt with my help he might get somewhere. And then I met Mummy,' she brooded. 'Two years at the front, a wound stripe, twice mentioned in despatches, and yet as soon as Mummy says "Jump" Francis jumps. Don't you find that?'

'Well, yes,' said Miss Hudspeth, 'but I honestly don't mind. I find it restful, you see.'

'Restful?' said Millicent. 'It nearly drove me potty.'

'I can see that it would,' Miss Hudspeth said. 'But let me explain. Try to, anyway.' She paused, then, 'I have three brothers and my father living,' she said. 'My mother is dead. Of flu, the death certificate says, but I think it was mostly terror. She liked calm, tranquillity, you see, whereas all the men were bossy. Especially father. I honestly think he was cursing the midwife as he left his mother's womb. Mercifully, he spends most of his time in Birmingham. The family business is there.' She paused again and smiled. 'When I met Francis he seemed as calm and tranquil as my mother.'

'You can afford him?' Millicent asked. After all, she'd answered some pretty nosey questions herself.

'Oh, yes,' Miss Hudspeth said. 'My mother was rich in her own right. She left me the lot. I can afford to marry him.'

'What about mummy?'

'Get rid of her,' said Miss Hudspeth. 'It's easy enough when one is rich.'

All right for some, Millicent thought, but then Dad never ever shouted at Mum and me.

'I wish you luck,' said Millicent.

'Thank you,' said Miss Hudspeth, and then, out of the blue, 'She's still after your diamonds.'

★ ★ ★

'We thought of sending a search party,' said Elena.

'Sorry,' said Millicent, 'but it was all so interesting.'

'Your revenge?' Harry Edwards asked.

'I rather think that's taken care of, and I shan't have to lift a finger,' said Millicent . . .

19

A marvellous night, really marvellous, thought Gertie. Just like the old days before Bert, except that it was better. They had eaten at the Arcadians, 'that club of hers', as Aylmer called it, and it had been the red carpet all the way. Well, of course it had. It was owned by Reg and Freddy, and nothing, they said, was too good for her. *And* they approved of Aylmer. Not only that, but after a bit of chit chat he approved of them. Real Edwardian food: Barnsley chops, even brown bread ice-cream, and waltzes to tunes she had thought she would never hear again, then back to Eaton Place and her room, which was as feminine and frilly as his was austere, and love that was easy and relaxing and kind, and after it the sort of chat she thought had turned to silence for ever after Bert died. He even approved of Millie. Gertie wondered how long she had. It was all so perfect.

'Brave as a lioness,' he was saying. 'And twice as beautiful.'

'A lot of people are afraid of her.'

'And so they should be, if they attack the ones she loves. She looks generous, too.'

'Oh, she is,' said Gertie. 'As – a friend of mine used to say: When she gives she uses both hands.'

Her father, he thought. You were going to say her father. And why not? Half the time you were together, I was bloody raving. He paused there. Change key, thought Gertie.

'About us,' he said. Here it comes, she thought. 'I know it's a bit short notice – just one night of bliss and all that—' Gertie clenched her fists, 'but I wondered if we might stay – together – at least for a while.' He hurried on before she could speak.

'I'm – fond of you, you know. You'll say it's a bit early to talk about love, but fondness too can be wonderful. And then I can take care of you – which would mean no more worries about your daughter.'

'Take care of me?'

'There's something you should know about us Channings. We're so rich it's disgusting. It won't last, it can't, but while it does I see no reason why we shouldn't have our whack. It works like this. In most families like ours the younger sons have to get a job. Nothing vulgar of course. No dirty hands. The navy, the army, the law, the Church. Stuff like that. But with the Channings even the likes of me needn't bother. Not unless we want to. Like me in the Coldstream. Remember Lady Mary and Lord Arthur?'

'Oh, yes,' Gertie said.

'Never made a day's pay in their lives, even if they did work like dogs. But even if they hadn't wanted to work the cash would still be there.

'Take my case. The Brigade doesn't need me so I live here. Or in Northumberland. But that's out of choice. I could rent a flat in Mayfair if I wanted. *And* I've got a house in Berkshire. Nothing grand – ten rooms – but very comfortable. What do you say?'

'You'd let me live in your house?'

'Love – or fondness – would find a way,' said Aylmer. 'Bit of staff work. But I think we should go jaunting first. France suit you?'

'Paris?'

'No,' said Aylmer. 'Not just at the moment.' He chuckled. 'You never know who you might bump into in Paris.'

What a darling clever clogs he is, thought Gertie.

'But Nice is pleasant too,' he said. 'What do you say?'

He even looks worried, she thought, and said nothing at all, but put her arms about him and lifted her face for his kisses . . .

Such ardour, thought Millicent. Very gratifying. And quite often she enjoyed it almost as much as he did. And between rounds, such chats. Miss Hudspeth, for instance. Oodles of the stuff. In America she'd be a millionairess. Quite an experience, swapping gossip in the Savoy Ladies' Room with a millionairess. In fact, she knew one who was even richer, but Elena was special. Elena was a secret. She found herself wondering at a quite inappropriate moment whether Elena and Richard would be as she and Harry were, then yelled a bit by way of apology, and continued her chain of thought.

Totally different, she decided. She and Harry felt no commitment except to what they were doing, but Elena and Richard would marry. Not that they wouldn't continue to have fun, any more than she would. She'd sell some of her houses – well, two, anyway. That pompous place in Knightsbridge that had belonged to her first, Toby Crick, where the memories were not good, and the Grosvenor Square house too, now that Pudiphatt had cast his shadow over it . . . Children, she thought, and nannies and schools. Would they ever dance again? But she was sure they would. Richard and Lord Aylmer enjoyed watching them, and they both enjoyed it so . . . Back to work. Noises. Harry liked them. This time she tried a sort of murmuring yell, followed by a gasp, and found that she was enjoying it too.

She and her mother took a very late breakfast together. Elena still slept. Lucky Elena. But at least it meant that Millie could get down to business straight away. Gertie had been sure she would.

'Have you been naughty again?' her loving daughter asked.

'Well, of course,' said Gertie. 'Have you?' and Millie smiled. Her mother could still give her a game, whatever the rules.

'Just asking,' she said. 'You and a lord.'

'Runs in the family,' her mother said. 'With you it'll soon be a duke.' She smiled in her turn. 'Worried about me are you, or are you thinking of your father?'

'Not Dad,' said Millie. 'Dad won't give a damn. Not from where he is. But—'

'Aylmer's all right,' said her mother. 'He needs someone to spoil – and I like to be spoilt. But there's more to it than that.'

'Goodness I should hope so,' said Millie.

'Top of the trees this one,' said her mother. 'Not just a gentleman. A man.'

'Golly,' said Millie.

'And not just that either,' said her mother. 'Sweet and kind and friendly too. Considerate, that's the word. And thoughtful with it. Treats me like I was a lady.'

'Well, so you are,' said Millie, and her mother blew her a kiss.

'We're off to France soon,' Gertie said.

'Not Paris?'

'No, no,' said her mother, then quoted, and chuckled. 'You never know who you might bump into in Paris.'

Then Tufnell came in, and not before time, Millie thought.

'Mr Boyce is here,' said Tufnell, 'asking for you, Miss Blenkinsop.'

But the underlying message was: Just say the word and I'll sling him out on his ear. Goodness, how soon servants found out what was going on.

'Better see him I suppose,' said Millie, words that Tufnell found pleasing. They meant that Miss Blenkinsop now saw him as a pest, which Tufnell always had.

Francis seemed agitated, which wasn't surprising: nor did he look as if he'd been committing naughtiness the night before, unlike every other person she knew well.

'I thought I'd better come and explain what happened last night. At least my part in it anyway. You see I—'

'No,' said Millicent.

'I beg your pardon?'

'We're back to the first person singular again,' said Millie, and we can't have that, she thought, even if my affections have been usurped by those of another. 'Was it an engagement celebration, by the way? I take it you *are* engaged, though not to me of course.'

'Miss Hudspeth and I do have an understanding.'

'Goodness, how sweet,' said Millicent. 'I trust your behaviour is seemly, Francis.'

He ignored her. 'But what I wanted to say was about the toast.'

'I think I might spare a few minutes for that,' said Millicent.

He didn't like it. Of course he didn't. Being allotted a few minutes by a woman who not long ago had made it delightfully obvious that she— Best get on with it.

'There you and your friends were. At the Savoy.'

As if we'd gone there to spite him, she thought. 'You knew we would be.' He made no answer. 'Why the Savoy then?'

'Miss Hudspeth wanted to go,' he said simply.

'Such devotion. Explain the toast, please.'

'I knew you'd never met. Never would, if I could help it.'

'Only you couldn't. We had quite a chat.'

'So you did. After I drank to you. I knew we were finished. Time we parted. Clean break. That was what the toast was meant to be. A signal. I wanted to leave. Had to, in fact.'

'Since there's no help, come let us kiss and part,' said Millicent, but Francis it seemed had no taste for quotation.

'Then there's Lord Aylmer. He's Elena's father.'

'I know who Lord Aylmer is. Do get on, Francis.'

'He'll know all about me, and I couldn't cope with that, just at the moment.' And then, 'Forgive me – there's gossip about him and your mother.'

'Can't you even listen Francis? I said get on.'

'He might gossip too. And your mother.'

He must know I'm off to Paris, she thought, and this is his

226

revenge. Clumsy, even for him, but not at all ineffective.

'After all, he's a Channing,' he said. Better. Much better.

'We all live in the same house,' said Elena, 'because Lord Aylmer likes to be with his daughter, and Elena and I like to dance, and my mother is our *maîtresse de ballet*. If your ears weren't made of cloth you would know that. Lord Aylmer doesn't dance: he likes to watch, and my mother doesn't give lessons in dancing. They are friends, Francis dear, just as he and I are friends, and he and Richard Milburn. And that's all . . . Now tell me – how is darling Evadne these days?'

Francis Boyce knew when he was beaten, and hunted about for his gloves as Millicent rang for Tufnell, who appeared at once, like a genie from a bottle.

'Mr Boyce is leaving,' said Millicent.

'Very good, Miss Blenkinsop,' he said, and turned to Francis. 'If you please, sir,' he said awfully, and Francis left at once. With muscles like Tufnell's there could be no argument.

The rest of the day, thank God, was quiet. Just an agreeable hour finding work for Mr Barnes (Mendip Estate, Farm Rent Arrears). Then a tranquil afternoon with nothing to occupy her mind except the kind of Real Property questions which her tutor assured her, were the first love of The Law Society Examining Board. Time to bathe then, and change, and as she did a call came from Harry. One of the many nice things about Harry was that he took an honest delight in gossip. A talent for it too. Miss Hudspeth's net worth for instance. He knew to a tenner what it was, and when he told her she whistled.

'As much as that?'

'Her mother left rather more than we'd suspected.'

But Somerset House would know to a ha'penny.

'And the rest?' she asked.

'Munitions shares. She sold at exactly the right time. An uncle left her them.' He brooded for a moment. 'She chose her relatives with care. Funny.'

'How, funny?'

All that financial ability – and she settled for Francis.

'I rather think he chose her with care, too.' Harry took his time thinking about it. 'At least he won't be in the way when she's bossing her bank manager,' he said at last.

Brains too. And ardent. Even a duke would have to work hard to match him.

'Which is precisely what she wants,' she said.

'A toy,' said Harry. 'A windy up, cuddly toy. Sort of a clockwork teddy.'

'If you're saying I had a narrow squeak, don't bother,' said Millicent. 'I've already worked that out for myself.'

In the drawing room Richard was taking drinks with the others. They were discussing poverty.

'You know about it?' That was Richard talking to mum.

'My God, yes,' said Gertie. 'At Black Sills there was nothing else. The only way out was brains, maybe. Or luck, like me.'

'Talent,' said Lord Aylmer. 'That's what got you out.'

'Luck too,' Gertie said. 'Lady Mary.'

'How could I possibly forget her?' Aylmer asked, appalled.

'You were away at your wars,' said Gertie. 'We all needed her but there was only one of her. That was my luck – just as Lord Arthur was my dad's. Without Lady Mary I could be dead by now, after half a dozen kids and a man who got drunk every Saturday because he couldn't stand it any more than I could – only for me there'd be no beer.'

'It's incessant. Unrelenting,' said Richard. 'Day after day – and in the winter not even seeing daylight. Pneumoconiosis – what the miners call dust disease – and the threat of a gas that could blow you to bits like a German shell.'

'And on pay day just enough,' Lord Aylmer said. 'Never more than just enough.'

'But can't anyone do anything?' Elena asked.

'Sooner or later it'll be the miners themselves,' said Richard. 'And they'll do it too.'

'You think so?' Millicent asked.

'They're men,' said Richard, 'and they can die like men. They proved that in Flanders. In France. But it won't come to that. Once they see it can be done – that they can win – they'll do it. But that could take a while.'

'And in the meantime?' said Millicent. 'Isn't there anybody?'

'Men like the duke you mean?' Aylmer asked.

'And don't look at me like that,' said Richard amiably. 'I've made a start. But we're outnumbered. Always will be . . . No . . . It may sound harsh, but isn't meant to be. I'll help, but they'll have to do it themselves.'

'God help them,' Lord Aylmer said.

Millicent thought: And how am I going to go to Paris with a duke after that?

★ ★ ★

The next day was nowhere near as quiet. It started after breakfast, or at least Mr Boyce did. Once again Tufnell announced a visitor like an undertaker's mute summoning a mourner. 'Mrs Boyce, Miss Blenkinsop,' but what he meant was: Oh, my God. Another one.

She had dressed with care. Neat silk suit, sensible shoes, a pearl choker. No diamonds. But then both women knew what she had come for. Now it's my turn, thought Millicent, but it didn't bother her. She always took great pains when she dressed for the office. So often there were visitors: impressive, or to be impressed. That day she wore Mr Bernstein's version of a Chanel day dress, in a silk at least as fine as that which Mrs Boyce had chosen: blue, but such a blue. It was from a dress of Elena's mother's after all. A blue that glowed like the skies she had seen in Andalucia: deep, and warm somehow, and never ever in danger of being thought demure. Neatly elegant shoes of a blue-dyed kid, and one diamond: on her third finger, Mrs Boyce noticed, but on the right hand. Altogether an elegant and graceful young woman, but what did she expect? thought Millicent. Something in drab bombazine, ink stained, frizzy hair? Or perhaps a flapper in a dress that showed her knees and more, and four feet of pearls to swing like a lasso every time she moved her neck?

'Good morning,' she said. 'Would you like coffee?'

Francis's mother detested her voice. It was pleasant and low pitched, and the Boyce creature hated it because it was as elegant as the rest of her. She shook her head. Millicent turned to Tufnell. 'Coffee for one,' she said. 'One cup.'

'Cup, miss?'

'Cup,' said Millicent.

Bang went to the chance to show off the Queen Anne coffee pot, thought Tufnell, but maybe this way is better. Miss Blenkinsop's up to something. He left the office as though leading a victory parade.

'Now, Mrs Boyce,' Millicent said. 'What can I do for you?'

'It won't take long,' Mrs Boyce sounded ominous.

'Just as well,' said Millicent. 'I do have rather a lot on today.'

She looked down at her desk: files neatly covered, but so many of them – and all of them put there just before Mrs Boyce appeared. On top was the current file: 'Mendip Estates'. Poor old Barnes, Millicent thought. I'll be in no mood for his golf nonsense after this harpy goes.

229

'It concerns—' Mrs Boyce began, but Tufnell, timing his moment, entered with a silver tray, a Georgian coffee pot and one cup. Undermining her confidence, he thought, and was glad to do his bit. When she'd arrived Francis's ma had looked at him as if he were transparent. He took his time. When he left at last Mrs Boyce said, 'It concerns some diamonds of my son's.'

'Francis is a collector?' Millicent asked.

Polite, gentle even, always the best way to begin, Mrs Boyce said, 'Some diamonds that were bought for me.'

'How very nice,' said Millicent. 'But then Francis, so I'm told, has always been a caring son. Diamonds. Very caring. All the same I fail to see—'

'One of which you're wearing at this moment.'

'My engagement ring, you mean?' said Millicent.

'It is on the wrong finger for an engagement ring.' My trick that time, her voice implied. My ace of diamonds in fact, but the hussy trumped it.

'How unkind you are,' said the hussy, 'to remind me of it. It's true your son and I were engaged – then parted.'

'Well, then surely—'

'Nothing was said about returning gifts.' On the contrary. Keep it all was his message. Keep the lot. I'm free. I'm Free!

'Nothing need be *said* about returning things,' said Mrs Boyce. 'Especially when he gave them to me.'

'You can prove it?'

A common person's question, thought Mrs Boyce. No lady would query what she had said. 'You have my word.'

'Ah,' said Millicent. One's word was one thing, that monosyllable told her, the possession of the diamonds another.

'And do I have Francis's word, too?'

'In a sense, yes.' To be subjected to such questions, like being in the witness box. Even so, it was time that she put an end to being ladylike. She took a piece of paper from her handbag and offered it to Millicent, who read it at once, then began again, when the telephone rang.

'Lady Mendip's legal office,' she said, and the receiver quacked like a demented duck. No chance of Old Mother Boyce understanding a word, but that didn't matter. It was Barnes and he could jabber by the hour. It was what he was for, after all.

'Yes, indeed, Mr Barnes,' she said. 'To go one's self is the only solution – but the Mendip countryside is still attractive, even at this time of year . . . Golf? I doubt if those farmers even know the game . . . Oh, Sunningdale! Rather up to you wouldn't you say? And the farmers of course. Litigation? . . . So I'm instructed. We can't tolerate debts of that magnitude . . . Time to define who has a right to what . . . Yes. Go to it, Mr Barnes. Sunningdale isn't completely out of the question. Not if you bring this off.'

She hung up. Barnes hadn't quite finished, but then he never had. She turned to Mrs Boyce.

'Well, I must say,' Mrs Boyce began.

'Must you?' said Millicent. 'I thought you said this wouldn't take long.'

Outside the door Tufnell listened, entranced. That cup was the start, he thought. Clipped the old bitch good and proper, and since then she was miles ahead on points. Francis's ma had hardly touched her – only please let there be a knockout.

'. . . Sort of a deed of gift,' Millicent was saying. 'Dated last week I see.'

'It's perfectly in order,' said Mrs Boyce.

'Well, it would be,' said Millicent, 'except that he gave me one, too. Dated three weeks ago.' And it was like pulling teeth to get it, she thought. That or thumbscrews.

'But since mine is the more recent—' Mrs Boyce said.

'That's what makes it useless,' Millicent said. 'The diamonds are mine. To become yours would mean a deed of gift in your favour from me, and you can hardly expect that, now can you?' She smiled pleasantly, almost gently, which somehow made it worse.

It had all seemed so simple when she set off for Eaton Place. The trollop dealt with politely but firmly, the promise of a reward – not vast, but adequate. The diamonds in her handbag as she went to consult with that diamond merchant in Hatton Garden. And none of it had happened. Mrs Boyce's own personal dam burst, and she began to yell, insult upon insult, and Tufnell all but rubbed his hands, as Mrs Boyce paused for breath at last, and Millicent said, 'Are you familiar with the law of slander?'

Mrs Boyce breathed deeply: grew calm. 'Well, of course,' she said. 'It's telling lies about people. Harmful lies.'

'Saying them,' said Millicent. 'Writing them down is libel, but the penalties for slander are equally severe.'

'I have told no such lies,' said Mrs Boyce.

'Oh, but you have,' said Millicent. 'Let's leave aside what you said here, in this room. There were no witnesses after all, but there were other occasions.'

'What other occasions?'

Leading with her chin, thought Tufnell. The knockout's just seconds away.

The dreadful creature produced a fat and somehow menacing notebook and leafed through it.

'A Miss Evadne Petworth on numerous occasions,' she said. 'The last one at Mrs Hinkson's tea party – the seventeenth of last month. Miss Daisy Hudspeth. Twenty-third of last month. Mrs Barber-Binns's party.'

But how could this dreadful woman find out? Mrs Boyce wondered. Daisy is important. She mustn't know. *Ever*.

Really, Duckhouse and Allnutt had their uses, thought Millicent, especially when it came to finding the right kind of detective. She waited.

'Please,' said Mrs Boyce. 'Please let me explain.'

That loud bang you hear is Francis's ma hitting the canvas, thought Tufnell. Eight – nine – ten – out. Run of bad luck at Deauville, the old girl was saying, and the total far in excess of what she had imagined.

But she had relied on Francis. He'd promised. And he *is* a dab hand at promises, Millicent thought. It's fulfilling them he finds difficult . . . So naturally Mrs Boyce was on edge. She said so many times. A vast sum to find, and only her son to turn to . . .

She knew all about Mr Boyce's aversion to paying his wife's growing debts, and longed to discuss it, but there simply wasn't time. Sling her out, thought Millicent. She's beginning to bore.

Outside in the corridor Tufnell was silently agreeing with her.

Millicent smiled kindly, sweetly. 'It's all very sad of course, but what can I do about it except offer my sympathy, which of course I do.'

What Mrs Boyce wanted was for Millicent to offer her the diamonds, but she had been humiliated enough for one day. Begging from this harlot would only increase the humiliation. What she would have to do was confront her husband and ask for enough to keep her creditors quiet, and what a price she would have to pay for that. No more gambling for months: perhaps a year. After she had finished with Boyce – or vice versa more likely – she would lock herself in her bedroom and cry . . . Millicent rang the bell, and Tufnell appeared after a suitable interval.

'If you please, madam,' said Tufnell and out she went. A jolly amusing half hour, Millicent thought, but there were far more important things to do, and once again Tufnell was in agreement.

20

Millicent flicked through the post at last. Nothing outstanding, though some of the Mendip farmers seemed obdurate. No holes-in-one for Mr Barnes . . . She took the notes on Real Property and got down to it. Never do to fail the law exams, and anyway she enjoyed it. Not like Mrs Boyce. The roses arrived just before lunch. Magnificent roses that looked as edible as peaches; fat and juicy, and the sort of colours that belonged with the Dutch flower piece in her bedroom. A card with the address of a West End florist, but no message. Just the single letter B. B is for Boyce, she thought, and the roses said all there was to say. Old Mother Boyce had been defeated not once but twice. He'd have to stump up for the good name of the family, but oh, the concessions he would exact in return. The thought was pleasing, and she smiled. At a side table a parlourmaid arranged the flowers and thanked God she was good at it. She was terrified of Miss Blenkinsop, especially when she smiled, though it was ever such a pretty smile, but then Miss Blenkinsop *was* pretty. And terrifying. She looked at the roses.

'Very nice,' Millicent said. 'You can go,' and the parlourmaid left, thanking God for she wasn't quite sure what.

More Real Property, and her mother came in. She and her Aylmer were off to Bond Street (where else?) after lunch at the Ritz. She loved the roses.

'And so you should,' said Millicent. 'They're just like you.' Pleasant and pretty and almost edible, she thought, but with more style even than the roses.

'Oh you,' said her mother. She was blushing, which made her more roseate than ever.

Her daughter told her their story, and Gertie looked at her with a kind of wary respect.

'You don't muck about, do you?' she said. 'Any more than your father. Sure you wouldn't like to join us for lunch?'

233

Now that was handsome. Middle-aged love cares even less for interlopers than young love ever could. There simply wasn't enough time.

'No thanks, mum,' she said, and nodded at the Real Property notes.

'What's it about?' Gertie asked.

'Land – who owns it, who rents it, deeds, titles.' The reason Elena employed her in the first place.

'Good God!' said her mother, and left her to it. And yet somebody owned the land they built the Ritz on, too.

Next it was Elena, off to lunch and a matinée with Richard. She too invited Millicent to play gooseberry, and tried not to look relieved when she declined and admired the roses instead.

Papa was just in time. Elegant but discreet, with a gardenia in his buttonhole.

'Off to lunch,' he said. 'Lucky I caught you.'

Elena waited.

'I suppose you know who with,' said papa.

'Well, of course,' his daughter said.

'And you don't mind?'

'Why on earth should I?' Elena asked.

'Mama . . .'

'Mama's dead, and so is Gertie's husband. You were both lonely. Oh, I know you both have a daughter but it isn't the same. You'll make Gertie happy and she'll make you happy. What's wrong with that? You've earned it, papa, and I rather think Gertie has, too . . .'

Her lunchtime at last. Real Property her only guest. Bliss. Then back to the office to work for Elena. The last post of the day was waiting, but Elena's work too was Real Property. The Mendip farmers still being obdurate. They were really rather good at it, but then so was she. The post could wait. Millicent worked on till the phone call brought her back to reality. Damn reality anyway. It was Miss Hudspeth, crisply delighted at what Millicent had done. No flowers, which was perhaps as well. She'd heard it on the Boyce grapevine: from mother to son to her; fiancée in waiting.

'How's Francis taking it?'

'Not too badly,' Miss Hudspeth said. 'His mother pushed him too far for once.'

'Did he—' Millicent said, then, 'Forgive me.'

'Did he ask me for the money?' said Miss Hudspeth. 'Yes, he

did. But only just enough to be able to go and tell mummy. I turned him down.'

'But that makes you a monster.'

'Well, so I am a monster,' said Miss Hudspeth, 'but I'm the monster who has the money.'

'And you don't mind?'

'He's the one I want,' said Miss Hudspeth. 'I can handle him. *And* his mother, which means my offer to you still stands.'

'Offer?'

'For me to be your client once you're qualified. You won't regret it.'

'I hope you'll feel the same,' said Millicent.

She hung up, and reached again for the Mendip Estates file. But it just wasn't on. The post wouldn't go away. More farmers, four requests for Elena and Rosario to dance, a bank statement, an invitation for a weekend with the duke 'some time before Christmas'. And after Paris, she thought. And then the sort of envelope that didn't belong with the others one tiny bit: brown but not manila, dingy, ink inclined to smudge – and addressed to her. Oh, my God, thought Millicent, who knew at once who it was from, and turned it over in her hands, but that was ridiculous. *Get on with it girl.* Her dead father's voice had never been more clear, and she reached for the paper knife.

> *To Miss Blenkinsop*, (she read),
>
> *To address you as 'dear' would be ridiculous, coming from me. Your fairy friend, Francis, no doubt, but not me.* (And even you are behind the times, thought Millicent). *Of course, I would have written to the Countess or whatever she is, but she's never where you expect her to be, so you'll have to do. Anyway, one bitch is as good as another. Or as bad.*
>
> *I've left the loony bin you sent me to. Not bad in its way but they refuse to fetch me whisky, which is as stupid as it's heartless. I told them I'd die without it but a fat lot they care. Acting on your instructions no doubt, or the other bitch's. Anyway, I've had enough. No whisky. That's horrible, which means you're horrible too.*

Well, really, Millicent thought. We had to move heaven and earth to get him in there, and even then, if it weren't for the duke being a patron . . . There there, girl. Remember he really is crazy and try to be sorry for him. I know you'll fail, but *try* . . . More abuse.

Screeds of it: some that made sense (Francis) and much that was pure fantasy, like their having to dance because they were broke. They needed the money. Even Pedrillito took a battering. The things he was supposed to get up to with his guitar were beyond belief, and of course she didn't believe him, but she was glad Pudiphatt hadn't gone in for illustrations too.

Then at last he got to the point, and for as long as it took appeared quite sane. *You may think, because you're a bitch, that I have nowhere to go, but you'll be wrong. I have my own place; still elegant, if rather austere after you two paid it a visit . . .* More abuse after that. The streets of Piccadilly the only place for them, except that they'd be corrupting pure British youth. Scouts? she wondered. Cubs? Guides? Then once again her father's voice, 'Get on with it girl.' Right as usual, dad. She reached for the phone, but Harry was discussing income tax with a junior minister at the Exchequer, Elena and Richard were at the theatre, but they'd forgotten to say which one, and Lord Aylmer and mum had just left the Ritz. Get on with it, it's the only way, she thought, and there's only me to do it.

She told Tufnell to get a cab, and Tufnell despatched a footman at the gallop. Miss Blenkinsop had made it sound urgent . . . On the way she thought of the late duke's passion for mediaeval history and the family's Saxon names, Oswin, Aylmer – and all because of his scheme to write a history of Bellingham in the fifteenth century, when the Channings had been mere barons. Mum had got it out of Aylmer. But mum was also the one who knew about talking to dad, there in that cemetery, and it was dad she had to think of now. Not that she believed her dad spoke to her, not literally, but when it came to action it was dad who knew what to do.

Like phoning the Grosvenor Square house, and letting the phone ring over and over, and getting no answer. So I needn't go up there, she thought, but dad wouldn't see it like that. There could be half a dozen reasons why nobody answered. The only sure way was to see for herself. Even so she was scared. Well, of course you are, dad said. What's that got to do with it? I was always scared, just before – she looked about her. The square was almost empty at that time of day, but a policeman was going round the corner. She could have called out to him, but her dad wouldn't have liked that. Wouldn't have liked it at all. So she strolled past the house instead, taking her time. Locks untouched, so far as she could see, windows untouched . . . 'Well, of course,' her father said. 'This is the posh end. Toffs passing all the time. Check the service entrance.'

Dad was right, as usual: door undamaged, but a window had been neatly broken (no jagged glass), and left slightly ajar. She tried the door. Locked. Whoever had done it was the neat and tidy kind – like the major. She went back to the posh end, and took the keys from her bag. Even to look calm was the bravest thing she'd ever done.

Well, he'd tried, he thought. Stuck it out at what the bitches called the nursing home for a whole week. But no whisky. Surely they must have known that was torture? So it was back to his digs in Earl's Court (the flat's rent still had a few days left) and make his preparations, pack his attaché case. First his notes (in case whoever was in charge would find them useful), then his whisky. An almost full bottle. And a glass. Mustn't forget his glass. Never, no matter how bad things were, had he drunk from the bottle. A little hammer for the break-in by him, who should have had a key, and his razor. He'd considered taking his service revolver, but this wasn't a military affair. The razor would do, after he'd strapped it again . . . Not the bicycle. Definitely not. He looked far too much like a door-to-door salesman anyway, because of the attaché case. A bike would put him beneath contempt, and so he took a cab. He had just enough money for the fare, one way, and what was left he gave to the cabby, who seemed surprised. Big tip from a bloke that shabby, the look said, and not all that sober either.

Pudiphatt broke in carefully. Never do to cut himself, and the window was awkwardly placed. Never do to break an ankle either . . . He went upstairs, to that part of the house where he should have spent his days, walking from room to room, but without furniture they were no more than elegantly decorated space. As he went to the main rooms the telephone rang. On the floor. Not even a table for the telephone. The whole place had been picked clean, like the skeleton of a straggler in the jungle when the ants had finished with it, but not his golden boy. Not Charles.

The phone stopped and he went to the stairs, sat and poured a drink. Nobody he wanted to talk to anyway, though he knew well enough who it would be. He poured again. It had all begun so well. Good plan of attack. Transport. All right a bicycle, but it got you there. Quickly too. Good look-out too. That feller Stobbs.

Close observer that one, but drank too much. Say anything for a
drink. And his friend had shell-shock. Shocking case. He'd written to the War Office about it because he needed help. But so do I
need help, he thought, and who would believe a chap with
shell-shock? Harry Edwards. He'd had high hopes there – except
he'd been to one of those dancing do's the bitch-pack gave, and
that meant he, Pudiphatt, had lost him. He sipped again. All
those half-lies about Lord Mendip. Best destroyed. He tried to
find them, but his eyes wouldn't focus. No matter. No coroner
would allow half-truths about viscounts as evidence . . .

And that was it, really. He'd tried and failed and he'd never live
in Charles's house. But he'd see Charles soon. He was sure of it.
The cuff links Charles had given him were in the suitcase, and he
took off his watch – another present from Charles – and put it
beside them, then poured the last drink, took the razor out and
stored the case on the stairs, three treads above his head. No
blood on his notes. The coroner might be squeamish. He drank
till his glass was almost empty. Time to get on with it. For what he
had to do he couldn't bear an audience; not even one of the
bitches. He opened the razor, then raised his glass high, like one
of his fictional heroes: 'The King, God bless him,' he said, then
hurled his glass away, listened as it smashed – at least he'd
achieved that. Firmly he grasped the razor.

She unlocked the front door, crossed the marble mosaic and
parquet, and there he was: stupid grin on his face, bottle nice and
handy, and for some reason a floppy red tie. Did the idiot think
that looking like some kind of stage revolutionary would be one
more insult to Elena?

'Major Pudiphatt,' she said, but he made no answer: just sat on
the stairs and grinned. Passed out, she thought. Drunk as an owl.
She took a step towards him and broken glass crunched under her
feet, then another – and then she froze. Not a red tie: red blood.
Arterial her Guide Captain had called it, when she did the
First-Aid Course, pumped out by the heart with remarkable force,
as the major was there to prove. Dead, she was sure, but very
recently. Well, at least he'd died in Grosvenor Square.

'Go on,' said her father's voice, but she shook her head. 'I can't
dad.' And this time her father accepted it. She'd been pushed as
far as she could go.

'Phone then.'

But even that wasn't easy. The phone had been left at the foot of the stairs. Warily she went to it, mindful of Pudiphatt's blood. The late Pudiphatt, Duckhouse would have said. Even then, even there.

'Get on,' said her father.

She picked up the phone, turned her back on the body and asked for the Chelsea number. Richard answered at once. They weren't in bed then. Not yet.

'It's Millicent,' she said. 'I'm at the Grosvenor Square house. You must come at once.'

'But what on earth—?'

'You'll see when you get here. Come now. The major's dead.'

He had known that something awful had happened, and was there in minutes, Elena with him. He went to the major and Millicent began to cry. Elena had never seen her cry and embraced her, hushing and shushing as if she were ten years old. From the stairs Richard said, 'He's dead all right. Not all that long ago. I think you two had better go.'

'But—' said Elena.

'There'll be police,' said Richard. 'Questions. Unpleasant questions. I can handle that far better than you.'

He was brusque – Richard of all people – but it made sense. There was simply no time to be nice. They left him.

First the body, but carefully. He mustn't be marked. The few flecks on his hands he could explain, but no more. And anyway there was nothing. The treasure trove was in the little leather case: a cheap notebook untouched by blood. He shoved it in his pocket and picked up the telephone . . .

'And this is how you found him?' Detective Inspector Raeburn asked.

'It is.'

'Do you mind explaining who you are?'

'Sir Richard Milburn, I told you.'

Raeburn's sergeant scribbled busily.

'And why you're here?'

'The house belongs to Lady Mendip,' said Richard. 'She's a friend of mine. Her legal adviser, Miss Blenkinsop, had word of a prowler, and Lady Mendip asked me to look in and check.' He nodded at the major. 'Looks as if I found him.'

'You know him sir?'

'I do not,' said Richard. 'Never saw him before in my life.' And that at least was true.

'Why should a prowler break into an empty house?'

'I've no idea,' said Richard. 'That's rather your department, wouldn't you say?'

Raeburn thought of baronets, ladyships, legal advisers. 'Then we'd better get on with it,' he said. 'If you wouldn't mind, Sir Richard.'

'Yes, of course,' Richard said. 'I'll leave you to it.'

His Frazer Nash was outside, and he drove off slowly, no hint of urgency.

In Millicent's office he read the notebook, then destroyed it. Abuse, some of it quite nasty, about the two women Pudiphatt hated most, and nothing more. Methodically he ripped the book to pieces page by page, and dropped them on to the fire. Elena and Millicent and he watched them burn.

'Destroying evidence,' he said. 'Is that a felony or a misdemeanour?'

'Felony,' said Millicent. 'Don't forget to break the pieces up with the poker.'

Richard grinned and obeyed. 'We ought to burn that letter he wrote to you, too.'

'I already have,' said Millicent.

The others drifted in: Gertie and her Aylmer, then Harry, his interview with the minister cut ruthlessly short at Millicent's summons. Once again Gertie looked at her daughter.

'My poor lamb,' she said. 'How could you do it?'

'Dad mostly,' said her daughter, and Gertie nodded. She understood at once, thought Edwards. I have to think hard.

'Trouble is he doesn't look like a prowler,' he said. 'Wrong sort of clothes. Expensive watch and cuff links – if he got them back.'

'He doesn't look like anything much under all that blood,' said Richard, and Elena gasped, but the men were oblivious. They were back in France, ten years ago.

'He could have got his clothes from the Sally Anne—' said Richard.

'Salvation Army,' Millicent explained to Elena.

'And stolen the watch and cuff links. No fixed abode, either. He had a few visiting cards but I burnt them.'

'Sidney Pudiphatt, MC,' Elena quoted. 'Major (Retired).'

'I checked his digs by phone,' Richard said. 'His lease was up. And anyway he was known there as Thomas Wilson. Looks as if he didn't care much for Sidney Pudiphatt.'

'Who would?' said Harry.

'So – a prowler dosses and steals where he can,' said Richard.

240

'Only today it all got too much for him. *And* he reeked of whisky. Dutch courage.'

'Expensive razor?' Millicent asked. Good girl, he thought. The worst day of your life but you're still using your brains.

'Not cheap,' he said. 'My guess is he stole that too.'

'It all fits,' said Harry. 'Fits very nicely. So long as they don't make the connection with Elena.'

'Explain that please,' Lord Aylmer said.

'Of course, sir. Other papers – ourselves too – love stories like this. "The Peeress and the Prowler." Front-page stuff for most of them – if the prowler turns out to be a relative – and a hard-up one at that. *And* a war hero.'

'Hero?'

'There is the MC, sir.' Lord Aylmer nodded. Pudiphatt might be awful, but he was most certainly a hero.

'So the thing to do is drown the baby at birth.'

'Not sure I follow,' said Aylmer.

'Do a piece for tomorrow's paper,' said Harry.

'Not front page. As modest as we can get away with.' He thought, then smiled.

'Prowler Picks Wrong House,' Millicent chuckled. First home as usual, thought Harry.

'This Weary Willy or whatever his name is sees this house where not much happens. Old people he thinks. Reclusive. Should be good. Knick-knacks, statuettes, maybe a nice French clock – and in he pops. Only the place is empty. Times are bad, he's drunk anyway and he's just made a colossal fool of himself and it's altogether too much. And so—' Harry left it at that.

Aylmer said, 'You can arrange this?'

'Oh yes,' said Harry. 'I'll talk to Raeburn – the man in charge. My guess is he'll already be thinking along those lines anyway. Then I'll show him the piece we'll use – mention his name quite a lot and Elena's not at all. Just a war widow with a place in the country – but a lot of space for Raeburn. Oh yes, we'll manage it.'

'But suppose his name does come to light?' Gertie asked.

'It won't. Not for another two weeks at least.'

'But why not?' Elena asked.

'Raeburn. He'll sit on it. Bound to. It would make him look idle, and he doesn't want that. And no more names in the papers, and he certainly won't want *that*.'

'Why ever not?' Aylmer asked.

'Promotion,' Harry said, and Aylmer nodded. 'So we'll bury it even deeper, and so will our rivals. And Raeburn will be grateful because he won't look a fool. Not that I think it'll happen. My money's on Unknown Prowler.'

Another bright young man, thought Aylmer. I'd better put in a word with Oswin for this one.

In the cab to Fleet Street, Harry thought about Millicent. She'd invited him to watch them dance that night, but that wasn't it. She was worried about her conversations with her father, but he'd told her not to. In moments of extreme crisis – and God knows hers had been extreme – it was good if you could isolate that part of the mind that would do the job, and blank out the rest. And if her unconscious mind had chosen her father as the means of doing it, what was wrong with that? He'd been a good man and she'd loved him . . . She had thought about it, frowning as she always did when the thought was deep: intense, then oblivious, and then she smiled.

'Francis,' she said.

'What about him?'

'He'd have been useless,' she said.

No time to think about that. The cab had pulled up outside the Mercury building.

'Nasty one,' said Sexton. His editor looked worried. And of course it's a nasty one, thought Edwards. If it wasn't he'd be in somebody else's bed not his office. Not at this time of night.

'You think so?' he said.

'I bloody know so,' said his editor. 'Chain reaction. Our readers love 'em, but his Grace won't, not this one.' Edwards waited.

One by one Sexton ticked off the links of the chain on his fingers.

'Pudiphatt,' he said. 'Terrible name, poor sod, but our readers won't mind. Not if he's badly done by. *And* he'd got an MC. Linked to Lady Mendip. Gorgeous and talented society beauty.'

And so is Millicent gorgeous and talented, thought Edwards but he kept his mouth shut, as Sexton struck his third finger.

'Lord Aylmer Channing,' he said. 'Lord Aylmer was married to Lady M's mother. Something odd about that marriage. Oh, I know, she produced Lady M, but they lived apart a lot of the time. Far more than they lived together. I know we buried that one once, of course we did, but we can't do it twice.' Sexton struck his fourth finger, but gently. He's getting very close to God, thought Edwards. 'His Grace the Duke of Bellingham,' said Sexton. '*Mercury*'s biggest shareholder. Doesn't like publicity. This thing screams of publicity.'

'There could be a way out,' said Edwards. His editor looked at him hard, then opened a cupboard, took out a decanter and glasses, and poured.

'MacAllan Twenty Years Old,' he said, and Edwards sipped. A sort of silken fire, he thought. Like Millicent – *Not yet*. She'll wait. Glad to. There's still a lot to do . . .

'Once upon a time,' he began, and told Sexton the story of the prowler.

When he had done the editor's first reaction was a scowl, as Edwards had known it would be. Good front-page stuff just thrown away. But that particular front page would never be printed, and the editor knew it. He examined what was left. Properly written, and Edwards would take care of that, it was even funny in a way.

'Fine,' he said. 'Marvellous in fact. Just one snag. You're expecting a hell of a lot of people to keep their mouths shut.'

'They will,' said Edwards.

'You seem very sure.'

'I'm giving them what they want,' Edwards said.

'They'll be quiet. For a couple of weeks anyway. No big story ever waited longer than a fortnight. And if I'm wrong you can fire me. You would anyway, and I can't say I'd blame you.'

Sexton poured more single malt. The young feller had earned it. Damn it, he even deserves to sit in my chair, he thought, but not till I'm ready to leave it.

'You've done well,' he said. 'I think you'll find the *Mercury* is suitably grateful.'

'That's nice,' said Edwards. 'I have a very soft spot for the *Mercury*. Always had.'

The editor thought: This is going to be expensive, but Edwards' kind of brains are never cheap.

'All the same, I've been here rather a long time, wouldn't you say? As I say – I like the *Mercury*, but I have to think about the future,' said Edwards.

This is really going to cost me something, the editor thought. He knows so much – and not just the duke. They wouldn't use that: no one in Fleet Street would. To attack another proprietor was unthinkable – might be your own master next – but Edwards knew so many. From Pudiphatt up. Francis Boyce, and his father, his extremely rich father, Lady Mendip, and now this Daisy Hudspeth, two of the richest women in the kingdom. A peeress, a baronet, all queuing up to sue, and Edwards' friend Millicent to show them how to do it, and Edwards writing it up for the *Mail*, the *Express*, the *Morning Post*. I'd be out on my ear, thought Sexton. The haggling began.

When it was over, Edwards had moved up to chief sub-editor, his salary had doubled, he signed his own expense sheet, a car from the pool would always be available. The editor made no further move to the single malt, but Edwards helped himself. After all, a baronet, a peeress, the uncle of a duke and the duke himself helped him to pour.

When Edwards had finished, Sexton rose and said, 'Mustn't keep you,' then added savagely, 'You'll be glad of a rest, after the busy night you've had.'

'It isn't over yet,' Edwards said. 'I promised to look in at Lady Mendip's. She and Miss Blenkinsop are giving a private dance recital.'

And there you had him, his editor thought. Clock him one and he'll clock you one back, and a bloody hard one too, and he'd get away with it. But that's what brains and influence did for you. If he hadn't had brains and influence it really would have been a taxi home and an early night instead of calling the car pool and saying, 'All right. The Humber will do. But next time make sure it's a Daimler.'

At Lady Mendip's he allowed himself one more single malt. Glenfiddich. Tufnell was very fond of Glenfiddich. Lord Aylmer came up to him. 'I trust your trip to Fleet Street was successful.'

'Completely,' said Edwards, and smiled.

Richard, walking towards them, caught the smile and nodded, and that was all. No need to draw pictures for that one. Then from behind the curtain the music began. Elegant and easy like Velazquez scribbling to loosen his fingers, before the serious business of the day. But has little Pepe got a friend with him? Sounds like two guitars, he thought.

His cousin's arrived at last. You can tell how pleased they are to see each other. 'Just listen,' said Aylmer. And indeed the music was all delight.

'Mind you, there was sadness,' said Aylmer, 'but that was when they talked.'

'You heard?' Edwards asked.

'Me? Couldn't make head nor tail of it even if I did hear. It was Elena. She eavesdropped.'

'*Elena?*'

'Well, of course,' said Aylmer. 'She thought maybe it might be about Gertie and she was right. Not at first. At first they just chattered like monkeys, but then the tempo slowed so to speak and he told Antonio he was off because he was in love and she didn't love him, and all Antonio said was, "Ah." Very tactful.'

'Didn't he ask who she was?' Harry asked.

'He would have done, only little Pepe said she was a grand lady – far too grand for him – and Antonio let it lie. Thought it was herself or Millicent, Elena thinks.'

'And all the time it was the third grand lady,' said Richard. Aylmer grunted approval.

'Anyway little Pepe's off to Bayonne and Antonio's taking over.'

'Will he like it here?' Harry asked.

'For a while. Gypsies only like places for a while, then they have to move on.' He thought of Bellingham Castle. Thank God.

The two guitars had been playing a sort of hide and seek, even flirting, then there was a soft murmur from behind the curtains and at once they played as they should, and Eaton Place became Granada as the audience took their seats. Private recital is right, thought Harry. All three of us.

The curtain rose and the music grew softer, gentler, and there the two of them were in their Goya painting pose now famous all over London, and the guitars throbbed, the dancing began.

My girls, thought Gertie. My lovely girls, who dragged me out of Pimlico to live in Eaton Place. My daughter and her friend, who isn't quite a daughter but a lovely sister for Millie all the same, and it was far too late to work that one out, but she knew it was true. And dancing so well. Never better, in fact, never even quite so good. And all for Aylmer, and maybe a little bit left over for me. Millie was naughty: of course she was. With a mother like me how could she be anything else? And perhaps Elena was too, just a bit. She and her Richard. But what they were after was marriage, sooner or later, and babies. Me a sort of grandmother to them. I'll love it, she thought. Two ladies in my life so far – Lady Mary and Lady Mendip – and both gorgeous, like an aunt and a favourite niece. That was what Elena was. The best niece a woman could wish for. Gertie Garnet among the nobs.

She touched the champagne bottle. Too cold – but that was fine. It would be just right for when they'd finished. Champagne meant darling Aylmer these days, and she stole a peep through the open curtain. He was eating it. She'd never seen a man so happy – and some of that was for her too. Lucky Gertie. She'd even had a tune written specially for her. They were playing it now, Pepe and that cousin of his. To remind her that the little man had loved her, but it was Aylmer she looked at, because Bert, she was sure, would have approved of Aylmer – his kind of chap. And anyway, he would say, where I am now there's no need of ladies, so why be selfish? Enjoy yourself girl. You were always good at that.

Millicent found she could now think about Pudiphatt without wanting to scream, and partly it was the dance, because when you danced nothing was more important – even Pudiphatt reduced to no more than images on a cinema screen – and partly it was dad. True, Harry had explained that the memories of dad had come from inside her, and if they did that was fine, but she wasn't so sure. It could have been his ghost, and that would have been even better. Dad still loving, still caring, even after death, and knowing exactly what to do, and telling her, but gently, because he knew how she must feel. And so she danced for him, just as Elena danced for her papa.

She had done it for Elena. There was nobody else she could have done it for, even with dad's help. But Elena – best friend, sister, boss when you got right down to it, even though they never did. How could she not help? Publicity like that would drive Lord Aylmer back into silence and Elena to despair – and because of Pudiphatt of all people. Far better to leave it to Harry. Francis would have been useless, but Harry had gone straight for the jugular. The only way . . . They'd be back in bed together soon, she thought. But not that night. That night she wanted her own bed, her own company, except for dad to keep the bogeyman at bay. But Harry deserved some loving from her. Not that she was first prize in a contest for bright chaps. Nothing like that. She was far too choosy – just like mum had been . . . which brings us to Oswin. Oswin and Paris and Cartier, and if there has to be a first prize, this time it's Harry. All the same she liked Oswin, for the time being anyway. Just as she liked Harry for the time being. Her true love was the law: the long road to knowledge she thought, and success, and chaps dotted along the road like milestones. Not like Elena at all, though I love her like a sister. Mary and Martha. But which is which? Then the music changed, she took off her hat and skimmed it to her mother, and shook her head so that the falling pigtail might have its own round of applause.

Sevillanas. Elegant, and by flamenco standards demure: as close to mama's dancing as it was possible to get: the guitars serene; Millicent's hands clapping . . . Papa was happy, she knew he was, and never happier than when Richard was with them. God had been good to her. And Millicent, and Richard, and Harry, but especially Millicent. But if papa retreated again into silence, even she couldn't coax him out, even with Millicent's and her mum's help. The thought bit deep, and almost she missed the beat, but the dance, the whole recital was an act of thanksgiving, and she danced on – radiant, elegant, serene, until the guitars crashed out a chord like twin doors slamming.

Zapateado. Millicent came to join her as the guitarists alternated chords with single notes like rifle fire. For the first time ever the two friends smiled at each other before they danced, a smile of such happiness that the three men in the audience found that they were smiling too, and then they danced: Millicent grasping the lapels of her jacket, Elena lifting her skirts as their feet stamped harder, harder. Or maybe it was fireworks, thought Elena. Explosions of joyous noise as guitarists and dancers worked, on and on, until at last the great rocket began to climb, up and up and ready to burst, to scatter its happiness on them and on the house. And then, thought Elena, will be the time to pray, and ask Mama if she saw it too.